Colour Scheme

John R Gordon lives and works in London, England. He is the author of four novels, *Black Butterflies*, (GMP 1993), for which he won a New London Writers' Award; *Skin Deep*, (GMP 1997), and *Warriors & Outlaws* (GMP 2001), both of which have been taught on graduate and post-graduate courses on Race & Sexuality in Literature in the United States; and *Faggamuffin* (Team Angelica Publishing 2012). He script-edited and wrote for the world's first black gay television show, Patrik-Ian Polk's *Noah's Arc* (2005-6). In 2007 he wrote the autobiography of America's most famous black gay porn-star from taped interviews he conducted, *My Life in Porn: the Bobby Blake Story*, (Perseus 2008). In 2008 he co-wrote the screenplay for the cult Noah's Arc feature-film, *Jumping the Broom* (Logo) for which he received an NAACP Image Award nomination. The same year his short film *Souljah* (directed by Rikki Beadle-Blair) won the Soho Rushes Award for Best Film.

As well as mentoring and encouraging young gay and lesbian and racially-diverse writers he also paints, cartoons, does film and theatre design, and is a student of Vodoun.

Colour Scheme

John R Gordon

TEAM
ANGELICA

Published 2013 by Team Angelica Publishing,
an imprint of Angelica Entertainments Ltd

Team Angelica Publishing
51 Coningham Road
London W12 8BS

www.teamangelica.com

A CIP catalogue record for this book is available
from the British Library

ISBN 978-0-9569719-3-7

Printed and bound by Lightning Source

To Rikki, Andy, Graeme, Baz, Philip and Guy-Mark; to my mother Isabel; to Deobia and Dibby; to Zion and Diriye: thank you all for your love and wisdom, your kindness, encouragement and time.

Chapter One

*Z*iggy is coming back today.
    Ziggy is coming home today. He won't say where he's been. All he'll say is this: You've got to bring something to the table. Bread. Or a knife.

A horn-note rises up above the humid city from an open window where curtains hang limp as corpses, pure and clear and rich in all that is human, in all that is worthwhile. Soft brown lips press muscularly against unyielding, curving brass to create a fusion of forms, and the note soars up past domes and church-spires, a gleaming ribbon of sound bearing heavenward all that God could want of Earth.

Ziggy cries.
    Ziggy doesn't cry anymore.

It's a blazing hot day in July. The tired dancers rag as they turn, turn to the pounding retro bass of Funkadelic's 'One Nation Under a Groove'. Braids flick, hair and sweat flies, muscle and sinew strain as they strive to release themselves into that present moment where the mind becomes the body and the body becomes the music. George claps his hands in double time then clicks his fingers as he snaps his lanky arms and legs out, marking with a precisely-pivoted wrist or ankle the full extension and most realised form of each movement, his long, dark, delicate fingers fanning, splaying, striking and sculpting the moment, electric-blue nail-varnish flashing like flung sapphires.
    Fifty years on. Fifty years here on Earth and I

don't know much. But I do know this.

For moments, in intense flashes of truth, it all comes together: rapport between him and the students and the music is achieved. They become part of that endlessly renewable revelation of spiritual connected-ness of which dance is both the fact and the proof, the heart-beat and the symbol. This is what it was always for, for George: a way to demonstrate the understand-ing that the spirit is in the bones and meat of the body, the muscles, sinews and shining pores of it; and that it is through the body and only through the body that the spirit can most completely and truthfully be shown.

Then the flashes of art, of truth, fracture and are lost in dissonance, in flailing inattentive limbs and minds. The movements are similar, so similar, to that true pitch, yet they signify nothing now but the terrible fragility of meaning most fragile in this, the most ephemeral of the arts. George snaps his fingers again pistol-shots, *snap snap snap snap Get on the beat get on the beat get on the* beat *yes yes yes.* He feels his students' pain and exultation and it creates a magnetic, energising field around his own half-centuried joints and tendons, that half-century a permanent awareness in him now. The pain - both his and theirs - is not only the price of self-creation, but also, and more impor-tantly, the price and proof of their faith.

All art is a gesture of faith, George thinks. *What-ever its form. Faith in humanity. In the belief that we can share what we feel and understand. All art is a sacrifice of the individual made to take the rest of us beyond what a workaday life of unreflective getting-by can give or even offer us.*

This life of sacrifice is, he hopes, what his students are working to dedicate themselves to, as opposed to one where anything that is too large or too difficult is blotted out with drink and drugs, TV game-shows and lottery dreams. They warp their bodies with extreme movements and extreme treatment in the search for truth in the physical human form, poisoning them for purity with cigarettes and black coffee, turning them out against the body's easy tendencies in defiance of nature.

All art is unnatural. All art rejects the naturally-proportioned life, the conventionally-proportioned life, if these two are the same. All artists are queer if only many are gay.

The sun streams in in hot yellow trapezoids through studio windows that have been designed to not be opened, and the air-conditioning has failed again. The humidity level is high and the solid air becomes another sort of flesh, wrapping and unifying fourteen sets of lungs that gasp for oxygen, carbon life expelling toxic carbon waste into the growing heaviness of the room, and the dancers' movements coarsen and gain weight too.

The Funkadelic track ends. The shining students stagger, rise, freeze in pose, then slump, projected into anticlimax immediately the number is over. The tape clicks off. The class is finished. There is ragged applause, then water is sucked greedily from plastic bottles and poured over upturned faces and heaving chests.

Libating the flesh.

George allows himself a smile. Moments of truth were more than he had expected from this class today, the day of his fiftieth birthday. And those ghosts that he has never, can never, and perhaps would never want to lay to rest were not resurrected in the impassive, eager faces or taut, toned, perspiring bodies of the young students now catching their breaths before him; were not revealed as implicit in the living, as the skull beneath the skin; were not channelled down. No mediumistic contacts today, only the living ones of body to body. *Life taking life's side. It is necessary.*

He wipes his sweaty face with a towel, then rubs it over his shiny shaven head. One of his students, a pretty, light-skinned black girl with an elaborate geometrical construction of braids exploding from the top of her head, thanks him for the class. And now, reflected in her clear, clear-sighted eyes, he does see ghosts, the vivid ghosts of the flesh: skin and bone and muscle crying out to skin and bone and muscle.

Oliver.

Jean-Pierre.

Felipe.

The memories do not return. How could they when they are never not there? They are only more or less consciously present, more or less in focus. Life and death are intertwined, after all. They define each other. Striving is born out of mortality. Creation - artistic creation - is born out of the knowledge and fear of annihilation, and as an act of resistance, defiance of God, if there is a God, which George doubts. Defiance of the callousness, then, the indifference and wasteful-ness of a Nature that cares nothing for any given individual and little even for the species. Defiance, and also the assertion - the queer assertion - that what is of value can be transmitted down the chain of blood and sperm without wombs or child-bearing; that art can be a different sort of procreation.

The girl is twenty, with a delicate thorax and strong thighs. Miriam. Hard-working but with only a modest natural gift. George has always admired hard work. He thanks her for thanking him and she smiles brightly with attractive too-large teeth. Other students drift out in knots, most saying goodbye to him, to others, a few not. Miriam joins a tall, long-limbed and very dark-skinned black boy with short dreads and they leave with hands lightly linked. George takes in the precise position of their fingers in relation to each other, that butterfly delicacy something to be captured in some future work, part of the dance of life; a small connection that reveals.

They are the last to leave the studio, and his eyes follow them as they go. It is the sixth of July and for so many reasons he feels alone today. His fiftieth birthday. Half-century. An apparent meaningfulness, a decimal illusion. The room is empty now, no class is scheduled for the next half-hour. Suddenly George feels he must move. He extends his left arm fluidly and inclines an ankle, creating the starting place, the angle that compels response of joint to gravity, limb to limb, breath to beat to rhythm. The snare is memory, the bassline heartbeat: secret time-signatures. That which can be heard is the thud and shuffle of his bare feet on the dust-impacted, subtly elastic varnished floorboards, and the compressed exhalations of breath his regularly-snapping diaphragm expels from him. He moves with the grace of wisdom and the grief of remembrance, for moments totally alive, dancing with unseen present partners.

Because the flesh remembers, the mind, the soul, the body, no true division between them, remember:

Oliver, Jean-Pierre, Felipe and me. All of us, our quest back then, our compulsion, our necessity was to turn weak flesh, weak will into some supple expressive human-transhuman tool, to become abstract so as to become completely present. It was Oliver who most understood the truth of that and of me. Angelito Negro. *He had that rare lightness that lifts a man above the banalities of craft and technique, he had the moves and when he moved he was transmitting life, his arms impossibly long his body so strong, so delicate, so beautiful it startled, conveying all that was human, all that was necessary, which is surely all that art can or ever should attempt to do. But I could see his double tragedy, I who know it so well -*

Dancing to industrial beats in Heaven with Felipe and Jean-Pierre after the show, Oliver en pointe *in crepe platforms and green sequinned hotpants, filled with a love of the music that was total, his movements a constant giving, his presence a tribute to The Kids, the unknown geniuses who never dance outside the clubs, who never turn expression to account, to profession, who never get paid, and who are our secret inspiration, we who know the truth of it. Perhaps he was repaying their gift as he simultaneously acknowledged their tragedy: that nothing is left behind in that place, in that dark ephemeral world, not even memory. There is only the music, endlessly repeating like some larger heart-beat, pulling the flesh, compelling the flesh, and the moment repeats over and over and when all is done, sweat, semen, blood and tears, nothing remains behind.*

How many times have I lain in my bed alone, my flesh screaming out to be touched, to be loved, to be nurtured? And I have put my hands over my ears as if the pain, the need was audible; and sometimes I have woken to the sound of my own voice, a high, flat child-like keening I do not want to own. And I know Oliver's flesh screams too as I watch him dancing over and over in my mind, gutting himself, exposing all that is deep in him Oh baby -

We need to love our flesh for they do not - *Toni Morrison somewhere - something like that. And Oliver's flesh screamed out for love as his youth burned within him, as he danced his life away, and that was his double tragedy, two tales of love, two tales of blood, a double tragedy of the flesh.*

And I leave his absence at the hospital, his husk,

the haunting death-mask I kissed, the weightless fragility I held and I too am a husk dry of tears, seeds rattling pith desiccated, fibrous, and I'm on the Underground and it's the rush-hour and the train rattles on and all around me life presses in, lives press in on me telling me that none of it matters, that organic matter is fecund, that no individual matters. I am assaulted, violated. A boy-girl couple kiss juicily and I want to scream but instead I retain my elegant artificial facade all the more rigidly: my grief is not for them, not for their indifferent - hostile - eyes. Germs multiply all around me. I can't turn it into art, not now, not in this close and stinking place. Later I will create a duet for two men, my first out gay piece, Double Helix, and dedicate it to Oliver.

Oliver, Jean-Pierre and Felipe. All gone. Felipe I knew least well, Oliver I knew best and he died last, and here. Felipe went back to Brazil, Jean-Pierre went to Paris. Oh, but they never left me.

George is tired now, and in any case he doesn't want to be watched while he dances, whether it's by passers-by, other teachers, or students arriving early for the next class with nowhere else to wait but right by the open door. He shakes his shoulders loose, moving through the stretches that have kept his sinews supple over the last thirty-seven years. His muscles are warm and aching and feel almost good.

Oliver.

The heat of his forehead smooth against the stubble of my chest as we lay together naked on his sagging single bed on dingy sheets in some other July. The scent of dope and beeswax candles hanging in the air of that poky rented room. The dust-striated linen blind lowered against the street-light that burned outside just eight feet from the dirt-webbed glass. A king of infinite space A queen of infinite space he seemed then, both of us maybe born to royalty and ruling - what? The countries of ourselves, perhaps.

George goes over to the stack system, ejects his mix-tape, picks up his sports-bag and leaves the empty room. The ghosts leave with him, embedded as they are in his flesh. This is a Voodoo truth: that we bear the dead with us; that we are marked and formed even by what has passed beyond our remembrance. It is a spiritual analogue both for our genetic heritage and for the endless intermeshing ripples of cause-and-effect that form our lives. We are not haunted by our past so much as possessed by it. We are made up of our ghosts. And it is a visceral thing.

He makes his way down the narrow stairwell, turning sideways to squeeze past stretching, bitching dancers and gay office boys and housewives waiting for aerobics classes, goes down to Danceworks' basement and showers. Afterwards he moisturises his body with cocoa-butter from head to toe with obsessive thoroughness. 'I reckoned you weren't over thirty-five,' a pick-up told him sometime last year when, after they'd had sex, he had asked George his age and George had told him - *(skin supple shaved head ageless his dancer's grace and leanness)*. 'Old enough to be my father,' the boy had laughed, not caring. A white boy, a barrow-boy from down Brixton Market. George had felt neither shame nor triumph. *Just a thing, just nothing, just life.*

The small café in Danceworks' basement isn't too crowded, and George gets a table to himself. To one side the tops of the windows slide up to street-level, so if he looks up he can see men's and women's feet going to and from Oxford Street, some fast, some slow. A slanting glass wall opposite gives onto a small sunken studio where a ballet class is in progress. He sips his espresso and watches dispassionately as the dancers execute their moves, thinking now not of the past but of the dance he is making, the dance in which he is striving to express, perhaps futilely, a thousand things beyond words, the dance of remembrance. All he has that is certain is its title: *Legendary Children*.

Malcolm drags a breath into his narrow chest and blows, setting the notes from his horn free, sending them spinning upwards to pierce the membrane of the relentless city sky, bring the deluge and end the heaviness.

> *Exhale*
>   *Inhale*
>   *Respire*
>   *Expire*
>   *Always mortality*
> *Life, death/*
>   *The breath*
>   *the spirit;*
>   *The city*
>   *the In*
>   *-spiration/sky burst relieve*
>   *Me*

The mass of air piled up above him feels like pre-destination, feels like the weight of history pushing down on the present, forcing out the future.

Ziggy is coming back.
  Ziggy is coming back today.

But Malcolm doesn't know Ziggy yet, doesn't really even know who he is, let alone that their lives will soon become so passionately entangled. Some friend of Luke's is all he knows. *A name, an old flame.* He breaks off to wipe the back of his hand across his mouth, puts the trumpet to his lips again.

It's the first time in three days he's picked up his instrument, a scarily long time for him. *Because to not be making music, to not be feeling it and having to respond to that feeling is to be dead. My fingers lay there like slaughtered things and all sounds were bleached. The Devil-fly insect-bite to the soul, the wound the old poison that is genetic social psychological that I can never fully suck out spit out.*

Yet despite that, and despite the enervating heat and humidity, something about today has energised him.

Ziggy, sending out secret, unconscious signals?
Whatever unknown reason I can run again
    Yeah I'm an athlete in my
    Spirit-head/I climb
    a Human Fly
    a speeding bullet in my lungs and lips
    Heart and hips/
But
    The Spider waits the Black
        Dog runs faster (No torn
    ham-string ever no not for it)/ the revolver-
    barrel sucks backwards &
        Like a pharaoh's buried
    slave mouthful of sand/I will soon choke again
    on gun-powder despair -

The aching emptiness that brought him to the bridge two years and two months ago, that made him look down into the grey-brown undertow, rippling, lit with night-sulphur, and see sirens beckoning him to join them, calling to him with throats that gargled sewage. *The currents strong, they say*, the dirty water colourless and cold. *They catch you and they drag you under and you don't rise.*

He had leant out over the parapet and stared down. And then he had leant out further, no longer thinking or even feeling, just tilting against the static, timeless moment.

Then *they* had come swaggering up behind him, vibrant with hate, flushed on drink, transcendent on drugs. Five of them bunched like a fist, those pale reverting others. And he had looked round and seen them and known at once that to them he wasn't an artist in existential crisis, he wasn't a human being in emotional pain, he was just a *Nigger on the bridge*. Their eyes had been transparent and shiny as broken glass, and all that is dead in the West was made manifest in them in meat and bone and sharpened iron.

Crossing the other way towards him, towards them, drunk and unsuspecting, another other then, another stranger, Luke.

And there had been shocking sudden violence and blood, Malcolm's blood, running hot and cold slantwise down his face as he hit the pavement *Five against one*. And in the face of that pumping mottled racist hate and rage he had struggled violently for life. *Boot in the gut expelling breath, sucking breath, spirit back into torn lungs Breathe, Live, Fight*. He had struggled violently against a violence that defied him to choose to die. And then Luke was there alongside him, making it five against two, Luke the naïve white boy who couldn't stop himself piling in, defying his skin - *Race traitor Nigger-lover* - paying off some obvious and obscure debt of history, but they were too many, and soon enough his blood was on the pavement in red coins too, and soaking black beneath the streetlights into his blond, blond dreadlocks. He lost a front tooth to a steel-capped boot that night. Every time Luke smiles Malcolm remembers.

Take it to the bridge.

They would both have been done for, done over, hospitalised, crippled, even killed, if a car hadn't pulled

up then, a battered white Bimma full of Nubian warriors on the high arch of the bridge in that empty pre-
dawn hour under the fizzing street-lights. Joe and his
spars, heading back from some party, some blues late
late late. And after they had fractured some Nazi skulls
and bloodied some narrow noses the skinheads had
broken and run.

Cowards pack-hunters.

'Fucking queers!' Joe's mate Levi had called after
the skins as they pelted away south, blood streaming
from his nose where a rose-slick forehead had slammed
against it, and Malcolm had noticed Luke's eyeballs
twitch at that, a twitching imperceptible except to him
who could sense the same flickering responsive com-
pression of his own sclerotic membranes -

Fucking queers -

No escape then, no mercy for sons who love sons.
But on that night and in those circumstances that
hadn't mattered much. They had ended up at some
whores' all-night café where they had bound their
wounds with headscarves and talked through split lips
stiffened with drying blood, pressed paper napkins over
barked knuckles and hunched over aching guts. They
had drunk strong bitter tea and eaten greasy all-day
breakfasts, and as they talked that hard-eyed morning
they had become something deeper than friends;
comrades, perhaps.

Malcolm, Luke, Joe, Levi, Royston, and Leonie with
her large, wise eyes. Leonie, who had stayed in the car
watching, witnessing, when they had been up there
battling on the bridge, and who watched them now,
witnessed their bruised, drawn, radiant faces transfig-
ured by the searing gold of the dawn sun as it broke
between the tall, tall buildings of the City. And Malcolm
had looked at Luke then, had studied the angles of his
face, the sea-greenness of his eyes, and seen something

there.

And the strangest of all the strange things that happened on that night was this: Joe offered to drop Malcolm and Luke off at their respective homes, leaving his friends and his future wife to go back and collect later, and Luke, who Malcolm had never met before, and to whom he had barely spoken even in the café, had turned to him and said, 'Come back to mine, yeah?' And without a moment's thought or hesitation Malcolm had said, 'Yes.' And that was two years and two months ago and Malcolm is still here.

He looks around the untidy, cluttered room. Their room, home. Squalid, but not. As a womb is squalid with blood-knots and foetal piss, with life and promise. Furniture that is saggy and marked with bright scars of oil-paint, but comfortable. Twists of dust among the plant-pots and in the corners. Rag rugs. Old vinyl records in a slanting row along one wall, gleaming unseen in their sleeves; piles of CDs and art books. A tiny universe. Sometimes the room is a source of wonder to him, sometimes it is a trap, sometimes just a room, the front room of a twelfth-floor tower-block flat off Ladbroke Grove.

And him and Luke? Sometimes he thinks they are lovers, and it is true that they share a bed, that they sleep naked together under the less than ideally clean sheets, and that they sometimes snuggle close as cats. They smell each other's farts and morning breath and feel - are casually aware of - each other's jutting morning hard-ons, and Malcolm plays his trumpet while Luke paints. But there is not, and never has been, any sexual act between them.

Sometimes Malcolm thinks they are friends. But it's never enough to say that. Nearer is that each is the brother the other never had. When questioned Malcolm says they have a zebra situation and leaves the questioner to decode that as they will.

No explanations, then, no accounts, and his music, fluid, sinuous, improvisatory and ever-changing, is the representation of his stateless state of being. Or perhaps it is the music that determines the indeterminateness of his life, that constructs the shifting structures of his mind, a mind that is at once both freed and slightly broken by the drugs he's taken that he mostly no longer takes, that in a profound although indirect sense Luke freed him from, as he freed Luke from other things. They both freed each other and so, paradoxically, remain indebted to each other. Because freedom is complex, and is both necessary and unbearable.

Malcolm has dyed his short hair orange and grown a goatee. He hides large, dark, large-lidded eyes behind blind man's shades, and has full, almost outsize lips. Bumper-car lips Luke once called them, approvingly, making Malcolm smile. He is between skinny and lean, and his skin is mocha-dark, and smooth. Even dressed as he is now, in a dirty white tee-shirt, grubby white Cargo pants and broken-backed deck-shoes, he comes across as sharp, as a cool cat with a bebop style, a Blue Note album-cover in waiting.

It's his style, it's what comes naturally to him, but it has a price. Because despite his being sexually attracted to men, despite the fact, the muscle, the cock and arsehole of it, the what-gets-you-hard of it that he is sure pervades his scent, chemically informs his pheromones and inhabits every cell in his body, something in his vibe gets him habitually taken for straight, drawing women to him, and not with the particular safe-scent of fag-haggery, but with real cunt-to-cock hopefulness.

He puts down his horn, wipes his face on his tee-shirt. *When I've never been straight in any way*, he thinks, remembering girls who've put the make on him, mistaken him for what they wanted him to be, who've made him feel invisible and filled him with silent rage. *Never been straight, always been a fucked up, night-working, cock-sucking, drug-taking outsider. Like Bird and Miles, Monk and Mingus - Never been inside the world of insiders. Well yeah, okay, I've been inside. I've seen it geographically, architecturally. But I never fitted there between those walls, never belonged in the houses of the holy or the houses of the rich, in the vaginas of white girls or black girls, or fuck it in the* anuses *of black girls or white girls. It was a different grip I needed,*

> *A harder, darker trip*
> *I had to take*
> *make*
> > *not fake*
> *To reach the Real Deal.*

So I was brought to the deep places, to the Mother-ship Connection, to the primal Black by the hard and the yielding realities: that my dick felt different in a woman's arsehole to a man's

> *(how?*
> *why? But it did),*

that my hips were flowing in line with nature - my nature - when I fucked a guy while the same act with a woman was a parody, grotesque, hard to keep it hard for, a performance, surface, worthless -

> > *Made me*
> > *Worth*
> *Less.*

The different riffs, different slides on the ring of muscle tightening round my dick revealed me. Getting laid

> *laid lies*
> *to rest*
> *Oh yes,*
> > *and it was ecstatic too, my dick like*

obsidian or
Some Osiran monolith
Erected inside/some other man's holiest place.
And so I was, you understand, brought by the mo-
tion of my hips down down to the Gay Ghetto Deep
where no straight man goes if he can avoid it, to face
the mystery of the generality of gender, to confront the
taxonomy of desire, to ask the question what it is in
the mind or heart of a boy, a youth, a man, that
decides 'pussy is what I want' or 'dick is best', a ques-
tion that for straight men has an answer clear (un-
seen) as glass troubled
(and then only rarely)
by provocative androgynes
with kaleidoscope genitals
     or
Cheap drag queens
Viewed through the gauzy stocking of
too much whisky, beer or wine: the answer being,
the begetting of children.
But they know this is no true answer, or we'd have
no pill no rubbers no rhythm method no abortions,
just an endless birthing.
Why do men get me hard whether I think about it
or not, and women don't? Is it the smell, the heat of the
male body, the pheromones? If I was blind and my lips
my fingertips brushed a smooth bare shoulder I know
I would know.
To the straight man or woman these questions are
invisible, or just perverse: to even ask why you want
to fuck who you want to fuck is something no-one does
except out of queer necessity.
To refuse to kiss the arse of the system that props
up and magnifies the centrality of reproduction in this
bi-gender species, to refuse to lap up all the shit of
binary opposition of male to female that that gives rise

to, to refuse to understand desire as apart from the pull of sperm to egg is something you do not do unless you are forced to. And one of the false and phoney binary oppositions that shit creates is gay and straight, as if gay and straight are clearly and simply divided rigid categories, opposed to each other in need and deed, politics and faith. But maybe there is no opposition. Maybe in the elaborate uniqueness of our construction none of us are the same, none of us are categorisable.

Why do some men want to eat pussy? Or arse? Why are some men breast men? Why are some men cock men? Butch men? Femme men? Perhaps there are a hundred thousand homosexualities and just as many heterosexualities and bisexualities. Maybe the formation of our sexuality is so subtle a process that any attempt to categorise it, to crudely and lumpenly divide it, can only impoverish us all.

So for me it had to be jazz: the only expressive form that can begin to touch on this, reflect and celebrate this openness, our improvisatory lives; reflect these complex permutations of preference that can only make sense species-wide, beyond the individual acts of necessary procreation; make sense in some secret way that satisfies something in the collective unconscious, the group mind, the soul, the heartbeat of humanity, and gives us art and music, other procreations.

Or perhaps Damballah is improvising it all, and all this life and all this richness and blood and death and madness is just a riff on Gabriel's horn.

Only jazz is not too basic. Or too cold.

Not only did the music convey something deeply real to Malcolm from the first time he heard it, but also the particular scene in which it was created, that heavily masculine, incipiently Black Nationalist Fifties-

Sixties world of hep cats hanging homosocially, was for him intensely and profoundly erotic. In its upfront hetero machismo it was a world that pushed women to the margins, and though they might loll provocatively there in the background fancying themselves muses, in reality it was about pure, raw male creative energies reflecting and magnifying each other; brothers inspiring brothers, (mostly) black men turning each other on with the newest truth-bending, truth-revealing sounds, driving each other on - bebop don't stop - a Muslim division, Islam without the crap. Miles, Mingus, Bird, Sun Ra, Trane, Ornette, Art, a spirit brotherhood. A world that was compelling for Malcolm in its male totality, in its exclusions and essentialisms, and the place where he had first felt both the reality of love and the pain of its denial:

Musician/

Faggot.

Luke found me in the gutter, lying there waiting like his destiny. My zebra brother. Waiting so later on his dark night I could bind his bloody wrists. And with each tight tug and knotting of the torn cotton duck I tied him closer to me. My younger brother by two years and many skin-tones.

And Malcolm looks at his horn and thinks, *Jazz is the way forward, the symbolic escape from these cycles of repetition, this paralysis of the soul, creating variations on a theme that break open the damning loop, that embody progression, that liberate us from the structures and language that have so often oppressed us, and lets us step outside them. It is a way of understanding, of seeing the truth not in an intellectual but in a felt way, it is a spiritual understanding made manifest, made physically present in sound -*

He puts his horn to his lips and sends another cool high note up out into the heaviness of the day. The piece is his own. It is called *Saviour*.

Does Ziggy hear Malcolm's music? Perhaps behind the clatter of the train's steel wheels across a million joints, ten thousand points, he does. The journey he is making is one that is small in miles but large in meaning. He stares out at the passing landscape not thinking, not feeling, just waiting. To begin again. To exist again. To reappear. For himself. To disappear. From them.

And George - George, who doesn't know Ziggy yet, who doesn't know where Ziggy went, or that he is now coming back, hitting the city panel-beaten and rewired - looks down on the ballet-class through the sloping windows of the Danceworks café, his body and spirit resonating softly as he watches.

Of all the forms of dance it was ballet that captured George first, unexpectedly and even perversely given that he grew up in a household filled with everything but classical music. Jazz and blues, calypso and soca, ska and reggae and Tamla soul and gospel were his whole world back then. And he loved them. No, more than loved them: he *was* them. That music was part of him, and not like a limb or hair or even memory, but like a syncopated inner nervous system: fundamental, primary, autonomic. No room for anything as remote as love: do you love your heart?

The sense of movement that music brought to him was so direct as to be impossible to detach from the fact of his body, encoded as it was in every cell, in every drawing of breath, every pulse of the heart-muscle. It gave him a rhythmic self that with total unexpectedness was to permit in him the profound love of something other, and a confidence that enabled him to bear to be the sissy boy in the rough neighbourhood who wanted to dance ballet. *Sissy ballerina. Nancy. Queer.* Only love could have made him push through that wall of spit and vitriol. Only love could have countered and overcome that corrosive contempt.

Why ballet? A question he's been asked ten thousand times, it was also a challenge with a threat wound up in it: why a form so remote from everything you know, everything you've experienced, everything that's touched your life directly? And more deeply: how could you, a boy so brown, so poor, so full of moves, acquire such a consuming fascination for an art so white, so bloodless, formal and effete, an art so intended for the titillation of the rich and powerful? The threatened answer being, of course: *because you've been contaminated, boy, because you've been corrupted, perverted, emasculated, coconutized, because you've given it up for The Man in every way.*

And George would say nothing because the real answer was too hard for words, too deep and subtle, and could only be given within the art itself, perhaps. But he understood that ballet touched on some necessity in him, some need both for order and escape, in a profound and personal way.

He had been brought all the way to England from Jamaica at the age of seven by his mother's sister, sent on ahead of his mother and following a father he had not seen since the age of four, (*searching for warm brown eyes, familiarity of blood, the prickle of a moustache - memories of his father's strong arms lifting him as he would later as a man be lifted by others, the movement always touching a sense of loss in him and briefly repairing that loss*). Expecting, needing family, a home, George had found instead a stranger, a man exiled from his former laughing self in dark and tangled ways. Shepherd's Bush Green, which had sounded so rural to George in his father's brief letters home, so filled with the resonance of goats, the parish, had turned out cold and grey and bare and poor, and the alien city was writhing around him, around them all, writhing and dead at the same time.

His father mostly either ignored him or actively resented him - *di pickney drain away me money* - and seven-year-old George had felt lost and afraid in that unfamiliar, unwelcoming place, under that lightless sky. He might have been helped by his older brother and sister, but though they had been in England for two years by the time he arrived, and so knew many of its ways, they had no more time for him than his father did, both of them preoccupied by then in dealing with their frighteningly-erupting and now culturally-unmoored sexual awakenings. *(Flung into a utopian slum, a concrete city in the sky raised cheap and high above bomb-sites left over from the War, the troops Jamaica sent to help the Motherland, the Empire then, and his sister's good hair counting for nothing in that white hell of hatred and pale, tight violence, Union Jacks and race-riots. No blacks no dogs no Irish)*.

The grey and threatening confusion of the world outside combined with the disunity within his family to make the young George long for order. Another young man might have fantasised about joining the army, or allowed his mother to persuade him into going to church and dressing smart in suit and tie. But not George. Slender, fine-boned Jamaican George who, at age eleven, on a school trip to see Swan Lake, had discovered ballet, and been transported.

His class-mates had behaved so rowdily on that trip that they and their idealistic, shame-faced teacher had been asked to leave in the interval. He had burned at the unfairness of it as they were escorted out, hating the way the theatre manager, ushers and afternoon balletomanes had looked at him and not seen that he was different from the others, had seen just another

ignorant yob. But still that day his life had been trans-
formed.

The rigour, discipline, stylisation and rigidity of the
ballet's traditions sank straight into George's receptive,
eager psyche. He was also overwhelmed by its assertion
of a purity that he had never seen or even conceived of
in the bleak and grubbing harshness of the lives around
him, or in his own life up to that point: the purity of
giving your life over to serving beauty. That it both
offered escape from the world around him and added
something rare and precious to it made it seem perfect
to George then, a higher calling that both embraced the
flesh and transcended it.

As it had to.

As it had to, because already for the eleven-year-old
George to express through the body, through its
muscles and sinews in abstracted moves and gestures,
was to escape being tormented by a dangerous awaken-
ing sense of other bodies, of the sexes of those bodies
and his own, and of his difference from other boys.
Throwing himself into the discipline of dance, the
physical stress and grind of it, was a way of blotting out
sensibilities that he already knew in his shrinking heart
were totally unlike those of his class-mates, the boys
who had laughed so loudly and coarsely and confidently that day at the male ballet-dancer's crotch and
buttocks encased in seamless white hose.

Holy. Somehow.

To me.

The Puritan.

Perhaps too he had responded to some prescient
genetically-encoded, acculturated or group-
unconscious impulse that steered him towards a
strongly homosexual environment. *Sissy ballerina not
untrue.*

And then there was the music, orchestral, elevated,

vast; rich and heavy with the history of a continent that had ruled the world. It moved him in a different way from any other music he had heard before, and that too seemed liberating then. To respond to that music, to be compelled to hear, feel, move in a different way, an external way untrammelled by the confining fear and poverty of the life he knew, somehow released him from himself.

He followed that cold white path with what seemed like all his heart until he reached the age of nineteen. That year he had his first love affair, and not coincidentally he realised that what had seemed like love had been at least in part a hatred of where he came from. So he turned from his now-tainted calling and spent the next five years of his life rediscovering from the outside-in the music that had formed him from the beginning. And in doing so he developed one of the many sets of double-consciousness that structured his being, although it was not the first. *No, that first revelation came faster, hotter, more violently, in kisses and bruises and semen: the revelation of my skin, my race, in itself, in myself, and at that moment as it was reflected back at me in my white lover's eyes. I met his gaze and saw mirrors masquerading as tunnels. Oh my eyes were opened then as he moved his lips and said the things you can never take back.*

Lucky, he said, you're lucky. Because most white men won't date black, they think it would be a step down, dirty.

This is 1969, clandestine, almost pre-Gay Lib, almost pre-Black Power, and I'm lucky, so lucky. I can tell by the look on his face he thinks I should be grateful, I should be kissing his arse or his feet. He is from money. He is being groomed to be the star of the class. The romantic lead roles come to him as a matter of course, of right, droit de signeur. *He is blond and has a classical profile. His body has what was then and what is still considered to be the anthropometrically correct proportions for classical dance. No defective steatopygous Hottentot butt. I am lucky to be granted such proximity to him. He doesn't understand why I curse him out and storm out of his flat, why I blank him at class the next day. He doesn't know how he split me open, how he made me despise myself for believing I could be what I wanted to be. What he is. He starts a whispering campaign against me, says I stole things from him and that I've had VD -*

George had been alone for a year after that disastrous first affair, wounded as he was, searching in other places and ways for healing, for wholeness. For a while he turned to drag, perhaps in self-loathing rejection of the overtly male aspect of himself that at that time felt tainted with failure, or perhaps hoping to access the wholeness of the two-spirited, the shaman, the witch-doctor, the *berdache*. And in a form that could be displayed. A presented form, because George is above all a performer, and no performer is whole without an audience: all performers need the suture of applause to heal their wound.

And for a while, as Laliqua Vase, he was healed. Elegant, haughty, long-leggedly athletic, as crazy as Grace Jones, she side-stepped his injured masculinity, side-swiped it and gave him access to a new power: as Laliqua he needed nothing of maleness. As Laliqua he was a lesbian. As Laliqua, for the first and only time, pissed and stoned out of his head, he went down on a woman, a drag king dyke, backstage at one of the gay pubs he was working back then. Laliqua intoxicated him; he was in love with her. For a while.

But drag has its own constraints, its own conservatism. Its brazen shallowness precludes digging deep, and it is not taken seriously as a vehicle for pain and anger. And George needed to dig deep. So he gave one last show, a grand diva finale for Laliqua, then put the sequins and boas aside and returned to serious dance.

At the age of twenty-two he choreographed his first significant piece, *Mulatto Hermaphrodité*. It is a solo piece he has reworked many times over the years, always concerned to bring out what is uplifting in it without betraying the defiant spirit that led him to make it in the first place: out of the movement from Negro to coloured to Black, through bitch, faggot, queer, homosexual, gay, *Rise up defy Deny nothing*. The death of Civil Rights the birth of Gay Liberation, feminism, Black Power. That uncertain, angry time producing uncertain, angry work -

Sometimes he's danced it himself, sometimes let others dance it for him, of whom Oliver was the first. His reworkings of the piece over the years have been necessary because revelation is relative, and must be constantly remade.

He has never believed in Christ. Or Mohammed. He cannot believe in a static moment of absolute revelation - Christ on the cross circa 33 A.D., Mohammed getting the good word from Allah, circa 622 A.D. - when everything suddenly became fixed forever and ever.

No: we begin from the body, we begin with the truth of the body, from the fact of the spirit being in the flesh, not first, not before the fact of the flesh. And we begin with music - the heartbeat, the voice rising up.

Recently he has become interested in Voodoo, or Vodoun, as he has learned to spell it out of respect for its practitioners, who wish to distance themselves from its Hollywood schlock-horror associations, drawn by its centring in dance and music. Its existence beyond, below and beside the establishment strikes parallels for him as a gay man, as does its co-option of, and resistance to, the established church. Its birth in Haiti, the first black state to win independence from the Europeans, adds a resonance of pride by association. And the concept of ecstatic possession - of being ridden by the ancestral dead, or by the *lwa,* the spirits - strikes something deep within him, a true note that neither Islam nor Christianity could ever reach. Moreover, in Vodoun all sufferings can be explained as being caused by the ill wills of men or spirits, and obeisances can be made and defences taken against them. There is no perverted all-powerful, all-loving God destroying his shrieking toys of flesh with rains of fire and agonies of plague and blaming them the while.

The spirits, the *lwa,* are not yet real to him, however, and since they must be fed in order to have power in the world, and his mere fascination doesn't constitute an offering, they remain buried below. But he gains strength from the fact of some other cosmology existing than the Judaeo-Christian one, some other way of understanding the world and humanity. Vodoun opens spaces in him that seemed closed before.

He dreams of a great work of life and commemoration that is perhaps beyond his ability to realise, the work he has already entitled *Legendary Children: Living Spirits Of The Dead.* But today he is tired, today he is lonely, and art doesn't feel so very important after all. Because what is the view from the mountain-top if you have no-one to share it with? No companion to urge you on on the climb?

Fifty years old and still dreaming of love.

He smiles to himself, tolerant of the sentimental yearning on this hot July afternoon, almost comfortable with it as he sits in the café and watches the ballet class end, smoking a filterless cigarette and sipping a strong black coffee.

Too hard now. It'd be too hard. I'm too hard.

*

Luke had felt the lowering hatred in the air the night that brought him to the bridge, to Malcolm. Living so long under the suffocating bell-jar of race-hatred, hypersensitised to it through overdosing, he retained a heightened awareness of its faintest presence, a pre-science almost. He believed himself immunised to it and yet he was still its product: he had still to struggle to transcend, or rather to transform into something useful, the fact of the whiteness of his skin, and escape the damning particularity of his history.

He remembers the title of a small magazine he saw in some Anarchist bookshop window once, when he had just turned eighteen: *Treason to Whiteness is Loyalty to Humanity*. He hadn't had the courage to go in and buy the magazine, but it had opened a window in his mind and let him know that he was not alone. Not mad.

'The mind-fuck soul-fuck of it is they tell us we live in a post-racist time, my Nubian.'

Malcolm, holding forth in their living-room six years later. Luke is twenty-four.

'It's all still there, the racism, the hatred. Black people are still getting beaten, killed, imprisoned, underpaid, discriminated against, kicked out of the country, erased. But the government says they're not racist, the media says they're not racist. Even the fucking *Daily Mail* says it's not racist. And because they say that - '

Malcolm drags on the joint he's been smoking, then passes it to Luke.

'Because they say that it makes certain truths invisible, you know? Shit to do with how power operates, with the way so much hasn't changed since the empire went under. And the intellectuals, the opinion-makers, the so-called liberals think they're above all that, too cool, too wise to be racist, and they look down on the

Nazis and the niggers from on high and they sigh because to them it's just boring. It doesn't touch them so they don't feel it. To them it's like, What's the problem? Drop the attitude and trust us and everything'll be just fine. But if you deny the reality of racism then you're calling black people deluded for seeing it, deluded for trying to resist it. And that's just another way to crack a black man's skull. Political trepanation, my brother. Post-racism.'

Malcolm had smiled at Luke then, watching him intently over rose-pink shades, his slightly buck-toothed smile half-warm, half a baring of teeth. 'Don't worry, my man,' he had added, in response to the anxious look that clouded Luke's face. 'You're at least a part-time nigger now. And that ain't a job you can quit, my brother.' And he had put his arm around Luke's neck and pulled him to him on their battered brown leatherette sofa, and kissed him on the temple. Luke had smelt dope-smoke and cocoa-butter, CK1, sweat and meaning. He had laughed, feeling both relief and a strong connection with the vital and the meaningful through Malcolm's words, in the heat of Malcolm's lean, bare arm around his neck, and they had kissed but as always with them done nothing more.

Battered Horn.

That was the title of the first piece Malcolm had made after he started staying with Luke. The motif, the initial sound, was the product of his trumpet having been kicked aside and stamped on by the thugs during the attack, splitting its mouth open. The notes were intentionally bent, splayed, flattened, fractured, as if played on the wrecked instrument, but rising up out of that wreckage into something pure and defiant. And so Malcolm called the piece Battered Horn.

Luke's thoughts return to that night on the bridge

and how to make sense of it. It is inextricably linked in his mind with another night eight years before, the night he ran, the night of repudiation -

Del is talking and the others are listening, shaved heads pale and flushing red, eyes hard, bright, the intensity erotic, repellent. The close room reeks of cheap aftershave and stale sweat. *He's a visionary your brother a fucking genius*, one of them says to Luke. Union Jack vests lace-up Doc Martens ball-crushingly tight butt-hugging jeans - *Oi Queers Keep your hands off our Boys* the stickers read on random lamp-posts, the erotic displaced into violence; and his brother, *twin, older by a heel*, is talking and they're all spell-bound and Luke realises he has to get out of that room, that flat, out of those streets, off that estate as the words pour down like hot blood over dark skin. Del is speaking, a cascade of words:

Whiteness is like a vast monument rising above atavistic roaming packs. You need someone to hate like you need someone to love. We are not no-one, we are not nothing. We are the continuation of history, of destiny, of everything great and massive and noble and visionary and callous. It's in our skins: we built an empire. We are the great, not the nobody nothing detritus of a shrinking industrial base, not the un-skilled third generation unemployed parasites on the system displaced by niggers and Pakis and Polacks and immigrants forever -

And Luke listens and burns, and his stomach clenches because there is a side of him that yearns to get caught up in the white-hot thrill of belonging even though he is excluded from it in every way, being both a queer and a nigger-lover. That truth is hidden from the others at that moment, however; is hidden in a handful of masturbatory drawings buried deep in a drawer in his bedroom, drawings of acts he has never yet commit-

ted with men he hasn't met, the longings and prefigura-
tions of a virgin queer, a long-distance nigger-lover.
*(What made me start to draw: that seized empower-
ment, that internal liberation, a world I could live in.)*
If they were discovered he would be dead. And in that
sick, dark, schizophrenic moment, empty of goodness
and despairing of love, he finds that he wants to get
caught up in the thrill of hating, half-wants to anyway,
which is why he will have to leave this room, those
faces, leave Del forever after this meeting is over, leave
it all behind him and choose life over the burning
parodic intensity of death. *Never see my brother
again.* Or at least not until eight years later almost to
the day -

Take it to the bridge.

This he never told Malcolm, this he kept as his secret: how he was unrecognised at first as he piled into
them in his baggy nigger clothes, blond extensions
exploding from the top of his head in a funki-dred style,
so different from the nondescript nothing whiteboy
clothes he used to wear, but not unrecognised at the
last as he rolled on the pavement after a savage knee in
the gut.

*I take one last kick to my face from my brother's
steel-capped boot before Del turns and runs like what
he is Lucky to only lose one tooth blood filling my
mouth. That saved Malcolm's face, maybe his mouth,
his lips, his teeth, his art.*

'We are supermen, we embrace destiny, we are pure
enough to be unafraid of getting our hands dirty, we are
the true white will,' Del is saying in the small, stinking
room, sitting legs wide apart below Union Jacks and
swastikas in ironic fusion, declaiming as if it all meant
something more than hate, than self-loathing turned
inside-out, the others hanging on his every word, loving
him sexlessly, obscenely.

'We hunt in packs, base, primal, unafraid of reality. We move in secret, underground. Make connections, flypost the truth: *Hang Paedophile Scum/Race-mixing Stinks/Repatriation Now.* Others commit to nothing, others reject purity, they lust for contamination, confusion, miscegenation. A white whore with a brown baby deserves to be raped. We must stand firm. For England. They see our signs and are afraid. To spread fear is power. Nothing exists except power.'

And Luke's throat constricts painfully as his mind fills with incoherent responses to Del's tirades that he is too young to articulate and would be too scared to say anyway, and he feels sick and has half a hard-on. He hates himself for being afraid of his own brother who is only a minute older than him and only a half-centimetre taller.

He is afraid of himself too, the nigger-loving queer. He is seventeen: his love is an insult. He tries to imagine a place where it won't be an insult as his brother rants on and on, a place like the world of his drawings, filled with fantastical black and white warriors, Conans and Blades side-by-side, swords drawn against a common foe, or face to face, hypnotised by each others' eyes, but he is trapped by his youth, his lack of experience and the poverty of his upbringing, and can imagine nothing that might exist in reality. And too he is trapped by the fear that he is nothing but a mirror to his brother and the others, right-to-left to left-to-right; that his loving what they loathe is somehow sick and perverted too, because it is toxically connected to the same need to find meaning outside himself, the same sense of lack.

Something to love. Something to hate. No difference. No, I don't believe that -

A further terror winds itself into his seventeen-year-old chest: *if I found the balls to do something - if*

*they caught me with someone what they'd do to him -
I've heard Del saying how he's seen the KKK in action
and how they've got the right idea and he'd chop off
any nigger's cock and shove it in his mouth and it
would be because of me because of me my skin pale
against his dark and we'd be torn apart and I
wouldn't be able to save him or save myself All red
under the skin Del says laughing and I'm at the wrong
end of a telescope retching with self-loathing.*

*That evening I knew something terrible was going
to happen, the thick build-up of hate was so heavy a
storm had to come. And maybe I shouldn't of, maybe I
should of done something more than I did, but I just
ran. All I could do was run.*

'Destiny,' Del is saying, his pupils pinpricks, his
gaze fixed on something beyond what is visible in that
low-ceilinged council-flat on the sprawling concrete
estate where he and Luke have spent their whole lives,
'destiny is what England felt in the time of Empire. And
now we live in an age of small men, devalued heroes,
our people unaware of their history, of the power in the
whiteness of their skin. I will pursue the red rapture of
the flesh, the violent conflict with alien flesh, the only
contact that matters or has meaning: the need to
master. Violence is the only contact that does not
defile, that cleanses. And even more than niggers,
Pakis, Chinks and wogs I hate with my divine ascen-
dant hate race traitors, nigger-lovers. I will stomp them
and their niggers into the ground.'

(Were those Del's words? Was Del ever that poetic,
with thoughts so well-formed? So Luke remembers it,
perhaps giving him power in memory, unintended
legendary status, *The monster to face and slay*).

Charged up on speed and hate and lager and vodka
they had left Luke *(at least I had the balls to refuse
that)* to hunt like dogs, and Luke had shoved his few

possessions into a sports-bag and walked out of the flat he had shared with his brother for the last eighteen months, walked out on the Union Jacks and the Nazi flags, the Combat 18 survivalist videotapes and the Skrewdrivr bootlegs, nothing resolved in his mind except that he needed to be somewhere else. He left no note, sent no letter. What would he have said? Nothing that Del could have heard. What did he even know to tell Del anyway? Only that he was going to look for what he knew he needed more than anything: primary blackness.

Before that had come a personality-stripping month in a homeless hostel followed by emergency housing, (he had still been just young enough then). Then a transfer to a progressive housing co-op and his introduction to the alternative world with its permissions and taboos, poverty-row bohemia. He had listened and learned. Six months later he had met Ziggy in a bar in the West End, and Ziggy was an artist who believed we are all artists, and so Luke became an artist too, not so much reborn as born for the first time, sucking life, nourishment out of Ziggy's mind and out of his dick like a new-born at the nipple.

'Fuck that mammy shit,' Ziggy had said when Luke had blushingly tried to explain the feeling to him. 'This is strictly one warrior to another, not *Gone With The Wind.*' - Ziggy administering an African Zen slap to Luke, one of the many thousand introductions he was to give Luke to the complexity of life, to the demands of stepping past delusion and living and loving in reality.

For a month after he left their - Del's - flat Luke scoured every paper, local and national, for news of some racially-motivated attack, battering, slashing, killing that had happened the night he ran, his throat constricted, fingers nerveless as he turned the pages, but there was nothing.

Nothing reported, anyway.

Chapter Two

*S*ometimes the voices go babbling on and on faster and faster louder and louder like a steam-train becoming more and more demanding until your rotating Exorcist head opens like a clockwork toy an anti-music box, slaughterhouse blades bloody saws gut-strings (your own stretched screeching vocal cords) the bow but They are playing not your clawed cat-mind. Then they float out and suspend themselves just above your head, persecuting you like owls or the police. You try to imagine something that would cut the wire the cord let them fall back up into the cold ink of space but you can't because that is part of what the babbling does, it strangles chokes off drowns the real you out defeating plans and will. You think maybe screaming might do it if you could only scream loud and piercingly enough but you don't dare to scream because what if it works but it is only while you are screaming that the voices shut up so you cannot ever stop screaming again if you want peace?

This is not what they call it, schizophrenia. It is not possession either. If it is anything it is the opposite, evacuation. It is being preyed on by secret subterranean crash-landed space leeches with silver sucker tooth-hole mouths crawling in and out of your skin metallic rotating radulas secreting enzymes thinning the soul-blood sucking out soul-content.

They don't understand these distinctions: soul-blood versus grey matter. Bone-shrines. Ancestors teleporting in versus hostile programming, tapes running discs spinning, drugs a wind-up wind-down: they don't understand what matters. But they have the

*power so what matters to them becomes what matters
to you and what matters to you you hide bury in cuts
not physical ones no Cuts in your brain transections
eyes on the slant otherwise you're trapped in mirrors.*

*Was I really only there for eight months? Man, I -
it felt like - Christ - (Don't think I think I'm talking to
Christ don't think I think I am Christ I know I am not
Christ. I know I am just a man Only half of what
Christ claimed to be The mortal organic tethered half
not the one that rose up to Heaven like a volcanic
eruption pyroclastic light a throne waiting). Somewhere radioactive isotopes decay at an absolute rate
but time is subjective.*

It feels like eight years have ground by since they
took him away, and his soul it is true is eight years
older than the world was when they dragged him strait-
jacketed, pinprick-pupilled, screaming and bloody into
the ambulance and slammed the doors. Eight years,
and not the eight calendar months the slow-motion
drive-by of the seasons beyond the reinforced security
glass told him it must have been. And if that was an
illusion for his soul, his brain, it wasn't for his body, all
the drugs he was doing back then, in the lead-up to his
crisis *(brain lungs liver kidneys aged decades beyond
their natural span, ruptured, burnt out, fucked in no
particular order by dope and alcohol, coke and heroin,
E, crack, ketamine, and every other pill and powder
going).*

Those were the bad drugs, the non-State-
sanctioned drugs, morally, spiritually different of
course from the drugs they pumped him full of when
they sectioned him: the good, obedience-inducing,
conformist drugs. Drugs that couldn't work on him, he
yelled and shrieked until his vocal chords were bleed-
ing, because they were in conflict with his true, free
nature. Drugs that could only poison him.

And they did: *toxic shock allergic reaction cardiac arrest - No his heart started beating again before they took the current to it No electric eels fastening their teeth on* his *nipples writhing on his pectorals No more drugs of either kind after that.*

I cured myself. Secretly I discarded them, their needles, their pills, their mind-controls, and reconnected with –

Ah, but I don't tell you that so easily: I don't know you and They could be listening Always are listening, recording but even their resources aren't unlimited and they are lazy-lazy.

Now I'm out but not fully because still I wear their clothes, their uniform: the piss-stained slacks and yellow-armpitted shirts of the unfashionable mad. (His own clothes blood-stained, soiled, were burned; he himself was stripped and thrown naked into an empty room. *Drug-induced psychosis, a voice said. Leave him like that. He'll calm down). And I was told by a voice behind a dazzling light that I was better off without those markers of dysfunctional deviant individuality, those kinking fetish fabrics with which I had adorned myself the metal rods and rings through my flesh.*

I wear the clothes they assign me from the communal bin. My hair is nappy. I look broken, and I have been. I stink with the sourness of those who endure inert confinement, the sweat of the immobile staining my African skin that is dry and thirsty and in pain: they never understood or cared.

The entrance to his flat is an anonymous dark-blue door on Portobello Road wedged in between a West Indian takeaway and a shop selling incense, Indian brass and hippie paraphernalia. Before he opens the door Ziggy uses his key to scratch a small pattern into its glossy paintwork, a *vévé* made of two interlocking Vs and four cardinal crosses bisected as if reflected in a mirror: protection.

'Is that your door you're marking up?' asks a large Nigerian woman in a yellow-and-orange headscarf with a young boy in tow, getting in his business, thinking him one of the local crackheads, maybe. He ignores her and slides the key into the lock. It turns easily, but he has to force aside a slurry of junk mail to get the door open. Eight months' worth of estate agents' materials, pizza flyers and credit-card offers. He steps over it and out of the crowded, pressing street. His flat was - *is* - on the first floor. The hall smells of dry rot and is airless. He climbs the narrow stairs and stands before his front door, produces another key, inserts it into the lock, and turns it. There is only a little resistance.

Inside the smell of oil-paint, linseed oil and turpentine is strong. Dust floats in the air, almost sparkling.

It's all there, waiting for him.

Without history we are nothing, like Malcolm X said. We are demoted to the lower animals. But to remember history too much, too intensely, to allow the past to be too constantly present to you, to allow it to possess your life, to forget nothing, to forgive nothing, it will drive you mad. A certain amount of forgetting is all that makes life bearable. But still I love you, Malcolm. From the first time I read you in that other hell, when you gave me back to myself.

He looks round the room. Everything is as he remembered it except dulled by a layer of dust, and the plants in their pots are desiccated sepia echoes of their former green selves. He closes and bolts the front door behind him *In case In case what? Just in case* and goes and forces up the rickety sash-windows. The air is as warm and motionless outside as in, and it makes no more difference than if he had opened prop-windows on a stage-set. Only the sound changes: the noises of the market come up with sudden clarity. Then the smells. He inhales sizzling meat, too-sweet fruit and rotting vegetables, baking, incense, car-fumes.

I'm back.

He thinks of the fridge. Opening it after eight months is not an appealing prospect so he doesn't. He tries the phone. Dead. At least the electricity and gas are still on, the standing orders slowly leaching away whether he was there or not. Lucky he had money in the bank.

Not much now.

The lack of change disturbs him. *Blood flesh mutilation madness did it really make no difference?* His right forearm starts to ache: it hasn't forgotten.

He tips the pills down the toilet, all three bottles' worth, and flushes. Then he kicks off the cheap, low-cut shoes that have been slopping off the backs of his heels and reduced him to a pitiable shuffler for his whole journey home. After that he strips off the identity-erasing clothes the hospital gave him to get home in: the ill-fitting beige slacks with the tide-mark stains around the crotch, the faded grey shirt that after a thousand boil-washes still has under its arms the darker coronas of unnatural sweating, both items cast-offs of the dead. He shucks off the saggy pair of market multipack briefs he was handed that morning - *I am a queen goddamnit, motherfucker, a queen and a black man, a Nigerian man, I do not* do *non-brand underwear -*

This one isn't cured No not at all We should keep him in longer much longer Indefinitely. Defiance, Non-acceptance are clear signs that further treatment is required.

But the paperwork is done. So get out before we wire you up again. Before we fry you again.

Now he is naked, the beginning of becoming free. He goes to the dresser drawer, gets out his barber's clippers, plugs them in and stands before the bathroom mirror and stares into his handsome-ugly, large-featured, battered face. Slowly and carefully he shaves the Mohawk back into his untidy, kinky hair, strength and clarity returning to him as the springy, interlocking rows of coils slide off in neat rolls onto the bathroom floor.

Maybe I'll dye it blond again later on today.

With the aid of a spirit-level Afro-pick he trims the top of the Mohawk until it is neat and flat and sharp-edged, then he cuts a vertical strip through one eyebrow. He runs the clippers over his chest, reducing the hair there to stubble, and gets a half-erection. Then he gets into the shower, picks up a loofah, and starts to scrub the institutional stink from his skin.

He is in the shower for a long time. Afterwards he moisturises his body with cocoa-butter, his aubergine-dark skin soaking it up, regaining smoothness, suppleness, vitality and resilience, regaining richness of tone, no longer ashy like the dead.

They didn't care if your skin split in there. In there they wanted your skin to split. They thought maybe the madness could get out that way, the way it got in, through the cracks. Or if not that, they could at least get their fingers in and open you up.

He goes to the over-full clothes-rail in his bedroom, chooses what he's going to wear, (*Not assigned at random out of the bin back from the laundry*), and dresses. A cut-off white tank-top, tight-fitting and navel-revealing, a black leather kilt, heavy black bike-boots with metal plates on the front. Rubber bangles on his wrists, a chain of cowries around his neck. The holes in his ears and nipples and dick-head have healed up - rape in reverse - so he wears no other jewellery. On his shoulder the *vévé* he had double-tattooed there so it would stand out like a raised scarified pattern gleams and glints. He stares into the mirror and for the first time in more than eight months sees not some confusing blank projection of the will of others but himself.

I'm back.

And with the one thing that I learned in there: what matters, what matters most of all, is to live your life from your own point of view, from your own perspective.

It's harder than you think.

He drinks a long, cold glass of water from the sink and heads out into the golden afternoon feeling light and wild.

The class George has been watching idly ends. Aerobics students, mostly women in their late twenties and early thirties eager to cram a bout with fitness into their lunch-hours, along with a few gay men, squeeze in past the outgoing ballet students as if there was a rush on, just like they do every day. Today means nothing to anyone except him. He lights up another cigarette as the aerobics class begins. Several of the women and one of the men struggle to keep up, missing the beat, missing the moves. George never used to understand this inability to do what was to him simply the only thing to do - respond to the beat - until one day when he was sitting in a café in Soho with an artist friend, Vernon, and Vernon had passed him a pad and pencil and said, 'Draw the street.' And George had tried, but scale and perspective had defeated him and he had thrown the pencil down in frustration after producing a graceless, cack-handed scrawl.

'All it is is just drawing what's there,' Vernon had said, picking the pencil up and making a series of deft, confident, almost casual marks on the paper. 'Just horizontals and verticals and slantways lines. Just looking and putting down what you see.'

And in the transparency of his friend's explanation George had seen both the transparency of his own talent and the opacity of what he couldn't do, and had understood that overcoming opacity could be harder than just being talented and making use of it. Talent was the easy bit. George hasn't seen Vernon in - how long? Twelve years? He wonders how it went with him, if he's even still making art. *So many of us need normality more.*

He stubs out his cigarette and turns the pages of the paper he bought to read on the bus, *The Voice*. He doesn't normally buy *The Voice*, doesn't feel part of the black community it defines, but today, on impulse, he picked it up from the newsagent's by the tube station, compelled by the front-page story, an inquiry into the death of a young black man in police custody. Not, painfully enough, because such a death was – or is - an uncommon occurrence in itself, but because in the article an expert was quoted as saying that the apparent choke-hold strangulation the youth was subjected to was in fact most likely an anaphylactic response to swallowing drugs (autopsy pending), and that the six police officers involved had used no more than reasonable force. Printed below that statement was a reminder of the (white) prison governor who had said recently that black men had different kinds of windpipes to whites, and were therefore 'predisposed to being fatally asphyxiated by a level of choking that would only disorientate and subdue a white man.'

Racism as cancer, he thinks to himself. *Racism as a tumour. Landscape as body, the post-imperial body mutating, poisoning itself with race-hatred. Cells mutating, cells of reactionary revolutionary racists underground, under the culture's skin. A motif of cell-structures as the backdrop to some dance-piece. Very Gilbert & George.*

He sighs. He can't focus properly today, can't conceptualise the movements that would be required to realise his ideas. Maybe he's thinking too pictorially and not spatially, not viscerally enough. *The choke-hold Vs of arm-locks, necks bent at unnatural angles, eyes bulging - connect with that. If you can bear to.*

'George, man.'

A warm hand grips his shoulder where his singlet has left it bare, and George looks up to see a short, handsome, light-skinned black man with a moustache smiling down at him, a towel slung casually over one broad, well-muscled shoulder.

'Joe.' George is pleased.

Joe slides his hand up to George's shaved head and rotates it playfully, mock-flirtatiously, making the back of George's neck prickle. 'What's up, Mister Choreographer?' he asks.

'Nothing much, sweetness,' George says, pulling out a chair for him. Joe swings down onto it. He has a clean, just-showered smell twined in with a light, musky-lemony scent. 'Just gestating shit for a new show.' The chance phrase reminds him of something and he smiles. 'So when's the baby due?' he asks. 'It must be soon.'

'Three weeks to the day, man.' Joe helps himself to a cigarette from George's pack, then decides against it. (*Need to stay alive my daughter to provide for, my wife, I want to see my little girl grow up go to university marry. Leonie smoked in the early weeks before we knew I hope she'll be fine not maaga It's all suddenly different*). 'If she arrives on time, that is. I mean JPT, you know? Japanese People's Time, no Soon Come.'

'So you know it's a girl?'

'Not really, man. We could've been told when Lee had the amnio but she said no and I went with that, with getting a surprise. It's just a strong feeling I've got. But it could be a boy,' he adds. 'Either's cool with me.'

George has known Joe for nine years now. The two men became friends through a ballet class George was covering for another teacher. Joe was the only black student in the class. Seeing echoes of himself in the younger man, and curious as to how things had changed since he trained so many years before, George struck up a conversation with him after the class ended. The talk had been easy, and for his part Joe had been pleased to find a black male forebear in the still predominantly white world of classical dance, a comrade and someone genuinely concerned for him and interested in him and not, even when George's sexual preference became self-evident, in any predatory way.

'Sweetheart, you're straight?!' *George exclaims, half-cut after a lengthy drinking session in the Brixtonian, trying to pretend outrage at Joe's admission even though he has seen Joe kiss the same pretty browning girl goodbye on the lips before class several times now, and Joe knows that perfectly well. But George feels he can be bold because he and Joe have allowed - encouraged even - a certain homoerotic frisson to build up between the two of them over the months of working together, a frisson natural if not inevitable in a world so entirely centred around the necessity of trusting and being energised by each others' bodies. George waves his hand to the barman for another vodka. 'That is scandalous, Joseph. It's a total betrayal of one of the first laws of ballet. No matter you is black or white you know how things them stand, star. In ballet battyman fi rule!' He swallows the contents of his glass, then bangs it down sharply on the bar to emphasise his point.*

'Ah so, man,' Joe agrees. He's drinking one of the thirty-five varieties of rum that is the bar's speciality,

an overproof blend, Wray & Nephew White. 'But I'm not even bi-curious. Don't tell anyone though, aright?' He grins lopsidedly. 'Or I'll get drum out the union.' He thinks for a half-cut moment, his brow wrinkling. 'So when you first met me you thought I was gay, then?'

'Sweetness, I have to confess I took it as read.'

'But I thought gay guys could always tell,' Joe says. 'With whatsit, gaydar?'

'Maybe I'm straight,' George faux-bristles, handing a folded twenty to the barman and pulling himself upright on his stool with an effort. Silver glints on his fingernails.

'Ah, man, I thought you'd take it as a mortal insult if I took you to be anything less than one hundred percent batty in the bedroom department,' Joe says. The bar, the Brixtonian, though predominantly black and straight, is laid-back and not crowded, and both men are at their ease enough to rib each other here.

'Bedroom? You straight children are so conventional.'

'City as bedroom, if you like. Clubs and backrooms for double-beds.'

'Yes, it's like that sometimes. But who's been telling you about gaydar, if you're so straight?' (This is years ago, before it was old news to the cognoscente).

'Man, every other guy I've heard bitching or dishing after class of course. Straight guy doing ballet, they don't see me. Roll over, Ralph Ellison.'

'Touché.'

They clink glasses.

'Doesn't it make you feel outnumbered sometimes though?' George asks. 'Because one reason I went for dance, for ballet, in the first place was that I wouldn't be, for once. Sexuality-wise, anyway.'

'Yeah, well I guess I always knew I would be,' Joe says. 'And even before I really knew on that level I

knew I was going to be outnumbered white-to-black if I wasn't going for jazz or streetstyle, and I didn't want to be pigeonholed that way, you know? Anyway, my cousin's gay and it just – it never bothered me, you know? But my uncle, my cousin's dad, couldn't deal with it at all. Man, that was a fucked-up situation.'

Joe's light-brown eyes defocus slightly as he re-members. 'You know, it wasn't even like my cousin was his only son or he was big on the Bible or nothing, it was just prejudice against two guys doing the nasty. Too much thinking about it. I never understood that. I mean, if you don't wanna do it why put your thoughts that way? It's kind of porno in reverse - '

'And you've never been tempted?' George inter-rupts.

'Nah, man. I mean I've thought about it, sure. Who hasn't? What it'd feel like to suck a cock or be butt-fucked. Or fuck a butt, a male butt. Because everyone's thought about everything if they're honest, haven't they? Because people are complex, you know? And deep. There's probably no end to how far you can dig down to the roots of it all. Why people want to do what they want to do. I mean to like genetics and shit. Or chemicals in the water of the womb. If I was ever going to go that way I suppose I'd've given it a go by now.' He gestures to the barman for a refill. 'It's been on offer enough times, and from fit guys. I can't speak for if I was on a desert island or doing twenty-five to life cos then you're in a whole different situation. But what about you and women?'

'My attraction to women is purely aesthetic,' George replies with an air of slurred certainty that is not quite honest, that doesn't admit the blurring at the edges of his identity that everyone feels and mostly denies, having enough shit to contend with centre-stage in their lives already. Perhaps also he wants to *revel in a separatist moment, in the power that rigid self-definition and exclusivity bestow. 'I internalise the male and female principles into my work, my art and myself. The business end of it's - abstract.'*

'Yeah, right,' Joe smirks. '*Man, you are so full of it sometimes.*' He downs his refilled glass in one. '*I guess I must love you one fuck of a lot to put up with it.*'

'*I guess you must, sweetness,*' George replies.

A cool brother. A good man.

Now Joe is a dance-teacher too, needing a regular income to support his wife and about-to-be-born child. He still drinks, but much less. For George it is strange to watch Joe, who must be thirty-three, thirty-four, moving through transformations that he himself, though sixteen years older, has never experienced and, bar some entirely unexpected change of circumstance, never will: marrying, parenting.

'Do you ever regret you've never had kids, man?' Joe asks, half but only half-misreading the sudden expression of melancholy on his older friend's face.

'I don't believe in regret,' George says. It is an act of faith as much as any other.

There have been women who've wanted to have George's cock, his seed, his baby inside them over the years. There've been drunken fumblings, half-erections, awkward proposals that could have ended up sending his life along a very different trajectory. (Or failed to, of course: *they fuck but she's infertile he's infertile the baby miscarries it goes to term but it's born dead she takes it and runs he sues and loses*). Anyway, his dancers are his children; his pieces are what he sends out into the world. His performances. And he sweats and bleeds and weeps for them. He once made a piece about those feelings he called *Parturition*.

But is that enough? *Children are the payback for having been a child*, he thinks, *and raising your own is the only repayment a mother will accept.* To be gay, exclusively gay as he has been, is therefore both to live in a particular sort of debt and to be judged for failing to shoulder its repayment. It is that exactly, and nothing more. It is not, as is sometimes said, and angrily, that gay men don't mature: they do, in their own way, and on the terms life allows them. It is only different. Not morally worse. But the debt remains, and is payable only on its own terms.

Knowing this, George still doesn't believe in regret. But he feels it nonetheless. And he has the first inkling that he may die today.

The studio smells of damp. It is a large, bare attic room with leaking dormer windows in its slanted roof and no heating, a housing association flat Ziggy blagged up in Westbourne Park, somewhere cheap for him to work until the association can afford to fix it up, which might be tomorrow or not for ten years. Until then, it's his.

Silk-screens are propped up against the walls. They're large, seven foot by five, and are derived from photographs Ziggy took of himself and then manipulated electronically, photographs of himself sprawling naked on a bed, arms and legs akimbo, legs thrown high and wide, his anal ring impossibly dilated because he's giving birth: a baby is sliding forth from his body. He tosses his head back in an ecstasy of relief. In the final image of the series - there are seven in all - he cradles the baby, bloody and shiny with sweat and mucus, the umbilicus still extruding from his anal opening. It is a boy.

The title of the series is *Parthenogenesis*. The boy is himself, adapted from an old photograph of him naked in his mother's arms, taken by his father when he was newborn.

These are the images he was working on when his

mind began to unravel most recently, although he does not believe they were the catalyst for that unravelling: rather they were an attempt at self-defence, a resistance to excessive external input, a looped ancestral chain that shut out nagging blood-claims.

Partly he had wanted to shock and provoke, as he had done four years earlier with a series of similarly silk-screened but far grainier self-portraits he had made from a succession of Polaroids of himself in profile sucking his then-lover Luke's cock from semi-erectness to explicit, messy climax. He had called that series *From The Nipple To The Bottle*, and he and Luke had recorded a demented (and very bad) cover version of the Grace Jones number to accompany the show. They had looped it so it played over and over until it drove the people running the small new gallery mad, drove out all the potential customers and led to No Sales.

The *Parthenogenesis* images are in black and shades of brown on a mottled gold relief. This attractive patina is perhaps self-defeatingly at odds with the visceral subject-matter of the screen-prints, although it does give them an icon-like quality.

An interview he did for a magazine that was never printed:

'Q: So whose baby is it?

Ziggy: Mine. Mine alone. I was inspired by the legend of the first Egyptian god, Atun-Ra. He split himself in two, fucked himself and gave birth to the other gods. Hence - Parthenogenesis. *Many cultures have some founding myth like that. And they usually call that first deity 'he' even though it's supposed to be androgynous. To be 'it' makes you less than.*

Q: Have you ever wished you were a woman?

Z: I suppose that like every man I have thought what would it be like to have breasts, a vagina, a clitoris, a womb instead of a cock and balls. Would I feel some primal connection to life, to humanity that men don't feel? Because what could be more primal than giving birth? But I like being a man. I love being a man, being male. I guess I wanted to channel the extremity of childbirth through my male body, to connect with that experience on a level that was visceral and honest but was obviously a fantasy.

Q: Someone I read said, 'he's equating having a baby with going for a shit.'

Z: Well, they probably only heard about the pictures because when you see them you realise they're not like that at all, they're very much about life, about celebrating life. But anyway women often do shit when they're giving birth because it's such an extreme thing for the body to go through. And you can celebrate that life is messy. You can honour that. It's hiding the mess that's dishonest.

Q: Do you self-identify as a gay man?

Z: Sure. Yeah. Gay, queer, same-gender-loving, whichever.

Q: Do you think gay men are closer to women than straight men?

Z: No. Gay men can get on with women easier because they don't have to deal with the really strong differences between men and women, the way men and women are incompatible on so many basic levels. Like, if you are having your period I can be accepting of that because I don't have to really deal with the details of it, whereas if I was sexually involved with you I would. So my being accepting is truthful, but it isn't the whole story. I don't believe in nature but if I did I would say everyone would probably be happier if men slept with men and women slept with women and the two sexes just came together for procreation. If you look at a lot of traditional societies the sexes are

*kept pretty separate and they seem to prefer it that
way. That whole Seventies unisex thing was a failure
because the sexes didn't really want to mix in. They
want to stand by their differences. Look at the way
now it's all lads together or it's all girls together
socially, and interaction across the sexes comes second
to that same-sex group thing. Now it's more about
bragging to your mates whichever sex you are. The
same-sex relationships are the important ones. For
men perhaps that has always been the case: Work,
colleagues, drinking friends have always been more
important, more real than the wife at home. Humanity is homosexual really.*

*Q: Do you really believe that or are you just being
provocative?*

*Z: I think you can't choose your sexuality. You
want to fuck who you want to fuck. And love who you
want to love. But I don't think men and women usually
make each other happy. Speaking personally, and out
of observation.*

*Q: So your art is a fantasy of completion, where
each sex could be complete in itself?*

Z: Yeah.

Q: So it could have been a woman?

*Z: Yeah. But of course it would be different because
it would have to be a woman fucking with, I don't
know, a female phallus. Anyway, that would be
something for a woman artist to do.*

*Q: Still, some people will see what you're doing as
misogynistic.*

*Z: When I was born I almost died because my um-
bilical cord was wound round my neck, strangling me.
They had to slap me into life to make me breathe,
which is a very violent way to start your life. I was a
blue baby. They say that can fuck you up because it's
such a primary assault, a really fundamental be-*

trayal. Maybe what I'm doing is a way of healing myself of that experience. Consciously I don't blame my mother, of course. But unconsciously perhaps it sets the way you see the world, it makes you see the violence and callousness of life, the randomness. And if you're an artist you have to work against that negativity, you have to force some order into the chaos. That is why I say I don't believe in nature.'

The phone rings. It is three in the morning. Ziggy is woken on the second ring and gropes for it in the close darkness.

'Ajyi Ezekiel?' The voice at the other end is serrating.

'Yeah? Who is this?' Then, recognising the voice is his father's, 'Daddy, what is it?'

'It's your mother.'

I don't love her. She's a cold place a lozenge-shaped blue light a steel disc with a razor rim No room for my plans inside hers The most extreme and intimate projection the hardest exoskeleton for my soft self to break out of.

'She's dying.'

The tumour fed on poison and radiation and thrived. Cancer of the womb.

It was six years before I could make this work.

I thought when I came here that I was going to have to destroy it but I don't have to. I thought the past in it would force me to paint over it. I thought that would be the only way I could break the steel circle unbend the spiral straighten the metal out and move forward.

Instead, the paintings liberate him. Their hidden narratives confess the complexity of the repeatedly betrayed connections between him and his mother, who in her own terrible way did mean the best for him, who in a frozen rage did pay for him to go to art school after he yelled in her face, 'Fuck business, fuck medicine, fuck law!'; and that confession, even if it is only he who is aware it has been made, nonetheless spits some of the poison out.

Luke had to get away from the flat.

More and more these days he finds it too claustrophobic being there with Malcolm: too much like a marriage gone stale that was never a marriage in the first place. Yet their friendship is not stale; their shared history, with its violent, almost mythic beginnings, their abiding pleasure in each others' company, is not stale. It's just that, as they are both increasingly being forced to acknowledge, it cannot give them that particular sustenance that a lover gives, a sustenance for which they both feel a relentlessly-increasing need. Neither of them wants to walk out on their situation, or even threaten it, but that makes it all the harder for them to look beyond it for anything other than impersonal sex.

Luke avoids the humid hell of the Underground in July and gets a rattle-trap open-backed bus up to the West End instead. He sits upstairs at the back, wraparounds shielding his eyes, and watches Kensington Gardens and Hyde Park pass by. An Asian boy-girl couple get on at Queensway, gelled, moussed and groomed, unsoiled as yet by the cloying heat. They sit near the front of the bus and start kissing with open mouths. Luke watches them blankly from behind his shades. He used to envy these unselfconscious, societally-approved heterosexual couples, but now he just sees them as curiously condemned: *he* must always fuck, *she* must always be fucked, half a sex-life. Luke can smell the boy's spicy, macho aftershave, which he dislikes.

At Lancaster Gate a gaggle of Italian girls in tight,

low-cut slacks and bra tops get on and spread themselves across the middle seats, talking loudly and glancing round at him, twisting their long straight hair round their fingers. From their gestures he can tell they're making remarks about his dreads to each other and trying to get his attention, and for a moment he hates them for presuming he's straight, for erasing him with that assumption. He sometimes feels the same hatred when white men eye him up, and for a similar reason. But the girls are only girls on holiday, and though they are part of a system that oppresses they don't deserve his hatred and he knows it. He looks away from them and tries to let go of his grievance.

A man in front of him is reading a newspaper and his eye is caught by the headline: '*Racist Thugs Set Me Alight.*' Beneath it is a photograph of a mixed-race youth who had once been good-looking. '*They sprayed me with paraffin. They laughed as I burned.*' Luke's skin feels suddenly raw. *It could of been Del*, he thinks. *It could of been my brother, my biological brother, doing that to my love-brother, to any one of my love brothers including those straight and those I have yet to meet. A very wise old black dyke on a TV show I once saw said, 'All gay and lesbian people are my family, not all kissing-cousins it's true, not all close but family nonetheless',* and that is how Luke feels about all black people, through black gay men to their black straight brothers, their black lesbian sisters, their straight women sisters, fathers, mothers, daughters, sons. Through gay to liberal even down to homophobic, they're all his in-laws, all family, a family that he has chosen that has sometimes chosen him, a family that gives life and soul to him, not takes it away.

(His father all meat drunk and brutal against his shrieking cursing mother and as he remembers it his silent brother and his silent self standing watching not

*intervening because by then they had learnt that
afterwards she would side with their father, her
husband to honour and obey; side with him against
her sons fruit of her womb of his loins even before the
cuts had sealed over returned to virgin skin and the
swollen bruises yellowed and gone down phantom
pregnancies composed of fists and trauma-fluid. And
they her sons witnessed what they could through black
eyes forced shut through swelling from his fists he had
been a boxer once she bled more than once a month -*

*Why do you let him do it, he asked his mother over
and over. Because I love him she answered over and
over. And he wanted to yell no, love wasn't that, had
to be better than that, or doing without love would be
better if that was what love was. But he didn't believe
it and he looked for a love that was different.*

And found it).

The girls laugh, oblivious to the weight and width of
cruelty in the world, and he feels they will never learn
even the small lessons he has learned in his twenty-five
years of trying to shed ignorance, shed whiteness. Why
should they? In the heat of the afternoon Luke feels
suddenly cold and overwhelmed. The girls are ignoring
him now, possibly pointedly. He becomes aware that
everybody on the upper deck of the bus is white now
that the Asian couple have got off. These days he feels
uncomfortable among only white people, as if he's
being a fake or a fraud, as if he's hiding half of himself,
the half that really matters, the half that makes him
exist.

The bus pulls over in front of Selfridges in Oxford
Street and the girls jump up and stumble over to the
stairwell, their progress hobbled by platform sneakers
and ungainly clogs. Luke looks down on them indiffer-
ently through grimy glass as they push past the conductor and step off the bus's rear platform. His eye is

caught by two black men waiting to get on, one stocky and mid-brown with a moustache and short hair, the other taller and darker, willowy with a shaved head. Both carry sports-bags, and the lighter-skinned man wears grey jogging-pants and a white basketball vest. They kiss goodbye lightly on the lips and the shaven-headed man steps onto the platform as the conductor dings the bell.

A small thrill runs through Luke's chest at the sight of the kiss, so bold, so public. He's mostly got over wanting to be black, but seeing these two, lovers he assumes, the meaningless, melancholy longing returns: *they look so good together, maybe better than I could ever look next to a black lover. Wouldn't he always look into my green eyes and look at my pale skin and run his fingers through my blond hair dreaded or not and feel a lack of revolutionary affirmation, a lack of fundamental affinity, of essential connectedness?* He exhales through his mouth, annoyed with himself for being so self-hating, and also, and differently, annoyed with himself for presuming and judging what another man, a black man, might want, might need.

To Luke's aesthetic gratification if nothing else, the man comes upstairs and takes a seat diagonally across from him. Luke gets a brief glimpse of his butt as he drops his bag onto the vacant seat in front of him. It is large and muscular, and encased in skin-tight black vinyl. The man sits back and looks out across the passing shop-fronts as the bus grinds along.

Luke studies his profile. He looks to be around forty, forty-five, although maybe his fitness is deceiving and he's older. Luke doesn't care about age anyway. His skin is aubergine-dark and smooth, and the long, bare arm that he drapes over the back of his seat is lean and sinewy. He wears a blue and white horizontally-striped tank-top vest that leaves his muscle-capped shoulders bare. From behind his Raybans his eyebrows are shaved or plucked upwards at the ends Vulcan-style. His face is clean-shaven and bony, his nose broad, lips large, mouth wide. It is a strange-looking, latently spectacular face, the sort of face, Luke thinks, that you would never get bored of.

As the man shows the conductor his travel-pass there's a kingfisher-flash of colour and Luke sees he's wearing blue nail-varnish. This excites Luke sexually, and also ideologically, because even in these times, even in the capital, even in the West End there is a defiance to it. *Maniacs bigots drunks. We've all been in cinemas swamped in laughter even now even here as the fag gets stomped, slapped, beaten, debased, and realised that tolerance is thin as skin and not as supple. We've all felt how little is really given and how easily it can be taken back, felt how much hatred is longing to break out, how much contempt. And what is internalised in us too. Witness on Compton Street the heartless eyes of those (think they're) straight-acting gay boys who are so easily shamed by anyone failing to make sufficient obeisance to the cult of so-called straight-acting masculinity -*

The man turns away to look at something in the street below and Luke imagines kissing the warm, dark, elegant stretch of his neck. *What if I just went over and did that?* He has been that impulsive and bold before, as he was when he first invited Malcolm back to stay with him that night on the bridge, not knowing, only guessing Malcolm's sexuality, Malcolm's emotional life. But he doesn't feel bold today.

Anyway, even if he didn't slap me down physically or verbally that other guy was most probably his lover so what would be the point?

The bus rolls through the lights at Oxford Circus and turns down Regent Street. Something about the man makes Luke think of Ziggy. Perhaps it's a sense of the unconventional as revealed in his shaved eyebrows and painted nails. Or the offbeat, lived-in attractiveness of his face. Luke isn't interested in conventional good looks, in conventional anything. In the man's face he sees intelligence and perhaps wisdom, qualities he's always drawn to, and he thinks he sees kindness behind his hard queen façade, and that too makes him think of Ziggy.

How long has it been since Luke last heard from Ziggy? Six months? Perhaps even longer, and then it was only a trivial chat about something inconsequential. *Perhaps he's dead.*

'Some journeys you have to make alone,' Ziggy said to him once, intentionally portentous or throw-away meaningless, who knew?

Luke still rings Ziggy's number once a week, missing his fucked-up friend. Even though Ziggy's mobile has been out of service for at least three months now, like a lapsed Catholic Luke can't help but keep on going through the motions.

The bus pulls over and the engine cuts out. The clatter of barely-visible lights being snapped on and off and the conductor calling up tells Luke they've reached the last stop: Piccadilly Circus. The man glances round as if surprised, jumps up and heads off down the stairwell.

It takes Luke a moment to notice that he's left his bag behind. Luke's chest cramps excitedly. He counts to five to make sure the man isn't going to realise immediately and come straight back for it, then picks it up and hurries down the stairs after him, imagining movie-style romantic scenarios. The bag is light, the seamed leather strap warm and soft in his hand.

Piccadilly Circus is crowded, and at first as he steps off the bus Luke can't see the man, but then he catches a glimpse of blue-and-white stripes crossing towards Tower Records, the block-wide music store that dominates the west side of the square. Luke hurries after him, dodging an aggressively-whistling cycle-courier and a U-turning taxi as he goes. He's just a few yards away when the man comes to a halt, clearly at that moment realising he's left his bag on the bus, which is now heading down towards Trafalgar Square at a gathering speed. The man's posture, which is surely that of a dancer, is unusually upright, and his butt is so amazing, so high, so perfect in its shape and muscularity that Luke has an instant hard-on. Since he is wearing skin-tight silver cycling-shorts and nothing under them, he is aware that the rod of his dick is crassly, criminally obvious to any passer-by who happens to glance down. He should, but he doesn't care: it's his nature and fuck them.

That butt.

Sanctified.

'The power of the African man is focussed through his powerful eye-drawing backside' - Ziggy monologuing, possessed of considerable back himself, sketching curves with a stick of charcoal to make his point. 'Twin power-pack piston-heads. Not the dick: that's a Mandingo projection, bullshit. The butt. Your butt's not so bad though,' he had added by way of consolation. 'In its perky Caucasian way very squeezable.' And he had squeezed it.

'Yeah but I want to worship yours,' Luke said. 'That's the difference. Your butt has the real power.'

'And I'd like to photograph you with your tongue up my arse, blow it up to the size of a wall and call it Reparations,*' Ziggy replied, and he had meant it of course, he always meant it, a bridge too far for Luke then, though now he would do it to prove he had no shame. Then he did it, but only in private. In Po-*

laroids. Only fun stuff.

The man turns abruptly.

With a shy smile Luke holds his bag up to him.

The moment he says goodbye to Joe and boards the bus, George's mood collapses. For no reason, for every reason, he finds himself thinking of Oliver.

He died the day after his twenty-second birthday, on my twenty-eighth, my arm around his shoulders, his mother's hand in his, his father, who'd struggled with his son's sexuality, touching him only once he was gone, pressing his lips to his son's cooling forehead. Outside it was raining. If I'd died at the age Oliver died I would have achieved nothing the world counts as worth remembering. I would be as unremembered, unremembered though I remember and in my work I do and will testify.

Joe was so happy today.

Is it enough, my life? My dance? Is it enough?

Joe's life, so approved of by family, church and state, suddenly feels like an assault to George. *The dream we still dream of love, nature and order,* he thinks. *As if those three were the same damn thing.*

He climbs the stairwell to the top deck of the bus, muscles aching from the class, joints feeling their age now even though he is more limber and supple than most men half his age. Still, he feels the loss of what he had at twenty-five, the stamina and resilience, the sense of open time, and the gain in wisdom from life lived seems a poor trade to him today.

He drops his bag on the seat in front of him, sits back and stares out blankly at the passing view. He has lived, if only briefly, in many places - Paris, New York, Berlin, Rome - but it's London that is his home. The title for a piece floats into his head, *The Free Movement of Peoples: a Dream,* but nothing beyond that.

Then a pornographic image of a row of customs officers in tight blue uniforms, all or mostly white, bending men in ethnic costume, Nigerian, Zimbabwean, Jamaican, Indian, Pakistani, Iranian, over piles of suitcases and fucking them.

George files the image away in his mind. The idea of being dead comes back to him: not of killing himself, just of being dead. Not having to decide, to struggle any more. No more painful endless subjectivity.

The bus-engine cuts out and the conductor shouts up that it's the last stop. Jolted out of his morbid state of mind, and remembering that he had been going to buy a Vodou CD from Tower, (research for a new dance-piece he wants to make using African animist motifs), he jumps up from his seat and hurries down the stairs. *And I could see if the new Janet album is out*, he thinks as he steps off the platform. He despises himself only slightly for using a shopping opportunity to blot out existential angst and anomie.

Have I done enough to leave this world a better place?

Oliver thought he was a revolutionary but time stole him before the world could put him to the test. And quickly enough back then just surviving became revolutionary, surviving then living something like a normal life, getting past the guilt of surviving. Oliver, what would you think of me now? Would you forgive me?

At least I'm still trying.

Tourists clump at the pedestrian crossing, presumably from countries where there are draconian jaywalking laws since none of them will cross against the red even when there is no traffic. Or perhaps it is just the bovine stupidity of the herd. *I am the cat who walks by himself*, George thinks, imagining something cool and jazzy as he pushes his way through snail-brained, hump-backed back-packers, then quickly crosses over to Tower Records while they mill and wait for the lights to change.

The moment he reaches the far pavement he realises he's left his bag on the bus. Feline hauteur punctured he turns on his heel, wondering how far down towards Trafalgar Square the bus will have got, whether he can face running after it in the baking heat; if there's any chance of the bag's not having already been stolen anyway.

Bizarrely and disconcertingly a young man is standing there holding his bag up towards him. The young man is white, athletic and handsome. He's wearing iridescent wraparounds that conceal his eyes, silver cycle-courier shorts and a torso-hugging silver lycra top, and has a small black rubber back-pack slung over one shoulder. He has a blond goatee and blond funki-dreds exploding from the top of his head, the back and sides of which are shaved, and a gold stud in his small nose. His mouth is wide and his lips are firm and full and red. His physique is lean and rangy. Knowing that his own eyes are shielded by his shades George finds himself glancing down at the young man's crotch and is disconcerted to see the outline of a substantial erection slanting there.

Uh -

George's sense of porn-fantasy dislocation is intensified. To one side of him a fat American is shooting video footage of nothing in particular on a state-of-the-art camcorder that must have cost several thousand pounds. To the other three Italian girls in blue plastic policeman's helmets burst into a discordant rendition of Robbie Williams' 'Millennium' as they stride along, tossing their long, straight hair like models on a cat-walk. The young man's thighs have a strong curve to them and his blocky calves are dusted with gold. He wears heavy black bike-boots and black rubber bangles on his wrists. George reckons him to be in his mid- to late twenties. The outline of his erection is large, although maybe its public display and George's embarrassment make it seem more prominent, more startling than it really is. He feels his own dick stiffen inside his skin-tight pvc trousers, and becomes even more embarrassed as its swelling head presses painfully against a seam that seems determined to cut into his piss-slit.

And so the two men stand facing each other like classical statues, like gladiators in the arena. The pedestrian lights change behind them and the signal begins to pip. Tourists start to surge back and forth across the junction.

'I think this is yours, man,' the blond youth says. His soft voice is husky, the accent working-class East London.

Chapter Three

'Thank you,' George says, taking his bag.

'You're welcome, man,' the funki-dredded white youth says, smiling as he relinquishes it. There's a strangely thrilling moment of contact at one remove between the two of them just before he lets go of the strap, then it's over. They stand facing each other awkwardly, getting jostled by tourists. George can see his face reflected in the boy's mirrored lenses, the windows to his own soul hidden by reflective plastic too.

'Well,' he says eventually, 'I'm going to - ' He gestures round at the glass-walled façade of Tower Records. 'So. Yes. Well, thank you once again.'

'My pleasure, man.' The young man keeps on smiling, but now he's shifting uncertainly from one foot to the other.

'Well, perhaps I'll see you around,' George says, half-trying for closure, half-evading it, receptive but perversely unable to make the first move himself, the fear of rejection too deeply embedded in him despite all his life experience, all his knowledge of love and desire. Despite the blatant stiffness of the young man's dick in his lycra shorts.

'Sure, man, I'm round and about on the regular,' the young man says. 'Anyways,' he adds, when George doesn't say anything more, 'I got places to be.' But he keeps on standing there.

George nods. Then, losing his nerve completely, he turns away and makes his way quickly through the glass doors of the store and up the steps inside. At the top of the steps he looks back but the funki-dredded

youth is gone. George feels as if he had been momentarily projected onto a movie-screen and now he is back
in the bitter dark. The movie, *Brief Encounter*.

At once regret kicks in. *I could have said something
done something instead of standing there like a damn-
fool idiot. I mean what more of a come-on could I have
asked for than that boy's obvious - I could at least
have asked his name -*

But the thought of what would have followed if he
had asked the boy his name depresses George instantly:
suggesting a drink, then going for a drink, making
desultory small talk while sizing each other up for the
prospect of a little mutual relief, then ending up back at
one of their places, most likely whoever's was nearer,
and getting that relief. Then nothing. *Because that's
what would have happened, isn't it? Because that boy
was too young for anything more. Too young regardless of any qualities I might or might not have or he
might or might not have. Because I am a quarter-
century or more ahead of him. But still I could have
asked his name. At least that.*

Yet despite his failure he feels lifted, challenged in
literally thrusting phallic Baron Samedi style for being
drawn too much towards death today. He goes up to
the World Music department, finds a CD by the Haitian
band Boukman Eksperyans, *Revolution*, and goes and
pays for it. Afterwards he wanders up Brewer Street
into Soho, ending up as he so often does in Old Compton Street, pulled by faggotry, his own and others,
unrepentantly.

The irony of the street having become a self-
promoting ghetto doesn't anger him today, nor its
decay from fought-for space of liberation to vacuous
marketing opportunity. He understands that as repression lifts victim identity vaporises and the oppressed
become as shallow as their oppressors. Shallower, even,

since they do not have the shame of having oppressed to grain their souls. But he remembers too how things were in the all-too-recent past, before advertisers were eager to chase the pink pound - *doing the Gay Pride march when it was only two hundred people and you were visible so visible and so unwanted* – and so he is thankful for the small, if hedonistic and apolitical mercies of this street.

And if the individuals who frequent it are shallow there is nonetheless depth in their coming together so publicly; in the history of defiance that is built upon. It is only one history among many for George. Effeminate. Immigrant. Black. Poor. Queer. But it's something worthwhile, this seemingly free street. And it can be taken away so easily.

The bomb.

The bombs. Brixton, Brick Lane, Soho. A single crazy bigot, a fascist, a loner. A reminder of how little it can take for the clock to start to run backwards, of how no progress is assured. Any good moment could be a Weimar moment, a peak before a collapsing-back.

He remembers a note among the wreaths and flowers and candles outside the bombed-out, boarded-up Admiral Duncan: *As a black man and as a gay man I know that all prejudice is connected and all bigotry must be resisted.*

At the time he had wondered, *how many others will make that connection?* But at least it had been stated in the face of the political apathy of the times. The street had been oddly quiet that day, the air compressed, and there had been a curious sense of dislocation between those like himself, the witnesses, and the passing tourists and theatre-goers. These latter were more oblivious to what had happened and what it meant than he would have thought was possible if he hadn't all his life been a black man in a white world,

their blindness surprising him only because of the
unusualness of its context.

He makes his way to Compton's Café, to pick up the
free gay papers.

Luke stares after George as he disappears through the
doors of the record store. Just as he's wavering over
whether to follow him in and try to get a conversation
going, his mobile starts to ring. He checks the number:
Caller Unknown. He turns and wanders up the street
as he presses 'OK.'

'Yeah?'

'Who is this?' a black male voice demands at the
other end of the line.

'It's Luke. Who are you?' Luke replies, although he
surely recognises the voice even after all the months of
silence: its clash of shifting registers - black Cockney,
amped-up Nigerian and R.P. - is unique.

'What the fuck do you mean, 'Who are you?''

'Where've you *been*, man?' Luke asks. 'And where
are you now?'

'I'm on my new mobile,' Ziggy says, 'and I'm coming up to town. Where are you?'

'Up here waiting for you, man. Outside Tower.'

'Spooky. You must be telepathic. Don't let the
shrinks know or they'll cut your brains up.'

'I won't let 'em know, man. Where you wanna
meet?'

'Ah – say, the *Waterlilies*? In half an hour?'

'Cool.'

Ziggy rings off. Luke heads down into the tube station, the underpass servicing it being the least tiresome
way of crossing Piccadilly Circus when it's this busy. A
busker, a bearded black man wearing pebble shades
and a Voodoo top hat, is singing *Ne Me Quitte Pas* in
one of the passages, accompanying himself on a guitar,

his voice magnified by the curving tiled walls. Luke flips a coin into his guitar-case. He always gives money to buskers, a habit he picked up from Ziggy. *Encourage art to be everywhere.* Luke often gives money to beggars too, a habit Ziggy has failed to break him of. *They are not crippled. They are not retarded. They're white. They should get off their flat arses and get a job.*

They're young, though.

Then they should rent, Ziggy says, loud enough for the two bedraggled white teenage boys sitting in the Elephant and Castle underpass to hear although they act like they didn't.

What, like you did? Luke says as they turn a corner and leave the boys behind, thinking he's making a joke. The rain beyond the mouth of the underpass is a heavy curtain.

Like I did, Ziggy says, shooting Luke a hard, depthless, defiant look. For a while I did that. Because it's all about pride: to do what it takes and feel no shame. Maybe in a better world someone else would save you, sort out all your problems, make sure you got a fair chance, a decent start, an even break. But in this world you'd better save yourself. Because why is anyone else supposed to care more about your life than you do yourself?

Ziggy the self-mutilating suicidalist full of life and ambition, overflowing with paradoxes, fuelled by them.

Ziggy's back. Luke feels an excitement flood through him that is almost sexual in its viscerality. Ziggy makes things happen. If he had called ten minutes earlier Luke feels sure he would have spoken to the man who left his bag on the bus. Ziggy has always had that effect on Luke even if too much Ziggy is – well, just too much.

Ziggy and Malcolm, Luke's adoptive brothers.

For some reason they have never met.
Not yet.

Malcolm is watching porn on his and Luke's clapped-out, scrapheap-salvaged VCR. *Should be out there*, he thinks as the fourth-generation bootleg tape rolls and bars unsatisfactorily. *Meeting men in the flesh. In my fucking prime and I'm sitting here on my own with my dick in my hand. Should be out there getting some sweat on my skin. Some salt on my tongue.*

But he's been doing that for the last eight months, and it hasn't satisfied him any more than the porn. Since the year kicked off he must have told a dozen men the morning after that he'd call them, then binned their numbers with only a twinge of conscience and no regret. Masturbation by proxy.

Flushed like Kleenex once you've
  Come/Release
    Mess and bad
    memories Hard-wired
Tension (de/
    tumescence) gone.

Increasingly he fantasises about rough sex but he doesn't really want it; it too is a proxy - for the emotional intensity he wants from another man, another man who isn't Luke.

A black man?
Not necessarily.
But ideally?
Malcolm adjusts the tracking of the tape with the remote. The sterility of American porn, whatever the colour of the performers, both fascinates and bores him: the steroid-beefy, hairless bodies; the groomed, gelled coiffures; the threaded eyebrows; even the way every man is circumcised. The lack of emotional contact between men who are, after all, penetrating

each other's bodies in the most intimate way. It is, in its rejection of dirt, disorder and even passion, the product of Puritan Christianity. Despite being about nothing but men industriously committing the sins of Sodom and Onan in fifteen-minute loops, it is oddly conservative, surprisingly unsubversive.

Increasingly Malcolm needs something that *is* subversive, something that will push him somehow, that will open new channels in his heart, his mind, his body. But what?

Recently he has been enjoying black-on-black porn most. In interracial videos he feels forced into identifying with one role or the other in a confining way, and it annoys his versatile self that the white guys almost never fuck the black guys: *Mandingo B.S.*

Sometimes he even prefers all-white tapes: being – in racial terms - purely a voyeur takes an internal pressure off him somehow. It is a pressure which is caused, perhaps, by that small piece of self-hatred that remains in him still that, like a coal, can be fanned or blown on till it glows and burns holes in his gut. *Watching them white boys doing them dutty business.* His father never gave a damn about what the white kids did. They weren't worth the bother. They had no capacity to be moral, to even be aware of their degradation. They had no souls. They were the enemy, just more or less deceivable. They didn't have the duty his son had to be a man, to fuck women, black women, that was; to procreate. Malcolm's father knows nothing of Malcolm's life. Malcolm half-wishes he did, or wishes for some parallel universe where his father could deal with his scene, even be positive about it.

Maybe I wouldn't be so fucked up now, he thinks. *Getting off on two white boys fucking like some straight bloke watching two fake lesbians diddle each others' clits.* Though subversive in this small way perhaps: *Me, a black man, watching two big-dicked bovine white studs all body no brain performing for me (for the dollars). Sometimes I do embrace the fucked-upness of it.*

The film he is watching now, however, is all-black and is called *High Rollin' - A Black Thang*. It features two of his current favourite performers, Bobby Blake, a beefy, bodybuilt, dark-skinned thug, and Richard Reyes, a smoothly athletic caramel-skinned Blatino.

Oh my Nubians, what is my life coming to? Obsessing on porn-stars. Though – truth - it's no more sad-sack than being a Star Wars fan fuck knows or obsessing on football or boxing: men are just obsessive and anyway all that sporting shit's just homoerotica for the totally repressed -

He hadn't been able to get up the nerve to buy the tape the first time he saw it on the shelf in the porn shop. Three black guys he assumed were straight were watching some football match on the TV set behind the counter, and he hadn't been able to face interrupting their heterosexual viewing pleasure by obliging them to play part of a fag porn tape for him to make sure the quality of the copy was okay. He had pretended to browse the straight porn, then left. It was bad enough that he, another black man, had come into such a place in search of porn, the province of the sexually inadequate, in the first place, without their witnessing his deviant appetites and judging him for them. Not a disruption of racial stereotypes they would have found liberating.

Brothers/not brothers
All
up in my business
   (their business)/tongues too free
      Skin family presuming/tongues
  Too sharp -

Frustrated, and in that place in his mind where the thrill of consumption is meshed in with sexual desire, he had gone to a nearby café, returning to the shop an hour later, chest tight, palms damp, determined to buy. A weaselly middle-aged white man was behind the counter then, and Malcolm couldn't have cared less what he thought of a black man buying black gay porn. He had even felt defiant as he handed over his money: *Yeah, I'm claiming this, what's it to you? Take my dollars and be glad.*

Bobby Blake is piston-fucking a writhing Richard Reyes over a car-bonnet in an LA chop-shop. His mind empty, Malcolm comes.

George sits in the window of a café on the sunny side of Old Compton Street, reading the gay papers and sipping a citron pressé. The glass frontage has been folded back so the café is open to the air, and he is pleasantly shaded from the sun by a striped awning. He adds a little more sugar to his drink and stirs the hazy liquid with a long spoon. Flaneurs stroll by, the gay ones dressed in the minimum their physiques can justify, sometimes rather less. There is a slight metallic tang of petrol fumes in the air although the sky is clear.

George flips idly through the pages of contact ads in the various papers. In *Qx*, the club-listings magazine, the personals are mixed in with advertisements for escorts in a wilfully-undifferentiated way that accents their sexual-services-on-offer aspect. In the other scene-oriented freebie, *Boyz*, romance is more popular, if by no means to the exclusion of casual sex. George has never placed a personal ad himself, although he has in bored or whimsically lonely moments called up and listened to them, even occasionally left messages for men whose voices he liked the sound of. No-one whose ad he has replied to in that way has ever called him back - well, no-one he turned out to be pleased to hear from, anyway. Just men with their own agendas, and little room for anyone else's.

(However suave he sounded, fuck it however fey or even frankly effeminate he sounded, how quickly they said some variant of I want you to fuck me with that big black cock, sometimes blurting it out as if confessing a taste for degradation, sometimes stating it boldly as if it would turn him on. How tired that endlessly-iterated demand had made him feel; how quickly it cut trust to a stump and Teflon-coated his heart. And yes, he had fucked some of them.

No saints here).

Looking over the double-page spread of contact ads in *Boyz* George feels as if he's spying on a glass-sided apartment-block. Anonymous lives of men, each exposing something about himself, even if it's only a capacity for self-delusion:

- *Me: Thick-set, balding, 57 y o, beer-belly. You: Tom Cruise-a-like, 18-25 for no strings fun.*

- *Sincere loving romantic successful professional ISO similar for passion, sincerity and lifelong commitment. No fats, fems, druggies, orientals or smokers.*

- *Gay guy, 20s, usual interests, seeks similar for whatever.*

- *GL WE BND, 6', NS, CS, OHOC, ISO GL GWM with GSOH, XVWE a +.*

- *White slave seeks black master for unlimited abuse. All colours except brown. No blood sports. Age, looks unimportant.*

- *Black master seeks in-shape white slave. Sane. Limits respected.*

A marriage made in heaven, George thinks of the last two. But the cumulative effect of the personals depresses him. At first glance there's the appealing impression that there's someone for everyone. But more deeply it feels to George like a succession of offerings on the auction-block, a reduction of self to product. *Still, it's no worse than meeting someone in a club or bar or on a heath or along a towpath,* he thinks. *Perhaps in some ways better. More civilised, whatever that might mean.* But stripped of the senses, stripped of the humanising fact of physical proximity, the personals are disturbingly revealing of the fragility and self-deception of male desire.

George's eyes drift over the categories: *Young & About. Firm Hand. Stocky and Stout. Just Friends.*

Men Of Colour.

In Search Of Men Of Colour.

Sometimes he feels anger at being categorised in this way, sometimes indifference, and sometimes even affirmation, conflicting feelings that are beyond any easy resolution. He has seen enough history in his now fifty years – his Negro, coloured, Black, Caribbean, Afro-Caribbean, African-Caribbean, Afrikan, Black British years, years as an auntie-man, battyman, poof, queer, queen, homosexual, gay, queer again - to bear a thousand paradoxes.

The last section in the personals is called *In Touch.* George's eyes move over more hopeless hopefuls:

Me: white tee-shirt, white jeans, number 2 crop, on E, you similar, blue tee-shirt, Heaven Saturday night, drinking Bud. You looked at me, I looked at you but we didn't speak. Give me a call.

Jack. I lose your number after we dance together at Trade. Call me. Renaldo.

You: black beefcake in Adidas sports vest, District Line to Upminister. Me: white skinhead, leather trousers. We smiled a lot but I was too shy.

Without letting himself think about what he is doing George fishes his mobile out of his sports-bag, flips it open and taps in the number at the top of the page. Looking around to make sure neither the waiters nor any of the few other patrons in the café can overhear him, he quickly leaves his details, notes down a pin number the service assigns him, and records his message in a dry, annoyingly unresonant voice:

'Blond boy outside Tower. Thanks for my bag. Call me so I can see what colour your eyes are. George.'

He flips the phone closed, self-consciousness flushing through him alongside an excitement that is almost adolescent in its intensity. *Not that anything will happen.* After all, it had seemed to him unimaginable that any of the other ads he had just read in that section would get a reply: why should his be any different?

Because I know he'll remember me. Because I know I turned him on. Because he might want to know my name. Because he might want to hear my voice again. Because I want to hear his voice again.

Luke is in the National Gallery. He is sitting staring at Monet's *Waterlilies*. One of Monet's *Waterlilies*, that is: there are many others. Luke has seen them reproduced in books, but this is the real one to him. The one where he can see the grain of the canvas, and the slight accumulated dirt of the years that depletes the luminosity of the paint; the one where he can see the truth of it: that genius is mortal, is part of the real world of blood and come and grime; that it does not float above us perpetually unattainable, mystical and out of reach. And that instead of being intimidated by it we should engage with it fiercely, allow it to penetrate us and bring us more fully into contact with ourselves and whatever brilliance we possess.

It was Ziggy who introduced Luke to this painting. It was Ziggy who overcame Luke's fear of galleries and museums. Before, Luke had felt they were for other

people. Ziggy had shown him that his feeling of out-
siderdom was something he had in common with all
the artists whose works were hanging on the walls,
even the most seemingly conservative of them, because
like him they knew they weren't really part of that
wealthy, confident world of patrons and dealers, even
though it only existed because of their energy, creativity and genius. Ziggy showed Luke that he didn't have
to reject the art, however uncomfortable he felt in the
hushed and airless spaces in which it was presented.

Ziggy made Luke want to be an artist.

Or more exactly, since Luke had always wanted to
be some sort of artist, whether he was drawing private
porn, doing spraycan copies of superheroes for the rag-
tag housing collective he had briefly been part of, or
reaching for something above and within himself that
he couldn't yet imagine, Ziggy made him see that it was
possible for him to be a capital-A Artist: that that didn't
have to be a life that only other people had.

'Look at Basquiat,' Ziggy says with a large gesture.
'He used graffiti, cartoons, straplines from ads and
made the most amazing art. Genius shit.'

'Bass-kee-at,' Luke repeats. He and Ziggy have only
recently become lovers. 'Is he like French like Van
Gogh?'

'Haitian,' Ziggy says. 'He's got a show at the Serpen-
tine. I'll show you. But you're a Londoner. Didn't you
go on school trips to the Tate and the National and the
Hayward?' Ziggy drags Luke in through the revolving
brass and glass doors of the National Portrait Gallery,
past uniformed commissars who, to Luke's surprise, do
not reach out a hand or a baton to bar his way, do not
detect that he is the enemy, working-class scum. Ziggy
is wearing leopard-print jeans and a fluorescent green
bra-top, a look that draws eyes to it, but not in a We
Won't Let You In Here kind of way.

'Our school never went on trips,' Luke says, looking around uneasily. 'You wanted a trip, you sniffed glue round the back of the toilets.' He knows by then that Ziggy went to some posh private school. He could read him on privilege, but Ziggy's so obviously been fucked up by his background that he doesn't.

Ziggy did a screenprint off a photograph once, a self-portrait called Mr Black Power. In it his eyes were overpainted a bright cobalt blue, his hair a garish yellow Afro. The title came from something he once said to me: at school I was Mr Black Power.

Always defying something. Always perverse.

Luke admires Ziggy's relentlessness. Ziggy is fundamentally restless too, and that keys into a restlessness in Luke: he and Ziggy share a state of mind that is always searching for something Out There.

Ziggy despises philistinism and ignorance. He sees them as collaborating with the status quo, with the mechanisms of power and oppression that torment and madden those like himself who see more clearly, who possess what he sometimes calls 'extreme opticality', and at other times, 'Extreme optical agony.'

Luke gazes into the *Waterlilies*, into the depths of its surface, blanking the two syrupy Renoir odalisques that flank it. The controlled air is dead in the room. Tourists drift about. The younger ones are mostly in college-trip gaggles. Taking their privilege for granted, on the whole they're indifferent to the art and more interested in flirting with each other; just a few are sketching in pads or really looking. Those Luke approves of. But who really looks except other artists? Luke doesn't understand what art is for unless it is a call to action, unless it demands a creative response from the viewer, and not just passive appreciation.

(Ziggy: *I have no aesthetic responses. I just look at things. And I make things.*)

The old people, those sitting resting their bones, seem lost in contemplation, although maybe it's their own lives gone by that they are really thinking about. Perhaps the paintings function as anamorphic mirrors, reflecting their interior psychic states back at them with a greater sense of scale and wonder than an ordinary mirror can do. Increasingly CD-Roms spin in bags, supplying a certain level of information, setting a pace and suggesting, if not actually controlling, the viewer's gaze and response. Luke dislikes them. Ziggy hates them.

Luke wonders what it would feel like to be old (*will feel like*); to feel you'd got what you came to do done - or you'd failed and it was now too late, and you would have to make your peace with that failure. He can't imagine it. For him the future is all there is, the past a dying thing left behind, a shrivelling umbilicus, some-thing to be repudiated even as its pain-rays propels him forward with a pallid, fading energy. *Maybe I'll always feel this way*, he thinks. But the thought is disturbing rather than inspiring, as it suggests being trapped.

A hand touches his shoulder. 'My brother.'

It's Ziggy.

They embrace hard in front of the wall-size Monet, body to body, drawing slight stares because when men embrace in the straight world their bellies and crotch-bulges do not press together, only their chests. Perhaps too there is revealed in the configuration of their bodies that they have been lovers; that the habit of fitting together in this way is ingrained in them.

Ziggy's body is burningly hot against Luke's.

They release each other and sit side-by-side facing the *Waterlilies*. Ziggy gazes into the painting, per-versely keeping on his pink-tinted sunglasses. Luke watches him out of the corner of one eye. *What does Ziggy see?* He both knows and doesn't. 'So how are you doing, man?' he asks after a while.

'I'm cool.' Ziggy's right knee jigs up and down, either because he's full of barely suppressed tension or it's the side-effect of some drug, prescription or otherwise. Maybe both.

'Where you been, Zig, man? Your phone's been dead for months.'

'Away,' Ziggy says, staring into the curving wall of canvas. 'Getting my head together. Trolling the depths. Putting some shit behind me.' He looks around sharply as if he thinks people might be trying to eavesdrop on their conversation. 'Let's get out of here,' he says. 'I've got my fix.'

(Drugs I love drugs To feel pleasure more extreme than any straight citizen feels, to know that you have more nerve-endings and are a stronger spirit, that you are Elite, you are the Thin Black Duke. And the highs push you above and beyond the mortal towards the divine, and the lows push you down below the bottom of the sea, and stretched between those two extremes you see like Ghede The Corpse At The Crossroads between the worlds of the Living and the Dead, and it is all golden on the ups, and later on the downs you pierce the grey shell of meaning and reach the oblate hell outside.

And you see the world is toxic.

And you see your blood is toxic.

The first time I OD'd I wanted to shatter into starlight, implode into a black hole and compress to the ultimate, or maybe it was an accident I don't remember. Anyway it was full of meaning or meaningless, take your pick.

Drugs I hate drugs They fuck with your sensibilities, rupture your pleasure receptors fist them to the elbow render them insensible to normal pleasures a kiss a rose a straight fuck – Sick I'm sick of the endless molecular fragmentations, imposed decomposed chemical recombinations atomic weight gain exponential neurochemical neurological reshuffling rewirings The plunge to the centre of the Earth I need to reinvent myself from there from that white molten core The world is beautiful My blood is beautiful Art oxygenates my blood, my life, reddens it in tooth and claw.

I fight. I'm free.

Don't unravel don't unravel don't unravel don't unravel Luke bind me like the wound I am -)

They wander up S^t. Martin's Lane together, passing the Victorian façades of West End theatres and the neo-classical portico of the English National Opera, ending up at The Box, a small gay bar off Seven Dials, although it being a weekday afternoon in July the outside tables are taken by tourists of whatever sexual persuasion, presumably mostly straight. Luke orders a beer, Ziggy a Diet Coke and a lemon cheesecake.

'So what have you been working on, man?' Luke asks once their orders have arrived.

Ziggy's head immediately starts to pound.

Q: So the art. Tell us about the art, Ziggy.

A: Uh, sure. Well... what do you wanna know?

Q: Just talk us through some of the pieces and -

A: Oh, okay, right. Right.

Q: I mean, like this series here, you call it the Cock-Sucking series, right?

A: Ah, no, I never called it that. Reviewers called it - this guy from some magazine, I think it was one of the gay ones, he called them that.

Q: So what's the proper title of the series?

A: Well, they've all got different titles and it was all concerned with ideas about the symbolic meaning of sucking a cock, a dick -

Q: For a man to suck another man's cock?

A: Yeah, well, mostly. I mean, for women it's a

whole different thing.

Q: And does race play a significant part in these images, which are quite mixed?

A: Sometimes. So like with 'Mammy' it's a white guy sucking a black guy's cock, which is a political - but on the other hand it's intentionally a beautiful image, I mean formally. So with that racial configuration I'm not condemning, it's not a - it's not critical in that way. It's more like something to question.

Q: And these silk-screens are taken from photos, yes?

A: Yeah.

Q: Do you use models or friends or...?

A: Well, in 'Mammy' it's my cock and it's a friend. But then in 'From the Nipple to the Bottle #5' that's me and the dick in my mouth is black. That's another friend.

Q: And that means?

A: Well, I guess to me it went slightly better if we were both black; I didn't want to be bringing in content that was extraneous at that point. It was an idea I'd worked on before. I think really a lot of our sexual identity goes back to experiences around childhood and breast-feeding and there's something primal about sucking: cigarettes, ice-lollies, cigars, heart-shaped drinking-straws... and for gay guys sucking on dicks. And maybe that cum is white like milk is no accident. Cosmically.

Q: Isn't that rather a depressing and sterile view of homosexual sex? A parody of the new-born experience?

A: No, no, not at all. It's – maybe it's got a jokey tone, but it's not parodic. It's about men nourishing and sustaining each other. My dick, my phallic aspect, comforts and feeds another man. It's kind of an emblem for single-sex wholeness. Resisting that image of sterility that as a gay man you're told you're only half of a straight couple even if you're in a relationship, you know? The tyranny of nature even when you're erupting and exploding with love.

Fuck nature.'

'Nothing,' Ziggy says out loud. 'I'm not working on anything right now.' He laughs shortly. 'Just myself. You?'

Luke shrugs. 'Just my usual, man,' he says, looking down into his beer. His work doesn't have the fuck-off abrasiveness that Ziggy's does; it's sensual, intimate, smaller-scale, and Ziggy sometimes makes him feel guilty about its lack of edge. 'Kind of neo-primitive, Harlem Renaissancey but not retro, not Burra. I'm trying to get a jazz riff into it. Cool, I mean, not trad, you know? Bebop. Charlie Parker, Mingus, early Monk. But twenty-first century. Kind of a cosmic Sun Ra style.'

He doesn't say, doesn't need to say because Ziggy already knows perfectly well, that all the figures in his paintings are black men. Ziggy likes Luke's paintings, even owns a couple of them – insisted on paying Luke for them - and Malcolm too likes Luke's work. But even so, at the back of his mind Luke is always afraid that he may somehow be offending his friends with his representations. Or if not Ziggy and Malcolm, his brothers, then those angry others who await him:

White boy, who do you think you are to fix us in your mind? To trap us in your history-sodden neo-colonial psychological projections? Thief, who do you think you are?

And his reply: *No-one. No-one special. Someone who wants to give, not to steal. If that is allowed. If that is allowable.*

If it was only white people who liked his art Luke would stop painting or at least do something different.

If black people liked his work and white people didn't he would feel he had reached some deep truth in the art and in himself. In the meantime, however, he needs his work to be liked on some general level, and whoever his ideal audience is he knows that most gallery-owners and buyers of paintings are white. He is forced to be realistic about this because, like the rest of the world, he has rent to pay and food to put on the table, and he cannot, after all, control who looks any more than a Black Arts Nationalist can. He has learnt how to charm those who do not interest him. He has learnt there is work to do after the work of painting and framing is done. He is young enough to waste energy grudging that work. But increasingly he does it.

Sometimes he feels as if Ziggy created him, or at least brought him to life, animating then filling him with language, ideas, images, and possibilities; and with that comes the corollary: that his art must in some way pay that gift back, both personally and politically.

'You could come see my new stuff now if you like,' he suggests. 'I'm kind of quite proud of it but, you know, it's only me who's seen them. And Malcolm, of course. He says they're my best stuff, but maybe he's too close to them cos his music's part of them, you know? It's like they're part of his life. Like furniture. Or the view out the window. Or a diary, where you look at it and think 'Oh, yeah, I was doing this and that when that was being painted.' So I don't know.'

'He's still there then, your mystery man?' Ziggy says.

'Yeah. But he ain't my mystery man, man. He's my other brother.'

'Maybe it's time I met my brother-in-law.'

'He might not be in.'

'Don't you want me to meet him?'

'Course I want you to, it's just -' Luke shrugs, feeling guilty that he has avoided having Ziggy and Malcolm meet before. Partly it has been easy. Neither of them have friends in common, Ziggy is erratic and hard to pin down, and Malcolm can be solitary and disappear into his own secret world for days at a time too. But the truth is that Luke wants to be the pivot in his relationship with them, not just one side of a triangle - or worse, find himself marginalised by the common ground shared by two black gay men. Behind that fear, and a paradoxical further reason for not introducing them, is his strong feeling that Malcolm and Ziggy will dislike each other on a dozen different levels anyway, and he doesn't want his brothers to fall out before they have the chance to really get to know each other.

'Come, man,' Luke says. 'We can get food on the way and I'll cook something. We'll get enough for three and if he's there he's there, and if it's just the two of us we don't have to eat it all.'

Ziggy nods, and they drain their glasses and go.

They catch a bus in Regent Street, sitting upstairs at the front and sprawling across a double-seat each like straight lads. There are stickers dotted around calling for a March in Defence of Islam, green and black on white. Luke gestures at the stickers without speaking. Ziggy grunts. His family are Nigerian Christian, and though he has little direct contact with them, the threat from Islamist fundamentalists in Nigeria is real, not just a matter for liberal hand-wringing or pious expressions of multicultural correctness.

Abstractedly Ziggy picks at one of the stickers, trying to peel it off. It shreds under his nails. His mind goes back to that strange day the Towers came down, some random day as it had begun, JFK day for their generation they were told over and over, and it was true. Where had he – had they - been?

Luke and Malcolm were bumming round Camden

Market when they noticed people gathering at the windows of shops selling TVs with *Invasion of the Bodysnatchers*-style silent focus. *Not football then,* Luke remembers thinking. *I'd bought a three-CD set of the Specials, Malcolm a pair of retro chequerboard shades. Rock Against Racism, Two-Tone: he'd told me all about that. The Moon Stomp. The Specials plus two.*

Ziggy had been painting and had only heard about the attack late that night. After working till his wrist and eyes ached, needing to shoot a load he had gone cruising in Holland Park. A skinhead had beckoned to him from the shadows, turning round as Ziggy approached him, shoving his tight, bleach-marked jeans and Calvin's down to his monkey-boots, pushing out his backside, eager to be fucked. 'Wear a rubber,' he had said, handing the pre-ripped foil square back to Ziggy. Then, as Ziggy rolled it onto his already-stiff dick: 'The fucking Towers, eh? Can you believe it? All those people – ah, yeah - ' Ziggy slid up into his slack, receptive hole, fucked him hard. Later he watched the endless news, upped his dose of Risperidone and went to bed at dawn.

George had been in the air, flying back from a gig in Paris, and had arrived to hear the news pouring like gas through the terminal, the scared, strained faces of officials and fellow-travelers: *it could've been us.*

And over the days that followed all of them had watched as the new angles were spliced into the reportage, until by the end of the third day the footage of the planes hitting and the Towers falling was as slick as any Hollywood blockbuster, and so both more and less real. And then – and now – the slow, abstracted crawl to war, a crusade without faith: war on an idea, a perverse echo of that earlier futile War on Drugs, a similar category error. And all of them remembered the

Reverend Pat Robertson saying the Twin Towers fell because America tolerated abortion and homosexuality, and that was a reminder to not get caught up even for a second in simplistic jingoism. Still, you asked yourself what would you fight for? What would you die for? Ziggy had talked about the animists, the Vodouists caught between the cross and the crescent moon, the hammer and the anvil, and Luke had thought, imagining body-painted warriors with spears and heart-shaped shields, *that's us*.

The market is starting to pack up by the time they get off the bus, stomachs queasy from the relentless juddering. *Not that hard to build a bus that don't shake and rattle every second it's standing still you wouldn't of thought, they can sew your dick back on and send back pictures from Mars, for fuck's sake.* Funny how rage at the little things is easy. With the big things it's too terrifying, too enormous. *What terrible things would you do? What if my family, I mean my real family, Ziggy and Malcolm, was in danger? Or my biological one?*

Enough stalls are still trading for them to get the things they want: fresh coriander and mint, pea aubergines, beefsteak, fresh spinach, vine tomatoes.

As they go from stall to stall they pass Ziggy's front door without Luke realising that that's where Ziggy's living at the moment. Ziggy moves around a lot, perhaps compulsively, and his friends are usually an address or two behind. *It's too much*, Ziggy thinks, picking out two ripe paw-paws and looking around for limes, feeling tired. *I need somewhere I can make a home. A quiet place that's not a grave.* But the thought, the longing, is disconnected, a dead line.

Even though Luke's his best friend, Ziggy still doesn't tell him that he's living so close by. *Maybe later*, he thinks, not analysing his reasons, which he knows are lacking. *Fuck addresses anyway. With my mobile I'm connected. Wherever I pick up my phone, that's my home. No-one can pin you down and mount you and fuck you over. You can always switch them off.*

Their shopping done, they stroll up towards the canal and Luke and Malcolm's block.

The block, which is just five minutes' walk from the hustle and bustle of Portobello, has recently been creeping upmarket: it has mutated from a vertical slum to a Sixties design classic, and has therefore become desirable despite the deteriorating façade, the lifts breaking down constantly, and the low-key but distinct criminality of the surrounding neighbourhood. Luke and Malcolm's flat is housing association but the others, council flats, are slowly being sold off to yuppies and investors. This has created an atmosphere of social and economic conflict within the block that mirrors the wider tensions outside.

On a sunny day and from a distance the block is beautiful: it's only up close that it disappoints. Still, it's home. It's sanctuary.

While Luke and Ziggy wait for the lift a pretty, light-skinned black girl with corkscrew curls enters the lobby, weighed down with candy-stripe bags of market-shopping. Carol, another housing association tenant. She has two young daughters and lives in the flat below Luke and Malcolm's. From time to time she drops in on them, and they share a joint and a beer and small talk.

Carol smiles at Luke and says hello, and they chat inconsequentially while the lift mechanisms whirr and grind randomly above them. All the while she's looking Ziggy over obliquely, trying to read the outré-looking black man next to her white, gay neighbour as to his sexual orientation, economic standing, prospects; trying to catch his eye and get a vibe. But Ziggy is blank: the shutters are down.

Eventually the lift arrives and they get in. Luke and Carol fall silent, their talk stifled by Ziggy's unfriendliness. Ziggy stares straight ahead, his chest tense, veins standing out in his thick neck. He only exhales once Carol has got out of the lift at her floor and the doors have closed behind her.

'What was that about, man?' Luke asks.

'What?'

'With Carol. She's really nice. And she don't care if you're gay.'

'You mean she doesn't care if *you're* gay.'

'Still, you could've smiled, Zig. I mean - '

'I don't like being sized up like that. That's all.'

'Why, because it's a woman?' Luke asks. 'If a woman fancies me it's a compliment,' he adds, conveniently forgetting the girls on the bus he had so disliked earlier.

'There's a particular expectation black women put on black men,' Ziggy says. 'You can't ever have the same shit put on you because there's no equivalent a white woman could put on a white man. It's like when they realise you're gay and in their eyes you can see they reduce you to nothing. That shit pisses me off. This body - ' he gestures the length of it '- is for giving pleasure to other men. My mouth's for dick, not pussy. My dick's for arse, not cunt. And my arse is for dick, not being ignored, disused.'

Ziggy's outspokenness makes Luke flush, and Ziggy's words give him a semi-erection. He realises that he is more tolerant of Carol than other straight women for the same reason Ziggy is less so: she is black. He slides his front-door key into the lock. Before he can turn it the door is unlocked from the other side and opened. Malcolm stands there, funky and glossily sweaty and dishevelled in a white skinny-rib vest and black lycra trunks, a joint hanging from one corner of his mouth, his large eyes hazy gold. He kisses Luke wordlessly on the lips, looking Ziggy over as he does so. Ziggy looks back.

'Malcolm, this is Ziggy,' Luke says. 'Ziggy, this is Malcolm.'

Malcolm leans out from the doorway and shakes Ziggy's hand, then pulls himself back to let Luke and Ziggy pass inside. Ziggy can feel the heat of Malcolm's body as, turning sideways-on, he slides past him, chest-to-chest.

'Go in the front room, man,' Luke says, disappearing into the kitchen. Ziggy glances round at Malcolm, who shrugs acquiescence, slips round him and leads the way.

The front room is large but cluttered. Luke's paintings, which are all different sizes, some just sketches on paper, some canvasses as large as six foot by four, hang on or lean stacked against every wall. They are vibrant with the oranges, yellows, turquoises, ochres and scarlets that Luke loves, and their technique is painterly and passionate. The black male figures that are their predominant subject are rendered naïvely but with loving care and endless fascinated delight. The scents of oil-paint, linseed and hemp fill the still air.

On a battered brown sofa in the middle of the room is an open instrument-case. A trumpet gleams immaculately there on faded gold plush. A weeping fig in one corner has reached ceiling-height and dominates that part of the room with its delicate, spreading branches. Dried leaves gather dust where they've fallen. Other plants are dotted around; mother-in-law's-tongues, Swiss cheese plants, a small palm with waxy, needle-like fronds. Paint-specked art books are piled up on a smoked-glass coffee-table and stacked under it. In a small book-case paperback novels are crammed. Next to it sit a portable stereo, a stack of CDs, a pile of mix-tapes, a long row of records, a small TV and VCR. Colourful rag rugs are scattered about. There are no curtains at the single window which runs the entire width of the room, as if the view of the wide open sky must never be shut out. There is the faint but pervasive smell of body heat concealed within the stronger ones of paint and turpentine and dope-smoke, and Ziggy notices a tape poking out of the mouth of the VCR. *High Rollin' - A Black Thang* is written on its label in biro. Porn, Ziggy assumes, tasting a resonance of semen as well as sweat on the roof of his mouth.

'Take a seat, man,' Malcolm says, closing the trumpet-case and setting it down carefully next to the TV. Ziggy does so, choosing the sofa not the armchair. Malcolm joins him on it, but leans back into one of its corners. Ziggy echoes his posture so their bare knees are only six inches apart, Ziggy's slightly bristly, Malcolm's smooth, almost entirely hairless. They study each other guardedly.

'You want some wine?' Malcolm offers, reaching for an already-open bottle that's standing on the floor by the coffee-table. Ziggy nods. Dragging the spliff back into life, Malcolm tokes and gets up. Exhaling a cloud of sweet blue smoke he passes the spliff to Ziggy, who takes it from him as he pads off to the kitchen. Ziggy watches Malcolm's butt as he goes, then looks at the spliff. It's almost finished. He takes a hit. Malcolm returns with an extra wine-glass, which he dries with the tea-towel slung over his shoulder, before filling and handing it to Ziggy. Then he refills his own glass. Ziggy passes the spliff back to him and Malcolm drags it to the cardboard then stubs it out in a stolen pub-ashtray. Ziggy takes a swig of the coarse, blood-warm red wine and looks round at Luke's paintings. Malcolm watches him. *So this is Ziggy*, he thinks.

All Malcolm knows about Ziggy is small stories Luke has told him over the years that he mostly doesn't remember. Of course he knows what Ziggy looks like - or rather looked like - from the snapshots pinned up among the bills and postcards on the cork board in the kitchen. In those Ziggy mostly has green hair, in one a bull-ring through his nose. Luke has talked to Malcolm about Ziggy's art, which sounds too extreme to Malcolm, too queer and complicated, too fucked up about race.

Malcolm remembers Luke telling him that Ziggy doesn't generally date other black men. That made Malcolm take against him - or the idea of him - even though he is himself fairly exclusionist in the other direction. (*But that's just natural, though*). It annoyed him politically, but since he never found Ziggy particularly attractive from the photographs - too crazy and bullish-looking - it didn't seem to matter much. But now, meeting Ziggy in the flesh, Malcolm finds himself unexpectedly turned on by him, leaning in towards him as he twists round to look at Luke's art, compelled by the solidity of his presence: the blockiness of his belly, the heavy curves of his thighs, the largeness of his hands, his big-featured, ravaged face; even the paganism of his short Mohawk, his black leather kilt, his rubber and metal bangles. It feels strange to Malcolm to be attracted to another man here in this flat, in the home that he and Luke have made together. Inappropriate. Or maybe it's exactly right and necessary, he can't tell yet.

'So you play music,' Ziggy says without looking round.

'Yeah,' Malcolm says, trying to push texture into his voice. 'Jazz.'

'You like Fela Kuti?'

'Sure.' Malcolm takes a swallow of wine. 'I got - uh -

Gentlemen and *Coffin for Head of State* on vinyl.' He gestures to the row of records even though Ziggy isn't looking his way, feeling a strong urge to reach out and grip one of Ziggy's thighs. 'So what's Ziggy short for?'

Ziggy glances round at him. 'Ezekiel,' he says. 'And I never liked Zeke. But I did like David Bowie.' He goes back to looking at Luke's art.

'So what d'you you think?'

'They're good,' Ziggy says decisively. 'Yes.' He looks round at Malcolm again. 'There's a lot of you in them.'

'You reckon?'

'You see the shoulders of that cane-cutter there?' Ziggy points to a figure in the foreground of one of Luke's larger paintings - a group of labourers sharing a beer in the purple-blue shade of a shack as they rest from their labours in yellow cane-fields that stretch out fantastically behind them. 'His shoulders, they're like yours. The structure of his chest. Even the way you rest your arms. Those kind of elegant lines - ' Ziggy marks the outlines of Malcolm's upper arms and torso with an easy gesture of his thumb. 'Are you.'

Malcolm takes a gulp of wine to hide a smile, pleased by Ziggy's observations, which are, he knows, true: he *has* become part of Luke's art, just as Luke's colours and forms and sensibility and rhythms with the brush have become a part of his music.

'They're the best things he's done,' Ziggy says as Luke comes in with a tomato, olive-oil and basil salad, a third glass and another bottle of wine.

'For real, man?' he says as he sets the things down on the coffee-table, obviously pleased: he made a point of staying out of the room while Ziggy looked at the art, and also he wanted Ziggy and Malcolm to have a bit of time to get to know each other without him being there.

'You know I don't lie,' Ziggy says as Luke tops up his glass, then fills one for himself. He is about to drop down between Ziggy and Malcolm on the sofa when he senses the subtle electrical charge running between them, so he perches on one of the arms instead, forcing Malcolm to budge up slightly and get closer to Ziggy. Malcolm's and Ziggy's bare knees brush then, and neither of them pull back.

Ziggy feels excitement rising in him, and the warm, sensual art and the ingrainedly intimate room and the wine and the man - Malcolm – sprawled thighs parted on the sagging sofa next to him, open and radiating heat and current, combine intoxicatingly. Ziggy didn't expect this, couldn't have expected anything less than this: to meet this man, slightly fey and vulnerable and cool, shy in his attractiveness and attractedness, and clearly surprised too. In Luke's flat on this the first day of Ziggy's freedom. He wants to kiss Malcolm's magical, musical lips, and bend forward and nuzzle his crotch through the soft shiny lycra that shields his mystery.

Luke goes back to the kitchen to fix the rest of the meal, pleased his two closest friends are getting on so well, if a little unnerved, as they too have been unnerved, by their surprise flirtation; and wishing as he briskly chops the onions that he had been bolder with the black guy on the bus.

Because suddenly, change is in the air.

Chapter Four

Two weeks have passed since that stoned, drunken evening when Malcolm met Ziggy for the first time, and since then his relationship with Luke has been subtly but profoundly altered. His and Luke's habits of feeling, their small and loving habits of physical interaction, their affections both deep and shallow, have been first energised, then slowly drained of significance by what that evening set in motion.

By heat connections, Malcolm thinks. *Sudden erections Me and Ziggy two lions The transformation alchemical, cellular/Flowing both ways Light rays Dazzling yet illuminating, and the muscle-rings of our obsidian pupils could take it as it realigned us both with Hot animal fag magnetism, reassuringly black on black.*

Not that Luke is white exactly, but -
It's different. And the feeling is different.

Malcolm looks down from the rooftop terrace of the Grove Café, where he and Luke are having a mid-day breakfast. The market below is crowded but everyone moves at a Third World pace in the dead heat. Idling the afternoon away in the lilac shade of an awning the glaringly bright sky and dusty humidity seem pleasant and holidayish rather than sapping and oppressive.

This is Malcolm's treat. The Urban Afro-Nubians, the jazz quartet he plays with, have had a run of decently-paid gigs lately - several weddings, a student ball and a club date - so for once he's got money in his pocket.

He's also feeling good because after the club date Trevor, the Afro-Nubians' drummer, introduced him to a man who was opening a café-bar in Soho and wanted a jazz aesthetic for the décor. 'Blue Note sleeve-art via the Harlem Renaissance,' the man said. 'Murals.'

Trevor is garrulously straight, a likeable punani-hound with a half-dozen fresh tales of conquest for every time the Afro-Nubians get together, but his contact Malcolm was sure was gay, so when he had a chance he mentioned Luke's art to him. The guy gave Malcolm his number, Malcolm told Luke, and Luke got off his butt and called the man up and went to meet him for lunch, taking slides of his largest and most jazz-themed work with him. The guy liked what he saw - 'loved it,' he said. Quite possibly he 'loved' Luke more than his art because Luke took a view and turned up wearing a midriff-revealing tank-top and hustler-tight hipster jeans. By the end of the meal he had a commission for three wall-size murals.

The deal is still up in the air - *never done till it's done* - but Malcolm has put hope on the table, and has given Luke the possibility of something at a time when he is threatening to take something else away.

Malcolm wonders about Trevor and his contact, an older, dark-haired white guy. Spanish or Portuguese, Malcolm thought when he met him, but maybe, on reflection, Brazilian. *Perhaps Trevor's relentless hetero bragging is just a front*, Malcolm thinks. *Maybe secretly he likes to take it up the arse.* Malcolm hopes not. He wants Trevor to be what he appears to be, totally straight, even though he finds Trevor's chunky muscularity and bullish shaven head attractive. Except for Luke, Malcolm believes he prefers the company of straight men to that of gay men.

Until Ziggy.

Gesturing to a waiter clearing a nearby table he orders two more iced coffees. Luke's blond funki-dreds cast shadows over his face like blue tribal markings. Eyes masked by shades he seems suddenly exotic to Malcolm, his thought-processes impenetrable.

Even if my thing with Ziggy goes nowhere we can't go back to where we were, Malcolm thinks. *Even if we wanted to.*

Even if we needed to.

If Luke is afraid, Malcolm is afraid too.

Nothing has happened. Yet. But they both know the rules are changing. Over the last fortnight they've been both more critical of each other and more loyal to each other, and to their friendship, than at any time in the past six months. Now it is in danger of slipping away they cling to what has sustained them for the last more than two years. If that is a troubling thing, at the same time the realisation is growing in them that their situation doesn't have to be a dead end or a trap; that what they have can continue to add to their lives if they accept it for what it is and don't try to force it to be a stand-in for something else. And both of them understand, have always understood, that for all its strengths their friendship cannot take the place of a loving, fully sexual partnership.

Despite that, Malcolm hasn't been able to bring himself to tell Luke that he and Ziggy have already been on a date. Partly he doesn't want to hurt his closest friend; partly he's afraid of still-birthing a potential relationship through too much picking over its possibilities in advance. Also Malcolm knows this is the one thing he cannot explore or process with Luke.

I'll tell him when something happens. If something happens. And if nothing happens then we carry on some way or other, me and him, on whatever new terms we carve out.

Permutations of notes flow through Malcolm, the

music freer in him than it has been for a long time, the liberation unexpectedly physical in nature. *Because even the way our lungs function is affected by who is around us, by the impact they make on us, dragging us down or lifting us up, making us push our chests out proudly or cave them in, weighing down our shoulders, making them hunch or pulling them back, spreading and opening us. How we walk in the streets, how we curl up in bed with who we curl up with, all of that affects our lungs' capacity, resilience, elasticity, our ability to give breath shape. Surprising the subtlety of what alters the exhalation, the art, or maybe not surprising at all.*

A title for a piece that came to him two nights ago: *Hot Animal Fag Magnetism.*

He taps out a filterless cigarette and lights it. Strange how this more obvious assault on his chest-capacity doesn't seem to affect what's important in his breath-control or impair the supple responsiveness of his lungs, even though he knows each inhalation coats their delicate membranes with tar and could be seeding tumours. Somehow, ludicrously perhaps, it feels to Malcolm that his smoking cannot damage his playing because it is not in opposition to his art. He tosses the pack onto the table. Luke helps himself from it.

'Gimme the *Qx*, man,' Malcolm says as he passes Luke the Zippo.

Luke slides it over to him from among the Sunday papers and gay freebies they've brought with them. Malcolm flicks through the club news to the contacts section, hoping to be pruriently appalled by brazen declarations of eighteen-inch-girth mancunts and seekers of wet and messy fun, but there's nothing new in the shock department this week.

'Same old same old,' he says, his mind on Ziggy. Strange there should have been such a rapport between them when they disagreed about so much. Like Malcolm preferring to pass for straight as a matter of course (the only giveaway of his faggotry his white male friend, his white male friend with a different visual style to his own, so that no onlooker would suppose they grew up in the same street, worked in the same shop, office or factory: that much he is prepared to carry), while Ziggy is compulsively perversely fetishistically up in straight people's faces 24-7, which is about the most fundamental difference they could have as two same-gender-loving black men of the Diaspora really, everything else in their lives spiralling outwards from that self-positioning, that refiguring of the old debates: integration versus separation; socialism versus Black Nationalism; group loyalties versus the freedom of the individual. Face to face horns locking skins sheening drunken and stoned they square off and make four:

'But look, man, look,' Malcolm is saying, 'it's childish to be loudly rebelling all the time, saying look at me, look at me like that achieves something in itself. It's adolescent - ' Challenging Ziggy as Luke slumps back out of his sight-line exhaling thin blue smoke, green eyes hazing to dull jade, half-listening to their talk, half-dreaming Malcolm knows of some black knight.

'It's childish to conform,' Ziggy says, dopereddened eyes burning, voice hoarsened by herb and constricted by wine. 'What are you, a schoolboy wearing what you're told to wear, going where you're told to go, saying what you're allowed to say, never questioning what that's all about? Nobody ever won freedom by knuckling under to the status quo - '

'Yeah, I agree totally, fuck that. But what's the point of getting ordinary people's backs up and getting shit off them? For the sake of what?' Malcolm reaches round and takes the spliff from where it dangles from

Luke's lower lip. 'What freedom is that? My way you can - ' Malcolm tokes. ' – move. Move on up.'

'What's the point of hiding yourself? What is the point of letting people only see a fake you?' Ziggy asks, rubbing his face with one large hand and reaching for the joint with the other. His fingers brush Malcolm's and Malcolm's chest tightens. 'Unless you can survive in no other way. They won't thank you for it when what you really are does come out. They won't be grateful you spared them the worry and grief for as long as you did. If they'd hate you for who you really are they'll hate you even more when they find out later you lied to them all that time. Because everything comes out in the end.'

'Yeah, but even granting that, that only applies to people close to you,' Malcolm says. 'Not every ape in the street.'

'There's never a good moment to stand out,' Ziggy says. 'There's never a good moment to take a stand, only a necessary one. If you don't get shit from the ignorant then you are not taking a stand.' He swallows wine and sits there hunched over, staring ahead. Malcolm stares at his solidly muscular arms in silence. 'Well, and are you?' Ziggy asks.

'What?'

'Taking a stand?'

Malcolm doesn't reply. He feels tremblingly alive. 'Luke says your art's pretty far out there,' he says.

'No,' Ziggy says, thumping his chest with a fist. 'It's in here.' He moves his hand down to his crotch, grips it through the leather of his kilt. 'And here.'

The drink and the humidity and the radiant heat of the three of them close in the close room have put a sheen on Ziggy's espresso-dark skin. A bead of sweat slides down his striking, gruelled face. Malcolm imagines running his tongue up Ziggy's temple to catch it, imagines the salty taste.

'Where does your music come from?' Ziggy asks. 'It comes out of you.' His flickering, red-rimmed eyes are fixed on Malcolm's. 'Nothing else,' he says.

Malcolm feels as if he is falling into Ziggy's eyes. 'There's something out there too,' he says.

'No,' Ziggy says. 'There is just us.' He is defiant, hotly cold with certainty, and he seems large in the room.

That moment is what Malcolm remembers most clearly from an evening hazy with drugs and alcohol, Ziggy saying, *There is just us*. And maybe he meant there's only humanity and human beings and no god, but to Malcolm it was like a declaration of something else, and he knew he would have to see Ziggy again.

It seems like a lifetime since Malcolm was last seriously interested in a man, since he genuinely wanted to engage rather than play the situation bebop cool. That it should be Ziggy surprised him as much as, if not more than it surprised Luke.

Falling for/in?
Maybe.
Love?
   A song lyric. A word. I don't know.
A lifetime
   /lifeline.

Luke is flicking through *Boyz*. Malcolm watches as his eye is caught by something. 'What, man?'

Luke flushes slightly. 'You know I said about that guy who left his bag on the bus and I give it him back?'

'Who you said had a quote 'inspirational butt'?'

'Ha! Yeah, him. Anyway, listen to this, it's in the *In Touch* bit: 'Blond boy outside Tower. Thanks for my bag. Call me so I can see what colour your eyes are.'

'You reckon that's him?'

Luke goes over the ad again, his mouth slightly

open in the way of someone who has struggled to learn to read. 'Nah,' he says after a long moment. 'I don't reckon.' He makes to close the paper but doesn't.

'Well, you spoke to him, didn't you?'

'Not really, man. I just said here's your bag and he said thanks and see you around or something. But not like *talking*.'

'I mean you'd recognise his voice if you heard it again, my half-speed brother.'

'Well, yeah, I guess.'

'So call.' Malcolm pushes his mobile across the table towards Luke. 'What have you got to lose?'

'But voices sound different on the phone,' Luke says, picking it up. 'I mean, I wouldn't even necessarily recognise it's him even if it is him, you know?'

'Yeah, but do it anyway, man.'

Luke thinks about it, then puts the mobile back down. 'It'll be someone else,' he says. He looks away from Malcolm out over the market, moving his head to a secret beat.

'What it is,' Malcolm says, 'the thing is - I met up with Ziggy last week.' Luke keeps on moving his head as if he hasn't heard. 'I was going to tell you - '

'When, man?'

'I'm telling you now.'

'So I'll call this ad?'

'Call it or don't call it, but you know what I'm saying to you, my Nubian. Nothing stays the same.'

The muscles in Luke's jaw clench. After a long moment he shrugs, picks up the mobile, keys in the number, waits a moment, then enters the code for the contact ad. Malcolm watches as he listens to the voice-message, all the while drumming the table with his buttery-pale, square-ended fingers. He presses a single digit, clears his throat, then speaks:

'Uh, yeah. It's me. Luke. My name's Luke. I saw

your message in *Boyz* and uh, I'd like to - why don't you call me and we can talk some more. Cos I liked you too. A lot.'

He flicks a glance at Malcolm, his face colouring. *Phone-number*, Malcolm mouths. Luke gives it, then snaps the mobile shut and passes it back to him. He grins lopsidedly. 'Now you know all my secrets.'

'Only the ones that matter.'

'So you saw Ziggy again?' Luke tries to sound casual as he folds up the paper.

'Yeah.'

'Well, *and*, man?'

'It was interesting.'

"Interesting?"

'*He* was interesting. *Is* interesting. It's kind of hard to talk about it, man. I mean, you're who I talk to about everything. But this - '

'I get it, man. No sweat.'

'Don't be hurt or pissed off.'

'Like I said, I get it.' Luke's smile is still there, but it's now a little forced.

'You sure?' Malcolm says. 'Cos I love you, you know? I'll always love you, my albino brother. In a way maybe more than anyone else ever. Just, this is something different, you know?'

'I know,' Luke says. 'And you don't have to talk about it. Just don't not tell me stuff you want to cos you think I won't be able to take it cos it's you and Zig. Deal?'

'Deal.'

They brush knuckles, palms, pull back into languid soul-brother finger-snaps.

'So you think it might be serious, then?' Luke says.

'Maybe, man. For the first time since - ' Malcolm shrugs. 'Since whenever. Time.'

Since Marvin. And wasn't everything after that

disaster just the long slow walk to the bridge?

Since then there's been sex, and Luke, though never together, but that seemed like enough back then, and true it was enough, for a while more than enough. And sometimes I'd catch that in my blowing –

Rubies set on/

My gold band -

But here's the lesson: you can't piece your life to-gether like a composite, with love here, sex there, meaning here, freedom there. In the end the pieces reject each other. No denial-drugs can suppress the immune-response. Some people don't notice but they're dying all the same. Suture yourself to them, transplant yourself into their mentality and it will kill you too. Marvin was a black and blue variation on that theme, ragamuffin beaten by the police Stone-disc eyes concealing the vulnerable jelly behind. Oh, and how you hated your name, my Nubian, because it was your father's, and how you hated yourself.

Three years seven months ago them fi chat in a minicab office down Brixton way, a conversation that to a straight man would have seemed begun without purpose and lacking in meaning, but not, of course, to Malcolm. And he had cancelled his cab and gone back to Marvin's yard ostensibly for a little sensi but really for something else, only looking for a little body-heat then, a little satisfaction and release and nothing more from this brother who despised queers and chichimen in his talk while returning repeatedly to the subject of man and man nastying it up.

But Malcolm had fallen for Marvin hard, harder than he would have thought was possible back then, at that time perhaps only half-believing that men could fall in love with other men rather than just fuck and be spars, love and self-hatred tangled up inside him two spitting cats in the sack of his guts -

Marvin. Younger than Malcolm in years but older in street time. Fucked up on drugs, Soon Come unreliable, intrinsically pornographic in the slant of his hips. Effortlessly naturally masculine he seemed, although Malcolm knows that that is always an illusion that must be worked at, guarded, defended by whatever means necessary.

Marvin. Effortlessly masculine battyman corroded with a self-loathing he externalised onto Malcolm.

It all felt so real.

It was all so clichéd.

But all clichés are true.

All clichés are true but never in the way we expect, and so we cannot learn from the clichés of other people's experiences. When he drunkenly hits us in the face and trashes our yard and then the next morning has eyes reddened by tears and equally red roses in cellophane and kisses and statements of undying love and makes love to us with a sudden passionate tenderness we think we're special, that this has never happened before to anyone else, or at least not in the exact same way, and so we will somehow be exempted from the rules, from the consequences. Being black, being gay, being Jamaican, working-class, clever, being a yardcore faggamuffin, it must all make some transcendental difference somehow, must push us beyond the obvious -

But no, we never are exempted.

And then there was Luke.

Perhaps it had to be a white man after that chasm of blackness, though that is a thought Malcolm cannot be happy with.

Just someone different.

Someone I didn't love. Someone who couldn't betray me because I expected nothing from him.

The love and the trust came later.

And now there is Ziggy. Maybe. And Ziggy is African, Nigerian. Born in Lagos. An African African, though brought here at an early age. Malcolm hopes that Ziggy can connect him with that authentic black essence he feels he needs now more than anything. It was that authentication he was looking for from Marvin but could never find, mistaking, it seems to him now, class for race in the essentialist equation as he searches for a validation he knows at bottom he will never find. Because Ziggy has already said 'Fuck essentialism!' and meant it.

Cracking me open, Malcolm thinks. *Letting in the light. Letting out the light.*

Ziggy.

Ziggy, ambling home below a palely lilac predawn sky after his evening - night - with Luke and Malcolm. Not far to go, and he had wanted to take his time and let his fox-thoughts roam in that sinking night, that rising morning.

Sounds were heightened at that crossroads hour: a burst of birdsong; a car starting up and pulling away; the hum of a rare electric milk-float, the particular clink of its crated glass bottles.

It was only now he was out in the open air that Ziggy felt his mind starting to work on its deeper levels. The ghosts of dawn stroked the outsides of his bare arms but the chill of their fingers felt pleasant, almost sensual.

Malcolm.

Maybe.

But I don't check for brothers.

Ziggy laughed at the thought, shaking his head like someone a little crazy. *I don't check for brothers and fuck your judgements. Don't fence me in.* It is both his standard in-your-face piss-off-the-politically-correct-brother line and a private joke between him and Luke, one that requires a deep understanding on Luke's part and extreme trust on Ziggy's. *My brazen shame: only you know how much I mean it.*

Yet his eyes, his dick, even his heart have all at one time or another been drawn that way, towards black men, towards other black men. Almost always he has refused to follow their lead.

What programming am I accepting? What programming am I rejecting? They say your attractions are formed by what's around you when you're coming to puberty though that wasn't true for Luke: for him it was all repulsions and what was attractive was what was elsewhere. I asked him once, If you were in a world where there were no black people no black men wouldn't you just have ended up with a white man and been happy? And he said would you be happy if you had quartz and you never saw a diamond? Probably you would, but it'd be a poor kind of happiness. And maybe it wouldn't even be that cos there'd always be this thing at the back of your mind or the bottom of your heart where you'd feel like there had to be something more to life or sex or love even if you couldn't figure out what.

And Luke moved from the dead white no-places of his beginnings and found life. And me.

My desire is the mirror opposite of his. I learned it from my environment. I was constructed by it. I lusted after peaches-and-cream private school whiteboys. They knotted lust and violence in my gut and cock and balls with their silky hair and well-nurtured skin, with their sense of certainty and entitlement. Their difference made them almost another sex to me in a school where everyone was the same sex. Blond was the most different. Blond was furthest from home. Blond was where shame was the least real.

*Does that make me bad? Does that make my de-
sires invalid? Their blondness, their whiteness made
my blackness matter, made it monolithic. Across the
playing fields and the quad, behind the sound of
leather on willow, beneath the spreading cypresses I
was Kunte Kinte and Eddie Murphy, Shaka Zulu and
Linford Christie, I was Mr Black Power, I and I alone
a kaleidoscope of shattered coloured pieces of glass, a
thousand Tarzan-bearer nigger-projections rolled and
tumbled into one. Externally schizoid living in mirror-
eyes.*

*This is the legend I am telling you. The legend of
me and the white boys. We begin with the legend and
then we burrow down into the truth below, isn't that
how it goes? Without the legend there would be no
curiosity about the reality.*

*When I first met Luke he was just another blond
boy, another in the parade of flesh and pleasure that
filled and failed to fill a need in me. My white-trash
wigger blond. But soon he became more to me than
that.*

And Luke had done his best when the voices came
roaring through Ziggy, voices different from possession, different from rapport with the spirits; voices
made out of damage not divine connection: mental
illness, not the remediable anger of the ancestors. And
in the middle of all that pain and self-loathing Luke
had loved him, and Luke's love had been the mirror,
the inversion of the self-hatred that Ziggy had been
fighting all his life, and he had loved Luke back, loved
him crazily, and for a brief time that love had worked as
a tie and bound the two of them together in their hot,
wild damaged youth.

*He didn't judge me when I turned the mirrors to
face the walls to stop the charged mercury from
making me invisible. We would share baths and shave*

each other's faces, the odd nick not mattering, each
spot of blood in the dirty, milky water proof that we
still existed on the material plane.

For that one brief summer they had balanced on the
high wire, floating it seemed above everything, safe. *As*
his cock slid up into my rectum with shocking sudden-
ness it was so different from those other times, it was
totally good. I felt for the first time that nothing else
mattered, and that feeling consumed me, simplified
me down to my prime number. This was right. This
was my nature. My mind was as quiet as light in
space. I was for a moment free. I was absolutely
connected to the flesh, to the earth, to everything.

Has Ziggy loved since that summer? He doesn't
think so.

Now it is that evening seven years later and two
weeks in the past, Ziggy intensely aware of Malcolm
next to him on the couch, sweatily excited in the close
heat of Luke and Malcolm's living-room, intrigued
against his expectations but wary and defiantly abra-
sive: not easily convinced he has been accepted by this
new black man. 'So when you push onto me that it is
most natural to prefer your own race,' he is saying, 'I
say fuck nature.' He is ragging on Malcolm's cultural-
conservative tip, bold both because it's his nature to
provoke, and because if Malcolm is Luke's friend his
separatist position must be half a pose. 'Why should we
be natural like it is some moral imperative? Are shoes
natural? Is hair-dye natural? Are holidays in the sun
natural? No animal dies in bed. A natural death is
being torn apart by carnivores or getting eaten out by
parasites - '

'Eaten out?' Malcolm adjusts his posture on the
sofa to accommodate the half-erection clearly visible in
his trunks, his hazy, darkly golden eyes on Ziggy's,
secret twin eclipsed suns.

'Eaten from the inside out,' Ziggy corrects himself, an image of Malcolm sitting on his face and yielding to his tongue flashing through his mind, making him tug at his own semi-hard-on through his leather kilt with stoned unselfconsciousness. 'A faggot talking about being natural is giving weapons to the enemy anyway,' he continues. 'Mankind has no obligation to survive. Don't push me to the margins because I'm not planning on having an exponentially-expanding family in a world filled with cruelty and famine. Don't tell me how to live my life. Anyway,' (relighting a joint), 'art is more important than life. All the millions of the past, all that is left of them is their art.'

Ziggy had expected Malcolm to disagree like all the dozens, maybe hundreds of dates and fucks he's had over the years, but he didn't. He just bent forward and toked on the joint where Ziggy was holding it between his thumb and forefinger, his irises dilating receptively as he inhaled, though whether that was from the dope, or in agreement with what he had heard, or out of growing desire Ziggy couldn't tell. But he leaned forward too, and he and Malcolm kissed hotly while Luke was off pissing, and Ziggy's heart pounded so hard in his chest he felt physically sick, and Malcolm's lips against his, sweet, firm, large and smoothly dry, stole his breath, made his cock buck and his stomach-muscles clench.

It had been only a brief kiss: Luke had come back a few moments later and they had broken it off, faces burning, before he saw. But it had been enough. Ziggy had known he wouldn't need to whisper 'Call me' into Malcolm's ear as he kissed his cheek goodnight three hours later. Instead, wordlessly and unseen by Luke, he had touched Malcolm's earlobe with the tip of his tongue as he embraced him, nipped the soft coin of flesh between his teeth as he pushed his scrawled phone-number into Malcolm's hand.

Malcolm had called Ziggy up the next evening, and they had arranged to meet the following day. Without discussing it, they both avoided telling Luke.

'You choose the place, man,' Malcolm said. 'Leave a message telling me where and when, and I'll be there. Choose somewhere that tells me something about you.'

'th London Aquarium @ 1,' was the text Ziggy sent.

(Somewhere different, somewhere twilit at noon, somewhere I'll feel calm. Somewhere cool).

'Til 1,' Malcolm replied. *'Abyssinia.'*

The studded leather belt Ziggy chose to wear for his date with Malcolm had the word FREAK spelt out in interlinked steel letters for a buckle. It is a word he likes because of the slipperiness of its connotations. A word embedded in his adolescent psyche through the song-lyrics and self-presentation of the pre-prison, pre-Born-Again Rick James, who was then all lycra and thigh-high boots, steel studs and long braids, kinky, male, hetero but deviantly fuckable. The belt-buckle itself is a copy of one worn by the rapper Scorpio on the cover of a Grandmaster Flash album, the man himself cane-rowed and lean in a black leather tracksuit and ski-shades, snapping an incongruous fan that at the time Ziggy failed to pick up on as a symbol of 1970s faggotry. But he listened to the cut on the album with that title and fantasised, though whether his fantasy was more to do with being Scorpio or being with him in some then-inconceivable male-on-male sexual encounter Ziggy cannot honestly remember.

(Mirror Marassa psychic twins kiss the glass split fuck yourself give birth to the world)

He remembers reading nearly a decade later of Scorpio's death from AIDS. It was after finding that out that he had the belt-buckle made, defying death with desire.

There have been others across the years who have given him energy, or freed the energy that was already within him, other idols, inspirations, fellow freak avatars. The Hot Gossip dancer Floyd, who was the first black man Ziggy ever saw with dyed blond hair. Prince, from the bikini-briefed, spike-heeled look on the *Dirty Mind* album cover to the butt-up, looking-to-be-fucked manifestation on the inner sleeve of *1999*. Jean-Michel Basquiat, pretty, dreadlocked, brilliant, wrecked by drugs, an ex rent-boy boxing with Warhol; Dennis Rodman, macho but pierced, tattooed, dyed, transvestic. Ziggy has had had flashes of liberation from all of them over the years, mixed in with the slightly removed but still inspiring freakery of white stars: Bowie as Aladdin Sane, Adam Ant, Boy George, Marilyn Manson.

In service to his chosen image as a freak, when he first went to college Ziggy initially flirted with men and fucked women, keeping what would threaten others within bounds, failing during that period to live his life from its own centre, embracing instead a self-defeating parody of it: bi-curious heterosexuality. Still living in terms of other people's projections.

Why I had to cover the mirrors. To put a stop to the accumulation of other people's visions piled up behind the glass pressing out towards my gaping eyes, everyone who ever looked at me exploding outwards in shards blinding me raping my pupil-holes -

In the bodies of the women he was intimate with he found only absence and no satisfaction. Because to Ziggy the principle of femininity is flesh, and flesh is soft and yielding. Whereas the principle of masculinity is muscle: hot, dynamic hardness. This he exults in. To heterosexual men the softness of female flesh is complimentary to their own hardness, perhaps even magnifies it through contrast, whereas to Ziggy that softness always amounted to a cancelling-out of energies.

It is strange how you can fuck someone, be inside her body with your cock, even please her with your tongue, go as deep in there as you can go, experience that intimacy and then forget it so completely it's as if you were never there, as if you're just remembering some porn you once watched, half-watched, without even that much interest.

It's as if Ziggy has never been with a woman, now. *Though you can forget men too, fuck knows*. And he has.

For his date with Malcolm Ziggy had his hair put in twists and bleached blond. From his wardrobe he chose butt-and-crotch-hugging orange pvc trousers with the freak belt slung low on his hips, orange metal-fronted bike-boots from Camden Market, orange wraparound shades, and a skintight turquoise lycra tank-top. It was a heavily-sexualised night-time ensemble that in the glare of the afternoon drew looks and remarks along Portobello Road, but because of Ziggy's hard face and obvious physical toughness, no negative action. Still, he knew it was another challenge for Malcolm.

Why do I do this? To turn him on? To put him off? To punish him for liking me?

No. To demand this: take me as I am or not at all.

Isn't that what love means? If this is - could be - love, the beginning of love.

And if it is love, and if it's love from me to him too, what will he ask of me?

By the time he was dressed and shaved and ready to go, Ziggy was, of course, already late.

Malcolm was on time, something he's been working on lately, and as a result he was nervous. Drum rhythms rattled through his head, his chest, horn-notes projecting beyond them.

Ziggy, oh -

The day was baking hot and he was dressed simply in an indigo-blue cotton jacket with nothing underneath it and tight, low-cut hipster trousers that revealed the smooth dive of his lean stomach and the sculpted, buttressing grooves of his pelvis. In the shallow disc of his navel a gold ring glinted. It was a look that at first glance was conservative, then not.

Like me. He hid his eyes behind blind man's shades and affected a nonchalance he didn't feel as he lent on the white stone parapet and gazed out across the glittering Thames. Behind him the elliptical shadow of the London Eye curved away mauve across the yellow pavement. Beside him a fanciful bronze dolphin with a lamp on its head looked down on him with a rolling, humorous eye. Malcolm smiled back at it. Everything seemed hopeful that afternoon. Even the hordes of tourists milling back and forth along the waterfront seemed to embody some positive notion of something: the freedom just to go where you want, he supposed.

Malcolm doesn't think in terms of holidays, but he spent a week in Harlem once, six years ago when he was twenty-two, intended as a pilgrimage to the haunts of his jazz saints. Despite being disappointed by the commercialisation of their relics, he had gained something only half-expected from the trip: a massive surge of liberation that came from finding himself exclusively among black people. In England such an experience would be overdetermined by negative externals: poverty, crime, violence, despair. In Harlem the citizens were of every class and type, and a fully-functional black world suddenly thrillingly possible.

The week had come to an end before Malcolm had had to confront the fact that they were also, and in reality first and foremost, Americans, and that he was, for all his fantasies of fraternal Negritude, irrevocably English, and that hanging your hat did not mean you were home. For all the healing energy he had received he had been a tourist in Harlem.

Malcolm dreams of Africa, and of a psychic integration he cannot imagine really experiencing. He longs to go, but is afraid of disappointment. Afraid to find that after all nothing can fill the chasm within him.

Ziggy is Nigerian.

Ziggy has no romance about Africa.

Afrika
  Afreaka
    Mythical Land
      Heal me

The only other burst of freedom Malcolm ever experienced that felt anything like what he experienced in Harlem was his first Gay Pride march. Still framed in terms of protest then, it linked arms at least symbolically with Martin Luther King and that deep vein of Black and Third World struggle for freedom and self-determination. Who remembers all that now? X is for ecstasy, not Malcolm Malik El-Shabazz.

He would have been twenty-three then, and every bus and tube-carriage, every pavement and park had been crowded with self-evident queens and queers and dykes. It was – still is - strange for him to feel even for an afternoon what he imagines straight people must feel, or what white people must feel, all day every day: that everyone around them, or everyone who counts, who is 'real', is like them. They don't even notice, don't even know, much less feel, the fundamental confidence that gives them.

On that first march, and at the party in the park afterwards, he had felt a burden of insanity being briefly lifted off him just as he had in Harlem. It was a chance to take a breath before being dragged under again, even while he did not, could not, would not ignore the complex, painful reality of existing where identities compete, something the grudging presence of a People of Colour tent among the other club-night party tents could not atone for or resolve.

Imagine being without that weight all the time -

He knows one reason he is drawn to Ziggy is that Ziggy forces him to be braver. He has been involved with men who have sex with men but don't incorporate that fact into their identity, men like Marvin, and while at first he found that disassociation perversely exciting, somehow authentically masculine in a way that calling yourself gay or queer failed to be, the thrill of living in the shadows, of performing heterosexuality on the streets, being heterosexual everywhere except between the sheets, soon proved itself a thin, starved thing.

Not just
antics
4 this
true romantic.

Turning from the river he saw Ziggy making his way towards him, threading his way through the candied-peanut and hotdog-sellers' stands, bulging pornographically out of skintight orange vinyl and electric-blue lycra. His freshly dyed and twisted blond hair made his skin look blue-black. His eyes were hidden by orange-framed iridescent sunglasses. His battered features - wide nose, large, strongly-defined lips, wide mouth - were full, voluptuous, spectacular. Some people have that quality, the intrinsically pornographic.

Malcolm's erection was instant and painful, and rammed all fear from him. He stepped down from the parapet and kissed Ziggy on the mouth. It wasn't a long kiss, but it was hard and charged with desire. As they kissed again, more deeply this time, Malcolm felt Ziggy's hand slide inside his jacket and grip his side.

The confident physical contact made him exhale into Ziggy's open mouth. He felt disconcertingly like he might come.

After a long moment they broke the kiss and stood back from each other a little. Like duellists lowering their pistols each man slowly removed his sunglasses, glancing down shyly as he did so, as if uneasy at what his eyes might tell that his lips did not. But when their eyes met they were brown and sparkling, and Malcolm smiled and Ziggy laughed. They replaced their shades and entered the aquarium, Ziggy leading the way.

Yes yes yes yes yes yes -

Beyond a bland merchandising area and the ticket-booth the interior was dark and cool. Malcolm had never been here before. The idea of visiting the Aquarium had always made him think of school and borinng science classes, and he was surprised to find himself impressed by the three-storey tanks, vast, glowing glass cases that housed sharks, conger-eels, lobsters, rays, and shoals of reef-dwelling fish, all living together in seeming harmony: a world of sinuous, silent beauty.

In the low light Ziggy took Malcolm's hand and Malcolm let him even though he was aware they were being watched disapprovingly by the black attendant in the navy blazer who stood by the doorway.

Probably Nigerian.

Don't be angry at him. His isn't the real oppression. We claw at each other at the bottom of the barrel. We have to try and undelude ourselves. A white man would have disapproved too. Ziggy didn't seem to notice. His hand felt good in Malcolm's. Physical pleasure and even pride suffused Malcolm as they passed tank after tank, coolly lambent environments with glass walls that were wide and tall enough to seem not imprisoning, and Ziggy pointed out the strange undersea creatures he liked, sharing small facts about them with Malcolm as they strolled through the dim, quiet corridors.

'This is my favourite part,' Ziggy said, leading Malcolm by the hand down a ramp into a low-ceilinged room containing a large, waist-high, U-shaped, open-topped tank.

Gazing down into the water Malcolm saw at the tank's floor golden-brown diamond-shaped skates the size of cymbals with figure-eight eyes. They glided smoothly about, or rested still as stones on the gravel. No-one else was in the room. Ziggy glanced at Malcolm, made a soft, low whistling noise and dabbled his fingers in the water. After a moment one of the skates detached itself from the bottom of the tank and flapped calmly up towards the surface. Then, its pale nose pointing up out of the water, it paddled towards Ziggy's fingers like an old man doing breast-stroke and trying to keep his head above water, until Ziggy was chucking it softly under where its chin would be if it had a chin, his fingers darkly pink against its marble-white underside.

'You can touch it too,' he said softly.

Malcolm reached out and very gently stroked the skate's muscularly undulating wing. Under the water it felt like silk, not slimy at all, just miraculously smooth, and firm and fatless; all muscle and alive, but cold. He stroked its back, which was unexpectedly ridged and spiny to his fingertips. He looked round at Ziggy and smiled, feeling young and innocent, and Ziggy was smiling too, his face underlit with silver like disco mascara by the reflected light from the pool, and they kissed again. Malcolm felt a tear slide from the corner of his eye at the intensity of the brief contact, at the heat of Ziggy's forehead against his.

The skate decided it was bored of their attentions and slid back to the bottom of the tank. Two small children came rushing in, followed by educating, loud-voiced parents from whom they were presumably trying to escape. Still holding hands, Ziggy and Malcolm moved on.

After leaving the aquarium they wandered up onto Westminster Bridge. At the apogee they looked back along the river. Dusk was falling, and the blue sky was deepening overhead. The glass-walled capsules of the Eye seemed to fill with summer lightning as the sightseers within tried to capture panoramic views of the city, rendering the curving glass opaque with flashes in defiance of optical science. The air was blood-warm, still as amber.

Don't think ahead Don't plan/Don't damn and paralyse/your heart. Uncurl, unfurl/the flag of you, escape/unwind/the spiral shell/Despair -

If only it was that easy, Malcolm thought. Then: *perhaps it is.*

From Trafalgar Square they got a bus to Notting Hill, sitting shoulder to shoulder at the upstairs front, playing at being tourists for just a little while longer. Then they ambled down Portobello Road, neither of them quite able to say the word, to make the move that would take things further.

Ziggy did let Malcolm see him to his door, a concession and a forward step Malcolm didn't know Ziggy well enough to fully appreciate, but he knew it was something nonetheless.

'Strange, isn't it?' Ziggy said, turning in the doorway, silhouetted by the yellow light behind him in the stairwell.

'What, man?'

'How much harder it is when you like someone. And you don't want to - '

'So you like me?' Malcolm said.

'Oh, yes,' Ziggy said. 'I like you seriously and smil-ingly.'

'Good.' Malcolm felt heat flush through him. 'That's good, man.' He took hold of Ziggy's chin and kissed him gently on the lips. 'Call me,' he said. Then a thought seemed to strike him. 'You be in later on, yeah?'

Ziggy looked at him sharply. 'Yes,' he said, but his eyes receded slightly. Malcolm nodded and turned away, smiling to himself as he did so.

The light, which was on a timer switch, snapped to black.

Ziggy lent out of the doorway and watched Malcolm go, hoping for a backward glance that didn't come. He sighed and pulled himself back into the hallway. A perverse desire to straight away go out surged through him. *Fuck Malcolm. I go where I like when I like Do what I like. So fuck Malcolm.*

No no no-oh.

I like Malcolm. Deeply.

Closing the door, he turned and climbed the stairs to his flat. Suddenly he felt exhausted, dizzy and slightly nauseous. He wondered about the pills he had tipped away. He was too tired even to smoke a joint. He stumbled through to his bedroom and without even unlacing his boots collapsed face-down on the bed. Thick grey sleep swept over him.

He woke in the small hours sweaty and restless, lured from dreams by something on the edge of conscious-ness, something that like a spirit summons made him sit up, put his still-booted feet on the bare boards and go over to the window. Earlier he had propped it open with a brick in futile hope of a breeze: both sash-cords had long given way. Now he pulled back the curtain and looked down on the neon-lit street below.

Like a performer in a spotlight a man was standing under one of the streetlamps opposite. A black trilby was pushed back on his head, and he was playing his trumpet softly, too softly in fact to have woken Ziggy, who felt he had been drawn to the window by other energies.

This city my shrine. My
Kalakuta show.

Malcolm glanced up as Ziggy pulled the curtain aside, his eye caught by the surely hoped-for but only half-expected movement, and he played on, finishing the piece he had begun ten minutes ago, blowing the notes more sweetly now, infusing their small-hours melancholy with a secret joy, or so it seemed to Ziggy as he stood there and the music flowed through him.

The solo ended. Malcolm lowered the trumpet and looked up at Ziggy, his chest rising and falling, his eyes bright and hard with the bravado of vulnerability. He kissed his fingertips and waved the kiss up to Ziggy. Then, without a word, he turned and disappeared into the night.

As if a spell had been broken, a few streets away a woman started to shriek abuse, and nearer to an argument between drunks broke out. Somewhere glass smashed. Ziggy stepped back from the window, carelessly tugging the curtain back into place, feeling strange, his skin electrified.

When sleep came to him the voices came too. These he knew were the true spirit voices, so different from the other, neurochemical voices that clacked like ghastly wooden puppets; that stole light and gave out only death-ray darkness from their painted eyes

The spirit voices first came to Ziggy shortly after he abandoned Luke, though at the time he had believed it was Luke who had abandoned him, refusing, as it seemed to him then, to bear what Ziggy couldn't, in any case, extract from himself and transfer across the void between minds.

I twisted the chuck until it gripped the black iron bit tight, plugged in the drill pressed the trigger like a gun It whirred I pointed the spinning metal spiral at the imploding exploding disc between my eyes and it was then then then the warrior came in my room and said Put up the spear, my son. And I said Grandfather, and he said No I am Ogun, I was hunting in the forest and I heard your cry. And I closed my eyes and I opened them and it was hours later and the drill was unplugged and lying away from me on the floor. And I cried and I couldn't stop but somehow knew I was embraced.

When he next woke it was a little before 2 p.m. He speed-dialled Malcolm. Malcolm answered sounding husky - evidently he had still been asleep when the phone rang - but pleased. 'So how you doing, my Nubian?' he asked.

'Good, I'm good,' Ziggy said. Then after a moment's self-consciousness he added, 'What you did last night was a beautiful thing, you know? A sweet thing.'

There was the soft sound of static and Ziggy imagined Malcolm smiling. 'When I started playing I wondered if you were going to hear me,' Malcolm said. 'I was playing real quiet because part of me didn't want to wake you up. I guess I wanted to infiltrate your dreams, you know? Go in there on the deepest level.'

'I like a man who goes in deep.'

Ziggy could hear the soft laughter in Malcolm's voice as he went on, 'But when I saw you at the window I was pleased, so I guess I meant to wake you really.'

'Wanting your applause.'

'True.'

'Is it your own composition?'

'Yeah, man, it's mine,' Malcolm said. 'Well, now it's yours.'

'I am honoured. Does it have a title?'

'I call it *Nocturnal Admission*.'

Ziggy's mobile rings, bringing him back to the present. He checks who the caller is. It's Malcolm. He presses OK. 'I was thinking of you,' he says, pushing a low, seductive tone into his voice.

'Good,' Malcolm says. A pause. 'I've been missing you, man.'

'Me too.'

'Were you asleep?'

'Just thinking about stuff.'

'What stuff?'

'Just stuff.'

'Like what?'

'The curve of your lips,' Ziggy says. 'The curves of your ass.'

He can feel Malcolm smile. 'I can't sleep, man,' Malcolm says. His voice is pillow-talk intimate as he whispers over the airwaves, as if he's just a breath away. 'It's too humid. I feel so... *restless*, man. You know?'

Ziggy glances at his watch. It's one a.m. The moon above is full, he knows, and heavy. It drags on oceans, lifts up seas. *We are 70% water*.

'So...' There is a catch in Malcolm's voice before he hurries on: 'So I was thinking, can I come and chill at yours?'

Behind his casual choice of words Ziggy can feel his aching need, the unevenness in his voice revealing how hard it is for him to be this direct when his feelings are so strong. 'Of course,' Ziggy says, after only the briefest hesitation. 'I cannot sleep either.'

'Sweet, man,' Malcolm says. But he doesn't ring off

right away.

Ziggy listens to the silence, trying to guess what it means. 'Is Luke there?' he asks.

'No,' Malcolm says. 'No, he's out.' A soft half-laugh. 'On a date, actually.'

'Who with?'

'This brother he met through the personals.'

'Anyone you know?'

'I don't think so,' Malcolm says. 'A dancer, a chore-ographer. Older than us. I don't know. He sounded okay.'

'Are you bothered about it?' Ziggy asks.

'No. Not really,' Malcolm says. 'Just, I always wait up for him, or he always waits up for me, or calls, you know? Just so we know we're okay.'

'But now it is different.'

'Yeah.'

'And he hasn't called?'

'No.'

'Do you still want to come over?'

'Yeah,' Malcolm says. 'I just don't wanna feel - guilty about it.'

Still he doesn't hang up.

'Malcolm, are you calling me up tonight about you and me or about you and Luke?' Ziggy says. 'Am I talking to a friend about his friend or - '

'You and me,' Malcolm says. 'I'm sorry, man, I'm jerking you about and I don't want to because you're the most - ' He cuts himself off awkwardly. 'Maybe I shouldn't come there.'

'I think you should.'

'Yeah?'

'Yes, I do.'

'Then I'll be there.' Malcolm rings off abruptly, as if he's afraid that Ziggy might change his mind.

We are all so vulnerable, Ziggy thinks. *The harder*

we seem the more we've been hurt. And love can be that razor-sharp blade that slides in with no pain but does such damage inside.

And now he wonders, *Luke, where are you? Is something happening for you too?*

Chapter Five

George suffered a crisis of confidence while getting ready for his date with Luke, brought on by noticing his nail-varnish was chipped. He debated changing colours - he liked wearing gold and silver too, and occasionally even red, although he always felt too drag-queeny in red - but decided to stick with the blue. Then the feeling swept over him, *He's a handsome blond kid, why in hell would he want to be seen with some hard-faced black queen who paints his nails and shaves his eyebrows and is twice his age?*

Strange and even terrifying how all the protective walls of self-love and self-approval can be torn down by a smile. Angry at himself for being undermined by conformist views of what is desirable, and also for projecting those views onto Luke, who did, after all, respond to his ad, George defiantly applied metallic blue eyeshadow to match his repainted fingernails.

Luke's response on his message-line had followed a confused, Spanish-accented one that seemed to have no connection with anything George had said in his ad: 'I would like you to show me some good times,' that first message had said. 'I can be quite open. You sound very nice. I am nineteen, student. I like pubs, clubs and to work out.'

Message deleted. You have - one - new - message.

He had recognised Luke's voice at once, and an almost adolescent excitement had stabbed through him as he scrabbled for a pen to take down the mobile number Luke was repeating with careful clarity.

The first conversation between them, when George called Luke back that evening, had been awkward, but it was the awkwardness of delight rather than the embarrassing realisation that the moment had passed.

After a handful of questions - Whereabouts do you live? Did you worry about leaving/answering the ad? Have you done the personals before? - which served to reassure them both that neither was an axe murderer or a crack addict, they had arranged to meet that evening for a drink and maybe a meal, and set a time, eight. Eight had a sincerity to it that a later hour would have lacked, signifying as it did the giving over of a whole evening rather than half of one to their meeting, and thus emphasising the romantic over the sexual.

'So it's a date, then?' Luke said, just before getting off the line.

'It's a date,' George replied.

An odd thrill ran through his chest as he snapped his mobile shut. *A date!* he thought later that afternoon as he went through his wardrobe. *How long is it since I've been on a 'date'?*

His longstanding partners he had mostly met through work, and he used saunas or cruising grounds when he wanted sexual release without involvement. Neither of which could be called 'dating'. The novelty was exciting in itself.

Once he had hauled his self-esteem up with the application of eyeshadow he began to feel unexpectedly optimistic and adventurous, and glad he hadn't died a fortnight before, on his fiftieth birthday.

Had it been sincere, the premonition of death that had been on him that day? Now it seemed a vanity. Perhaps it had just been weariness: so many endless battles. He felt almost robbed of some obscure grandeur that he could have risen or fallen to: some final, absolute moment of insight that can only be gained as the curtain creaks down for the final time.

But what's the point of an insight if you can't share

it? And how can you allow yourself to die if you have a duty to remember the dead? And being a black fag and surviving is a duty too, a proof of the possibility of bearing it all. 28% of gay teenagers attempt suicide even now, even here, 42% of black gay teenagers compared with 4% of straight ones.

And some succeed.

More ghosts. More spirits to commemorate.

And there is too a duty to the young, to those arriving now, to make the world a less hostile place for them, or if not that, if that is too much, to at least create and maintain the spaces of release and freedom they will need. *And in this I am a parent. In this I pay the debt we owe our mothers.*

He looked over his face minutely in the mirror. 'Young as you feel,' he said out loud. 'Yeah, right.' He sighed, seeing his face then not as he usually saw it, with all the years from boyhood on built up inside it, something that was almost an achievement, but as Luke would see it, stripped of all that vital history. Just old.

Why people who've been married for a long time stick it out: they're the only ones who see the youth in each other, the full colours of each others' faded handsomeness or beauty. If either of them left the marriage both of them would lose that window on the past; and to anyone new they met their most youthful moment would be that moment, would begin with age.

Well, he's seen my fifty-year-old face and he liked it.

Apparently.

Once Luke had learned that George lived in Brixton he suggested meeting at the Juice Bar, an offbeat, liberal, semi-Afrocentric café which had walls lined with books by black authors and hosted jazz and cultural evenings. It was on Coldharbour Lane, just past the arches of Brixton market, and was somewhere George went for breakfast sometimes, enjoying as he did its relaxed atmosphere and vegetarian menu. So he agreed to meet Luke there, though he had rather wanted to get away from the insanity of Brixton on a broiling July evening.

My manor.

George's flat is just two minutes' walk from the Juice Bar, on the top floor of a house in a curving Victorian terrace behind the Ritzy cinema. As a result of a steady run of work in a series of West End musicals in the mid-Eighties he had the good fortune to be able to buy just before Brixton became irrevocably yuppified and property prices went through the roof.

His sell-out period, he thinks of it now, remembering the spirit-destroying realisation coming upon him at thirty-four that life wasn't going to shit him a miracle; that he, George Defries, wasn't going to be exempted from the colourless world of mortgages, tax demands and pension schemes. Nor was he immune to a growing psychological need to have money in the bank for once, a washing-machine, a properly-upholstered couch and a dozen other mundane status items that regular working stiffs take for granted. As a result, and despite the pounding anxiety induced by not knowing if he would - or could - ever go back to doing serious or committed work, he had gone up for the most commercial jobs he could find, and had won roles in *Cats* and *Starlight Express* among others. It had been necessary, and it had been a relief so strong that it had literally made him shudder, but it hadn't been a happy time for him.

Not that he regrets having done those shows now, of course, or the money they brought him. Being shot out of star-traps in body-stockings or careening around arenas on rollerskates night after night, matinee after matinee: that repetitive, artistically meaningless and physically arduous work bought him his home.

Dr Dre's *2001* began to pound from a neighbour's wide-open window, drowning out the roots reggae and pop trash that was blaring further down the street. It put George on a homeboy tip as he rummaged through his racks of clothes, and he quickly picked out a shiny red Dennis Rodman basketball vest, black knee-length Dexter Wong shorts, a high red leather baseball cap and a pair of chunky black old-skool hi-tops.

He checked his reflection in the mirror critically. The vest showed off his lanky arms and broad shoulders nicely, the shorts flattered his butt and bunched sexily just above his strong, hairless calves. No way did he look fifty.

Forty-five maybe. Forty. Maybe even younger.

He nodded to himself, pleased with his appearance, but somehow not quite satisfied. After a moment's consideration he decided it was his eyes: even without the eyeshadow they gave too much away for the streets of Brixton on a Saturday night. Eyes that are too readable, eyes that are looking for queer love, can draw knives instead of smiles towards them. They can draw hatred from the damaged, frightened souls who see their longings mirrored there too nakedly.

George dug a pair of brown-tinted ski-shades out of a dresser drawer and slipped them on. *Wraparounds at night. Tres Kool Moe Dee. Tres Old Skool.*

He glanced at his watch: 7:58.

Time to go.

To his irritation Luke managed to arrive at Brixton tube station twenty minutes early. There was nothing for him to do but go straight to the Juice Bar and sit there and wait and get nervous.

He managed to get a small table just inside the door

that gave him a good view of the street. Groups of drug-dealers, several of whom had off-handedly offered him Black, Red Leb and sensi as he passed them by, loitered under the arches. Ragamuffin boys with fresh cuts, fades and cane-rows, and flygirls with newly-done processes, weaves and extensions hung out in posses around the many black barbers and hairdressers that were scattered along that part of the street. Older West Indians and African men and women in traditional dress went about their respectable business, mingling with Rastas, bohemians, wine-bar yuppies, derelicts and students.

Luke feels at home there, and not.

In the café Thelonious Monk is playing. Luke knew nothing about jazz until he met Malcolm. Well, he knew the greats - Louis Armstrong, Billy Holiday, Nina Simone, Ella Fitzgerald: it was mostly the vocalists he liked then, not the beboppers, the birth-givers of the cool, men - and they were all men - like Miles Davis, Mingus, Monk, Bird, Trane, Ornette Coleman, Wayne Shorter and Sun Ra. It was Malcolm who got him past their overt, albeit male-bonded, heterosexuality and let him discover the dynamic spirit-intensity of their music.

'The spirituality of masculinity, of maleness,' Malcolm said, knowing how to intrigue his friend, 'it's all in there, man. That richness. Open your ears and cash in.' And Luke had listened, and had been enriched. The piece playing now is *Round Midnight*. Each note makes him feel a little more at ease as he waits for the clock to creep round to eight, at which time he can legitimately start waiting for George to appear.

He takes from his pack a new biography of Jean-Michel Basquiat, an artist he loves because he went from homeless street hustler to star artist in New York in the crazy Eighties, but finds he can't concentrate.

Instead he looks out at the passing scene, his eyes drawn to youts in mesh vests and do-rags whose butts rise enticingly above their sagging jeans.

Normally the sight of so much brown male skin, so much Afro-physiognomy, would induce in Luke a generalised but painfully intense sense of longing and alienation, but tonight these homeboys are just atmosphere artists, setting the stage for the man he is meeting, hopefully very soon now, building him up with their sexual energy.

If he turns up, that is.

Luke smoked a joint before setting out, but the calming effect of the sensimillia has passed from his system. Perhaps a little paranoia has even set in. He is wearing a v-necked sky-blue glittery lycra tee-shirt that shows off his arms and chest, soft, dove-grey knee-length military-cut shorts, beat up black army boots and, around his neck, a black leather choker that presses, he hopes provocatively, on his Adam's apple.

'Does this look too faggy?' he asked Malcolm earlier that evening as he dithered over what to wear. 'Too G.A.Y. air-head?'

'No, man. You look good. Buff.'

'I don't want him to think I'm no bog-standard queen, though.'

'You don't need to worry on that score, my brother. Not once you open your mouth.'

'You reckon, man?'

'You look good, man. Relax.'

'This choker, you reckon he'll think I'm into S&M though?'

'Queercore skatepunk, that's what he'll think, man.'

'Yeah?'

'Yeah. Now smoke this and chill out. You're giving me a migraine, my Nubian. And have a good time when you get there.'

'I'll try. And if I don't - '

'Blame me.'

And Malcolm kissed him on the forehead, a bene-diction.

Sweet Malcolm.

Luke smiles to himself and glances at his watch: 7:55. He swallows the last of his drink, a blend of carrot, pear and ginger named after Jean Toomer, a Harlem Renaissance writer he's heard of but never read anything by. Other drinks are named after Claude McKay (banana), Wallace Thurman (blackcurrant), Alice Walker and *Yardie* author Victor Headley.

George arrives at eight minutes past eight, looking shy and unexpectedly streetwise in red basketball drag. His face is both stranger and less strange than Luke remembered it. The blue eyeshadow is more artificial, the shaving upwards of the eyebrows more pro-nounced, and yet its humanity is also more fully present, revealed in the sadness and warmth of his large brown eyes as George takes off his ski-shades and slips them into a shorts-pocket.

Half-rising, Luke extends his hand for George to shake. They maintain the contact, enjoying its affirma-tive intimacy, as George takes his seat. 'Am I late?' he asks. His voice is pleasantly grainy.

'No, man,' Luke says. 'I was early.' His own voice sounds light and flavourless to him. He swallows down self-loathing.

George releases his hand gently. 'Are you hungry?' he asks.

Luke glances at the menu the waiter left with him earlier and nods. 'Is here okay?'

'Here's fine.'

'Cool.'

George is looking straight into Luke's eyes. He smiles and Luke smiles back, then Luke blushes and looks down. His eye is caught by George's nail-varnish.

'You've got beautiful hands, man,' he says. And they are beautiful: large and long-fingered, dark and tapering and strongly-veined. Hands Luke would like to kiss, fingers he would like to suck, to feel slide inside him.

And George is struck again by Luke's offbeat handsomeness, the greenness of his now-lidded eyes, the angularity of his jaw and the sensuality of his mouth, the slight but provocative gap between his front teeth. One of them is a shade lighter than the other, suggesting a bridge. He is also struck by the extremity of Luke's youth.

The waiter arrives and takes their order. George and Luke become slightly awkward during the wait for the food, the free flow of their talk hobbled by the fear of being interrupted in some moment of intimate disclosure. Their drinks - a Claude McKay and an Alice Walker - get brought over promptly.

'He was gay,' George says. 'Clause McKay. A gay Jamaican writer during the Harlem Renaissance.'

'Yeah?'

'He wrote poems and a book called *Banana Bottom*.'

'Yeah?' Luke smiles. 'And Alice?'

'A womanist, to say the least.'

Good smells come from the kitchen. A boy-girl couple sit at the table next to theirs, but because they're chatting in Italian, not English, a sense, perhaps false, of not being overheard is created, and George and Luke experience the sudden, exuberant feeling of being on holiday. The food arrives.

'So you live alone?' George asks, digging his fork into an oval clay dish of lasagne.

'No, man,' Luke says round a mouthful of salad. 'I live with a friend.'

"Friend?"

'Yeah.' Luke munches rocket and lambsleaf and baby spinach: all day he's had no appetite, now he's extremely hungry. 'We're not lovers or anything. I mean it's not like I don't think he's beautiful, cos I do, but we never went that way. But we're as close as you can get with someone you're not having sex with, or in love with, but you love. He's like my brother. No, more than that, cos my real - I mean biological, not real; biology ain't destiny - my biological brother's crap. Malcolm's like a brother's supposed to be, you know? Really he is my brother. To me.'

'And he's black?' George asks.

Luke nods, only slightly avoiding George's eyes. 'Yeah. He's a jazz musician. A trumpeter. But what am I going on about Malcolm for? Tell me more about you, man.'

'Well, what do you want to know?'

'Everything, of course.'

George laughs. 'Even I don't like the sound of my voice *that* much.'

'I just want to know you, man,' Luke says.

'So ask me a question,' George says.

'Do you believe in love?'

George is pleased by the question: not *What role do you play?* or *How big are you?* or *What drugs/pubs/clubs do you like?* Not a bad stab at depth.

'I do,' he says. 'But I also know love is complex. And it's the most wonderful thing, but sometimes it's still not enough.' He feels old saying that, but what's the point of avoiding what you've learned from your life? 'I don't mean that in a cynical way,' he adds. 'Love between two men, yes, I believe in that. I've experienced it. And then there are other loves. Love of Man, the idea of man, or humanity. Love of art - '

'Do you think they fight each other?' Luke interrupts. 'Loving a man and loving your art?'

'Well, you're a painter, right?'

'Yeah, I am,' Luke says, surprised. He hasn't said anything about his art to George. 'But how did you know?'

'There's paint under your nails. Pigment colours not household ones. Ultramarine, scarlet, Prussian blue, maybe. Vermillion, cadmium yellow.'

'You must of looked at my hands pretty close.'

'I did.'

'So what d'you think?'

'I think they're beautiful.'

Luke blushes. 'I mean about loving art and loving a man.'

That exact formulation of words - 'loving a man' - isn't one Luke would normally use. Usually he would say 'loving someone' - the defensive habit of never specifying the gender of his sexual partners to someone he doesn't really know. But saying 'loving a man' to this man in front of him, to this particular, remarkable man, seems almost intoxicating in its specificity. It seems to cut to something essential, something profound that the less gender-specific phrases evade or even deny.

Monk is still playing in the background, his staccato piano technique embodying some particular masculine spirit that fits perfectly with what Luke is feeling at this exact moment.

'I've known people who are threatened by me being a dancer and a choreographer,' George says. 'People who aren't in the arts. It made them feel worthless in a particular way because they didn't create anything, even if what they were doing was actually more directly useful. You know, nurses, electricians, bin-men.' He sighs. 'They thought I'd think they were boring because of what they did for a living, and sometimes they'd get angry about it, angry with me, I mean. With their idea of me. And they were wrong, except that their fear of being boring made them try too hard, or not try hard enough - out of defiance, you know? - and that *was* boring. Maybe there's an inevitable difference between people who have a vocation, whatever it is, and people who are just getting through. D'you want another drink?'

Luke shakes his head.

'Then there've been others who didn't do anything artistic themselves but could appreciate it was an essential part of me, like my sex or my skin. So there doesn't have to be an opposition, just a genuine desire to embrace what the other person really is. They don't have to be in competition with my vocation because it's not like my love for dance and my love for another man are slices out of the same limited pie. Maybe in some ways they even amplify each other. Does that make sense?'

'Totally.' Luke is a little breathless. So much of what George has just said resonates with him. How often do we meet a sexually intriguing stranger and discover a real mental or spiritual affinity? He is excited and afraid. This date, begun almost as a dare, half-instigated by Malcolm, is now becoming something else.

'So tell me something about you, sweetness,' George says, twiddling the straw in his bottle of Perrier.

'Just ask me a question,' Luke says. 'Anything you want to know.'

'Are all your lovers black?'

The question. Well, he has the right.

'Yeah. They're all black. And men. Well, so far. But I'm not planning on any changes. I mean, why should I?' He finds himself speaking more rapidly. 'I mean, if you're doing what you wanna do with who you want to, and if they wanna do it with you - '

'Do you know why?'

'Do any of us know the why of anything?'

'We can guess at some things fairly certainly,' George says. 'About ourselves. About others.'

'And what would *you* guess, man? About me, I mean?'

George laughs. 'I'd guess you're afraid of answering my question in case you say what I think is the wrong thing. And maybe you're wavering between what you think I'll be comfortable with and trying to tell the truth, when you know the truth is flawed and messy and might not be appealing.'

'You're scary, man,' Luke says with an uncertain smile.

'I'm a pussycat,' George says. 'But I've been around too many years and I've seen too much to be appalled, and I like you, sweetness. I like you a lot. So tell me.'

'Okay.' Luke swallows the last of his drink. Eryka Badu is playing over the speakers. He doesn't know how to begin.

'Was there a moment?' George prompts, and Luke wonders what has been said to him in the past in answer to a question he has perhaps asked many times.

'A bunch of moments, I guess.'

Luke's eyes haze as he looks backwards and in-wards, trying to be unselfconscious, trying to be honest. Trying not to avoid George's gentle yet penetrating gaze.

'So?'

'Well, I don't know, man,' Luke says. 'Like, it sounds stupid, but I remember when I was a kid and seeing this black Action Man. And for some reason I really, really wanted it but I knew I couldn't ask my mum for it. Dolls were for homos anyway, although Action Man was halfway okay. And I knew my brother, he'd despise me for wanting it. And if I got it, he'd twist its head off. Looking back that seems like kind of a big-deal moment. Like hitting some intense taboo thing. But it was just a toy I wanted and I couldn't have. No,' he corrects himself, 'couldn't ask for. I guess that means something, don't it? I mean it was weird to feel it so strong. But it don't answer why. I would of been like seven or something.' He looks into George's eyes, seeking a response.

'I always coveted my sister's dolls,' George says. His eyes reveal nothing except reflective amiability. 'I was envious of Barbie for some reason, I suppose because she had Ken. He was her toyboy; he didn't have any function except to be decorative. He had some kind of latex skin that covered his legs so there were no joints, and I remember even as a kid knowing that was a sensual decision by somebody to make it so he'd look good in shorts. And then there was just a disappointing bump under the Bermuda shorts when you peeked. Which I did, of course, the first chance I got. In retrospect it's mildly creepy and puritanical, I think, to deny the sex of the body like that.'

'Action Man was really sexless,' Luke says. 'No cock, no butt. I think half the reason those Billy dolls are a success is they're what every gay boy wanted his Action Man to be.'

'But not you?'

'You know what's really embarrassing?' Luke says. 'When they first come out I was real judgemental about 'em, cos they was so blond and there was all this 'every gay man's fantasy' label put on them and, you know, it made me feel like I didn't exist, which happens all the time if who you like is pushed to one side - and also, which matters a lot more than what *I* feel, all these black guys was made to feel like *they* don't exist or ain't wanted. And then' - Luke's face flushes - 'And then they did – you've seen it, right? – this black doll, Tyson -

and I'm not even gonna go into how come Iron Mike can be so popular after literally being in the slammer for rape – or maybe it was probably also supposed to be that supermodel guy, that Tyson Beckford, or kind of both, but anyway they did it, and I saw this doll in Prowler in this like macho little army outfit and it all come flooding back to me, wanting that black Action Man and not being able to ask for it.'

'Did you buy it?'

'I just *couldn't*, man,' Luke laughs. 'Malcolm bought me one in the end, like for a birthday present. It's on the top of my easel like a Voodoo doll. But did it bother you, man, when you were a kid, that all the dolls were white? I mean, I guess they were?'

'That would have been the late Fifties, early Sixties,' George says. 'At the time it just felt - we'd come to this white country full of white people, and we were terribly poor, we had so little of anything - it was just what you'd expect. And my parents' plan was to come here, make a decent pile of money, pick up some skills they could use back home and go back there and become part of the well-to-do middle-classes. They didn't expect representation here because it wasn't a place they planned on staying, so we didn't either. Not to start with. Also the political battles that were happening, the Civil Rights and Black Power movements over in the States that were having some impact here too by then, were about much more direct things: No Blacks, No Dogs, No Irish, not issues of representation.'

'When were you born, man?'

'1952. Eighteenth July.'

'A Cancer?'

'Yeah. You?'

'1978.'

'*1978?* Ow. I was twenty-six by then. Date?'

'Eleventh December. I'm a Scorpio.'

'Ah-hah,' George says. 'Not that I believe in astrology, I should say.'

'Me either.' Luke looks away for a moment. 'You've seen some times, man,' he says. 'I mean, from Enoch Powell and all that shit to now and a new millennium.'

'Yeah, but those things only come clear when you look back,' George says. 'At the time you're just getting through. The Rivers of Blood speech on the radio - which wasn't about the Brixton riots to come; it was Powell saying the whites would rise up and massacre the black and brown people if there were too many of them, and it never went *that* way, sugar, you know? The man was a damn fool, and wrong, whatever people started saying at his funeral about him being a great mind, rewriting shit. But at the time it was a deeply frightening thing to deal with, some bug-eyed politician saying the white citizenry were going to murder you in your bed. And you've got to remember he was *elected*, sugar. But time passed and it by and large didn't happen and the fear faded and he faded. Then there was the end of empire, the Commonwealth, Rhodesia becoming Zimbabwe. And you cheered and you started to feel proud to be the descendant of Africans and you pricked up your Afro, but you still had to go to school or do ballet practice or work at some shitty job to put food on the table. So you don't feel like you lived through it the way it was written up at the time. Only later on you think, Well, I was around for that.'

George reaches for his cigarettes, surprised to find himself talking this way. He never talks this way, except in the context of his choreography, where the grandly and the personally historic have to be stated and wound together to make sense of his intentions as an artist. But not to lovers, or even friends. Lovers are rarely interested in the deep past, and friends either already know your story all too well, or the parameters of the friendship preclude them from asking about it.

'Did all what happened ever make you - hate white people?'

'Oh, yeah, baby. Sure. Sometimes. Directly towards a few individuals who were explicitly racist towards me or my family. But mostly I hated white people as an abstract mass. They were 'the oppressor' - and that was even when I had white lovers.' He laughs softly. 'I was rather hard on them from time to time.'

Ah those times of anger, defiance and desire Hope heightened by the intensity of youth in those incandescent years when change seemed possible and even our black gay liberation seemed possible within the words of freedom spoken by others then in other frameworks. The revolution.

And yet George is not, will not let himself be, nostalgic about that time when the struggle was clear just because it was clear: so many things are better now, however much the old poison works its way outwards. 'I've made myself sound like the Grand Old Man of the Diaspora,' he grumbles.

'You're not old, man,' Luke says quickly. 'You've just - seen stuff.'

'And done stuff, my dear,' George says. 'But enough about me. For the moment, anyway. Tell me more about you.'

'Well, um, what d'you wanna know?' Luke asks. He feels his life lacks the epic sweep of George's.

'Everything, sweetness,' George says with a laugh. 'Why would I settle for less?'

'Where d'you want me to start? Everything's a tall order and I don't want to bore you right off.'

'Well, you mentioned you had a brother,' George suggests.

'Yeah,' Luke admits grudgingly.

'Is he older than you or younger?'

'Just a little bit older.'

'And are you close?'

'Close?'

'I mean are you out to him, or to the rest of your family? Is he - are they - in your life at the moment?'

Shame flushes through Luke. 'I don't see none of 'em, man. Not no more. Especially not my brother. I don't have no brother.' He is glowering now. 'Except Malcolm.'

'You don't have to talk about it, you know,' George says, shifting in his seat. His bare knee brushes Luke's. A thrill runs through Luke's loins at the contact. George extends his leg so the shaved skin of his shin slides across the soft fuzz on the side of Luke's. Luke's balls prickle. 'There's no obligation to disclose,' George says. 'This isn't Court TV or the confessional.'

'I know, man,' Luke says. 'It's just I - I just wanna - ' And he leans across the table and kisses George on the lips. 'I've been wanting to do that all evening.'

He sits back down breathlessly, glancing round to make sure nobody noticed. George does not look round and Luke wishes he was as brave as George, brave enough to really not care, to not fear the judgement of the mob.

George tilts his head to one side, hoping he looks cute and flirtatious, not old and ravaged and queeny. *If you can be 'cute' at fifty, that is.*

Luke smiles.

I guess you can.

They sit in silence for a while then, enjoying just being near to each other, minds idling in neutral. India Arie floats out over the speakers. *Brown skin, you know I love your brown skin...*

'I need to use the toilet,' Luke says eventually, obviously regretting having to break the mood. The outline of his semi-erection is eye-catchingly evident in his baggy shorts as he stands. George checks out his butt as he goes. It looks firm and muscular.

Love. When was the last time you were in love?

Four - no, five years ago.

With James.

Odd how he never thinks about James now: the most recent and yet somehow least present of the men he has been seriously involved with.

A fit, cultured, mixed-race businessman, he had struck up a cautiously flirtatious conversation with the obviously gay George on a red-eye flight from Berlin. George had just finished choreographing a pseudo-avant-garde fashion show and was returning to London exhausted, but with money in his pocket.

What was its name? He forgets.

It had been an artistically unchallenging but mostly enjoyable and certainly well-paid seven days, and he had been only half looking forward to getting home, as he had no other work lined up and no lover to get back to. He had insisted on being flown business-class as a condition for taking the job, and that was how he had found himself sitting next to the Armani-suited James, making small talk as the sun came up, its reflection flaring dazzlingly on the curve of the plane's wing.

James had been negotiating the rights to an internet portal into a substantial tranche of formerly-communist Eastern Europe. He was well-groomed, handsome, confident and charming. He'd been married twenty years ago for seven years, and had two grown-up children. He'd worked and lived in the Middle East, South America and East Africa. He was well-informed about the arts, and had a liking, if no deep feeling, for dance as an art-form.

Business cards exchanged as the plane touched down and a lingering handshake had led to them meeting for drinks a few days later, then dinner at the

Ivy, then, a few days after that, dinner again, at Nobu this time, and after *that* the first of many nights spent together at James' river-view warehouse loft conversion in Docklands.

Everything had been easy between them - talk, sex, the stretch of shared history - and after so many hard years that ease had felt like love to George. James having money and being free with it meant that the props of romance - fancy dinners, bouquets, glinting gifts given on glittering weekends in Paris, Rome and New York - had rolled on like stage-sets with painted backdrops.

It had been, at least for a while, indistinguishable from love, and even now George will admit that on some level he did genuinely love James. And yet behind that love there had been something fearful and clutching, a sense they had better make this performance real because it was their last chance for happiness.

Last chance.

One of the many lies of life, of gay life in particular, George thinks. Lies like if you're an older man then nobody wants to be with you sexually. Nobody wants to offer you love. You know it isn't true and yet you start to believe it in this culture where youth is all that is presented as desirable, where the old and even the not-so-old rip off their faces and yank them back on their skulls, slicing out lines, erasing the evidence of life lived, and cultivate youthful folly and excess. No wise elders in the gay village of the West, then; nothing passed down. In fact the reverse: the young now teach the old, who are assumed to have so lost touch with the energies of life, with the ecstatic, ephemeral, all-important ahistorical present that their views are without worth, ignorant as a child's but without the golden excuse of youth.

Lately George has come to believe it is the absence

of a desirable vision of themselves as old, as venerable and revered, that has made younger gay men so careless about fucking without rubbers, the risk of death of no consequence to them it seems, or even, from a distance, a desirable evasion of the banal.

Because they haven't yet seen the skeleton emerging from beneath the skin.

Screaming.

And too the early deaths of so many artists and visionaries - Rotimi, Essex, Marlon, Assotto – have robbed us of our tribal elders. Those who we would revere if they were still with us. But it's not just the queens: all of society is suffering from this dislocation, this fantasy that you can opt out of aging and death, though it is among gay men that the delusion is the most intense.

He had felt old with James, a last-chancer, impossible as that seems to him now, seven years later; and their relationship had seemed so credible in its externalities that he had felt he must hold onto it, however hollow it was.

What I hate most: the unfelt performance.

Once he had made the decision, leaving James had been easy, even nerveless; and in his quick, almost pre-emptive acceptance of George's decision George realised that James too had been battling a sense of defeat and compromise. Still, for a year after they broke up George had felt lost emotionally, the needle on his internal compass spinning. *Birds fly south for winter but where is my south?*

He had never really found out what James's dream partner would have been like, though small signals and chance remarks over the seven months they were together suggested it would have been someone considerably more straight-acting. And what had George wanted? *Wildness ecstasy the unexpected.* Yet hadn't he been a hypocrite? Hadn't he enjoyed being squired around town by a high-status, straight-acting, conventionally-handsome man? *Yes. Of course.* But that was only one form of masculinity among many for him, and any form could work, could turn him on, if it was inhabited with passion.

Luke returns to the table. 'Penny for 'em,' he says.

'Just thinking how long it's been since, well - since I met someone I really liked,' George says.

'Me too,' Luke says. 'It's hard,' he adds, then he cuts himself off, because he had been about to say, *It's hard to find someone who can compare with Malcolm*, and he doesn't want to put his closest friend between himself and George. 'It's hard just meeting people,' he says instead, and after all that's true too. 'I mean guys who are looking for more than just sex, you know?'

George nods. 'And trust me, it doesn't get any easier as you go along.'

'But you can't just sit at home and wait for the doorbell to ring, can you?' Luke says. 'I mean, you can't just expect your knight in shining armour to pitch up on the front step like you're entitled, like all them straight girls do. It's like they don't think they have to do one thing to deserve love, not even be nice, nothing. But you've got to earn love, man. Like you've got to earn luck. It's like my other best mate Ziggy says, 'The more you do, the more you're around, the luckier you get.' It's kind of obvious but it's a hard lesson to learn. I dunno why, but it is.'

'Most lessons in life are simple in principle and hard in practise,' George says. Luke watches as he tugs gently at the petals of the lone white chrysanthemum in the vase between them. Every time George lowers his eyes Luke is struck by the glittering blue coating their sculpted lids. He imagines gently pressing his lips to their cowry-shell curves, sensing the slight tremor below, and feels exhilarated. Yet shadows loom behind him. And inside him. The jade of his eyes darkens, striated by some other, indefinable, sea-stormy colour. 'What's wrong?' George asks.

'Sorry I was weird about my family when you asked before.'

'That's alright, sweetness.'

'It's just they're not nice people.'

'You don't have to tell me, you know.'

'I know,' Luke says. 'But I do want to.'

'Okay.'

'You can say any time if I'm boring you.'

'I will.'

'Promise?'

'Promise.'

Luke nods, takes a breath. 'We was always brassic,' he begins. It is like confessing, and not. And he is ashamed, and not. 'Growing up on a rough estate out East, Poplar way. Sounds like trees, don't it? But there weren't none. My old man was second-generation unemployed. He'd do odd jobs, legit and dodgy, but he was never off benefits. So never that legit, I suppose.' Luke smiles wryly. 'His life was shit, and he made our lives shit too. He used to get hammered whenever he had the dosh, and he'd lay into me and my brother just to let off steam. We were his punch-bags. I guess having us there made him feel even more trapped than what he did already. The trap was all inside his head, cos you don't need money to be someone or free, Ziggy and Malcolm showed me that, but - ' Luke shrugs. 'He'd batter my mum too. He'd black her eyes on the regular, he broke a couple of her ribs plenty of times, one of her arms one Christmas, and even her neck one time. Her fucking neck, man! It was a spiral fracture though, not the sort what paralyses you. She didn't even know till they x-rayed her in Casualty. She still sided with him afterwards though. Against us. Like she always did. We was always wanting her to kick him out, but she never did. Dads.'

Luke spits the word out. George thinks, *If I'd had a son he'd be your age now*, and wonders how he'd have done, what that son would have ended up thinking of him.

'Maybe she thought having the actual biological father of her kids stick around was a achievement compared with a lot of the other mums. Like sure, he was violent and a lousy provider, more like a leech actually, but hey, he was there. He was a drunk, a homophobe, obviously, and a hardcore racist. He'd get pissed out of his skull and go on and on and on about niggers and queers ' - Luke's voice falls on the n-word - 'and my world felt so tiny it was like being the wrong end of a telescope or dropped into a garbage compactor. I knew there was this whole other world out there, a world of colour. But it was like a dream, you know? Like a fantasy, like TV.'

George nods. Luke's eyes are glittering.

'It seems kind of mad now,' Luke says. 'Cos I could've just got on a bus or the Tube and come up the West End and mixed it up a little, but back then that all felt like it was as far away as the Moon.'

'It's hard to break out,' George says. 'Even if you get some education, or some aspiration to go somewhere beyond your home streets. You don't feel you have the right.'

'Did you go through that too?'

'Sure. Differently, because race was part of it, but yeah, I went through it,' George says. 'And you do go, eventually, and you look back and you see your friends who accepted the walls, who thought they needed them to hold the sky up, stay where they are, and that's painful because there's still a tie.'

'Stupid, ain't it, man?' Luke says. 'Back then it felt easier - or no, more realistic, that's the fucked-up thing - more *realistic* to kill yourself than to get on up and out of it, even just for the day. Like when I was fourteen I took a bunch of antidepressants my mum was on - figures, don't it? How could *I* get up and go when she never could? She'd rather take pills and sit there staring into space than sort her life out, and I was her son, half my genes were hers. And then there was my old man. What did he sort out? And half my genes were *his*. I needed gene therapy, man. Anyway, I blew it: took too many and chucked 'em up.'

'I'm glad,' George says, giving Luke's hand a gentle squeeze. Luke blushes.

'There's other shit operating too,' he says, returning to an earlier thought. 'Like you don't leave your area except to maybe go Ibiza or shit. That's your identity, and you think you'll like disintegrate if you read a book or have a point of view that ain't the usual. And on top of that you know, and it's true, ain't it, man, *they* don't want you out there, and you don't want that rejection, that pain, so you beat 'em to it and turn your back, make out like you despise all that. Culture, learning, looking outwards. You call it pride but really it's self-hatred. And if you're queer on top of that - ' He shrugs. 'It's a lot to drag on up and out from under, ain't it?'

George nods. 'I came from rough places too.'

'Was you always like you are now? I mean, uh, flamboyant?'

'Even before I knew I was gay other people knew I was going to be,' George says. 'My brother, who's six years older than me, half-protected me from it, and half-despised me for needing his protection from the white kids in our street. Now, *he* hated white people with a passion. There were lessons he learned that I never knew about, things he went through that I wasn't aware of because I was younger and we were on the cusp of changing times, you know? But I saw the damage done to his psyche. He blamed white people for every adversity, for all his inner torment. Sometimes, maybe even often, he was right, but partly he also needed to exonerate our father for his failings.'

'Are you close? You and your brother, I mean.'

'Not really,' George says. 'He moved to Canada twenty years ago, but we hadn't been close since he left home, and that would have been over thirty years ago now. He would have been seventeen, and he left angry, after a big fight with our father, I've no idea what about. I felt betrayed for years afterwards. Deserted, I suppose, because unlike my father he at least wanted to protect me, however shame-faced he was about it, and however angry he'd be with me after yanking me out of some scrape my manner had got me into. I would have been thirteen, fourteen when he went. I can't remember exactly because it took a while before it was evident that this time he really wasn't coming back. He'd blown up and bounced plenty of times before.'

'Wasn't Canada a weird choice though, if he hated white people?'

'He married a Canadian girl,' George says, 'a white girl, a student, Lorelei.' Luke looks puzzled. 'Really he only hated white *men*, like a lot of the young black men then. He was from that generation just a little ahead of mine who felt they were getting one over on The Man by conquering and possessing His Woman. This was only a little post interracial relations being actually illegal in the States, you know. But the heart can betray you in funny ways. I suppose he set out to use her, but he fell in love with Lorelei. If he hadn't I imagine he would have gone Afrocentric, changed his name and married a sister on point of principle. Maybe moved to Ghana. Anyway, they've got three children. All boys.'

George avoids stating the ages of his brother's sons, (thirty-three, thirty and twenty-nine), since none of them are younger than Luke.

'Do you ever feel like you've missed out?' Luke asks, meaning both generally on the joys of parenthood, and secretly on the joys of being an uncle to three growing nephews, three young black – biracial - men. And Luke does imagine them as young, as teenagers. A particular excitement is thrilling through him now, a heightened state that he always feels when any black person trusts him enough to talk about race and racism, about the hate, passion, fascination and ambivalence that trail in its wake.

'I've visited them quite a few times,' George says. 'So I haven't missed out entirely.'

'When was the last time you went?'

'Two years ago. The boys have turned out well. They're bright, good-hearted young men. They live in a basically all-white suburb outside Toronto. It's comfortable, well-ordered.'

'Do they have, like, white partners?'

'Two of them do. One's single. Was single, the last time I visited.'

'Are they all straight, d'you reckon?'

'As far as I know.'

'D'you think he's happy? Your brother, I mean. I mean not going back to, like – Jamaica, right?'

'Jamaica,' George nods.

'So being like among white people all the time?'

'I think he's as happy as he's going to be,' George says. 'He'd never admit it, but in the end I don't think he likes other black people much. He's happiest when he's the only one. He feels the most certain of himself then. We get on now, but seeing me always reminds him of what's toxic and unresolved in himself, I think.'

'What's his name?'

'Yohan.'

'And you've got a sister too, you mentioned?'

'Four years older than me. Her name's Eunice. She's – she *was* a nurse. She took early retirement last year. Our father kicked her out for getting pregnant. Our mother used to go behind his back and give her money. They made up later, but by then I'd left home, so I've never been that close to her either.'

'Where does she live?'

'Birmingham. She had the baby but he had bad health problems.'

"Had"?'

'He died – wow, fifteen years ago. She ended up having to put him in a home so she could work. His name was Peter.'

Luke nods. They sit quietly for a while. India Arie has given way to Lauryn Hill.

'But you were going to tell me about your brother,' George says. 'He's your only brother, right? No sisters, stepkids?'

'No. Just my brother and me,' Luke says. 'He's still back there, I guess, where we grew up. I've only seen him once since we was seventeen.' *Boot in my face That blood-dark moment of recognition.*

'You fell out?'

'I left.'

Luke can't talk about this, about Del, not yet.

'And does he prefer black partners too?' George asks, inadvertently giving him an in that he could take, but he doesn't. He can't bear to risk tainting his attraction to George with the revelation of his twin's revulsion at the notion of contact with brown skin. Still, he can't just sit there and say nothing.

'It's not like a family thing,' he says. 'I don't know where it came from. Like, how come I ended up finding these people who weren't even around me so beautiful and - and I know this is gonna sound stupid and lame but - kind of magical as well. Like, did you ever read *Lord of the Rings*? I mean, before they did the movies?'

'Oh, sure. We all did. Back in the Age of Aquarius when medieval cloaks were big for five seconds.'

'You liked it?'

'Yes. To my surprise. Not as much as the Brontes, say, but yes, that very English romance I liked very much. So - ?'

'I was like the way Sam saw the elves. Like they were above his likes and dislikes, and he knew he was dull and they were special, and he was ready to jump up and risk his life to go off with Frodo and see elves. Shit, man,' Luke blushes. 'I know that sounds so lame, but forgive my kid-heart, yeah.'

'I forgive you.'

'Don't get me wrong, man: even from when I was like ten I knew there was a reality chasm between them kind of feelings and like actual black people I'd see out on the streets.'

'And you never tried to - interact with them?'

'There was never a space,' Luke says. 'It really was Them and Us back there, you know? And there was a lot of things I was afraid of.'

'Like what?'

'Rejection. From both sides. And it *was* sides there, man, believe me. We was all in boxes. Or cells. My estate was a white estate. That controlled what you were allowed to do. What you were supposed to think. Who you was allowed to know. The streets controlled your brain. And white skin ended up meaning death and hate and closed minds and being trapped to me. Everything ugly, you know? And brown skin, black skin was life and sex and love and freedom. I know that sounds like hippy bullshit. But it's brought me a lot of friendship and a lot of love and beauty. So in a way I was right, weren't I? Even though I know life's a lot more complicated than that. Not so black and white.'

'Colour, in fact.'

'Exactly, man,' Luke says. 'Exactly.' His mind drifts back to his breaking out, his breaking *in* to something new and needed, beginning in bars up the West End, his seventeen-year-old self nerving himself up to be bold as anyone whose attractions are specific must be bold, knowing mere receptivity would not bring him one to whom he is attracted.

Sometimes he wonders what it would have been like to have been born in a country where the majority were in the category to which he is attracted: what difference that would have made to his psyche, to his identifications and alignments, to what he rarely calls, but nonetheless is, his politics - some fantasy homo-friendly Africa or Caribbean; what freedom that would have brought him. But he is no more sexually-frustrated than most, no more deprived of love or lovers than most, no less free.

He decided on Soho on the grounds that any black guy drinking there would be open in his attractions. Or perhaps more precisely: not separatist.

Luke has a heightened and paradoxical emotional response to black separatism. He himself, after all, is not sexually or romantically interested in white – or even Asian or Arab – men: why should a black man be? And why should a black man risk the heart- and headache of distorted perceptions that can be involved in having a white partner?

Later Ziggy would point out to him that of course it's not that simple or pure: that black people have race-distortions inside themselves. Malcolm would say so too, though he would inflect the point differently, removing it from being a confession of fucked-up soul-damage and telling it as another battle to be fought in the endless war against racial oppression.

Still, to Luke there was always this: why would a black man fail to notice that black men were the most beautiful of all? Why wouldn't he be won over from the uneasy and often-betrayed fraternity of interracial love to the embattled warrior politics of unity? He could feel the power in such unity even though he was simultaneously aware that, as a politics forged in reaction to white racism and colonialism, it was a construct as much as, if not more than, an essence: potentially no more than the obverse of what Fanon called 'the hyper-valorisation of the Negro.' That was a text Malcolm had hipped Luke to, about white people who were overly infatuated with black culture and black people, a romance to which separatism is a twin.

Still Luke is drawn to essentialism: how can he not be? He believes in it – or no, not *believes*: it is as foundational to his sexual nature as his homosexuality. However much Ziggy and Malcolm tease him for it in their different ways the two terms are, at bottom, the same to him: Black. Man.

And that romance he wouldn't discard even if he could, because he has learned this much: that behind our narratives of desire there is not some raw, clear reality but a Russian doll of competing romances and operations of power. And though sometimes, privately, in the best and worst of times, he does ask himself why, ultimately it doesn't matter to him. Because why does anyone love or desire this or that configuration of features, physical elements and personality traits, whether particular to the desired individual or symbolic and emblematic of some wider web of associations? The real question is how we love.

'I bet your young years must've been rougher than mine,' he says, coming back to the present. 'Racism being legal and being gay being illegal - '

'Stop before I feel a *hundred* and fifty years old!' George laughs. 'But yeah, it was hard then, sweetness. Materially hard. Shit people wouldn't put up with now, however poor they were, that would make them say their rights were being violated.'

'Like what, man?'

'Like the bath being in the kitchen under a big lid. Like having no fridge, no washing-machine, no central heating, and no TV. Feeling lucky to have an inside lavatory.'

'Jeez.'

'But we did have a Dancette though.'

"'Dancette'?'

'A record-player radiogram the size of a sideboard. And a pile of singles and albums to play on it. Music was the one thing we did have.'

George falls silent. In the café kitchen plates clink in the sink, water whooshes and something sizzles. In the sudden absence of words he and Luke are shy again, and both of them look down. When they look up and meet each other's eyes their pupils dilate receptively, as eager for the interpenetration of souls it seems as their bodies are for the interpenetration of bodies.

'You know what I'd like, man?' Luke says. 'What I'd really like?'

'What, sweetness?'

'To see you dance.'

George raises one artificially-extended eyebrow.

'No, really, man.' Luke reaches across the table and takes George's large, dark hand in his own square buttery-peach one. Blood pulses against blood.

'Well,' George says, looking down at their interlaced fingers. 'On one condition, sweetness.'

'Anything, man.'

'You have to dance with me.'

'Try and stop me, man!' Luke grins. 'I've been wanting to wind it up with you all evening. But I ain't no proper dancer or nothing, though,' he adds. 'Just a club kid who likes to shake it, you know?'

'And I can't wait to see you shake it, sweetness,' George replies.

They wave for the bill. George pays it over Luke's protests, and they head back down Coldharbour Lane to the high street, bumping shoulders as they go. Most of the hairdressers have closed by now, but some of the barbershops are still open and lively with customers, creating an atmosphere of saturated, if predominantly heterosexual, maleness. The dealers still loiter.

Brixton Road is thronging even though it's gone eleven, the racial and social demographic tipping there towards mostly white gay club kids, wine bar yuppies and white drunks and junkies. The club, Substation South, is off a side-street just across the way. Queer Nation is a long-running, predominantly black gay night that takes the venue over each Sunday.

The queue to get in isn't long at that hour, and Luke makes a point of paying for both their admissions before George can reach for his wallet. The night air smells of hair-gel, Emporio Armani and Ck1.

Inside there is little oxygen, and the smell is of cigarettes, spilt beer and dry ice.

The club is divided into three dance-floors on three different levels. The largest, playing all the obvious gay pop and club anthems, is the one to which most of the white clubbers flock, peeling off their tops as they go. Of the other two, one plays hip-hop while the other, the smallest of the three, plays ragga and reggae. The dancers in the latter are almost all black.

As they cross the first dance-floor, which is to neither of their tastes musically or aesthetically, Luke wonders if George will feel awkward being here with a white date, while George wonders to what extent Luke's eye will wander with so much black temptation on offer.

As far as Luke's worry goes, George has been through too much bullshit in his life to feel the slightest self-consciousness at being seen with a white partner, and he leads Luke straight onto the ragga dance-floor. *(This is my music, Jamaican music. I claim it and take what I need from it the meat and the marrow and spit out the bones without apology).* And as George leads him onto the dance-floor Luke's eye doesn't wander at all because he knows that no-one else in this place could possibly be as remarkable as the man he is with.

And they dance...

Hip to hip, crotch to crotch, bodies arching back at gravity-defying angles, fused at their aching groins, fingers interlocked, body-weight cantilevered, they wind it up and down, their movements synchronous, primal, muscular: both the pump and the piston-head. And for that brief time they are at the centre: for the length of a song the world outside is beyond irrelevant.

And after they have danced until their bodies ache and their clothes are sodden with sweat George gives Luke his solo, spinning in the centre of the dance-floor, his charisma in full effect, his face an impassive African mask, long arms, long legs flung out, sweat flying from him like diamonds, momentarily immortal, playing with the music, playing inside the music, and Luke is spellbound and watches with expanding sight until he is drawn into George's arms as surely as if he was falling from a high, high place.

He puts his hand on George's waist and feels it firm and trembling through the hot, damp, silky fabric of his basketball-vest and they dance together again. Time slides and elides in an oxygen-depleted blaze of body against body, in a tidal pull of beats and blood. Luke is so intoxicated that he is barely aware of being led out into the sudden, ear-popping chill of the early morning hours, days, years later; is hardly aware of George taking him by the hand to one of the minicab offices on Coldharbour Lane, or of his address being asked for and his lips giving it; or of being led to a waiting cab a few minutes later by a stocky, bored-looking West African man with melancholy eyes.

George opens the passenger door for Luke and Luke climbs in obediently. The smell of cold leather, faded pine air-freshener and stale cigarettes is strong and soberingly particular. Behind it is the tang of bleach-expunged vomit.

George pushes the door shut. Luke winds down the window to say goodnight but before he can speak George bends in and kisses him on the mouth. It is a kiss long and deep and drenched with the melancholy of parting, even though parting is a choice they've made – or George has made for them - tonight. The intensity of it makes Luke feel almost sick.

Then the contact is broken and the cab is pulling away and Luke is left looking through the rear window like Bogart or Bacall as George holds up a hand in a gesture of farewell. The cab turns a corner, George is gone, and Luke finds himself fighting back sudden, hot tears.

Malcolm is standing in front of Ziggy's front door, his hand hovering indecisively over the bell. He notices the *vévé* Ziggy scratched in the midnight-blue paint with his key on his return from the mental hospital. Malcolm doesn't know about the mental hospital yet, but the *vévé*, with its obscure symbolism, is a reminder there are many things about Ziggy that he doesn't know. That he wants to know.

Marks

In the dark/secret scars
    Braille tales
        Tender to the touch -
He glances at his watch: 2.25 a.m. Luke's cab is pulling away from Coldharbour Lane. It will take half an hour to cross town. Luke will find their flat empty, their bed cold. The air is close, and there is a prismatic haze around the streetlights. Malcolm presses the bell. It rings loudly on the other side of the door. The moment seems eternal. Will Ziggy answer? There is the feeling of no movement within.

Even though I'm expected/
    Erected
    (Cock head slid –
    ((Aint it always
        this -
The buzzer sounds noisily, making Malcolm start, and the door clunks open. He goes in. The hallway is dark and musty. Narrow stairs lead up into obscurity. He gropes for the pop-switch, finds it and presses it. Nothing happens. At the top of the stairs a slit of yellow light appears, broadening into a trapezoid then a rectangle as to one side a welcoming door is opened. Excitement rising in him, Malcolm climbs the stairs.

Because of the heat of the night he is wearing only low-cut black lycra trunks, hi-tech sandals and a white shirt he has left unbuttoned and open to show off his smooth chest and flat stomach. A sapphire glints in his navel, and he shields his large eyes from blades and hatred with night-shades.

Talisman/
    Talis-
        men
        see
The fuckable
Me

When he left the flat he was oblivious to how provocative this scanty ensemble was, how blatantly it
revealed his nature and desire, because after speaking
to Ziggy he felt he would be doing no more than crossing from one bedroom to another: he forgot the streets.
It was only as he walked slowly, almost dreamily, down
to Portobello Market that his self-awareness returned.
Yet he found himself feeling neither ashamed nor
afraid but bold and whorish.

In a good way, that was.

A whore for my man.
(What he has is
   the only payment
   /I will take/
              and I don't mean
   the cash -

Even at that hour there were people in the streets,
the restless ones, those unable to sleep in a humidity
that had perversely grown worse after the sun had gone
down and the baked aching buildings had with a sigh
released their store of heat. Some were drunk, some
high, some crazy, but no-one bothered him, no-one
taunted him, no-one tried to touch him. A girl in a
canary-yellow   bra-top   and   micro-miniskirt,   lace
leggings and spike heels waved to him from across the
street as if he was an old friend and he waved back. He
felt curiously invincible.

Trailing
   An inno-
       cent
       Scent – all the world
          Loves a lover tonight

And now he is here, climbing Ziggy's stairs. Cas-
cades of notes run through his head but they don't fill
his mind; they are just the soundtrack to his movie.
Ziggy fills his mind. His mind, his groin, his heart.

He reaches the landing. The door is half-open. He stifles an urge to knock - *I'm invited* - and pushes it open wider and goes in. It's almost hot inside, and there is a close, waxy smell that reminds Malcolm of birthday cake, childhood parties, and church. The room is lit by at least one hundred candles. They line every shelf and cover every surface. The effect is at once romantic, ritualistic and obsessive. Like everything Ziggy does it both charms and disturbs. As Ziggy does himself.

On the walls are hung African masks heavy with a symbolism that Malcolm cannot access. Potted palms and other houseplants with glossily-polished leaves rise up from corners casting shadows like spears and shields, and a large ceremonial drum stands by the black-iron fireplace. An over-stuffed zebra-print sofa sits on white-enamelled floorboards. In front of it is a faux-leopardskin rug. Several large canvasses are turned to face the wall. The room is, like Ziggy himself, somehow other, dislocated, latently magical.

And there in the doorway to the bedroom stands Ziggy, for a moment like some guardian of the threshold, or a witch-doctor servant of the *Orishas*, waiting to initiate Malcolm into the ways of the tribe. Malcolm sees an image of himself speeding across the ocean's black surface like some great bird, low and fast and always at night, being drawn backwards across the water by strange powers. But drawn back to where?

Africa?

Afri*k*a?

The heart of his own black queerness?

Notes swoop through him like swifts or bats.

But of course Ziggy isn't a spirit, he isn't a priest. He's just a man, a black gay man in the West in the new millennium. A black gay man who isn't afraid to tap into something others shy away from or cannot reach.

Something essential, Malcolm would say, and Ziggy would agree, but would deny him one half of his use of that word; would refuse Malcolm that implicate essence of Negritude he so longs for; would allow it to mean only 'that which is needful.' Something Malcolm has need of, then: at least that. And something, regardless of what Malcolm knows would be Ziggy's disavowal, that brings him home on a racially-felt as well as a personal level.

Home despite Ziggy's refusal to present himself as what Malcolm would consider a natural black-Afrikan man and thus a suitable partner for himself. Home despite Ziggy's determination to be a freak both sexually and racially. Because in his style of dress and self-presentation Ziggy rejects not only the general trammelling-in of peacock masculinity but also the particular policing of black male self-expression that is enforced in a world in which sweatshop-manufactured, white-designed sneakers are presented as manifestations of authentic blackness, and where he has been told his bike-boots cut him off from his roots and powers like Grendel.

Ziggy's need to freak is persistent, urgent, and never refused. Two days ago - the last time Malcolm saw him - his hair was blond. Since then, he has shaved it into a Mohican again and dyed it a vivid parakeet-green.

Malcolm's cock stirs in his trunks.

Because the freaky
  is a part of
(a fuck of
  a lot of)
The
  Turn-
    On
Here

If I'm being/ (Yeah &
I'm finally tryna be)/
   Honest.

'So you came,' Ziggy says with a smile.

Malcolm nods, feeling the increasing weight of his rapidly-stiffening dick as, constrained by his lycra trunks, it pushes its way across his hip. *He only has to smile and I'm hard.* Malcolm's asshole tingles. *That too.* His face goes hot.

'I was going to give you till the candles burnt down,' Ziggy says.

'Then what?'

'Then I was going to come and get you.'

'Yeah?'

'Yeah.'

Ziggy's smile broadens to reveal large teeth. He is wearing nothing but army-boots and a pair of camou-flage-pattern trunks that fit snugly but in no way contain his bulging physicality: *sex warrior.* The quivering candle-light casts a shadow under the thick line his own engorging erection is making as it forces its way along behind the tight green, cream and black nylon. On his right thumb he wears a steel ring. He lifts a joint to his lips and tokes deeply. Then he steps to Malcolm and, before exhaling, kisses him on the mouth, sharing the sweet smoke with him, doubly intoxicating him, the hot proximity of his body sending Malcolm's heart-rate soaring. They hold the kiss until shortage of oxygen forces them to break it, coughing and laughing, hearts hammering greedily.

'Sweet,' Malcolm says. 'You're sweet, man.' Sweet like dope he'd meant really, just a play on words, but Ziggy is sweet in another way too. Vulnerable behind the front: wanting to give something precious of himself to another man. To Malcolm. Frightened as perhaps we all are frightened but giving what he can nonetheless -

Like some star of the silver screen, Malcolm lets his unbuttoned shirt slip off his shoulders and fall to the floor, revealing his lean, smooth arms and torso. His nipples – shamefully long and bullet-like, he often feels – are now in their erectness a vanguard announcement of what is in his trunks. He is a wholly sexual being and proud of it.

He and Ziggy kiss again, tonguing deeply, and now they move into a full embrace, hands sliding tentatively then confidently over charged brown skin, lycra-slicked rigidity sliding electrically over nylon-slicked rigidity as they grind intently against each other. Nothing has ever felt this right to Malcolm. Piercing horn-notes fill his mind, and tears fill his tightly-shut eyes as he feels Ziggy's hand grip the back of his neck with an assurance that is both total and totally liberating.

Oh baby I am yours Pause there Don't pause Your ass is mine My ass is yours Till dawn and more My all is yours -

And as Malcolm's tongue pushes into his mouth and Malcolm's hands grip his butt and pull his buttocks apart inside their nylon sheath, making his freshly-shaved sphincter clench and unclench in tremulous anticipation, Ziggy feels both possessed by Malcolm and bound together more strongly within himself than he has for the longest time. The love and desire of this man, this unexpected black man, will never, he feels sure, make him fracture and fall apart. The possibility of healing, of wholeness, floods through him.

For tonight at least.

He slides a hand down the back of Malcolm's trunks and Malcolm moans into his mouth as Ziggy's index-finger finds his sphincter and pushes confidently into it.

'You like that?'

'Yes.'

A shudder runs up through Malcolm's body, and his voice is choked.

'You want more?'

'Yeah.'

'Yeah?'

'I want it all.'

'You sure?'

'I'm sure.'

Ziggy is in him to the knuckle.

Chapter Six

I t's so late, or so early, that Malcolm can hear the sounds of the market setting up as he drifts off to sleep in Ziggy's arms. The sky outside is already lightening, promising another bright, metallically-hot day, and the curtains glow soft yellow. The air in the bedroom is sour and sleepy and intimate. Malcolm's body is aching and bruised, but in a good way, an attended-to way. He floats in and out of consciousness, the calls of the stall-holders penetrating his dreams.

Soft rustles thumps of cardboard boxes, bananas from the Windward Isles, avocados from Israel, Spanish oranges English coxes empires, russets, the produce of the world slid from the backs of vans. Shivering clatter of wheeled metal trolleys on thread- bare streets, peekaboo cobbles Too early for the clothes-sellers' magpie stalls, designer handmade Oxfam-wear, the space below the canopy just up the road empty now, reverberant. Come Carnival bands play there sound systems I've only got a pair of trunks and a shirt to wear in the street when I go backyard but I don't care I want to be seen I want the outline of my cock and balls and arse to be seen -

Defiant/ly myself &
filled to overflowing
    (yeah, that too but also)
  with/ The wild free
        inverted-perverted
  Spirit
Of Carnival -

Malcolm and Ziggy sleep like spoons, Malcolm be- hind Ziggy, his crotch welded to Ziggy's butt. One of his arms is round Ziggy's waist and his fingers rest on Ziggy's warm, tremulous belly, the strange relief of knowing Ziggy isn't dead pulsing through his fingertips one heart-beat at a time.

Malcolm has always remembered being told how his grandmother, his mother's mother, woke up next to his grandfather one morning and found him dead. 'Forty years them did married and one happy marriage,' his aunt Grace said with a shake of her head. 'An still she end up pon shi own for di las fifteen year a shi life.' Aunt Grace's glasses-frames were white and flyaway, Fifties in the late Eighties. Malcolm was eleven years old. 'And she say notin save you from loneliness in di end except Jesus, except di Lord. Him is the only comfort.'

Does Malcolm believe in Jesus? No. As a child he did, or at least he believed in a force vague and mysterious, half-reassuring, half-frightening, that was present where the sunlight slanted through stained glass on women who had on their heads hats of an inexplicable size that they never wore on any other occasion except weddings and funerals. Malcolm never questioned then, he played the part of a good boy, but he never understood either. Never experienced the leap of faith. And his grandmother said, 'For four years or more his dead face it haunted me, his last face erasing the rest of him. But slowly, through memory and photographs, the living face return, like bread rising in the pan. But I knew for sure when I realise him dead that there is a soul. Because it had clearly left him, you know? Left the house and moved on.'

To where, though? Malcolm finds it easier to imagine dancing with the ancestors than taking the chariot to Heaven.

Swing down sweet chariot-star, let me ride...

His other arm frames Ziggy's head on the pillow.

His shoulder-socket and bicep ache, but he doesn't want to disturb his lover. As he lies there he feels the particular freedom of the night-worker liberated from convention, from the banality of daytime routines. He has always loved this. The street-traders are already hawking their wares to the earliest shoppers. Shift-workers are going on and off shift, and all across suburbia alarm-clocks are shrilling, radio-alarms are babbling, and commuters are levering themselves out of bed and into the gridlock crawl, bracing up for the next eighteen-hour block of consciousness between themselves and the next vacation, a pension if they're lucky, and the grave. He almost loves them.

I'm free.

He feels it with an absoluteness that boosts his spirit and his sense of himself as beautiful, desirable and talented, things he rarely feels about himself and almost never all at once. Ziggy has given him this, for however long or short a time it lasts. He gazes at the back of Ziggy's head, and wonders what it is that makes one human being become suddenly so special to another; what subtle alchemy of pheromones and energies it takes to make the transformation happen, when after all we are all so very much the same.

He leans in so the tip of his nose is touching Ziggy's scalp, then rubs it gently up and down against Ziggy's glossy, freshly-razored skin, the movement slick one way, rough the other. The sweetness of cocoa-butter fills his nostrils, mixed in with the clean smell of the salon hair-nourisher on Ziggy's Mohawk. Malcolm realises he now sees its jungle-bright, graffiti-art artificiality as Ziggy's true hair-colour, the colour that Ziggy's vivid inner nature reveals.

Malcolm inhales deeply and the music starts to flow, keying synaesthesically to his senses of smell and touch, and picking up on and echoing the street-noises rising from the market. A title emerges for the forming piece: *Urban Hymn/Urban Him.*

Art, love and sex all energise and magnify each other. The lips that play the horn so supplely, the circular breathing that enables endless sustaining notes and fluidly cascading scales, last night gave Ziggy pleasure as Malcolm pumped his mouth on him without pause for breath and with sublime assurance, swallowing Ziggy repeatedly and holding him there at the back of his throat, like ganja smoke transubstantiated into throbbing, nourishing, rigid muscle, making Ziggy gasp sharp and loud with each swallow -
An mek him feed me
An mek me feed him
  Maasai-stylee
Milk and
  blood
Down mi troat
Down him troat
Di blood in we
  Bobandeh
Di milk in we
  balls-dem
    floodin -
  Seen!
Malcolm thinks of Marvin and how he never had with him what he already has with Ziggy. He feels a small ache for what, despite all their sharing of roots and desire, he was robbed of by Marvin's hung-up backyard masculinity. And for the first time he thinks that perhaps there is such a thing as a homosexual masculinity that is truly male and that stands apart from aping straightness. A masculinity that is something to be proud of. Ziggy is unreservedly and unapologetically a homosexual man, resisting and denying nothing about himself: kissing or touching

another man, sucking or being sucked by another man, fucking or being fucked, Ziggy sees no relevance in straight men's manliness, feels no need for their approval. Reflected in Ziggy's eyes Malcolm sees as never before how many shackles he has been dragging around with him.

Thoughts and memories flash through his mind like lightning strikes: TOK's anti-chichi-man anthem, *Bun Dem*, Buju Banton's *Boom-Bye-Bye*, the pronouncements of Louis Farrakhan, Frances Cress Welsing, Eldridge Cleaver, the rasping hellfire declamations and defamations of the preachers from his childhood church. And most vivid of all his father's voice tight with compressed loathing as he spat at his brother, Malcolm's uncle Milton, 'Man, I'm telling you, if any son of mine was - *that way*, I'd cut his throat.'

(*No comfort then for sons who love sons*, as Essex Hemphill wrote, and Malcolm was to read ten years later, and find the comfort of recognition in the poet's words).

He had been fourteen when his father had said that, standing at the open door of the fridge, skinny and shy and holding a bottle of sorrel pop perhaps a little too limply in one hand, with no clue as to what the run-up to that particular statement might have been. His father and his uncle were playing dominoes at the kitchen table as they did most Sunday afternoons, drinking beer and holding forth loudly over the clatter of the tiles. His entire body had gone instantly damp with sweat as he stood there, and his hands had turned icy and started to prickle with pins and needles.

Does he think Does he guess Oh Jesus Oh Christ help me I play with myself at night thinking thoughts I don't tell no-one. I pray every night too But it's You his anger comes from Jesus his hate his rage so why would You help me?

He had stood there not daring to turn around, not even daring to move, nausea at the thought of finding his father's eyes on him pulsing through his gut. And then his uncle had laughed in the face of his father's fury, a boisterous laugh that dispelled the tension in the room and made Malcolm feel a little less afraid.

The first piece of music he ever properly composed - worked out, resolved harmonically, melodically and thematically - he played in front of his father and his uncle before anyone else, wanting approval from them both, if for very different reasons.

'It's called *This Way, That Way*,' he had announced, his large eyes flicking between them as he put the trumpet to his lips, his chest shot through with fear and pride and defiance. He was seventeen then, and challenging his father on many levels. Not only by staying out late and drinking, going to blues, smoking and smoking weed, but also by studying music instead of the mathematics he also had a talent for, and jazz at that; and moreover daring to write it, to create his own music and not just interpret the acknowledged-as-worthwhile work of others. He had been going to gay bars too, but that happened in some other place within him that was nothing to do with his father, and in any case his sexuality was a fact, not an act of rebellion.

Sun had been streaming in through the plate glass of his uncle's barbershop as he played. His uncle was cutting his father's hair, moving over its soft waviness with flashing scissors. There were other men there, old and young, and they seemed pleased by Malcolm's blowing, the piece a light, summery melody with a tint of melancholy, and when he finished they didn't applaud, but nodded by way of appreciation. He felt a rare moment of belonging then, a moment he has sought to return to many times in the years that have followed, but has rarely succeeded.

Looking shyly round the barbershop after he finished playing he avoided his father's face, both out of
fear and habit, and so never saw his reaction to what
Malcolm, his son, had created. He regrets that now: his
squeamishness.

He only sees his father rarely these days, once or
twice a year. It seems to suit them both.

Uncle Milton died three years after that, of stomach
cancer. He liked his food, and his belly was as big and
taut as a kettledrum under a pinstriped shirt that was
pushed out not only by well-nourished intestines but
also, as it turned out, by a tumour the size of a grapefruit. Malcolm played at his funeral. *This Way, That
Way*. Milton had remembered his nephew's very first
work, and had requested it in his will.

Malcolm hasn't played the piece since. It became a
votive offering for the dead that day, and was sent out
across the water, and cannot be recalled. Not not
recalled in memory: he can remember every note of it.
Just sent and gone.

Uncle Milton always told Malcolm to be himself: to
refuse to be dominated by his father's vision of what his
life was for.

My father. Tyrone Alfonse Jones. Milton was five
years older than Tyrone, and could give Malcolm a
perspective on his father as a boy, a youth, a brother
that Malcolm would never otherwise have had, unless
perhaps he had met and got to know his paternal
grandparents. But they lived back in Jamaica and had
no intention of travelling to England, and Malcolm,
though full of ambivalent longing, born here has never
been there. *Bun dem*.

Too, there were allusions to some family disagree-
ment that had cut the generations off from each other,
over money, an inheritance, Malcolm had come to
believe, but neither Milton nor his father had ever told

him whether that was true. And now Milton was dead, and Malcolm couldn't imagine asking his father about anything that personal. Or his birth-mother, his father's ex-wife, who had shutters behind her eyes, and something in her soul that, like an optical illusion, seemed to retreat if you drew too near.

She left them when he was sixteen. 'Your father's been seeing another woman,' she said. 'I won't stay under this roof.' And because he had his father's eyes, in her fury she offered him no consolation, just left him standing in the narrow hall, hating her, and hating his father too.

Cold people.

Not like Uncle Milton, who believed among other things that all prejudice was absurd. Malcolm remembers a particular night when he went to see Milton late-late, needing to trust someone who was kin, needing to believe that he had an open mind and heart, and finding it was so. It had been August, and hot, and there in the windowless backroom of his barbershop Milton had held Malcolm as his skinny seventeen-year-old frame was racked with sobs. Malcolm had been distraught, drunk and bruise-eyed over a fight with his first lover. Not that he had told his uncle that; not that he *had* to tell it. His father's brother was no fool: Uncle Milton could read his nephew's sexual nonconformity in every gasping breath he took.

Different, it would have been different if I'd been straight. There would have been no fear no shame nothing to hide. Cocksman not Battyman, Punani Don not battyhole bitch. How much does that disfigure us, that constant knowledge we will receive no validation?

Milton, another time, holding forth in his barbershop to some autodidact bigmouth youth schooled on rap and ragga and a certain strand of Afrocentric chat, kicking at the tight coil of his certainty.

'Don't sit there an try tell me AIDS is God's pun-ishment for a homosexual guy being the way he is,' Milton challenged the youth with a wave of his comb. 'Or doing what he does. No tell me dat. Cah you know that in the USA is black women, straight black women, who is becoming infected at the mos rapid rate. An lesbian di least. And in Africa HIV no a gay ting, or is you saying that in Africa half the men that way?'

'Fuck that, no, man - '

One of the old men kisses his teeth at the disrespect and the boy flushes.

'So - Or disya 'homosexuality is a white ting'. I knew fellows backayard who were that way and they didn't have nuttin to do with white people. Less than you, I daresay,' he adds, jabbing the comb in the direction of the young man.

The barbershop is called Milton's. His uncle opened it twenty-seven years ago, and has run it ever since. Back then it was called Milton's 'Fros, the name staying on well into the Jheri-curled Eighties, before he even-tually painted out the second part and left it just plain Milton's. He was married once, for a short time, but Malcolm was too young to remember his wife, and she is long gone and little spoken of.

Malcolm watches as his uncle moves his clippers over the inclined head in front of him with the economy of long practise. His movements are almost fastidious, but Milton remains somehow altogether a man's man, whatever that means exactly; a man you would not take for gay, anyway. And Malcolm listens as his uncle speaks, declaims almost, motivated by some inner anger or drive for truthfulness that Malcolm will never understand:

'So don't go tellin me they deserve to be beaten or killed or disrespected by ignorant fools who half the time hate *themselves* and that is what motivate their rage. That is not morality. And don't give me none a that *Isis Papers* line about a homosexual not being man enough to reproduce cah tell me, what the hell is manly about getting a girl pregnant? Not taking precautions? That is not manly. It is all the rest that proves you're a man, if that's the path you're taking. Looking after your children and your woman. Taking responsibility.'

The older men nod in agreement with his castigation of the feckless young whatever they think of battymen, which is not much, maybe, but isn't necessarily obvious either, because not all of them would disagree with what Milton goes on to say:

'More people than you might think have a aunt or a uncle who don't have no pickney themself but help raise dem nephew or niece, an some a dem aunt and uncle-dem there is gay or lesbian. But them fulfilling that responsibility, which is a responsibility di birth-parents sometimes failing pon.'

'It ain't natural though, man,' the youth says, taking the usual fall-back position in the face of Milton's scattershot attack.

'So what it ain't natural? You use a condom when you make love if you're smart. Is that natural? Syphilis an gonorrhea soaring amongst our young people. Is that natural? If she on the pill, is *that* natural? And I know you're not going to tell me when you go a dentist you don't let him inject you with anaesthetic cah it natural to feel pain. In my chest, in my heart is a plastic valve from when I have a heart attack six years ago. The plastic it mek outta was part a di research for di space shuttle. Without it I would be dead. Should I be dead?'

'But the Bible says - '

'You ever read the Bible in Hebrew? Or the Koran in Arabic? Even if you read them sacred texts there, an in di original language dem written in, they are only words written by men for their own reasons whatever, two thousand years ago.'

'So you don't believe in nothing, then,' the youth says sulkily, glowering under the torrent of Milton's words. Dust floats and sparkles in the rays of sun that cut slantwise through the window behind him, making the back of his smooth neck sweat.

Sat out of the direct sunlight next to the shop's wedged-open door Malcolm leans back and watches the sullen young man watch his uncle. A purple shadow like an eye-mask is cast across his face by the peak of his baseball cap. Malcolm is cramped with tension, and only his shoulder-blades make contact with the chipped, clammy, mint-green gloss paintwork behind him, jutting backwards through the fabric of his damp tee-shirt like a bird's pinions.

'I believe in the human spirit,' Milton said, and Malcolm knew that his uncle was speaking to him too that afternoon. 'I believe that in di end humanity is all there is for certain. I believe we have to work out our own salvation right here on Earth. There are no rules, only guides and fellow-travellers. You look at this, you look at that, you take what you can use an you go on. You take. And you give back. That is all.'

Malcolm wonders what collision of experiences brought his uncle to the place he reached philosophically that afternoon, this very Jamaican man who only came to England when he was twenty-eight; who spent the formative years of his life in a country with the highest percentage of churches per head of population in the world. He wonders too what made both Milton and his father fall out with and split off from their parents, his paternal grandparents, the grandparents he has seen in old, hand-coloured photographs but has never even spoken to. His ancestors, from whom he is sundered, who perhaps even now do not know that he exists.

Who certainly do not know that he is gay.

So much is irreconcilable. So many fantasies of completion to resist because they will get you nowhere but side-tracked down some blind alley of sentiment.

They would never accept me.

What were they escaping from, his father and his uncle? What violence of the body or soul or mind were they both suffering under to fill them with such different forms of the same anger? Later that day, and unnoticed, Malcolm will spill a little wine for Milton – a libation for an ancestor, inspired by Ziggy. And perhaps the spilling of seed the night before was also a libation, an assertion of connection between the generations without reference to reproduction.

Malcolm stares at the back of Ziggy's head, at the fluorescent-green strip arching over his shaved mocha scalp. *Is this the answer,* Malcolm wonders. *Is this what I've been looking for?*

Someone who can build bridges in me

Someone who is never ashamed?

Before he knew Ziggy, if he had seen him on the street Malcolm would have been judgemental of that lack of shame; would have considered Ziggy's brazen self-exoticisation sad evidence of a colonised mind-set. He would have silently condemned Ziggy for dragging down the race. The race, and implicitly and subordinately, the sexuality.

Subordinately. Yeah, I'll own that. I called it political prioritising.

Now Malcolm can see the danger to himself in placing of one part of his soul below the other: *submissive, self-loathing sissy. Subordinate. Fucked*

Up.

His response to Ziggy on the street, he sees now, wouldn't have been a liberated Afrocentric challenge to a mentally-colonised brother. It wouldn't have been revolutionary. It would have been imprisoning. The mindset he thought so radical stands revealed to him now as little more than a claustrophobic continuation of the lower-middle-class, Church-and-Empire-influenced, fundamentally conservative West Indian upbringing he received.

West Indian.

And Ziggy is African. Malcolm feels Ziggy's Afri-canness powerfully, and feels not only his own Black Britishness in contrast to it, but even more strongly his West Indian-ness, his Jamaicaness.

Stolen, we became something else.

Ziggy stirs. Without seeming to wake he takes Malcolm's hand in his and clasps it to his chest. The freshly-shaved skin there is oily-smooth and hot, and Malcolm can feel Ziggy's heart beating through his fingertips as he drifts back off to sleep.

When Malcolm wakes up again he finds Ziggy sitting on the edge of the bed, holding out a mug of steaming green tea and smiling. He is wearing silver and black rubber bangles on his wrists, and has pulled on a pair of leather briefs that hug his bulging crotch and are cut so low on his large, muscular arse that his buttocks sit like brown peaches in a shallow black dish. Malcolm feels the power of fetish rise up in him - psychoanalytical fetish, that is, not African-spiritual, though there is a reverence there too: the way the moulded leather stylises and magnifies the bulk and mystery of Ziggy's manhood, the mystery of his cock and balls and even his arse and arsehole, which is part of his manhood also. Under the duvet Malcolm's dick stirs, starts to lengthen.

'Aren't you ever off-duty, man?' he asks, returning Ziggy's smile, his voice sandpapered by sleep.

"Off-duty'?'

'As in dress-down day.' Malcolm gestures at the provocatively-styled briefs with their vulcanised rubber detailing, half-accidentally brushing the leather with his fingertips. It is soft and warm, like skin. 'As in sweats or raggy old jeans.'

'Never. You like?'

Malcolm is surprised to be asked: he is sure Ziggy rarely asks for approval. He feels the thrill of being offered something both precious and slightly danger-ous. 'I like,' he says.

'Good.' Ziggy bends over Malcolm and kisses him on the mouth. He tastes of Freshmint. Malcolm worries that his own breath will be sour but Ziggy doesn't care, tonguing him deeply until Malcolm is fully erect and gasping for air, writhing with rekindled excitement and electrified anticipation.

We didn't do so much last night, good as it was, he thinks. *There's a lot more in Ziggy's freak-box.*

And in mine.

Ziggy makes him feel unashamed of his kinks and quirks and fantasies, and he knows he can ask things of Ziggy sexually that he would rather have died than ask of Marvin.

Rather have died. Yes, the repression had been that intense, that painful, that ultimately ludicrous. Yet at the time somehow it had felt like liberation, because isn't liberation always painful? The pain was what made it convincing - a passing through fire into a zone of genuine, non-faggot same-gender-loving maleness.

How could he have been so utterly mistaken? So easily suckered, like so many men who desire men have been, by an ideal of masculinity that is in all its trap-pings heterosexual? That led him, as it had to, to the self-defeating pursuit of the supposedly authentic - that is, straight - male, and its corollary: condemning himself to the role of the faggot. Either that or, at best, and as had happened when he was involved with Marvin, condemning himself to having no identity as a gay man at all.

The low-down
            On the
Down-low/ So hot
  Doin it
  wit a bro
Claiming no
      lying or
  denial
while
    posing as/
              passing as /(Self-hating/ab-
              negating)
  Strictly
  Hetero -

'You're beautiful,' Ziggy says.

'No, I'm not,' Malcolm blurts, then instantly hates himself for being unable to simply accept the compliment. He flashes back to being fourteen, skinny with an overbite and big-eyed ugly, forever on the outside looking in.

Ziggy shakes his head. '*Iwa l'ewa*,' he says.

'What did you say, man?' Malcolm asks.

'It's Yoruba,' Ziggy says. 'It means 'character is beauty.' It's a Yoruba saying. To the Yoruba beauty comes out of two things, being and character.'

'Oh, right, okay,' Malcolm says, managing half a smile. 'So I'm, um, *characterful*, then?'

'Why disbelieve me when I say what I'm saying?' Ziggy asks. There is a long, awkward moment, a sense of wobbling on the high wire.

I must not resist this man, Malcolm thinks. *I must resist what remains in me of self-loathing, the bullshit serpent of internalised homophobia, and whatever it is in a man that tells him he can't be beautiful, he can't be deserving of -*

(Say it)

- Love.

'I believe you,' he says.

Ziggy searches his eyes for evidence, then nods slightly.

'So teach me some Yoruba, man. Take me back to my roots.'

'Your roots?'

'My spiritual-rhythmical-linguistic roots.'

'Ah, yes,' Ziggy says. 'Those.'

'My legendary roots,' Malcolm goes on. 'The essence of African - '

'Do you believe there's an essence of European-ness?' Ziggy interrupts him.

'No,' Malcolm says, slightly irritated by the question. 'Well, yeah. Yeah, of course. Everywhere's got an essence, hasn't it? So?'

'Isn't that European essence part of your essence?' Ziggy says. 'Aren't you part of its essence? You were born here and you've lived your whole life here. Isn't there more of your true essence here than in this overall African thing you think is so romantic because it's vague and far away?'

'I thought you didn't believe in essence,' Malcolm says.

'I don't,' Ziggy replies. 'Or in Afrocentrism. That is a dream of African-Americans, not Africans. But I do believe in legends.'

'So humour me, man,' Malcolm says. 'I was good at French at school. I even did some German. Teach me something. Like what's Yoruba for - '

'Ah, I can't really speak it, you know,' Ziggy says. 'I can understand it when someone speaks to me but it's not my language. I just know some sayings, things I picked up from my grandmother when I was young.'

'Doesn't it feel weird to be - divided from yourself like that? I mean, they say language physically structures the brain and that's got to - '

'It's not a loss,' Ziggy says. 'Not in the way you mean. You don't start from some point of magical African purity and then grind downhill to this, to me, the dirty hybrid.'

'I didn't mean that,' Malcolm says quickly.

'No?'

'I was just trying out a thought that's to do with what I feel about - connections. You know?'

'Yes,' Ziggy says, but he is looking away now.

'Don't bring down the shutters on me, man,' Malcolm says. 'Don't shut me out.'

There is a long silence. Then Ziggy says, 'I won't if I can help it.'

If I can help it. There is a threat in that, intentional or not, and Malcolm wonders what he's getting himself into. 'I can go if you want me to,' he says quietly.

'I don't want you to go,' Ziggy replies, and without hesitation he pulls the duvet aside and slides on top of Malcolm, and Malcolm opens his thighs and offers his crotch, pushing down Ziggy's briefs as Ziggy kisses him on the mouth. They are naked against each other now, erections jousting, sex-energies charging, discharging, recharging in shortening loops as they move and flex, muscles tautening, skin fusing to skin -

I remember William, my first lover, who sent me shaking to my Uncle Milton's door after opening me up in ways I wasn't ready to be opened up back then. Use, I know use is a subjective thing, and to be used as the site of pleasure by your man can be a joyous thing, but it wasn't for me then. Not when he pushed his way into the virgin depth of me for his own satisfaction, and if not exactly without my permission then certainly without my understanding of what it meant, if in any case you can ever understand what a thing means without doing it. And he didn't, wouldn't, he would claim couldn't stop till he was done, but he would reach round and feel my dick and it stayed hard whatever he did to me and so my protestations of pain could be discounted as maidenly pretence. And it is in this that the use ultimately consists, when you're a young man at least, and think it must mean love to share this secret act with another boy: how the other changes towards you once he's come. Does he melt into you, or does every aspect of him but his dick harden against you and resist that warm, quiet fusion? How I realised I meant nothing to William, though he wanted us to do it again soon enough. I cried from the pain. I cried for reasons I couldn't explain. And I ran to Milton.

Marvin was a retread of that primal scenario, a scratched vinyl skip-repeat a sapphire-tipped bastard.

Ziggy is something else.

We go deeply into each other. There is no denial. No evasion. No shame. Everything opens.

Afterwards, glazed and glued with sweat and come, they doze in each other's arms, Malcolm's face buried in Ziggy's chest, Ziggy's nose buried in Malcolm's soft, clean-smelling box-cut fade. *When I first saw him,* Ziggy thinks, *when I first spoke to him I resisted him, his skin, his hair, the texture of his spirit, I resisted the symbol in him, the danger of the mirror. But he called to me electrically across that resistance and I crossed the water to him I waded in not knowing how deep it was how deep I would have to go to reach the other side.*

To reach him.

I remember when
When they said I was
When I was sectioned and they said I was -
Don't name it don't give it power over you. That European power that classifies, defines, places within systems of control and subjugation What's the word

Taxonomy.

I've studied it. The Age of Empire. Victoria on the throne, queen and empress. Some fool went up the Zambezi in search of its source hoping to curry her favour, a white Englishman. He passed through the realms of many tribes and sometimes he would have to account for himself to their chiefs, to their priests and wise men. And he would say he was on a mission to find the source of the river. A taxonomical mission. Eventually one of the chiefs has the Englishman killed because he thinks he is lying, he's some spy with a particularly lame alibi. Because why would anyone imagine finding the source of a river, the random point it first begins to bubble up out of the ground, would mean anything, never mind mean enough to be worth risking your life over?

His bones bleached in the sun but the chiefs failed even as the scavenger birds picked at them: their world was swept away on every level.

Classification, medicalisation, reduction: taxonomy. Control the definitions and you control the mind. The priests and witchdoctors who channelled the ancestors and the Orishas became just schizophrenics. The radiant was reduced to a thing of cogs and mechanisms.

This I resist.

Being with Malcolm makes me kiss the mirror. I once made Luke kiss the mirror kiss his own lips while I fucked him from behind. That was careless of me: to kiss your reflection risks an interpenetration of self and inversion that can start an ink-print spirit folding over. I run that risk with any black man: to become a Jew doll with swastika eyes A mammy doll with a fixed split watermelon axe-grin One of a pair Eyes thrust into eyes A cancellation. But now I am here I am glad, even though there is none of the reassurance Malcolm believes there should be between us because we are two black men.

It is past noon. Sunlight refracting through a geometric glass vase on the windowsill casts a soft spectrum on the ceiling. Ziggy wriggles round and kisses the broad tip of Malcolm's nose, waking him and making him smile. Malcolm has a large overbite that verges on the goofy when he lets himself be innocent. 'I'll run us a bath,' Ziggy says.

'That'd be nice, man,' Malcolm says, sniffing an armpit. 'I'm kinda funky.'

Ziggy rolls out of bed and pads off to the bathroom. As he goes Malcolm notices, tattooed at the base of his spine, a rose. A moment later he hears the squawk of taps and water gushing. Shortly afterwards the scent of some aromatic oil Ziggy must have added to the water reaches his nostrils, carried on drifting steam. Lemon and coconut mingle with linseed-oil and oil-paint, the latter smells that have dropped below the level of Malcolm's conscious notice. He can hear Ziggy pottering about in the front room, then Howlin' Wolf's voice comes rasping from the speakers:

'I'm built for comfort, honey, I ain't built for speed.'

The music sinks into Malcolm, and he wonders as if it is a new thought why it is he responds most deeply to African-American music when he is not, as Ziggy would be quick to point out, American; why it conveys to him some quintessence of blackness that no other music does. What trick of the light has been pulled that makes him feel that African-Americans are somehow more

African than people of Caribbean descent? Or even, and more perversely, through embodying the grief of the defining modern African trauma, slavery, more African than Africans themselves? For Malcolm Nina Simone, say, taps into something fundamental that Manu Dibango does not. It is a strange and paradoxical monopolisation of essence.

Just occasionally Malcolm is afraid that he is as much of a tourist as all those bearded, broad-brim-hatted white jazz afficianados for whom he has so little time. But no: the music that is his very own, and that they cannot claim, is first and always a response to a slave's holler. *Mine and not Ziggy's.*

Feeling lazy but wakeful he sits up and looks around the room. By daylight it is messy, even a little dirty. Malcolm likes it anyway. He likes the way that Ziggy's art intrudes on every part of his life: there are even paint-marks on one corner of the duvet-cover, turquoise and viridian. Canvases face the walls in here as they do in the living-room. Clothes are strewn about, as are art books and art and fashion magazines.

One of the magazines, a smallish, square one called *ArtIn/Sight*, catches Malcolm's eye because Ziggy is on its cover with his hair dyed blond. He wears blue contact lenses, which dehumanise him with their fixed, non-light-responsive dilation. The contrast with the darkness of his skin is brazenly unnatural. He is billed as just 'Ziggy'. The strapline is, *'Ziggy Speaks Out.'* It makes Malcolm realise he doesn't know Ziggy's sur-name, although Luke must have told him it at one time or another.

The magazine is two years old. Malcolm picks it up and flicks through it. From the glossiness and weight of the paper and the amount of colour inside he guesses it's quite prestigious although he's never heard of it. Luke will have done. He'll probably have browsed through it in some bookshop where you can sit and read without having to pay. Luke rarely has the money to shell out for pricey magazines; he can barely run to paint and canvasses, brushes and simple frames.

This is probably the longest time Malcolm hasn't thought about Luke in more than two years. The realisation is poignant. He hopes Luke is happy wherever he is right now. The gods feel kind today.

He finds the interview opposite another photograph of Ziggy, black and white and dramatically side-lit this time. The columns of text are bordered by reproductions of silk-screened multiples that at first glance look like brightly coloured flowers, but Malcolm realises after a moment are in fact close-up images of anal openings. One series is printed in candy colours over progressions of concentric circles. Malcolm reads:

ZIGGY: Anally Fixated Avant-Garde African Artist?

Q: What makes you want to deal with the anus as a motif - I'm thinking of the two shows you did -

A: 'Pleasure Zone' [1998] and 'Targets' [1999], yeah.

Q: What does that subject-matter mean to you?

A: Well, it means don't believe all that Freudian crap about anal sex equals death or a death-wish and is the opposite of vaginal sex, AIDS notwithstanding, because that's to do with blood contact, not with anal sex per se.

Q: Whose asshole is it?

A: Mine. And the photograph was taken by me. And then for both series I used pleasant colours because to take that kind of material and make it look aesthetically appealing seemed like it was working against the obvious associations for most viewers.

Q: The images are quite abstract. Apparently quite

a lot of people went round the exhibition [Pleasure Zone] without knowing what they were looking at.

A (laughs): Did they? Shit. Well, I wanted the images to be attractive, to operate aesthetically. I shaved my asshole for the original photos so they're very clean. Very close-up, so no context. What did they think they were looking at?

Q: Some people said maybe flowers. Poppies were the most popular.

A: I suppose the wrinkles must have made some people think of petals. (Laughs again).

Q: There are people have seen your work as pornographic.

A: People who haven't actually seen it, usually. But is it bad, to deal in that area?

Q: I thought it was the reverse of pornography, where everything's made explicit. In these shows you don't immediately know what the subject is, and when you realise you go 'oh,' and respond on a conceptual level, considering the titles and ideas. But you're not shocked or turned on: that isn't the response -

A: Yeah, but even if it was totally pornographic, I mean graphic like my 'Mammy' series, that doesn't make it not art or not meaningful. And it might turn you on or it might not, but to me that's irrelevant. I mean irrelevant as to whether it's strong work or not. If that was the only end, to turn you on, then it would be pornography in the boring sense.

Q: Erotica?

A: Erotica's for people who are too spineless for pornography. They want to put a gauze over it. I don't understand that. If you look at something directly the mystery still remains. That is the mystery.

Q: Could you talk about the different readings we're meant to give to the two different shows.

A: 'Pleasure Zone' is about presenting the male

asshole as a site of sexual pleasure. The images are cheerful and even enjoyable, even innocent. 'Targets' is like saying, this is the target of heterosexual hatred of gay men, this in particular, taking it up the ass. And if you look closely and reflect on it - and like John Waters said, the asshole isn't something most people get to see who don't look at gay pornography - then you can vibe that this is an asshole that has been fucked. It's had cock up it. It's not some straight guy's asshole. And gay men are still the targets of violence, hatred and contempt here and everywhere. But here, the UK, is my focus. Look at the bullshit rise of Islam, faith schools, the persistence of American-backed evangelism, Catholics lying about condoms and all that shit. In both shows I was trying to resist socially acceptable representations of gay men. Being penetrated by another man is still seen as the ultimate degradation. And I wanted to say fuck that, it's a pleasure, it's a more intimate pleasure than any straight man will ever know.

Q: Do you consider yourself a gay artist?

A: I'm dealing with certain things as a man, as a gay man, as a black man, as a black gay man in this culture. And within that as being of Nigerian descent. That makes certain things more immediate to me. Like where a lot of my family live there's real violence between Christians and Muslims. It isn't some abstract liberal debate where the real power is secular. These things reach me in a way they don't maybe reach a lot of people. So I can't say I'm a gay artist before any of those other things, even if that's what some people see first because of the overt context.

Q: Who do you see as your audience?

A: The discerning, of course! (Laughs) People who like some challenges, who like to think and see stuff they maybe haven't seen or thought about before. It's *not about shock value, or only so far as you're jump-starting a flat battery.*

Q: Could you envisage your work getting any sort of mainstream notice?

A: Probably not.

Q: Why?

A: Because of what it's about. It's too direct for most people, even though it's aesthetically attractive. Which is the opposite of pickling cows in formalde-hyde or nailing kippers to tables and saying that's a feminist commentary.

Q: So you're critical of the contemporary art scene?

A: They're doing their own thing and getting paid. Good luck to them. But what they're doing isn't any-thing I can use, you know?

Q: I notice you don't use your surname on your work on in your publicity.

A: No.

Q: How do your family deal with your art?

A: They aren't aware of it.

Q: How do you think they would respond to it?

A: With anger and shame. Relief I do not use the family name, at least.

Q: Is that conflict or tension something you plan to address in your art?

A: I refuse to be a slave to tradition. But also I don't want to drag them into my head-zone. I don't answer to them, I don't involve them. I am an individ-ual with my own challenges that I must meet.

Q: Ziggy, thank you for talking to us.

A: Thank you.

'What do you think?'

Malcolm starts: he had been so engrossed in the article he hadn't heard the taps being turned off or Ziggy coming back into the room. 'What was it with the peroxide and the blue contacts, man?' he asks.

'The blond was a Warhol tribute.'

'You weren't trying to fuck off black people?'

'I'd already had it in the neck from certain black people by then about my politics and appearance. I didn't care what they thought by then. I didn't go looking for their approval, but I didn't care about antagonising them either: that'd still have been giving them power. The blue contact lenses was a Grace Jones-Jean-Paul Goudé homage. Blond hair had no shock value by then: in Jamaica the most macho ragga stars were dyeing their hair blond.' He shrugs.

'I liked what you said, though,' Malcolm says.

'When?'

'In the article.'

Ziggy picks up the magazine and flicks to the interview. 'I can hardly remember,' he says. 'I don't lie because my memory is so fucked I would never manage to remember what I said if it wasn't true. But what's true changes.' His eyes move rapidly over the columns of text, then he closes the magazine and puts it back down. 'Come,' he says.

Taking Malcolm's hand in his, he leads Malcolm through to the bathroom. The steamy air is sweet with coconut and vanilla. A large age-speckled mirror leans against one wall, reflecting the two of them back at themselves as they step into the water, feet, ankles passing through cool, crisp foam into amniotic warmth. Malcolm almost slips on the slick enamel beneath, but Ziggy's hand tightens around his and steadies him.

Facing each other, slowly they sit down. Ziggy, the gracious host, takes the end with the taps. Their skins prickle and their balls loosen. Muscles tense then relax, pores open to the steam. Rivulets of condensation run down the mirror's surface and the turquoise tiles on the walls.

Strange how things you've done ten thousand times can seem like revelations when the feelings are new. It is as if neither of them has ever shared a bath before, or at least not since childhood, and doing so now reconnects them with that earlier state of innocence, as well as with some dreamed-of but rarely-attained spirit of romance. And as they soap and rub each other down, cleansing and honouring each others' bodies, they both embrace the flesh and transcend it, and are aroused and pure at the same time.

Ziggy moves a flannel in the shape of an octopus over Malcolm's smooth mocha skin, and curiously it is only now that he experiences the sudden ecstasy of recognition, of colour shared. The recognition thrills him, though still he resists being claimed by that thing from which he won't accept a claim, the commonality of race. He thinks of the *marassa*, the cosmic twins, the primary homoerotic: the androgod who splits himself in two and fucks himself to give birth to the world. And Malcolm is his twin on another level, on Plato's level: the lost half he has longed and feared to find, and found.

After the bath they moisturise each other's skin with cocoa-butter, dot each other with cologne, spears of glass touching glands, the sophisticated primal. A breeze, the first of the day, stirs the living-room curtains. Looking round at the canvasses, the paints and brushes and tins and jars, Malcolm is home. Since knowing Luke he has come to associate the smell of oil-paint with safety, with being cared for and cared about. He couldn't imagine being easy now in a place where art isn't happening. His stomach rumbles and he realises with a pang that he hasn't eaten for fifteen hours.

'You want some breakfast?' Ziggy asks.

Malcolm nods. 'Or my belly's gonna stage a coup.'

'I'll go and see what's in the larder,' Ziggy says. A moment later he's thudding down the stairs and out of the front door. Malcolm watches from the window as, wearing only black Speedos and flip-flops, Ziggy buys fruit from the stall next to his front door.

Village life in the big city, Malcolm thinks. *Perfection.* He pushes the window up. 'Get plantains, man!' he calls. 'You have olive oil? An is dat saltfish dere?' He points at something yellowy-brown piled up in a styrofoam container on a neighbouring stall. Ziggy looks up, follows the line of his pointing finger, and nods.

They breakfast on saltfish and ackee, fried plantain and sweet potato, and afterwards fresh pineapple and strawberries, feeding each other, licking and sucking the juice from each others' fingers. Then they make love again, on the living-room floor.

They go further this time, sixty-nining deep, Malcolm eventually breaking off to do what he has been longing to do since he first saw Ziggy, a longing intensified by the art in the magazine in which Ziggy was interviewed: tongue Ziggy's shaved hole. Ziggy moves his mouth on Malcolm's heavy erection and moans chokingly as Malcolm rims him, offering up his large, muscular arse, swallowing Malcolm's cock-head down his throat and pushing four oil-slicked fingers up into Malcolm's body as he does so. Malcolm gasps and writhes excitedly, experiencing an elasticity that was never there before, that is there only for Ziggy. Ziggy pushes his fingers into Malcolm to the knuckles, and Malcolm comes abruptly in Ziggy's mouth. Ziggy starts to jerk himself off fast while Malcolm's tongue is still up his arse, and a moment later he explodes too, his come spattering hotly over Malcolm's chest, his thighs clamping Malcolm's head until Malcolm's ears pop.

With a shuddering gasp they roll apart, flopping

onto their backs on the cooling painted floorboards, gasping for breath like caught fish, staring up at the ceiling with wild, wide eyes, minds blank, at first seeing nothing, then, as their heart-rates slow, taking in details without judgement: amber flecks of old paint around the light-fitting; trickles of sweat inching down the grooves of their armpits, the sides of their temples; the smooth clamminess of the floorboards against their radiant skins. A ladybird on a yellow curtain, creeping slowly upwards. Six spots on its shell. The halves of the shell flick open and it takes flight, a tiny miracle.

Like dancers mirroring each others' movements they sit up and look at each other with large eyes that at that moment let everything in and out.

'Sorry I came in your mouth, man,' Malcolm says.

Ziggy shrugs. 'I made you.'

'I mean, without - discussion.'

'Our mouths were full at the time,' Ziggy says with a half-smile.

Malcolm smiles too, but there is a pain in his heart that is caused by the impossibility of innocence. *Was there ever innocence,* he wonders. *And if there was, when? That window between syphilis being curable and herpes not? The grubby, grimy mid-70s which was in any case really the incubator of what was far worse -*

'Maybe we should - ' he begins, then stops.

'What?'

Malcolm looks down shyly. 'What it is, I really like you, man. I like you a lot and I feel serious about that feeling, you know? And I don't want that feeling to always have to go through - barriers. Not unless it has to, you know?'

Ziggy nods, says nothing.

'I don't think I'm positive,' Malcolm says. 'I had a test about eighteen months ago and I haven't done anything risky since, though there's always little slips, aren't there?' He sighs. 'I just don't wanna think - wherever we go with this, whatever you feel - I don't want to feel like I've got to go to this grey place if the condom slips off or whatever shit happens, chosen or unchosen, you know? And I don't know if you know your status - ' He stops. '*Do* you know?'

Ziggy shakes his head. 'The last test I had was five years ago. That was negative, but it doesn't prove anything now.'

'And since then?'

Ziggy exhales. 'Like you said, I have been mostly okay, but I admit there have been slips.' *There have been*, Ziggy does not say, *acts of wilful self-destructiveness*.

'Didn't any of that make you want to get tested?' Malcolm asks. 'Like, it was a rubber splitting that made me go. And what I knew about the guy - '

'In you or on you?'

'On me. Maybe if it had been in me I'd have been too scared to go. I mean, I know the facts, man: in this part of the world it's not a death-sentence, there's triple combination drugs coming through now that mostly work blah blah blah. But still it's one fuckin' paradigm shift, ain't it?' And he doesn't say, *From fought-for healthy to categorically diseased*.

'I decided I would rather not know,' Ziggy says. 'Not know if I am, that is. If I am *not* - I thought I could go on not knowing. I thought I could live at that level of uncertainty. And I could, Malcolm, if it was just for me. If I was just fucking various men I wasn't really involving myself with, and we never get to those kind of questions, and you protect yourself, most of the time, because it's transient, and anyway your life's your own to throw away. And I don't know if it's necessary to know now, but I feel like maybe it is.' He sighs. "Love means saying you'll test'.' He gestures vaguely. 'They should make a poster of it.'

'Love?' Malcolm's throat tightens.

'A figure of speech,' Ziggy says. Then, meeting Malcolm's darting eyes, he corrects himself: '*Not* a figure of speech.'

They kiss softly, and it's as if their lips have expanded, as if the field of contact is magnified by the emotion behind it. And for the first time in a long time Malcolm finds himself thinking about the future.

His future.

His and Ziggy's.

Suddenly he wants to travel, to go somewhere new. But where?

Africa.

The two of us.

Without and within.

Chapter Seven

Luke scrolls down to George's number, presses 'OK', and waits nervously for him to answer. He's spoken to George twice since their date four nights ago, but both times the conversation was awkward.

But awkward cos both of us was trying to drag it out, though: we didn't wanna break the connection once it was made. That's gotta be a good sign, don't it?

Needing reassurance, he had asked Malcolm that same question when Malcolm finally reappeared, bruise-eyed and subtly radiant, after being away from their flat for a second night without calling in. After, of course, they had swapped accounts of their respective dates with the shy intensity of the suddenly blessed, and the relief of those whose good fortune hasn't come at the expense of another.

'Sure, it's a good sign,' Malcolm said, going through to the kitchen. Luke heard him rummaging about in the fridge. 'Zere any Diet Coke left?' he called.

'We're out, man,' Luke called back. 'I shoved some Buds in the ice-box earlier though.'

'Good thinking, my brother.' The freezer-compartment opened and closed, then a bottle-top popped. 'You want one?'

'Yeah, man. Thanks.'

Malcolm popped a second Bud and came back into the living-room. Art Blakey's *The Witch Doctor* was playing at a low volume, Wayne Shorter's sax floating lazily over Blakey's sinewy drumming. The day outside was overcast and glary. Inside it was still and warm.

Malcolm dropped onto the sofa next to Luke and

handed him one of the Buds. They clinked glass and swigged. Luke smelt unfamiliar scents on his friend's familiar skin, moisturiser and antiperspirant, coconut, witch-hazel, lemon, sage. None of these were scents or brands Malcolm normally used. They were Ziggy's: his body smelt of Ziggy, even if the exact fusion of perfume and biochemistry was Malcolm's alone.

Luke felt oddly disorientated by this echo of his other friend and former lover on his best friend's skin. He also became vaguely sexually excited: he was suddenly more aware of Malcolm as a man than he had been at any time since the night they first met - *Crammed in the back of the car shoulder to shoulder with three other brothers and the girl up front, adrenaline-high, reeking of pheromones, machismo saturating the air, masculinity thick and tangible even above the iron tang of blood in my mouth. Right then I was in love with you all but Malcolm, Malcolm, I knew there was something else there calling my name -*

As if for the first time, Luke wondered what it would be like to have sex with Malcolm.

'But really, though,' he said, getting back to his worries about George. 'D'you think it's got somewhere to go? It was so fuckin' - *awkward* on the phone yesterday. I mean, we flowed the first night, you know? We couldn't stop talking when we was face to face. But now I don't know.'

'Well, there's two sorts of awkward, aren't there, my Nubian,' Malcolm said. 'There's the 'I wanna fuck you but first we've got to get through a whole evening of chit-chat and, oh shit, we've got absolute zero in common, so it's a struggle to get to the booty.' And if you don't knock boots that evening then it's dead in the water. And then there's the 'I like you so much I'm watching every word I say in case I blow it.' And if it's that one then you get self-conscious and you hobble yourself and talk boring or awkward and accidentally send out the wrong message.'

'For me it's that,' Luke says. 'But for him I dunno.'

'If he'd just wanted to make the beast with one back he wouldn't have packed you off in a cab that night, would he?'

'Maybe he just didn't fancy me.'

'He put that ad in in the first place, didn't he? You don't do that unless you're highly motivated desire-wise.'

'Maybe I palled on exposure.'

'Man, your self-esteem is so fucked sometimes. He's twice as old as you. He was probably nervous as fuck that'd put you off big-time so he avoided making a move. He probably still is nervous.'

'It's funny, you know,' Luke said. 'Like in the abstract the age thing would put me off, you know? But when it came to it, it didn't. There was almost something to it I liked, actually.'

'Okay. So that's not a problem. And who called who?'

'He called me the first time. I called him the second.'

'Well, there you go, man. He put in the ad. He invited you on a date. He acted classy. *And* he called you the next day to show he was keen.'

'Yeah, but - no, you're right, man.' Luke sighed. 'Funny how hard it is when you really like someone, ain't it?'

'Yeah,' Malcolm said.

They fell silent then, and let the music fill the space. Luke didn't ask about Malcolm's nights with Ziggy, and Malcolm didn't volunteer anything, for fear of laying them all – Luke, Ziggy and himself - too bare.

'Kiss the mirror, lesbian bitch!'

Ziggy is fucking Luke from behind, his fingers a

vice in Luke's dreads forcing Luke to meet his own lips through glass and mercury, a kinky reinscribing of his twinnedness, his biological twin replaced with a reparative porno fantasy one as Ziggy rams his dick into Luke hard, head hitting the second sphincter, gate to his gut, then slipping past it; a twin of himself as he is now, a twin of the man he has become. Luke gasps and tries to toss his head to give himself some small relief from the depth and fullness of the penetration but Ziggy holds him in place. His breath misting the glass Luke is now nose-to-nose with his perfect twin, who is also taking his black lover's dick and loving it. He has a studded collar round his neck and he and Ziggy wear bike-boots and nothing else. Ziggy's Mohican is red. His large hand slaps the peach globes of Luke's butt with stinging sharpness.

Kiss the mirror lesbian bitch Silly provocative trashy pervy Ziggy liberated him from what had till then been a pointless rectitude, a sort of – blackness, Malcolm would say later, in another context: the need to self-police, to avoid the games of sex allowed to others, to be above all respectable, a gesture as futile as imagining that going to church would cause the BNP to forget your blackness. And for what? To spare his partners? But that was to judge their wants and needs with a needy, wanting spirit. Because of their race.

'Just do what you like and fuck the others,' Ziggy said of letting a former partner piss in his mouth as if it was nothing. 'Then at least one person is having fun – you.'

It was after that that Luke let Ziggy photograph him sucking his dick for the *Mammy* series, albeit in soft-focus and identity-obscuring close-up.

George answers his phone on the fifth ring.

'It's me,' Luke says.

'Luke.' Luke thinks his name is said warmly. 'How's it going, sweetness?'

'Yeah, man, good. I got a call yesterday - you remember that mural gig I was telling you about? It's come through, it's happening for definite.'

'I'm happy for you, baby. When do you start?'

'Next week sometime. The plaster's got to dry properly first. But anyways, in the meantime I've got some free time and I noticed there's this exhibition at this gallery up Shoreditch of like Vodou art from Haiti that finishes like tomorrow and I was wondering if - '

'Sure, sweetness, I'd love to see it.'

'Cool. You free this afternoon?'

'I am.'

Luke checks his watch. 'We could meet at, say, um, three at Old Street tube? I'll be on my bike.'

'Till three then, baby.'

George rings off. 'You finished in there yet, man?' Luke calls through to Malcolm, who is in the bathroom.

There is the sound of water sloshing about, the rush of a tap. 'I'll be done in five,' Malcolm calls back. 'So you got a date, then?'

'I do, man.'

'Irie. You wanna eat wit me an Zig later?'

'Like, up in town?'

'Yeah, Soho, wherever.'

'Sure. Bell me on the mobile when you got a plan.'

The pollution-levels are high as Luke cycles across town, although it being late August there are less cars on the roads than there are the rest of the year. He's wearing the skintight silver lycra George first saw him in, along with silver-framed wraparounds, and this time silver bangles and rings, a Celtic tip. He got Malcolm to shave the back and sides of his head with their Wahl clippers and he feels clean and sharp, even if his scalp was left slightly reddened by the closeness of the cut. He wonders if George shaves his body like many dancers do. He hopes so.

The mountain-bike's narrow saddle rises firm and warm between his buttocks, its prow pushing up against the back of his balls with provocative insistence. His mind goes to Malcolm and Ziggy, how strange it is to think of them becoming a couple, how strange it will be to see it.

'Bring George,' Malcolm said.

He will if it feels right.

If George even wants to meet Malcolm and Ziggy, that is. Luke hopes so, although he doesn't want to seem to brag, though it is simply true, *my best friends are black,* and thus the corollary: *I must be sincere, implicitly admirable in the depth of my attractions.* Still, he *is* proud of his friends, and he is proud of George and, despite his uneasiness, he does want them to meet.

He feels then the intensity of his particular need, a need that is both visceral and conceptual: *without a black lover I don't exist.* This is his truth, and not a pose. Not a kink or fetish or peccadillo, and he has plenty of those - a fondness for lycra for instance; for Speedos instead of underwear; for shaved arseholes; for certain sexual scenarios, certain words shouted out in the heat of passion. But without a black lover his sense of himself slowly drains away: he feels his humanity and his sense of involvement in the world fade, and his art becomes pale. Black friends are a bulwark against that, in some ways a stronger one, but they are never quite enough, as friends never are for anyone.

He pumps his way across Edgware Road fast as the lights change, heading east, parallel with Oxford Street, his muscles by now warm and charged, his chest and crotch heavy with anticipation.

*

The train judders to a halt just short of Old Street tube station, and the lights dim then go out. There is the deflating whine of an engine powering down. A wave of anxiety passes along the mercifully only quarter-full carriage. *Terror attack. Person under a train. Terror attack.*

George stirs in his seat, glances at his watch. He is already ten minutes late, the result of combining BPT, (Black People's Time), with LTS, (London Travel Syndrome), which consists of taking the shortest time a given journey has ever taken you, then pretending it's the average. And then setting out ten minutes late anyway. At least now he can blame his slackness on public transport. And, more legitimately, on a call from his agent Patricia telling him he'd got a job choreographing a soft drink commercial. Sorting out various contractual matters had kept him standing outside the tube-station for more than quarter of an hour.

He'd met with the soft drink people three months ago, shown them some videos of his work. They'd been polite but no more than that, and he'd assumed the gig was a bust and had totally forgotten about it. *Funny how often those are the jobs that come through, while the meetings where you feel there's a real enthusiasm there somehow burn themselves out within the course of the meeting.*

The work wouldn't be very challenging, but it would be money, and it wouldn't be teaching.

Must get my own show together. Think about funding.

The train jerks forward as if a chain has been yanked somewhere ahead, and the lights flicker back on as it pulls into the station in underpowered spurts. There is a delay before the doors open. A few men in suits and George get off.

The only person George has discussed Luke with is his oldest friend Lester, who George has known since he was fourteen, since before he knew he was gay. But Lester, who was five years older, knew, and always looked out for him.

It was Lester who took George to his first black gay house-party, up in Notting Hill, safely away from streets where he was known. George would have been around twenty then. To his almost-alarm and excitement the party had rapidly degenerated – or evolved - into an orgy. It was Lester who introduced George to what he would now call The Life, appropriating the African-Americanism, but would then have had no name for. The introduction proved both liberating and cathartic. The year was 1972, and George was at that time beginning to struggle against what he felt had become a whiteness of mind in both his dance and his personal life.

Nowadays Lester counsels addicts and alcoholics, and in his free time helps organise the Notting Hill Carnival. He has taken the path of community, modesty, involvement in straight life. He is neither in the closet nor out. He has helped raise his cousin Sandra's three children, all boys, and has been a role-model to them. None of them are in jail, two are working and the other is at university. He feels comfortable among the people he's grown up with in a way George never has, kin or skin.

'So what do you think, Les?' he asked, cradling the receiver under his chin as he reached into the fridge for a pot of Greek yoghurt. 'Am I just deluding myself? Projecting all this rubbish onto a boy half my age?'

'What rubbish, my dear? If you mean the belief that these things matter, that they mean something, why are you calling that rubbish? To believe that love can happen, is that rubbish? No. Or I certainly hope not.

What are you eating?'

'Yoghurt.'

'So virtuous,' Lester sighed. He is perpetually strug-
gling with a paunch. 'But why do you fight the notion
that God might be giving you something you need?'

'It's not that I don't think life – I mean my life -
means something,' George said.

'Something apart from *art*, Georgie,' Lester said.
'You try to put all the meaning of your life onto art,
onto creativity, like a mother who lives only through
her child and not for herself, and is miserable and
doesn't understand why. Your life means something
apart from art. Never mind God - I know you're not a
church-goer - but because you're a human being. And
anyway, if you're miserable the whole time it'll poison
your art.'

'True,' George conceded. 'But - '

'Okay, so he's white, half your age, good-looking,
athletic, *blond* - '

'Thank you so much.'

'*But* you're wise, handsome and sexy. And he *likes*
you. He likes *you*,' Lester repeated, shifting the empha-
sis. 'When you consider it, *any* falling in love seems
unlikely. Why this person and that person hit it off and
not someone else? And any sort of love that goes
against what is approved of is forced to justify itself,
and that makes those involved in that love question
themselves in a way others don't have to. But that
doesn't make it any less real. I'm speaking about love
here. Should I be speaking about love?'

George didn't answer for a moment. Then: 'Yeah.
Fuck it. Yes, yes you should.'

'Well, then. It just has to be fought for harder.'

'Sometimes I feel too damn old.'

'I bet you don't feel too damn old today, though.'

George laughed. 'No, I don't. And I feel horny as

hell.'

'Then I'll pray for you, my dear.'

The escalator creaks as it rises sedately, one of the few wooden-slatted ones left. The leather of the hand-rail is worn down to the threads in patches. George is wearing gold nail-varnish and gold on his eyelids, which are concealed behind black wraparounds. He has on a black mesh cut-off tank-top, silky black runner's shorts, bright white socks to the knee, and chunky black trainers. His head is freshly-shaved, as are his legs, which are dark and smooth and long, all grey depilated. He knows the lump of his crotch looks good in the shorts. His keys, wallet, and a very lightweight tracksuit are in a small red vinyl heart-shaped pack on his back.

He passes through the barriers and emerges into a dazzling sunlight that is at once burning hot on his bare skin. Luke is there waiting for him. He looks fit, hand-some, ruddy from exertion and hi-tech in skintight silver. Infinitely desirable. George feels his cock expand inside his flimsy shorts. He moves quickly to hug Luke, to conceal its brazenly-obvious extension from besuited passers-by, but the feeling of hot skin against hot skin only adds to his excitement as he and Luke kiss greed-ily. His dick is rock-hard now, thrusting forward and up in the middle of Old Street. Luke's own erection pushes stiffly against it, it too ludicrously conspicuous.

After a long, thrilling moment of hard-ons sliding over hard-ons through slippery nylon and lycra, they move their crotches back from each other a little.

'I think we're gonna have to think turn-offing thoughts,' Luke says, his face flushed.

'Yes,' George agrees.

They laugh, wait, laugh again, eyes on each other.

'Okay,' Luke says. 'Seriously.'

'Okay,' George echoes. 'Art.'

'Art.'

'Deep breath.'

'Yes.'

'Shall we?'

'Okay.'

'Okay.'

Tentatively they disengage. Glancing down, they laugh again: their dicks are still jutting. They stand there in silence, hips hovering, trying to disassociate from animal desire, waiting on detumescence. Eventually it comes.

Holding hands against cat-calling streets they set off for the gallery. It's in amongst several others, up a narrow side-street just a few minutes' walk from the tube station. They have to buzz to be let in, which makes Luke uneasy. He struggles to let go of feeling out of place. George enters ahead of him, seemingly totally at his ease. A woman with straight hair and a good figure smiles at them both and hands them leaflets that explain the art and price each item. She does so, it seems to Luke, entirely without prejudice. Perhaps she is even pleased to have someone black coming to see the show, regardless of whether or not he looks like he's going to buy anything. Not that you can tell who has money and who doesn't. The more ceremonial pieces aren't for sale in any case.

Glancing about him at the work on display Luke's first thought is how much Ziggy would love it. If he was here on his own he would call Ziggy up, tell him to drop whatever he was doing and come to the gallery straight away. And Ziggy would have faith in Luke's excitement and come. Their friendship is like that: full of the impulsive sharing of enthusiasms, novelties, passions. But Luke isn't on his own, he's with George, and Ziggy is with Malcolm. *It's on one more day*, he thinks. *I can tell him tonight and he can go tomorrow*. He feels almost treacherous.

The Vodou art takes several forms. There are large, ornate metal silhouettes of the *lwa*, derived in part from French colonial wrought-ironwork. There are paintings of spirits and historical scenes like Bois-Caiman, executed in a naïve style; ritual flags – *drapeau* - embroidered with sequins; ceremonial gourd rattles, mesh-covered spirit bottles, and painted drums. There are also several elegant black-and-white photographs of Vodou believers taken by a European photographer. The collision of the two worlds is strongest here: black art, white gallery; the looked-upon and the onlooking.

'There should be music,' Luke says.

George nods. 'Drumming. And bells.'

'It'd drive the staff mad.'

'Or take them somewhere new.'

Luke nods. Apart from the woman behind the desk, they are at the moment the only people in the gallery.

'So do you know much about Vodou?' George asks as they gaze up at a glittering blue and white flag the size of a tablecloth embroidered with the name *Labaleen*.

'A bit,' Luke says. 'Ziggy - he's my best friend, apart from Malcolm - his family's Nigerian, so he knows about African Vodou from stories his granny told him, legends and stuff. But he collects stuff about Haitian Vodou too, books, pictures, movies, whatever. I reckon I relate to Haitian Vodou more than the African type, you know? It's got more of a angry, fucked-up side to it, like it comes more out of pain, out of – I dunno - being broken. But what do I know, man? Zig even likes weird old black-and-white flicks like *White Zombie* and *I Walked With A Zombie*. Even *Live And Let Die*, you know? Cos he says the look's authentic. And sexy. He likes to wind people up sometimes, though. What about you?'

'I don't know much,' George says. 'What I've picked up on is what I think applies to dance. The idea of bringing up the energy with dance and music till the spirits come. Achieving that heightened state where you become a kind of psychic tuning-fork. Dance functioning not only as worship - which is quite unusual in itself - but also as communion. The spirits coming into the body, manifesting through the body - '

'Yeah, it's not like the Greek myths, is it?' Luke says. 'Where you come across like Hera bathing in a pool and think it's just some mortal girl and all that.'

'Or Zeus as a bull or a swan.'

'Yeah. It's more - I dunno, man. More *real*, somehow. More psychological, but not in a bullshit Freudian way. Them Greek and Roman or whatever myths feel like just made-up stories. But Vodou feels like something real.' Luke feels his heart beating. To be talking this way excites him. Everything he knows about Greek myths he got from Ziggy and Ray Harryhausen but it holds up, it isn't fake, he doesn't feel like a fool.

'Beautiful, isn't it?' George says, admiring a large purple flag with black and white sequinned motifs, obviously a starring piece. *Baron Cimetiere* is spelt out in black beads under a cross.

'That's another name for Baron Samedi,' Luke says.

'As in *Live And Let Die*?'

'Yeah. *Lwa* of the dead, lord of the dead. Promiscuous fucker. And protector of children.'

'How so?'

'Well, who'd you want protecting your kids? Someone with power over death, right? Or at least influence. And fucking is like pushing life up against death and making death back off.'

George nods. In his mind he is wearing a white top-hat with a blood-red cockerel-feather in it. *Oliver,*

Felipe, Jean-Marie. I couldn't protect any of you, not in the end. He remembers a phrase he read somewhere: *This fragile scarlet tree we carry within us.* Fucking, life and death, all intertwined. The flag is priced at £3000.

They wander through the other rooms of the gallery. Not all of the work on display is equally good, but every piece is imbued with the particularity and power of the culture it comes from. Even if it's tourist art, and some of it surely is, for what believer would make and sell genuine devotional artefacts? - it's still Haitian art made by Vodou artists: it still has an energy that is genuine.

To think and process thoughts differently, how liberating, George reflects as he takes in these representations of a different spiritual landscape. *It's so easy to get trapped, to follow the furrow, the plough, the mule's backside.* A desire to make art wells up in him. Movements fill his mind. 'Thank you for inviting me to this,' he says.

'You're welcome, man,' Luke replies, pleased.

They spend just over an hour in the gallery. Afterwards, being in no hurry, and having nothing in particular to do, but half-thinking of cafés and food, they stroll over to Soho, Luke wheeling his bike. On the way he gives Malcolm a call, to see if he and Ziggy still fancy meeting up, and since it turns out that none of them have eaten yet they arrange to meet at Balan's in Old Compton Street for supper at seven.

The rush-hour has begun by the time George and Luke reach Oxford Street, though in the sulphurous humidity no-one can drag up the energy to actually rush. A few try to enjoy the heat, but most just look beaten down and soiled. Luke feels a burst of compassion for the men in their constricting ties, buttoned-up shirts and tight, hard shoes, and the women in their tie-neck blouses, tights and calf-compressing court-shoes, their make-up melting in a heat that only intensifies as the sun creeps down towards the horizon.

Having time to kill, Luke and George saunter down to a sunbather-crowded Soho Square. Luke chains his bike to the railings, then they find an unoccupied patch of grass to sit on. Although he's fifty George sits straight-backed and cross-legged with supple ease while Luke, for all his youth and fitness, has to sprawl to get comfortable. He changes positions several times in quick succession like a hyperactive child, then stops shifting about to look at George admiringly: his up-rightness, his stillness, his dark skin glinting in the blaze, mocha shadowed with indigo. And so smooth –

To run my tongue over your thigh to roll you onto your back spread your legs wide with magical ease plunge my tongue into your shaved, sweet –

'D'you fancy an ice-cream, man?' he asks, interrupting his own train of thought as a girl passes licking an old-school ice-lolly. Luke imagines sliding the shiny, orange, red and purple length in and out of George, George gasping in response.

'Sure, sweetness,' George says. 'If you're having one.'

'Cool.' Luke jumps up, turning quickly so George won't see his half hard-on, and goes over to an ice-cream van that is parked just beyond the railings.

George watches his arse as he goes and wonders if he likes to be fucked. *Not the sort of compatibility the straight children have to worry about*, he thinks: *who wants to take what role when*. Although it can lead to obvious problems, he finds it hard to imagine being deprived of that variety in lovemaking. Of everything he found dull about sex with women, that rigidity of presumption was the worst.

Luke returns with two Mister Whippys. 'I'd of got

us 99s but they were out of Flakes.' George grinds out his cigarette on the parched grass and takes one of the already-dripping cones from Luke's outstretched hand. 'You don't mind it's not premium-grade whatever, Ben & Jerry's, do you, man?'

'How could I resist the synthetic taste of nostalgia?' George says, extending a provocatively long pink tongue to lick the rapidly-sagging grooved vanillin dollop. He watches Luke watching him and starts to get turned on again. In Soho Square he doesn't care if his thickening dick is visible in his flimsy shorts; in fact he almost wants it to be.

My dick my queerness and this good-looking white boy who wants Me I could strip and sit on his dick right here Put on a show -

The small ornamental park is crowded with loafers and queens, bohemians, beggars and derelict drunks, and office-workers putting off the commuter-crawl home, all of them lolling like seals on a rock beneath the brilliant sun. Pigeons move jerkily as they search for crumbs in purple shadows under benches. Small talk and the clink of glasses comes floating across from a gay bar on the north side of the square. A woman in a gypsy headscarf tries to sell out-of-date Big Issues. Someone buys one. George and Luke nibble at the rims of their cones like leaf-cutter ants.

Time passes.

A wasp that has been hovering lands on Luke's thumb. He watches it without concern as, abdomen pulsing and antennae switching, it bows its head to taste the patch of shiny sweetness there. He thinks he can feel the touch of its tiny tongue as it forages in the grooves of his thumb-print.

A breath of breeze stirs the heavy air without cooling it. Careful not to disturb the wasp, Luke checks his watch. 'Time we made a move,' he says. He doesn't move, though; nor does George. The wasp flicks away. More time passes.

George checks his watch: 7:10. 'Okay,' he says. With a fluid ease he gets to his feet. He offers his hand to Luke and pulls him up, and hand-in-hand they stroll down to Old Compton Street.

The glass frontage of Balan's has been folded back. Ziggy and Malcolm haven't arrived yet, but George and Luke have the luck to get a table right in the middle of the window-space that will just about sit four. George orders a white wine, Luke a Diet Coke.

'So Ziggy and Malcolm are your two best friends, and they're also going out with each other,' George says, lighting a cigarette with a paper match. 'Isn't that awkward sometimes?'

'It's so new I don't really know yet,' Luke says.

Diagonally opposite the restaurant is a gay bar, one of several in the area, Compton's. Skinheads cluster outside behind a velvet rope, holding bottles and glasses, drinking and chatting, ranging in manner from the apparently authentically laddish to the paradoxically camp. The two bouncers on the bar's door are black. One, the more beefily muscular of the two, is chatty with the clientele; the other is impassive.

'I mean, I don't even know they'd say they *were* going out, it's so recent,' Luke says. 'I mean as opposed to just hooking up on the regular, you know? This is gonna be the first time I've seen them as a couple. I guess I worry it's gonna turn my two best friends into one not-so-good one, because now they're together all the time and you can't barely bitch to one about the other when they piss you off. And they didn't even know each other a month ago.'

'Nor did we, sweetness.'

'Freaky, ain't it, man?' Luke says. 'Bum us a fag, wouldya.'

George passes him the one he's been smoking and taps out another. Before he can light it Luke is waving to two black men coming hand-in-hand towards them along the far side of the street.

'Ziggy! Malcolm!'

A few moments later the pair are stepping over the threshold and joining them at their table. Malcolm has on a midnight-blue jacket with nothing underneath it. Around his neck is a thin gold chain that glints on the curves of his bare clavicle. He wears snake-hipped, low-cut trousers, and sandals. He has a big-eyed, skinny, almost boyish vibe to him, although there is a certain pain behind those eyes, it seems to George. Ziggy wears a cut-off orange tank-top that exposes a solidly-muscled belly, an orange and turquoise sarong and bike-boots, and has on his wrists black rubber and silver bangles identical to the ones Luke wears. He carries a folding fan in one hand. His hair is a green Mohawk. George initially takes him to be in his late forties, but quickly revises his estimate downwards by fifteen years or so: Ziggy's striking features are, he sees, gruelled by drugs and drink beyond the passage of time. Yet he is handsome.

Luke stands to kiss his two best friends hello, Malcolm first as he's nearest. Normally he'd kiss them on the lips, but today that feels inappropriate so he kisses them each on the cheek instead. This registering of the shift in their relationships seems right and natural, and acknowledges that Luke is here with his lover too.

'This is George,' he says, turning to George, whose hand he has been holding throughout the greeting. 'George, these are - this is my best friend and flat-mate Malcolm.' George lets go of Luke's hand to shake Malcolm's. 'And this is my other best friend and fellow artist, Ziggy.'

George and Ziggy shake hands. Ziggy slides into a

chair Luke turns round for him from a just-vacated adjoining table, his movements constricted by the fabric wound around his thighs. Malcolm corrals another chair for himself as the waiter comes over to take their drinks order, a good-looking Spanish boy with a pumped physique. Ziggy orders red wine, Malcolm a Beck's.

Malcolm lights a cigarette. He can feel the restaurant bending in their favour as places do sometimes. Their being obviously gay is enough to ensure them attentive service here, over and above that offered ephemeral tourists and theatre-going straights; and their party being mostly black works in their favour too for once, lending a cachet of cool to a culture that has long ceased to be vanguard.

Liberation through liberation from meaning, Malcolm thinks. *If nothing means anything there can be no judgement, or judgement itself becomes a caprice. Is that freeing or is it an evacuation of the soul? Does it just replace*

The
Shit with/
More shit?

They order food and the food arrives, and as they eat and drink and talk the sky passes from pale cerulean to hazy indigo. One by one the streetlights come on, and the waiters light candles and set them floating in dishes of water on the tables. The theatre crowds arrive, go in to see their shows, mill about on the pavements in the intervals, then go home. Beggars pass in twenty-minute loops, working their beats as assiduously as the Nigerian traffic wardens.

At some point the talk turns to suicide, and there is at once a shared understanding between them. All of them know someone who has taken his own life, either intentionally, or by doing something so rash it was suicide in everything but name; and, although it is not said out loud, all of them, whether seriously or not, have attempted suicide.

There is a further bond between them: they are artists, and to be an artist means destroying your life for your art, if not melodramatically like Michelangelo, who ruined his back and his health painting the ceiling of the Sistine Chapel, then more mundanely by throwing away financial security, orderly career progression, conventional social standing, all the markers that most people cling to to reassure themselves that their life has shape and meaning. Repudiating these things is a form of suicide particular to both artists and revolutionaries, and that is another affinity, a parallel paradigm: the desire to risk all to remake the world.

'The first time I cut my wrists,' Ziggy says, and at the frankness of his disclosure the others shift in their seats, 'it felt like clarity. I saw the world stripped of everything false. I think that is how God sees the world. It was unbearable.'

'Were you serious when you did it?' Luke asks. 'I mean obviously putting a razor to your wrist is serious, but - '

'It was a piece of broken mirror. I don't know,' Ziggy says. 'I thought I wanted to take my energy level down into the negative. Reach some ancestral underground level. I felt like people were pounding me with waves of hate. I would hear voices chanting Faggot! Faggot! Faggot! I couldn't see any escape except down in the ground.' He takes a swallow of wine. 'But I learned from that. I stopped staring longingly at God's turned-away back and said Fuck Him.'

He falls silent. No-one says anything. They're all a little drunk now, and, at that moment, family. Luke watches as, without looking at him, Ziggy reaches out to Malcolm. Malcolm takes his hand and Ziggy exhales as his fingers close around Malcolm's.

'Black Americans used to have the lowest suicide rate,' George says, pulling the conversation round from the excruciatingly particular to the more bearable general. 'Until after the Civil Rights legislation was passed. From then on it started to ramp up till now they've got the highest rate. Particularly young black men.'

'Why?' Luke asks.

'Because you find bigotry is still everywhere,' George says. 'But now you can't fight it, except on a personal, fragmented level: after all, the law's on your side now, isn't it? And it becomes harder to prove where the prejudice really is for exactly that reason, so when you fail you're thrown back on your own despair: maybe it really is you, not society or the system or whatever. So now you're mistaken *and* paranoid. And that's a hard pit to climb out of. Like if you're gay: you're told that no-one except the Daily Mail, the Catholic Church and the mullahs seriously hate you any more - in this country, anyway - but you move through your life feeling prejudice everywhere anyway. For instance, has anyone at this table *not* been abused – verbally or physically - at some point over his sexuality by some random stranger?'

Heads are shaken.

'It's the deep effects that kill, though' Malcolm says. 'Being denied is what knifes the soul.'

'So what keeps us going?' Ziggy asks.

'Love,' Luke and Malcolm reply simultaneously. They meet each others' eyes then, and smile.

'Yes,' George says.

The waiter comes by to offer them dessert menus and coffee. Once they've ordered and he's gone George sighs. 'In another way I think suicide's infected the whole culture,' he says.

'How d'you mean, man?' Malcolm asks, offering him the last of the wine before refilling his own glass.

George gestures at the front page of a *Pink Paper* he and Luke picked up from the Admiral Duncan on the way to the restaurant: the headline is about soaring rates of HIV infection. 'This barebacking shit. The kids demanding the freedom people thought they had in the Seventies but never really did, that led to a lot of death, as if it's a right.'

The others nod agreement, but not unreservedly. There is the sudden sense that George is speaking for and from another generation, the generation of the late Sixties and early Seventies who did exactly what the gay youth of today are doing, but unknowingly and so freely; and that because he survived he is now moralising from a position that isn't really moral.

Still, survival is not nothing.

'A bunch of the kids think there's a cure for AIDS,' George says. 'What, ten percent think the drugs are a cure? They've never seen sick people, never mind buried anyone.'

'But there are older guys in their thirties and forties and fifties doing it too,' Malcolm says. 'Okay, so a lot of them are positive already, or take it for granted they are. And I get that they want to get away from thinking about it twenty-four seven and wanna act like it doesn't exist for a couple of hours, but still they're sending it round and round - '

'But you cannot blame people for needing that escape,' Ziggy says. 'Whether they're youngsters or older and should know better.'

'Plus it's not just gay people, is it, man?' Luke says. 'I mean, straights are slutting it about big time, fucking in gutters and up alleys, and they're a thousand times more careless about rubbers than gay people.'

'But creating a jargon – barebacking, bug-chasing,

raw this-and-that - going looking for it as if it's some exciting, fetishised thing in itself instead of just not bothering with rubbers, that *is* a very gay thing,' George says.

'Straight men pay prostitutes more to have sex without condoms,' Ziggy says. 'Even though they know someone who is a sex-worker is likely to be full of STDs.'

'I think part of it's a rejection of the previous generation who were so militant about safe sex,' George says, remembering a screening at a gay film festival where the director was scolded at the Q&A afterwards for not showing his characters using condoms for oral sex. 'If you want to be a rebel you stick two fingers up at the AIDS activists because they're the patriarchs now. Defying the fathers who did what they wanted and now they're sorry and preaching about it.'

'It's to do with age too, I reckon,' Luke says. 'Cos our culture's not like them traditional ones, like in Africa, where you honour the elders. Old here is like you don't know what's going on, and what you do know is about dead stuff what don't matter.'

'So we live fast and we die young,' says Malcolm. 'Or we try to.'

'That's different from suicide though,' Luke says. 'I mean, both ways you're looking ahead and seeing a big nothing and feeling the horror of it, right? But partying and smoking and barebacking is all about avoiding facing up to that nothing, ain't it? And topping yourself *is* facing up to it. Well, in one particular way, at least, right? To me it's more like, have you got a vision of yourself as a old man that's something you feel like, yeah, that's okay. Even good. That's where I wanna be, in time. A wise old man. I don't feel like we've got that.'

'With straight people it isn't much different,' Malcolm says. 'That's why they're having kids later and later. Because once you've got kids it can't be all about fun anymore: you're gonna start to feel the generations. And it doesn't necessarily make your life more meaningful to follow the biological imperative, the animal function, because it doesn't need a brain or a soul. It's how come they sometimes think they envy us.'

'Even though some of us do have children, of course,' George says.

'Wanted children,' Luke says. 'Not serial accidents,' he adds, his cheeks flushing.

'They don't want to feel old anymore than we do,' Malcolm says. 'And they don't have any more time for old people than gay people do. Maybe less, even.' And it is true: all of them have seen older gay acquaintances get pressed into caring for declining parents while straight siblings plead parenthood as an excuse for offering no help. 'We should reinvent ourselves,' he says. 'And become our own elders.'

Ziggy lifts his glass. 'To surviving,' he says.

'To surviving,' Malcolm, Luke and George echo, raising their glasses also.

'And to loving,' Luke adds, and they drain the dregs just as the coffee arrives, along with the two desserts they ordered, and four spoons.

Malcolm tugs a sugar wafer from a ball of coconut ice-cream, snaps it in half and feeds one half to Ziggy, catching the shards that fall from Ziggy's lips in his cupped hand. Luke offers George a spoonful of frozen mocha cake. Then he and George kiss, and Ziggy and Malcolm kiss, and for a moment they're double-dating teenagers, young and foolish and bold.

> *This to claim/re*
>   *claim*
>   *Let*
>   *Self (consciousness)*
>   *Go*

Where love is -

There is a sudden rumble of thunder although the sky above is clear. The lights around the streetlamps haze, and the pressure drops. A sudden inrush of air sends the candle-flames flickering; several go out. Bare skin goosebumps. A suppressed excitement passes through the crowded restaurant. The chill passes and is replaced by an oppressively heavy humidity as, with disconcerting rapidity, the sky clouds over. The waiters huddle together in conference, the maitre d' gesturing towards the restaurant's folded-back fronting. Before they can come to a decision to close it the rain begins, heavy drops splatting then hammering down, within moments a diamond-white downpour. George, Luke, Malcolm and Ziggy pull their table and chairs back a little so they're under cover, though splashback water-vapour still drifts in over them, thrown up by the impact of the raindrops on the abruptly-sodden pavement. It's oddly exciting, this sudden violence of nature. In the street all except the defeated and the defiant are running for cover.

'Joe!' George calls after a figure dashing past in a grey tracksuit with the hood up. The figure pulls to a stop and turns, dove-grey soaking to charcoal as he searches for the source of his name. George waves vigorously. Seeing him Joe runs over, hesitating on the threshold of the restaurant getting wetter because he doesn't know the others. With welcoming smiles they reach out and pull him in under cover.

Malcolm begs a fifth chair off a neighbouring table and Ziggy waves to the waiter, who comes over as Joe pushes the tracksuit-hood back off his head. Luke recognises him as the cute friend George was talking to at the bus-stop the day he and George met.

'What can we get you, man?' Malcolm asks, indicating the hovering waiter with a tilt of his head.

'Uh, just a cappuccino please, man,' Joe says. The waiter nods and withdraws. Joe peels off his sodden tracksuit top to reveal a skimpy basketball vest and muscular brown arms. Immediately the wet fabric is away from his skin he feels warmer and his spirits rise. 'Gimme some sugar,' he says to George, and he leans across the cluttered table to kiss his friend lightly on the lips. Ziggy quickly moves the candle so it won't set the hanging nylon of his vest alight. Joe sits back down, then looks round at the others inquiringly.

'This is Luke, Ziggy and Malcolm,' George says, indicating each in turn. There is general hand-shaking. 'This is Joe, one of my best friends. He's a dancer and dance-teacher - and he's due to be a father any day now.' He looks to Joe for confirmation. 'I haven't missed the main event and you've failed to tell me, I trust?'

'As if I wouldn't tell my fairy godfather the second it happened,' Joe says, smiling, just a little self-conscious at being outed as straight in front of a group of gay men.

'When's the baby due?' Malcolm asks. 'Is it your first?'

'Yeah,' Joe says. 'Two weeks now. To the day of nine months, that is, so it's only approximate: you know black people and time-keeping.'

'D'you know if it's a boy or a girl?' Luke asks, for many reasons thinking of a boy first.

'We could've found out when we went for the scan but we thought we'd let it be a surprise. Too much planning and definiteness...' Joe tails off with a slight shrug, unwilling even to speak the idea that too much forward planning provokes the fates and can bring on misfortune. 'Just a lot of yellow baby-clothes.'

'Do you have a preference?' Luke asks. And as he asks Ziggy thinks: *I am the firstborn son the only child*

*and male and there is a weight a great weight to that,
and it is a burden and a power. There are certain
energies that pass through me through my maleness,
energies denied here in this culture and in this fem-
inised time. I cannot believe you would not prefer a
son -*

'I really don't mind,' Joe says. 'Either is good. And
it's not like we plan on only having the one anyway,
so... Do any of you guys have kids?'

(Joe is no fool, he thinks to ask that question).

They don't, as it happens: none of them are fathers,
although there are connections with nephews and
nieces for some of them that are important. But these
things can't be spoken about concisely, and so they
aren't spoken about at all.

'How's Leonie?' George asks. 'Leonie's Joe's wife,'
he adds.

'She's doing really well,' Joe says. 'She's *big*, man.
But in a good way, you know? Kind of magnificent.' In
his evident love for her he is suddenly immensely
attractive.

Strangely he doesn't recognise either Luke or Malcolm then, and they don't for the moment recognise
him. It's true that his hair was in cane-rows that night
on the bridge, not shaved as it is now, and Malcolm's
hair was short and black, not orange and box-cut. Luke
didn't have a goatee back then, and was dressed more
hip-hop, less lycra cyclist. And George wasn't there,
and Ziggy wasn't there with his distracting sarong and
fluorescent-green Mohawk, and the fan he flicks like a
black bird-wing. And Luke and Malcolm had been
strangers to each other then, and had none of the
rapport of language or body-language that is so strong
in them now.

Perhaps too the surge of adrenalin that night carried the specific memories away as it receded, leaving

behind only general emotional impressions. Certainly none of them could recognise any of Malcolm's attackers now. *Except Del.* Nonetheless, and without knowing why, beyond his being George's friend, Malcolm and Luke feel kindly towards Joe.

The cappuccino arrives. Joe cups his hands around it reflexively although he isn't really cold. The rain is falling solidly outside, but has lost the smashing intensity of before. The waiters have closed half the glass shutters, leaving alternate ones open in deference to the night's still-intense humidity.

'So are you celebrating something?' Joe asks, taking in the shared dessert-plates, the accumulated empty glasses crowding the small circular table.

'In a way,' George says. 'Yes, yes we are.'

'What's the occasion?'

'Just meeting,' George says. 'Meeting lovers and friends.'

Chapter Eight

L uke sprawls diagonally across George's double-bed, the duvet pushed down to his ankles, face-down and nude. He rolls over, stretches and arches his back, his morning erection jutting. George's bed is low and wide, a futon-mattress on a cherry-wood box-base, a Japanese simplicity and harmoniousness of design that Luke likes. After two years of sharing sagging springs with Malcolm he finds its firmness surprisingly sexually energising. Idly moving his fist on his dick he wonders where George is, whether he might be up for some pre-breakfast love action.

'George, man?' he calls. 'You up?'

No answer.

The flat is silent.

But not in a way that makes him feel uneasy.

Yet.

Probably gone jogging, he thinks, plumping the pillow under his head and feeling lazy. It is eleven days since they met in Balan's the night of the thunder-storm. The scent of George is on the pillow-case: sandalwood accented by lavender, his aftershave; and behind that other, subtle human elements. Luke's heard it said that black men smell different to white men, though to him his lovers simply smell like his lovers, and in that sense he doesn't know how white men smell. With his dad, his brother Del and his mates he remembers beer breath, cheap aftershave, sour body-odor: generic smells. He doesn't think there is a difference; suspects it like the story put about at school that Japanese girls had their vaginas on sideways. And he's been with light-skinned – biracial – guys and felt no convergence of their scent and his own; felt no consequent recognition or cancelling of desire.

The thought puts him in mind of biochemistry and neurochemistry and how these things impact on the sweet subtle mechanisms of attraction. He's read that desire is pheromonic, that chemical response is the key trigger for arousal, the invisible truth that like pupil dilation reveals what claims in words can hide. There is a certain subliminal scent he needs that he doesn't, it seems, smell on men who aren't black.

These are the scents of my lovers, he thinks. And perhaps even more importantly, *these are the scents of my friends, of trust, of home.*

At times the question excites him: how can he have become imprinted to be fired with desire on this physiological level that is outside his conscious control, that being chemical cannot be the product of cultural conditioning, for a group of people he was never among, had at that point barely even met? Yet he had felt it, and later it had proved to be so.

Looking round his lover's bedroom Luke is struck - and not for the first time; this is not the first night he has spent here - by George's embeddedness in his environment. This is his home in a way that Luke has never yet had a home. Everything is anally tidy. The sisal carpet is freshly vacuumed, the leaves on the rubber plant and a large banana-plant are polished. Shelves are built-in. Prints and posters are in hardwood frames, not cheap clip-front ones. It is an older man's home: established, resolved. And it is the record of a life: most of the posters that crowd the walls are of shows that George has either danced in or choreo-graphed, or both, across the years.

Luke's eye is drawn instinctively to the cheapest, most hand-made-looking programmes and flyers, the ones he assumes have come from nearest the start of

George's career, when George was closest to Luke in age and circumstances.

One dog-eared A4 photocopy shows a young George with a large Afro standing next to a fine-boned, middle-class-looking white girl with long, very straight blonde hair. Both of them stare blankly out at the viewer, holding in front of their chests a banner on which is painted *Mulatto Aphrodite*. From the Afro and the age George looks to be in the rather grey photograph Luke reckons it was taken in the mid to late Seventies.

Luke himself was born in 1978.

That fact, and the fact that therefore George was a man and fully sexual when he, Luke, was a baby and his mother's breast was his whole world, interests but does not disturb Luke. To him George's Afro is just a look, and not a marker of the potentially overwhelming difference of years between them, any more than the wet-look Jheri-curled Mohican George sports in another, surely mid-Eighties poster.

This one is a large, full-colour landscape strip. Four male dancers stand in a line, posing and pouting in fingerless mesh gloves and black vinyl shorts in front of a brick wall on which has been sprayed *NF Area Wogs Out*. George is leftmost of the four. Turned sideways on, he looks out at the viewer with Kohled eyes full of secrets. His lips are glossy.

Next to him a shorter black guy in a vinyl trilby has kicked his leg up into a vertical split. His calf is braced against the curve of George's chest and George's hand grips his ankle. He is pretty, boyish and dark-skinned, and looks at George intently in profile. Leaning against him but turned front-on is a lean white youth with blond spikes bursting out from the front of his trilby, which is pushed back on his head. He wears a studded leather choker and pushes a waistcoat back off his bare shoulders to show off well-defined upper arms. Silver rods glint in his flaunted nipples. Next to him, bracing back against him and pushing his crotch out in a provocative silhouette, is a sulky-looking South American youth, eyes Kohled to match George's. The title of the show is *Tears For a Crown*, and scrawled over it in silver marker-pen are the dancers' autographs: George, Oliver, Jean-Pierre, Felipe, each name below its respective owner.

One of the few posters that isn't of a show George performed in or was involved with is for a commemorative exhibition of the work of Rotimi Fani-Kayode. In it the photographer's face tilts upwards, eyes closed, skin blue and flawless, features sculpted like a death-mask. Next to it is a print of George dancing naked, whirling long neon-orange plastic tubes that have been sewn into his then cane-rows to make a firework-bright pattern of lights. The image has an incised block mount on which is written in pencil, *R F-K 1983*.

'Wow,' Luke said when he noticed the lettering, the morning after the first night he spent at George's. 'You knew Rotimi Fani-Kayode?'

'Timi?' George said. 'Yes, I knew him, sweetness. Not well, just a little. He was a friend of a friend who came to a show I was in, and he liked my form.'

'It's kind of legendary to have been photographed by him.'

'Is it?'

'To me it is.'

'Then bless you, my dear,' George said, and he kissed Luke on the temple.

George invited Luke back to his flat for the first time after the meal at Balan's. The rain passed off at around one, and its cessation felt like a signal for the evening to come to an end. And Luke said yes without hesitation, thinking only afterwards about the risk of leaving his mountain-bike chained up in Old Compton

Street overnight.

The five of them had loitered in front of the restaurant for a while, not quite wanting the evening to end, restarting fragments of earlier conversations then not following through. The air was by then almost chilly, and their body-warmth slowly drained away as they shifted from one foot to the other, resisting goodbyes. At no particular signal from anyone hugs and kisses were exchanged and the evening was over.

Joe went to catch a night-bus west with Ziggy and Malcolm: it turned out he lived just five minutes' walk from them, in the direction of Latimer Road. George and Luke went to a nearby gay-run minicab office, and after only a short wait were driven down to Brixton by a pretty young dyke with a DA. In the back of the cab they kissed and caressed like teenagers. The night's streets slid by in a way that seemed to Luke almost magical in its effortlessness and privacy, and for the first time in his life he felt the freedom that is yours when you have just a little money to burn.

No waiting at bus-stops on empty train-platforms exuding fagginess magnetising trouble hatred violence towards you towards the one you are with No you glide past as if above. That he was experiencing now what he had never experienced before, the particular safety that wealth provides, both thrilled and angered him. *The protection I never had. The innocence I weren't allowed.*

And am I allowed this? This - future?

Most of his life Luke has lived eyes-down and one day at a time. It's a survival strategy often adopted by those poor and without hope, and it had worked, it had got him through. It had a price, of course, though he had never really understood what that price was; perhaps even imagined he had paid it already, in advance. But now, in the back of that effortless cab, with this man who opened something in him like a flower, he felt the full burden of attempting to control his life that way, and realised he had never really understood.

Ziggy had understood. Ziggy always understood. 'To avoid hope does not free you from despair,' he said to Luke some endless drunk, stoned evening, his words uncomfortable as splinters of glass. 'Denial is not defiance, it is not heroic. It burns up your spirit-head, and refusing to face where your life is going – or not going – is not the same as embracing the moment. Life is a donkey. It is not responsible for itself, it is on you to compel it. Be the whip. And crack it.'

Luke hadn't understood what Ziggy meant back then but he did now, feeling in the bone what before he had known only in his mind. A weight fell from him then, the paradoxical weight that is the refusal to take responsibility for your own life.

The cab turned into a curving terraced street, George's street, though Luke didn't know that yet, and anyway his attention was all on George's hand kneading his aching crotch. He spread his thighs as George kissed him on the mouth, tilting his hips to encourage George's fingers to probe the sensitive area behind his balls.

'Um, we're here, guys,' the cab-driver said, once it became apparent that neither of her passengers had noticed they'd reached their destination.

They broke off from their exploration of each other with difficulty, breathless and blood-rich and bright-eyed with desire. George paid the driver, Luke chipped in the tip, and George led Luke into the waiting house.

His was the attic flat. The blinds - expensive, wooden-slatted ones - were down in every room. Carefully-placed milk-glass lamps glowed softly on polished floorboards, and the skylights in the sloping ceilings gave onto the star-strewn sky above. In the living-room they kissed again, hungrier for each other than ever, and soon they were stumbling about as with near-comic urgency they tugged roughly at each others' clothes, stripping, almost ripping off tee-shirts and vests, yanking down shorts and briefs to liberate bouncing, tensile dicks, kicking off shoes, peeling off socks.

And as they moved against and with and in and out of each other Luke felt the mysteries strong in him, in them both, the mysteries of muscle, of sex, of skin and race and difference. He felt the particular mystery of male energy, its kinetic power building exponentially as his and George's mouths moved on each other's rigid, aching dicks; and the mystery of George, this particular man who he has met, who has met him. The mystery too of George as a black man, as a descendant of slaves, and what that means to Luke, both as himself and as a white man, descendant perhaps of slave-owners and, however poor he has been in this life, beneficiary of the trade in black ivory, as indeed and ironically George at times has also been the beneficiary.

Sometimes I feel so fucking false, Luke thinks. *I need my man to be black, I need that energy, I need that difference, but sometimes in the face of history my need, my desire, my love feel like thin, weak bloodless things because I should wish so much more that history had never happened and I don't. And I tell this to Ziggy like I tell him everything, I confess to him because he's him and I wanna be able to express it all to a black man, a black gay man, a black gay friend so no-one can say I never concealed nothing. And he understands me like he always understands me, and he says fuck history, fuck what can't be changed let it go, and he tells me you've got to work on your love and feed your fascination even feed your desire. 'Look*

at straight people,' he says. 'They have the biggest
mystery there is, Man and Woman, all the depth of
difference in that, the way it's connected to bringing
forth life, one and one makes three, that crazy miracle.
All that deep shit to explore. But it doesn't just keep
itself going. Women have to work 24-7 at being
women, waxing their bikini-lines, wearing make-up,
wearing suspenders and push-up bras, having silicone
implants to be really feminine. And men have to work
on being men, always trying to be in control, repress-
ing emotion, drawing the line at this or that colour,
this way of standing, speaking, cutting your hair,
policing the boundaries with gender sjamboks. And if
the two sexes don't continuously prop up their differences and keep on making man-woman interaction
glamorous with movies, music, art and books, then it
starts to fizzle out: the magic drains away and you're
just left with two groups of human beings who do not
like or understand each other regardless of the draw
of their different genitals.'

Another thing Ziggy said was a really deep thing
that made me feel strange inside. One night we was in
a club, Heaven, I think, or Queer Nation, checking out
men but also noticing things more generally, like who
fancied who, who we thought was going to fuck who,
the dynamics of attraction. And you know who I like,
and Ziggy, well, he likes the white guys so, different
from him. And we was watching and noticing how
many guys go for doubles of themselves. Like the same
style of dress, the same general cast of features, same
hair and, definitely, the same race.

It was one of those moments where I felt like what
it must feel like to be black in a white world. And
Ziggy said that people like me (and I think he meant
him too) are literally a different sexuality from those
kind of gay men, and I think he's right but it made me

feel strange because it was like saying we was nearer to being straight. Because we need the mystery of difference on that categorical level. I said that and he said, 'Don't worry about it.'

And then some attractive brother walks by and I check the Negritude of his profile and the curve of his butt and it's all in me again, my love for what Malcolm, my Malcolm, calls the sanctified butt and the miracle of melanin-rich skin, the miracle-coil of hair, the fullness of lips, the flatness of noses and smallness of ears, certain body-lines, and life, my life, means something to me again.

See, when I see two white men kiss, I don't feel included. It's what it is, gay, and yeah, I'm gay, but I feel abstracted from it. And that's the beginning of a bond between me and those who are not white, because it matters to me to see black men represented everywhere, and that becomes a sort of politics.

They make love on George's wide, wide bed, on freshly-laundered sheets. And George's dark skin against Luke's pale skin is a beautiful thing, it is alchemical, and in their passion, on that bed, in that room, they find a moment of simple equality, even though to George the contrast of their skin-tones is just one combination of the palette, is not loaded the way it is for Luke. But something in Luke reconnects George with energies deep within himself, because he overflows with the nowness of his life, and is filled with the sense that the balance is still tipped towards the shining future.

After making love that first time they had looked at each other with eyes wide open, frightened and excited and absurdly filled with joy. George's arsehole felt slack and warm and achy and good from where Luke had fucked him deep. He wouldn't normally give it up the first time he slept with someone, but with Luke he'd wanted it so badly that holding back had become impossible, senseless.

They dozed until late morning, eventually waking facing each other, sharing each other's breath. George reached up and toyed with Luke's dreads, which he now saw were painstakingly tied and knotted and glued. 'It must be work keeping them in shape,' he said.

'It is,' Luke said, enjoying George's attention. 'They're my one big pain-in-the-arse financial drain vanity. But worth it.'

That first time in the chair down Portobello Road I closed my eyes. The girl was Japanese, she wore Wicked Witch-type striped tights, a baggy tee-shirt with plastic neon studs on it, black and white extensions arching out from her head and hanging to her waist like a Star Wars alien. A nose-stud and a lip-ring. The other stylists as world-wide and heightened in appearance. You sure, she asked, pushing her hand experimentally through my thick ex-skinhead-hair hair I'd kept hidden under a beanie for six months. Yeah, I said, and I felt the hum of the clippers pass up her arm down the other one through her hand into the bones of my skull.

She shaved the sides first. It was a relief. Like but different from the skin ritual with Del and the lads. Different cos it was the beginning of a different turn, and also because of the where of it: a fag avant-garde hair-salon between shops selling Rasta bangles and Bob Marley and Tupac posters, opposite stalls laid out with sweet potatoes, okra and yams.

And Luke had closed his eyes as she plaited and knotted the hair on the top of his head, trimmed and tied the ends and fused in the golden funki-dreds. There was a muted burning smell, an altar-candle lit to propitiate the small gods of hair, though hair isn't a small thing: hair can get you beaten or killed – or laid.

The clothes had been the easy part: from BNP white-boy to Hip Hop National one garment at a time - albeit with a scary tipping-point in the middle, after which he could no longer have returned to his old manor even if he'd wanted to, because his visible new declaration of allegiance would have invited assault as much as if he'd dressed in drag.

The hair took his self-transformation further, and when he opened his eyes he saw as he had hoped a new self literally tied and fused into the old one, and was quietly ecstatic: yes, this was what he wanted. Not to be black, but to move towards it. To not be white as he had been white. Sipping the coffee the salon provided, finally he was on his way. The dreads cost a week's wages at the wholefood shop where he worked as a shelf-stacker. *My real hair.*

They were worth going hungry for.

'Some guys think it's wannabeing, though,' he says.

'And is it?'

'Well, it's my personal flavour, but... it's a homage, I guess I'd say that.'

'Like drag.' George tugs on one of Luke's dreads playfully.

'Yeah, man. And in kinda the same way drag becomes its own thing, don't it? I mean like a woman could do a look and you'd know she was trying to look like a drag queen, right? So white dreads are kind of a thing in themselves now too. Like crusties and beach-type white guys: you don't look at them and think they're trying to be black, do you?'

'And are you? Trying to be black?'

'Not no more. Just trying to show I'm on-side, you know? I did kind of used to want to. I felt like it would solve something, be a kind of harmony. But then the first time I was kissed – by a black guy, obviously – that answered it, you know?'

'Answered what?'

'That I could be who I was and still be – found attractive by who I needed to find me attractive.'

'Extremely attractive,' George said. And he gripped a handful of Luke's dreads and pulled Luke on top of him, and they kissed long and deep.

Later, after showering, they sat down to breakfast in George's kitchen, and among other things George asked Luke about the first time he'd had sex.

'That come just a bit after I'd left home, so I woulda been seventeen, maybe eighteen. Which was pretty late to be losing your virginity round my way, but...'

'Black and a he, I'm assuming?'

'Yeah and yeah,' Luke said. 'It's not much of a story, though.'

'The first time usually isn't.'

'So what was your first time like then, man?'

'I asked first, sweetness.'

'True-dat.' Luke dug into a grapefruit George had deftly segmented for him earlier. 'His name was Denver. I was club-crazy then. A club-crazy virgin.'

'So innocent.'

'Nah, never that.'

I wanked so much I never felt like a virgin I'd touched myself so much I was too hot and sticky and constantly horny to be pure and still held back by a choking inferiority which could be reduced to this self-imprisonment: I don't deserve what I want. I looked at the white boys with their tops off and their tits out and thought how easy it'd be to go that way, so many of them, so uncomplicated.

So empty.

Though why the fact of sameness should feel like such a nullity to him he couldn't say. Yet he felt this too: that his desire made him somehow epic. That simply to desire as he did was some sort of revolution.

He would blush to say this aloud.

Yet this is his politics, a politics that was at first as inchoate and unworded as his desire; that was articulated for him first by Ziggy and then Malcolm: the fusion of resistance - to homophobia, to racism, to the pitting of class against race by the masters, to the deep programming via religion of gay self-hatred – with love. *To change the world.*

And we try to never talk about self-hatred, he thinks, *for all the scars on our wrists, the damage to our intimate linings from swallowing pills and corrosive agents. Our tattooed pain is hidden in private places, like the rose at the base of Ziggy's spine you'd only see fucking or rimming his ass.*

So much inferiority though we don't admit it. Just turn our warrior faces to the world. I call that courage.

It was in Heaven, Luke's first contact, on the dance-floor. Luke was wearing baggy Sean John jeans gangsta-low, belted under his butt to blazon tight white Calvins; a skinny-rib vest with shoulder-straps and scoop neck constructed to emphasize chest and shoulders, the sculpted interlock of biceps and pectorals, Timbs on his feet, and a dark blue bandana knotted tight round his still-shaven head. *Get Your Freak On* was ramming the dance-floor, it was a hip-hop night so more brothers in the club than usual though still they were a minority. Until that night he had lived in an African-American projection of what it meant to be black, a Tupac-Fifty Cent romance, if even then cut with flashes of sudden joy - at the sight of Busta Rhymes in a pink crushed-velvet jumpsuit, say: a draw towards the enjoyment of what normally was only permitted to women, another defiance.

A hand touched his hip. He turned, unexcited, because what were the odds? – and found himself crotch to crotch with a pretty, ebullient and shaven-headed black youth who wore only a black lycra one-piece like a wrestler's leotard. *He was nineteen I was nineteen Dancing and a cigarette shared and JD and Coke shared and back to – Denver he said his name was – Denver's, and I finally felt real in the world as I kissed his lips as he pushed his tongue into my mouth as he sat on my face as I sat on his cock And yeah with rubbers despite that I was quite pissed and he got me to fuck him too and I loved it both ways from jump.*

The next morning Denver had had to get up early to go to work. They had shared a quick shower, a scrappy breakfast, a kiss on the door-step, and it was surreal to Luke to see Denver in a suit, though the way his trousers hugged his butt provoked Luke almost as much as the leotard had done the night before. 'Fucked me slack, bitch,' Denver said, breaking into a smile and tapping Luke on the chin before heading off to get his train, and Luke had gone to catch his bus fragrant with Denver's fragrance. Why hadn't he called him? Luke doesn't remember now. Perhaps because the split between before and after that night felt so absolute.

'Was it like you expected?' Malcolm asked him years later, one stoned evening when they were talking as Luke is to George now of first love, first sex. Later Malcolm would tell Luke of his first love, of running to Milton, and Luke would hug him as he cried.

'It was better,' Luke said. 'It was a confirmation.' And he didn't say, but might have: it was an earthly miracle. Because this is a sort of religion: this is where his faith is.

'And Denver didn't hit any myth-buttons for you?' George asks. 'Any fetish archetypes?'

'If you mean having a foot-long dick and me wanting him to Tyson-fuck me, no, man.'

'And finally having that real experience didn't drain

the attraction of meaning for you?'

'Funny, ain't it?' Luke said. 'Cos you'd have thought it might. That he weren't doing none of them cliché things someone white who fancies someone black is supposed to be looking for. Yeah, he wanted to fuck me, but he wanted me to fuck him too, so - But no, it stayed what it was before. Having that real experience changed it, but only like a change of perspective gives you a new view of the same exact thing so you see a whole lot more.'

'What Gerard Manley Hopkins might call the ground of your being,' George said.

'Who's he?'

'A poet.'

'Malcolm calls it my backbeat.'

George nodded. 'That's apt too.'

'What about you, man? Your first time?'

'Ah, that was so long ago I'm not sure I can remember,' George teased.

'Course you can, man,' Luke said, leaning over and kissing George's bare shoulder where his dressing-gown had slipped off it.

'I would've been fifteen,' George said. 'It was with my best friend, Lester. He would have been nineteen. We were both tough but we were quite flamey with it, so - I think we cancelled each other out sexually. It certainly wasn't romantic, more of a case of oh, why not? We were both there, and horny. It was mutual masturbation and some half-hearted oral. We didn't revisit it. But we stayed best friends.'

'What about love, man?'

'As in when was I first in love?'

'Or last love. Who were you last in love with?'

'My last love, my last definite, real, painful love was a dancer called Oliver.'

'What happened, man? If you don't mind me asking.'

'He died, sweetness. Nine years ago. On my birth-day.'

'Shit, man, I'm sorry.' Luke got up and went round the table and embraced George, holding George in his arms, a pieta. *I stand he sits inclining his bowed head resting it on my belly Let my warmth the pulse of my life heal him. Nine years ago was the year I ran I was seventeen. Oliver's ankle on George's shoulder his name silver in flamboyant loops AIDS I guess -*

The kettle, which George filled and switched on ear-lier, came to the boil, framing them in steam. Gently they let each other go. 'And you, sweetness?' George asked.

'Last love or first, man? My last love was Ziggy, five years ago. Really he was my first love too.'

'What about Malcolm?'

'He's always been more like a brother to me,' Luke said. 'I mean, he's good-looking and sexy and all that, but...' He shrugged. Explaining how he and Malcolm met was too connected with ugly things for this daffo-dil-yellow morning.

'You don't much like to talk about your past, do you?' George said, turning to make the coffee.

'Cos my main memories are bad,' Luke said. 'Like, where you grew up you were surrounded by shit, right? Bigots and whatnot. And you could say, I don't belong here, I ain't like these people, I'm better than this and I deserve better. But we *were* the shit.'

'Don't say that, baby,' George said. 'You were never that.'

'It's true, though, man,' Luke said. 'We were the shit and we were in the shit and we never did nothing heroic to get ourselves out of it. Where I come up it was just a lot of bone-arse idle losers shitting on about how white culture was getting swamped, like culture was this stuffed fuckin' dodo you couldn't add to. And they didn't mean art or literature or history cos they didn't know jack about none a that. They didn't even mean fish and chips cos it was curries every Friday night, fags from the Paki shop, sweet an' sour down the Chinky. Fuck knows what they thought they meant.' Luke's accent was stronger now.

'But you were different,' George said.

'I was still ignorant though,' Luke said, spooning sugar into his coffee from an ornamental bowl. 'Just, I noticed there was a hole in me.' The sugar-bowl was highly-patterned, deep blue with a gold rim, and one of a set. The others were displayed on a shelf above the fridge, flanked by cut-crystal vases with yellow silk roses in them. Other dishes and ornaments were placed or hung decoratively around the walls, and the cloth on the breakfast-table was lace. Unlike the rest of George's flat, the cluttered, colourful kitchen was intensely West Indian. Luke felt at home sitting there, as if George's culture was his culture too, and if this was not yet his home, already he felt welcome here.

'It's the weirdest thing,' he said, stirring his coffee, looking down into its shimmering blackness. 'You're living in this big-arse city and the whole world comes here and there's all that brilliant difference that's here to turn you on on a million levels. But if you grow up where I did it don't mean nothing. You stay in your manor and you act like that's an achievement. It's like whatsit, locked-in syndrome.'

'Not everyone can deal with the wide world, sweetness: it can be a scary place.'

'Yeah, but it's not just that though, is it?' Luke said. 'There's hate too.'

'I know, baby,' George said, and Luke fell silent because George did know.

'So tell me a memory of your childhood that's

happy,' George said.

'I've got memories, or I think they're memories, of being like three or four,' Luke said. 'If you know enough back then to know how old you are. Like, I think I remember feeding the ducks in the park. But it's more like someone else's home videos. Maybe half of the nice things I think I remember were just stuff I saw on TV and wished it'd happened to me.'

'You still haven't told me one actual specific thing from your past, sweetness, good or bad, except your booty-busting tryst with Denver.'

'I told you my alkie dad broke my mum's neck and he used to beat on us.'

'True.'

'I'm not playing games with you, man,' Luke said. 'Don't get pissed off with me cos it's hard for me to get it out.'

'I'm not pissed off with you, baby. I just don't get it, that's all.'

And Luke wanted to tell George everything, but he was so afraid of the past poisoning the present that he couldn't bear to start. *But maybe talking about it is the test: if I can speak it, if he can accept it, then I'm free. If not* - 'I told you I've got a brother, right?' he said. He had no idea where his words would take him, hoping only that with George's help he could shape his past into something both of them could use, or at least survive. 'Did I say we was twins?'

'No, you didn't,' George said. 'Identical twins?'

'Yeah. Well, we used to be.'

'What do you mean, 'used to be', baby? Did something happen to him? An accident?'

'Nothing like that, man. Just, I reckon your life ends up being written on your face: what you are and what you done. And the way he's gone and I've gone I don't reckon people would even think we was related now.'

Malcolm didn't. On the bridge. I never told him this.

'How do you mean?' George asked.

'We went opposite ways in our lives.'

'He's straight?'

'Far as I know. I mean, I ain't seen him in time. But nothing ever made me think he weren't.'

'Just they say that where one twin's gay it's likely the other one will be too,' George said, matter-of-factly.

'Not in this case, man. Well, or I doubt it.' Impulsively Luke reached out and took George's hand in his. 'Maybe we're mirror-twins,' he said. 'Cos everything one of us loves the other one hates. The opposite I meant is he's a Combat 18 neo-Nazi. My brother's a psycho racist thug who goes Paki-bashing and thinks white women who marry black men should be sterilised.' Luke said this quickly and almost brightly, the only way he could say it, almost like it was a joke, every nerve-receptor in his pale pale skin horribly alert and ready to detect the slightest shrinking away of George's fingers from his, but George neither let go nor tightened his grip.

'Oh, baby,' he said, a weariness in his voice that was surely the weariness of history itself.

'I'm not,' Luke went on haltingly, 'I was never drawn to that, that pathetic skinhead swastika shit. I mean, sometimes I felt like a pathetic urge to belong, but I never felt no hate. He did: he needed to hate something outside of himself to make himself real. Funny, ain't it? I needed to love something outside of myself.' Luke sighs. 'I don't reckon he can love at all. Because of our family. Our upbringing. Anyway it was in me before that. Who I love, I mean. Who I'm drawn to. It feels like it's always been there. So I'm the lucky one, I guess.' He smiled. 'And I don't hate myself no more. Well, not most of the time. Or not more than anyone else in this fucked-up world who's not oblivious to themselves and everything around them.'

'That's good, baby,' George said. And this time he did give Luke's fingers a small, reassuring squeeze.

'Can you - I don't mean can you forgive me,' Luke said. 'Because I didn't do none of those things and I got out as soon as I found the guts to break and run. It's more like...'

'Can I still see you as innocent?'

'Yeah. Well, innocent enough to - '

'To love?'

'Yeah,' Luke said. 'Because I love you, man. I'm seriously in love with you.' He hadn't meant to say that, but once it was out he knew it was true, and he was afraid. *Will he say who do I think I am to put that on him on – what? - our second date? Will he tell me I'm some know-nothing kid good for a fun fuck but -*

'You're saying you're in love with me?'

'Yeah, I am,' Luke said, a look of boyish defiance on his face.

George lent across the table and kissed him on the lips. 'I'm in love with you too, baby,' he said.

'White trash baggage and all?'

'Yeah, but don't take me for no porter, sweetheart,' George said with the ghost of a chuckle. 'I've got my own shit to carry.'

'I'll lug yours if you lug mine.'

'Deal.'

They kissed again, and to Luke the kiss had the taste of a welcoming-in.

Strange how someone can be afraid even when they know you love them, he thinks. George laughs easily but every once in a while Luke sees him catch himself in the mirror, discomfited by the laugh-lines that don't go, frightened perhaps that Luke will suddenly see the fifty years he has lived on this earth as an immutable obstacle, and be not so much repelled as simply detached from his attraction to George by the twenty-five years that will always stretch between them.

It's true that it is when George laughs that Luke is most aware of his age, but that's only because in most other ways George is ageless to him: there are no grey or snow-white coils of hair on his glossily-shaven scalp, and none on his shaved dancer's body either. He dresses youthfully, and is fit and limber enough to carry it off. And if he was moisturising his skin fifteen years before Luke was born the investment has paid off: it is smooth and flawless on his body: his age shows only in his face and hands, and Luke loves George's face and hands. He loves George's age as much as he loves his still-exuberant physicality; loves the connection it gives him with a certain history that feeds and fascinates him.

'But baby, what about *your* history?' George asked him when he tried to express that thought.

'I need a history to connect me with black people, gay people, black men, black gay men - and white gay men too, you know?' Luke said. 'All of that.'

'You need a history that puts your story at the centre. I understand that,' George said. 'But part of your history is your own personal biographical shit and what it evolved out of, and you have to deal with that too.'

'My parents were just pig-ignorant,' Luke said. 'They didn't have no history. They were a blank. Why'd you think my brother fell for the BNP and all that bullshit?'

'But you came out of that blank,' George said. 'It produced you, like it or not.'

'I suppose,' Luke said grudgingly. An intense need surged through him then, to immerse himself in

George's black male physicality, to penetrate George with his tongue, take George into his mouth, to give this black man, his lover, ecstatic pleasure and through his responses make himself real. Pushing his tongue into George's shaved arsehole frees him from the control of a past he loathes.

No-one ever told me to do this: this I freely chose.

My history, okay:

My father beat me up. He was a drunk and a self-ish whiner who thought the world or at least the Social owed him a living. But me, I'm one of Thatcher's kids, it turns out: Do It Yourself. On Yer Bike. Not owed nothing. Punk at heart, even if I missed it by a decade plus. Ziggy did too, but it was him played me old Sex Pistols records and told me shit about Thatcher and AIDS and Section 28 and the anger and queer resis-tance and politics what come out of them times. History I can use. Punks didn't act like they was owed. I liked that. Not like hippies: with hippies it was all flowers and nature and heterosexuality and then if they got sick they demanded the latest high-tech shit to sort it like they was entitled. I never thought I was entitled. If I ever deserved anything it began the day I run - the day I showed some bottle and made my life change. Then, maybe, I deserved something.

Sometimes I wonder if I'd be any good as a parent, I mean given what I had. Have I changed my life enough to turn shit into gold? What would I use to replace the shit? Books? Stuff off TV? Dreams? And would George even want a kid with me? Or am I his kid on some level? And then he thought, *He's fifty now,* and he thought about the decades ahead and felt strange. *Maybe he'd think I was too much of a kid to have a kid. And even though straights are dropping 'em at fourteen maybe he'd be right.* He tried to picture a child that would be a fusion of the best features of himself and George. He could imagine a boy or girl quite easily, but not, for some reason, a baby.

'What's Leonie like?' he asked. He and George were sharing a bath one morning. Luke was sitting behind George, carefully shaving his lathered head.

'Attractive, bright, self-possessed,' George said, closing his eyes as Luke passed the razor over his scalp, making himself trust. 'Not easy to get to know. She and Joe went to school together.'

'So they was childhood sweethearts?'

'Well, I should have said, 'went to the same school', because they weren't involved then. That happened later, after Joe started training as a dancer.'

'And that was in, like, ballet?'

'Which was when I met him. I was teaching the class. She would come and meet him afterwards.'

'If their kid takes after him it'll be very cute,' Luke said, flicking a line of stubble-speckled foam from the razor's head into the bath-water.

'Or her,' George said. 'She's rather lovely-looking. Are you done yet?'

'Nearly, man.' Luke quickly finished shaving the back of George's neck. 'Keep your eyes closed, yeah.' He scooped a jugfull of water over George's skull. 'Want me to do your eyebrows?'

'I think I'd better, sweetness.'

Luke handed George the razor, and, looking in the small extendable mirror by the bath, George deftly nicked their outer edges, enhancing their Vulcan sweep.

'D'you think you're gonna have much to do with the baby when it comes?'

'As 'fairy godfather'?'

'I mean, will she be cool with that, Leonie?'

'Why shouldn't she be?'

'Well, you know, gay men and kids. When it comes

to the crunch.'

And there passed through them both a sudden un-ease, a sudden fear that nothing is really let go of; that the loathing of the deviant is only ever repressed, and that what is repressed will always return. George stood up, reached over and pulled a towel from the rail. He handed it to Luke, who was also getting to his feet, and took one for himself. 'She'll be alright,' he said.

It had taken her time to get there. To accept his kiss on her cheek without a flinch. To be comfortable with his flamboyancy of dress and gesture. And although it was she who had invited him to their wedding, and had phoned several times beforehand to make sure he was coming, he felt that insistence arose from will not heart, and possibly out of behind-the-scenes pressure from Joe. Still, she *had* accepted him, as fully, it seemed to him, as anyone accepts anyone.

'What d'you reckon to two men having a kid?' Luke asked as they dried off.

'It can be a good thing,' George said. 'If they're both going to really commit to that being what they're doing with their lives. Otherwise they should get a puppy.' He considered. 'Though I would worry about the absence of a mother, especially with a new-born.'

'But being a woman don't guarantee you'll be a mother,' Luke said, memories of his own mother's hard, flat face flashing into his mind, glassy-eyed with drink and impassive as her husband beat her sons with a belt in front of her. 'I mean more than just pushing the kid out.'

'True.'

'But I bet Joe and Leonie'll be good parents though. Their kid's a wanted kid, ain't it?'

'Very much so, sweetness.'

'We can be the cool uncles, spoiling it and always getting told off for spending too much on gifts and shit.'

George laughed softly at the idea, and Luke experienced an odd counter-projection, imagining how his
life might have gone if in some impossible way Joe and
Leonie had been his parents, loving, good-looking,
artistic, progressive, black, wanting their kid, good
people full of modest dreams. *What sort of man would
I have grown up into? Not this,* he thought, and the
thought was strange and chilling.

A memory sprang into his mind then. 'My mum and
dad give me a radio for Christmas,' he said. 'There you
go, man: a happy memory.'

'How old were you?'

'I'd of been fifteen. Me and Del shared a room till
we was fourteen, then we got a transfer off the council.
Only to the block opposite, but it meant we got separate
bedrooms and we could wank in peace. It was that
Christmas. It was nothing special, second-hand cheap,
but...'

How could he express what that moment had
meant when in the privacy of his new bedroom he had
for the first time extended the silver aerial, pushed the
jack of the cheap foam headphones into the socket,
turned the dial and found forbidden sounds? In that
secret world he had discovered not only Kiss FM and
other commercial stations, and caught up with Boyz II
Men, Tupac, 50 Cent, Busta Rhymes and Snoop Dogg,
immersing himself in the minutiae of their West Coast-
East Coast beefs and particular African-American
hegemony of blackness, but also pirate stations that
came and went like ghosts, from which dub, old-skool
soul and funk poured into him each night as he drifted
off to sleep, headphones hugging his ears, dreams of
the Afrosphere.

One weekend in the town hall there had been a record fair and he had gone in – he would have been
sixteen then - and flicked excitedly through the catego-

ries: Soul, Funk, R&B, Hip-Hop – this before the catch-all deracialised category, Urban. There he found illicit visual thrills: Prince in bikini-briefs on the *Dirty Mind* cover; Rick James licking his lips provocatively, pvc bunched pornographically round the bulk of his crotch; Prince Charles of the Stone City Band, buff in fetish black leather; and a host of other bulging-crotched, snake-hipped funkateers in satin and lycra, studded leather and pvc, Afro'd, Jheri-curled, flat-topped and shaven-headed, thrillingly latently sexually open.

He had no record-player, and even if he had had one he would never have dared bring back discs with such self-revealing sleeves. Still, the simple fact of their existence opened possibilities in him. In the heat of his adolescence he never questioned that his response to the music was so entirely defined by the gender of those who performed it. And only later did it strike him that almost all those performers, all those black men were American, and that his sense of essential black-ness was therefore African-American. Reflecting on that began a certain evolution in him, a movement towards embracing the reality of where he by then was, with Ziggy.

Luke gets up and pulls on a pair of Speedos. He stands in front of George's full-length bedroom mirror, considers his reflection, and feels attractive. He always feels attractive when he's at George's. His cock stirs inside the Speedos. He imagines George kneeling behind him, pulling them down at the back and push-ing strong, lube-slick brown fingers up into him, making him moan and push his arse back and down as he yields, staring into his own eyes and watching the minutiae of his reactions as George slips a third finger in.

The telephone starts to ring, interrupting his fan-tasy.

He doesn't know whether to answer it. George has never told him not to, but still he feels uncertain: after all, he doesn't live here. 'D'you want me to pick up?' he calls.

No answer.

Luke knows the ansaphone isn't working; it's been broken since he knocked a glass of red wine over it last week. The phone keeps on ringing.

On the seventh ring he answers it.

'George?' asks a voice that Luke doesn't recognise. It is male, breathless, odd-sounding.

'No, this is, um, this is his friend, Luke.'

The front door bangs open.

'Is George there?' the voice asks.

'He's just coming in now. Hold on, yeah. George?' Luke calls. George comes into the bedroom wearing silky red shorts and a red basketball vest that is darkened with sweat. His aubergine skin is gleaming and the veins stand out in sculptural relief on his long, smooth legs: he has been out jogging in Brockwell Park before the heat of the day becomes too oppressive, leaving Luke to sleep in. 'Phone for you, man,' Luke says. 'Who can I say it is?' he asks the caller at the other end of the line.

'Joe.'

Luke is surprised: he's answered the phone to Joe several times before, and they've always chatted a little before Luke hands over to George. But something in Joe's voice this morning makes Luke pass the phone to George without another word except to say, 'It's Joe.'

'What is it, sweetheart?' George asks his friend, picking up on the frown on Luke's face.

In the still quiet of the room Luke can hear Joe's staticky, whispered reply, but not the actual words.

George's face sags as he listens. 'I'll come over right away,' he says. Joe says something in reply, and George says, 'Yes,' and hangs up the phone. Then he turns to Luke.

'The baby was born dead.'

'Shit.'

'Yeah.' George sighs. He and Luke hug, sudden tears starting in their eyes.

'I'll shower then go straight to the hospital,' George says. The sense of emotional urgency he feels is dissipated by the knowledge there will be nothing to do when he gets there. He thinks of Baron Samedi, *lwa* of the dead, protector of children. Dance-steps form in his mind, then fly apart. There is drumming.

He and Luke hug again, chilled despite the rising heat of the day.

'You want me to come?' Luke asks.

George considers, shakes his head. 'I want you to fuck me,' he says. 'Hard.'

Chapter Nine

Joe lies in bed, next to Leonie but not touching her, and stares up at the ceiling. *My wife*, he thinks. *My wife, my child.* He can't go beyond the symbols, not yet, and even the symbols make his tear-ducts itch and swell. *My son.*

Pride before a fall, George. Cos I thought I was better than you, man. Oh yes I did, behind my kind face. Because I knew that what I had, what I did was natural, was of nature. We were man and woman, our acts of love were creating life like they were supposed to. I knew we were centre-stage. However much I loved and respected you, I knew what me and Leonie had was the deepest, most valid part of human inter-action. And you used to say to me to never confuse nature with order but I did. And I watched people - friends of yours, although they were only faces to me - I watched them die, die of AIDS. And I felt so safe so fucking secure because that wasn't going to happen to Leonie or me. We weren't violating any order so we wouldn't get violated.

Strange what life makes you face. What death makes you face. In the world. In yourself. I thought Nature would keep us safe, how stupid is that? When Leonie got pregnant it was the right time for both of us and we were happy. She was healthy, I was healthy. There was no genetic deathblow, no un-wanted gift from our ancestors, no sickle cell, nothing like that. Nature and order. Order and nature. One and the same.

He stares up at the ceiling. In the half-dark it is en-tirely featureless. Leonie rolls over in her sleep, snuffling softly. Her hot, soft, bare arm touches his. He feels only a sinking in the pit of his stomach.

Nature doesn't care. Nature is wasteful. Nature is chaotic. Nature is meaningless. There's no God. My son was dead in the womb. I'm - we're - tested like who - Moses? No: his son was spared. Nothing more despised, more shameful than a barren woman, a woman who can't bring a baby to term. Except, of course, a faggot.

Now Joe is up against it. Now he is stripped of something he never knew he had until it was gone and he understands George as he never did before. Strange that that should be foremost in his mind tonight. An evasion, perhaps?

He slips out of bed and goes barefoot to the kitchen, not looking to his left because that's where the nursery is. Was. Is. In the colourless predawn hour, when the soul is least attached to the body, its being on the left seems somehow symbolic.

Don't let that shit get a grip on you, he tells himself, which is a piece of advice Ziggy gave him. Ziggy has an old soul and Joe feels as if he has known him for a long time. *Don't count coincidences*, Ziggy said. *Don't count cracks in the pavement.*

Joe takes milk from the fridge and drinks it straight from the carton, and that too seems both symbolic and not: an adult man drinking milk. He thinks of the fullness of Leonie's breasts and belches and feels slightly nauseous.

With death the event has already happened. There are a few things that have to be done, but only a few. All the rest is waiting. Not for anything in particular, just for the sharpest edges of your pain to dull, and the old perspectives to reassert themselves enough for you to carry on with your life.

A large, dark moth has got into the kitchen. It

bumps around noisily inside the ceiling lightshade. Sometimes it gets right up next to the bulb, clattering its wings frenziedly against the unbearable glass until, stunned by the heat and glare, it loops down and shoots off into some dark corner of the room to regain its strength. Joe feels a vague disgust at its activities.

He thinks of phoning George. It's five a.m. but he knows George wouldn't mind. Luke will probably be there, they're all but living together now, but Joe knows Luke wouldn't mind either. Both because Joe is George's friend and so, in that particular gay way, family, and also because Joe is black. Joe doesn't really understand why that should make the difference to Luke it does, but it doesn't bother him in the way it might have done before, back in the world of natural order and affinities he used to take for granted.

Not anymore.

It's worse for Lee.

But if he can't sleep, then he can at least not think about her pain as well as his own; he can be that selfish.

A son.

No, don't go there.

But it's already too late: just the word is too potent, too resonant. Even the gay men feel it, he knows. Every man has been a son. Every man wants to see himself replicated through his woman's body. Would he have felt the same about the loss of a daughter?

Yes.

No.

Yes.

It would have been different.

The milk sits heavy in his stomach. His head is aching and he is weary but restless. He moves through some stretches, feeling somehow old. *Child then adult then parent*: death has slammed two generations together in violation of that simple progression.

So fuck nature, Ziggy would say. But Joe can't accept the savage liberation Ziggy offers today.

Strange the way Ziggy has become someone important to him. And not just Ziggy: Malcolm and Luke too. Three men he didn't know at all a few months ago. Three men offering male nurturing. That they are gay is an incidental thing. Except in this, maybe: that they permit themselves a candour of intimacy straight men are not allowed.

The house feels stifling even with all the windows open in defiance of burglars. *What is of most value is already stolen.* Joe goes to the front door and opens it, hoping for some coolness, or at least a little motion in the air outside, but there is none. Still as brass the night-leaves furtively suspire, stealing oxygen, and the streetlights glare relentless as surveillance machines: it can't even be dark. He imagines walking out not looking back but knows he won't.

He imagines himself talking to George on the phone, but the image is purely retinal: the words they would be saying to each other he can't imagine. At one further remove he imagines having sex with George. Or perhaps more exactly, although the details are vague, making love with him. He has the feeling it might somehow be comforting, having attention flow towards him as his attention flows towards Leonie. He inhales the entropic air, a gesture only, closes the door, and goes back upstairs.

Leonie is now sprawled diagonally across the bed. Either out of compassion or from some other motive he doesn't want to think about, rather than disturb her he goes and sits in a small armchair in one corner of the room. From there he watches her.

At first he sits very upright. Time passes or doesn't pass. Slowly he sinks back into the chair and closes his eyes.

His dreams are confused, unpleasant and unmemorable. He wakes up more tired than he was when he fell asleep, but it is bright morning and there is nothing to do but get up. Leonie looks panda-eyed, bloated with sleep yet unrefreshed. They don't speak as they move through their morning routine, proximate but totally apart. It's not that they blame each other for what happened, but perhaps both of them feel that minimising their interactions now will somehow prevent the grief reverberating between them, magnifying until some avalanche begins.

Too, certain ancient patterns assert themselves: she turns to her female friends and family members for support, he to his male ones. He gets little he can use from his father, under the weight of whose disapproval he has laboured ever since he chose dance as his profession. His older brother is in jail; and his younger brother, five years his junior and the feckless baby-father of several children by several different mothers, none of whom he supports consistently, what insight or sympathy could he offer Joe in his bereavement?

His mother offered what she could. But sometimes the blood is too much: you are too known, in ways that don't help.

So Joe turned to his friends. To George first, and then and oddly to those new friends he had made through George on that rain-soaked night in Soho: Luke, Ziggy and Malcolm; them, and not the guys he grew up with, who still hung out around the Grove and All Saint's Road, his manor. Too many harsh jokes shared over the years, perhaps, too many put-downs. The most they could offer him in his grief and pain was a beer, a joint, and a very masculine lack of obligation to talk about anything that mattered. Which was not to be discounted, but it wasn't enough either.

The strangest thing that happened during that

numb time was this:

Leonie had gone to her mother's to recuperate from a haemorrhage, their own home being no longer a healing place for her. This left Joe, to his guilty relief, on his own for a couple of days. He called George and they arranged to meet that evening in a bar on Soho Square, but when he got there George hadn't arrived yet and Luke and Malcolm were there instead. It turned out that George had arranged to meet them earlier, then hadn't been able to reach Luke to put the time back. Joe would, should have been annoyed, but the moment he saw Luke and Malcolm without George he remembered: *The black guy on the ground getting his head kicked in, the white guy jumping in to help him getting battered too. We pulled over and peeled out with the speed of righteousness. Leonie watched it all If she'd met them she would have remembered right away but we were too dazzled with adrenaline and the image of our own warrior hearts.*

He almost said something but didn't. The talk between them was halting and awkward at first, but beneath it there was something strong and vital. And with sudden knowledge Joe realised that if anything or anyone is ever sent to us, Luke and Malcolm had been sent to him then. That they would be there for him as he had been there for them that night on the bridge. And it seemed to him that Luke and Malcolm felt that duty of reciprocation even if they didn't know why, because they gave him attention in a way usually only old friends can. Which is to say, with a lightness of touch that comes from deep understanding.

Joe sighs.

Leonie has copied a line from some old poem onto the kitchen pad, pressing heavily, the biro-point incising the sheets below: 'And all is dreary, dreary, dreary.' Joe has never had much use for poetry. Before today he would have shrugged a line like that off as banal, almost meaningless. Today it seems simply and exactly true.

He has to see George.

He waits in the living-room for Leonie to go out, as if to leave the house before her would be a betrayal. She takes ages, then slips out while he's using the toilet, avoiding goodbyes, kisses, plans. He spends half an hour cleaning the already-clean kitchen before going out himself, only calling George when he's out in the street, away from that contemplative, passive, female space where breath has stopped.

My son's breath.

Murdered future dreams pour through him as he waits for George to answer, battering him like the sea, cold salty eye-water, beautiful and ludicrous: his son would have been handsome, athletic, popular, intelligent, kind and sensitive and strong.

He was so small, so pale. So perfect. Dead.

'Joe?' George's voice is husky, warm.

'Yeah, it's me, man,' Joe says, trying to keep his own voice halfway up and bright. 'So, what you doing, me idren?'

'Just my stretches. How are you doing, baby?'

'Um, not so good actually, man.' Joe is suddenly close to tears. 'Uh, can we hook up?'

'Just give me half an hour to rise from the ashes.'

'Zat enough time, though?' Joe manages a half-smile that helps push the tears back.

'Don't worry bout yo mama.'

They meet at noon in Kudos, a gay bar off Trafalgar Square behind the church of St-Martins-In-The-Fields that is mostly quiet in the day. They arrive together, both on time for once, Joe on foot, George on Luke's bike. He is wearing a black lycra one-piece and a black do-rag on his shaved head. Round his neck is an antique jet necklace, and he has on plum nail-varnish: camp mourning. He gives Joe a hug, and to Joe he seems larger and more vivid than he ever has before, except perhaps the very first time Joe saw him, teaching stand-in for that ballet class back in the day.

Their hot, sweaty hug gives Joe a little of George's strength, the damp, dark highlights George leaves on Joe's vest traces of one man's body charging another, electrospiritual battery-contacts.

It was Joe who suggested Kudos, unusually for him as he doesn't particularly like gay bars. He feels perfectly at ease in them, and finds it easy enough to deflect the occasional pass, but he knows that, after all, they aren't for him, even though he has, at times, enjoyed flirting with other men. But that is precisely because he knows that nothing will happen; that he doesn't want anything to happen; and so it doesn't feel like he's being disloyal to Leonie in the way it does when he flirts with girls.

Perhaps Joe suggested a gay bar today because subconsciously he needed to get away from family, from nature, even from women. Perhaps especially from women because it is so much worse for them: the child, his son, dead inside Leonie's body. Her child, who has taken so much from her in substance and sustenance. Joe knows his mother feels Leonie's loss in a profounder way than he will ever do, even though he is the father and the husband, the giver of half the genes, the necessary seed. Next to Leonie's loss his own feels like placing an appeal for funds for a donkey sanctuary alongside one for Rwanda or Sierra Leone.

But still he feels it, and deeply, and it is a particular thing. And only another man, another man who is not his father or his brother, can really understand it, even though George, as far as Joe knows, has never got a girl pregnant or been a father. But George has had a lover die in his arms. Oliver, who Joe knew just a little. Who was a very good dancer. Who was too young.

George watches Joe with gentle eyes. He knows that Joe's older brother, the one to whom he should have been able to turn, is in prison; and that Joe's father has never respected his son's choice of profession, has always seen him as a failure, a *de facto* homosexual, and that this, the death of a son and heir inside its mother's body, will be to him another failure, another proof of Joe's lack of true virility. So George knows he must be father, brother and friend to Joe today.

There is a sofa free in the window and they take it. Joe stares out at passers-by but doesn't see them. He stirs his already-cooling coffee and takes a swallow that gives him no pleasure.

'So, how *are* you doing, sweetheart?' George asks.

'I don't know, man. Since the funeral - ' Joe sighs. 'Mostly in life you do something and then it's done, you know? There are consequences, and you deal with them as they come up, and there's some kind of sense and point to it. But with this you just have to carry on. Like the dead carry on being dead. And carrying on isn't even something you do, is it? It's just what happens. You're not earning anything by doing it. You're not building up anything. And then sometimes you're happy for an hour or two because you've forgotten, and shit, you know the rest of the world doesn't give a fuck about your pain, it just carries on, so you need to forget, you know? Just to keep functioning and make it through. And you know that nothing has ended for anyone else just because something's ended for you. And then you remember and you hate yourself for forgetting.'

'Don't hate yourself, baby,' George says. 'Never hate yourself. But especially don't hate yourself for being in pain.'

'No,' Joe says colourlessly.

George shifts along the sofa and takes Joe in his arms. Joe yields to him, closing his eyes as he does so. It is comforting to be in George's embrace, to rest his head on George's chest. Joe smells cocoa butter mingled with something lemony. George's skin is warm and slightly oily, and the stubble between his pectorals prickles Joe's cheek. Being there in George's arms Joe knows he won't cry. And being in George's arms he finds that at last he can think of his wife and not just himself.

After a while George feels the muscles shift in Joe's back and releases him from the embrace.

'Leonie's not doing so well, though,' Joe says after pulling himself upright. He keeps half-holding onto George's hand, not wanting to relinquish all contact between them.

'Well, it's a harsh thing, to go through a whole labour when you know that - ' George gestures ineffectually.

Joe nods. 'It's like everything's in reverse. You're doing all the right things but you're still going to be punished for it. No cigars, no smiles, no celebration, no relief. Just carrying out a medical procedure, and when it's done there's a coffin the size of a shoe-box waiting for your kid, who's doing everything a newborn should do except breathe.' He sighs. 'Sorry, man, I know it's a heavy thing to lay on someone over and over, even a good friend. Just, there's no-one else who I can really - '

'Sweetness, that's what good friends are for,' George interrupts. 'No apologies needed.'

Joe nods again, and falls silent. A couple – a Thai youth in a tight vest and denim short-shorts and a much older white man in an expensive suit – come in and sit down at a small table across the way. A waiter brings them a bottle of white wine in an ice-bucket and three glasses.

'Three glasses,' Joe says blankly.

'Yes,' says George.

'I just don't know what to do for Leonie, man.' Joe stirs his coffee again, then downs the contents just to be rid of them. 'It's like there's nothing I can do that will help, you know?'

'Do you believe in God?'

'You know I do, man,' Joe says. 'But not in a way that does any good. Like, we had - Leo - baptised, but that was more for my mum, and for Leonie's mum and dad, than for us, you know? Or for him. And it wasn't a hopeful thing, you know? It was more like you were stopping something evil from coming on. Like otherwise this kid, this innocent kid who didn't even have a chance to - ' He falters, kisses his teeth. 'Like if you didn't do it he would go to Hell, man. For no reason. Because of original sin. I mean, what the fuck's that about, man? Anyway, it was like having Leo baptised, was avoiding a curse, not doing anything good or positive. It made me angry. Just seeing the pastor going through the motions made me want to punch a wall.'

'Did you tell anyone how you felt?'

'Who *could* I have told, man?'

'Leonie?'

'That would've just turned it inwards.'

'She might have been feeling the same way, though.'

'Maybe. But I think for her it *was* protection. Like what she couldn't do for her - our - baby in real life. But why add on this whole extra level of shit? 'Your baby's dead. Now if you don't do this and that in church he's also gonna go to Hell for ever and ever, how about that?' I just felt it was sick, man. Vampiritic.'

George nods slightly.

'You don't have to say anything, man,' Joe says. 'It's not like I'm expecting you to come up with the answer.

Just I know – well, that you've had people die on you who meant a lot to you. You get it.'

'But this is different.'

'Still, man. People dying before their time.'

'Yes.'

Joe looks at George. *What if Leo had grown up to be a gay boy?* he wonders. *How would I have dealt with that?*

Well, gay would have been one thing, he thinks. *A thing that might or might not have been visible, a man-on-man not man-on-woman thing that could have been conducted on the Down Low not requiring nothing because never pushed up in your face. But a sissy kid – auntieman, chichiman - to be hated despised from whatever first revelation of effeminacy every hour every minute by your father year after year a heavy cross a bitter gall a corroding poison I had a taste of that though I could always say Yeah but I'm not a fag so fuck you. I wouldn't have done that to my son however he'd turned out. I'd have been proud of him. I'd have only ever wanted Leo to be his own man.*

And Joe finds he believes this is true, and is comforted.

A very fey East Asian boy with a slick DA sashays in, smoking a cigarette. He joins the other youth and the white man. The two younger men kiss on the cheek, then the boy with the DA shakes the white man's hand - or, more exactly, holds it briefly - before sitting down.

'Do you fancy some wine?' George asks, watching Joe watch the white man pour the boy with the DA a glass.

'Wine's for celebrations,' Joe says.

'And for commemoration.'

'Still,' Joe says. Then: 'I reckon I could go for a beer though.'

George goes to the bar and returns with a Bud for Joe and a white wine for himself. They touch glass to bottle in a silent toast. The beer tastes cold and clean to Joe.

A cloud passes over the sun. It is a relief. For a moment everything seems symbolic again. *But this reveals no truth*, Joe thinks. *My baby dies and it tells me nothing. There is or there isn't a God, is or isn't a higher purpose. And even if there is a God maybe He just let my baby die with a shrug like He does every day in Africa. Why should Leo be different? Why should a nigger in England be exempt? They were colonised and exploited, we were enslaved. They were exploited but they sold us. And now they're starving and we're here with colour TVs, Nikes and plump protein-heavy muscles, the sons of sons of sons of slaves. Rich by the world's standards even in inner city slums. Who can make sense of it?*

God?

And still my son is dead.

Is there nothing I can do?

Joe went out drinking with Ziggy one night, just the two of them, going from one straight bar to another – Ziggy's choices, not his - and on that night he felt Ziggy's Africanness and his own Africanness heavy within him, and Ziggy talked of firstborn sons and the death of firstborn sons, and said there were rituals, things you had to do, but the next day Joe couldn't remember what they were. He just remembered that whatever Ziggy said had in some way seemed right, and blessedly free of the perversity of baptism. And Joe understood that Ziggy lived in a world of spirits that were dark and strange and frightening, but also reparative and restorative, and on that sweaty, stoned and drunken evening that world made all the sense to him there was.

Something to do.

Because the dead are with us always.

The crossroads. The interpenetration of the worlds of the living and the dead. The Christian cross overlaid this, Ziggy said, a lie laid on top of truth.

The next morning Joe had been horrendously hung over and oddly confused, as if he was a character in a folk tale who one night had met a spirit in a country lane, and Leonie had been angry with him for being out so late without calling her.

'Typical male,' she had said. 'Out on the piss with your mates.' He had wanted to say no, he was consulting the *griot*, the *houngan*, he was out there with a fellow warrior on the hunt. But he didn't. He felt he had failed her, again. He sighs.

'There is something you can do, you know,' George says. 'For Leonie and yourself.'

'What, man?' Joe asks, feeling half as though George has read his thoughts.

'Make a dance.'

Joe thinks about this. 'But I can't choreograph,' he says. 'Not really, you know? Just shit for getting through a class. Not - *art*.'

'If you can dance, you can choreograph,' George says, both encouraging and merciless in his certainty.

'It ain't that easy, man, and you know it.'

'I can help you,' George says. 'I can make sure it all pulls together. But it's got to be from you: your seed.'

And there it is: the power of art. You can't do much but you can do this. Not just sit there waiting: make it into something. Maybe all art started off this way. Protective dances, rituals to control symbolically what humanity cannot control: death and pain; pushing hope out of the dead womb of despair -

Joe's face brightens. *Make a dance. Yes.* His eyes haze as thoughts dart through his mind fast and uncatchable as minnows. An energy he hasn't felt for weeks surges through him, the particular energy that is only accessed when your emotional life and your vocational life slide into synch. His posture lifts. 'Let's walk and talk,' he says, draining his beer abruptly.

'Yes,' George says. He takes a swallow of wine, leaving most of the glass, and they get to their feet.

'I've got a title,' Joe says as they make their way through Soho, heading for the western end of Oxford Street and Danceworks, where Joe is teaching a class later.

'What is it?'

"A Small Thing".'

'That's a good title.'

'I should ask Leonie first, though,' Joe says. 'It's her life too and she might find it too – personal. I mean, she gets art, she gets the idea of using your life to make art, but that's different from really, you know - '

'It's what we do, baby,' George says.

'Yes,' Joe says. 'Yes.'

They go into one of the discount music stores in Berwick Street, Mister CD, half-hunting for bargains, their minds abstracted.

'Luke sends his love,' George says out of that abstraction as Joe pays for a disc, Missy Elliot's latest.

'How's it going between you?'

'Well, I think,' George says. 'Very well, actually.'

'You sound like you don't quite trust it though.'

'In some ways it all gets harder as you go along. And he's very young.'

'Yeah, but you're young too, man,' Joe says as they leave the shop. 'I mean, you've hit the half-century but you're in better shape than most guys of forty or thirty-five even. And how many men can do the splits whatever age they are, you know what I'm saying? Can *he* do the splits?'

George laughs. 'No.'

'Well, so what you worrying about, man? The sex good?'

'Very.'

'And *he* loves *you*?'

'He even says he loves my feet.'

'*That*'s dedication,' Joe says. 'And you love him?'

'Yes.'

'So...?'

A van passes. They cross the street behind it.

'You worried you don't have enough common ground?'

'It's hard to express exactly.'

'Is it cos he's white? I know you've dated white and black guys in the past. We've never really talked about that, the difference it makes.'

'Well, you dated black and white girls before Leonie. Did it make a difference to you?'

'No, but - it could have, you know?' Joe says. 'If they'd had an attitude. I mean, whether they were black or white. Like when you get black girls who think you've got a duty to be with them because you're black, or white girls who fancy a jungle-fuck and that's it. But mostly they were just girls and you had to deal with them on a girl-by-girl basis. And maybe the difference between men and women is bigger than all the other stuff anyway, race, class, where you're from. I don't know. But you're bouncing me off, man.'

'Luke grew up on a very white, very rough council estate not knowing any black people,' George says. 'But then he left it, and now his two closest friends are black, and his lovers have always been black. So there's an odd kind of romance there he can't really explain. Not even to himself, I think.'

'Zat bother you?'

'It would if he had a head full of stereotypes. But he

doesn't, so - '

'Can I say something personal, man?'

'Why stop now, baby?' George forces a smile.

'Maybe you don't think you deserve someone who ticks all your boxes and is sort of societally-approved at the same time. Like, Luke's young, fit, good-looking, your kind of straight-acting, white and blond. *And* he's in the arts, and he's interested in you and your life and experiences.'

'My friend Lester said the same thing. But then I'm wondering too, how well our lives could possibly fit together.'

'Well, why shouldn't they, man?'

They are outside Danceworks now. George shrugs.

'It sounds to me like what you're wondering is, can he be a comrade?'

George thinks for a moment. 'You know, that's exactly it,' he says. 'It sounds so Sixties, but that's exactly what it is. And I think he can. But I'm not sure.'

'So follow your advice to me, man. He's an artist, right?'

'A painter, yeah. And a good one, actually.'

'So connect through art. Work together on something.' Joe glances at his watch. 'I better go in and shake my tail-feather. I bell you later, a'ight?'

He gives George a quick, tight hug then hurries inside. There is a lightness to his movements that wasn't there before.

A comrade.

George gets out his mobile, scrolls to Luke's number and presses 'OK'.

Ten minutes' walk away Malcolm and Ziggy sit side-by-side in the reception-room of a doctor's surgery in Harley Street. They hold hands. Both of them stare at but don't register the pastel wildflower prints on the wall opposite. Any view from the window between the prints is screened out by a translucent blind. The room is stuffy and there is an antiseptic tang to the air.

So you're waiting for the results, Malcolm thinks. *Luke and George were tested last week and they were okay and you're glad they're okay but them being okay only adds to your dread because there's a symmetry, a balance of forces at work in the universe and there's only so much luck to go around. Good luck, that is. You sit holding hands in the waiting-room of the surgery feeling very gay and very black, the crooks of your arms aching from the puncture-hole the needle made in your skin, your eye caught repeatedly by the small round plaster that, being a lurid pink, not even Caucasian flesh-colour, fails to conceal the invasive procedure you've just undergone. You half-resent the £120 you've paid between you to get a fifteen-minute test done,* payment upfront please, *but socialist radical or wannabe revolutionary you're also so fucking thankful there was a way you could cut an NHS week's wait down to that and save yourself at least some of the torture, even if it turns out you're positive and it would have only been the torture of truth deferred. At least there are drugs that work now it's not flash-flood death like it was it's a slow-motion crawl and pills pills pills with side-effects Oh fuck -*

And Ziggy thinks: *Joe's son Leo (Sun) firstborn I am the firstborn Dead to my family Dead as I really am Faggot Generation-slayer Unnecessary Disposable. Leo solar sun son black sun black son radiant blackness You are my twin My psychic twin. There are things that must be done so his spirit can rest I look in the mirror and see his reflection in my face The dead are always with us within us. Is his death now in my blood? Is that what I feel and fear? Obatala give my hands the power to make art. To do what must be done. To speak for the dead not from the dead.*

'Ezekiel?'

Ziggy looks round. The doctor has a kindly expression but it's only professionalism. Behind the glitter of his glasses his eyes do not admit to empathy. Ziggy gets to his feet uncertainly, feeling like a faggot and a freak.

Even money does not buy respect-o.

Malcolm watches with large eyes as Ziggy follows the doctor into his consulting room, his mind blank as the door closes on his lover. He has no new thoughts to think, and the old ones are temporarily frozen by dread.

To surviving. A toast that seems so long ago already.

Were Luke and George this afraid? *Had they been as foolish as Ziggy and I have been?*

Yes. And yes.

There is no music in Malcolm's mind now, just noise like a radio jammed between stations. There are shapes in the noise, and they are ugly. He clears his throat and the receptionist gives him a quick, kind look. He hates himself just a little for being grateful for her kindness.

The minutes inch by. Ziggy comes out of the consulting-room. He looks sick but his chest is swelling. He crosses quickly over to where Malcolm is sitting and sits down next to him.

'I'm okay,' he says.

Still his face is full of dread. Malcolm understands it: the dread that he, who's been drunk and careless, who's sold sex, who's been a junkie, or almost a junkie, will have used up all the quota of luck the gods have assigned them, and that it is Malcolm who will have to pay the price for that reckless over-consumption. Perhaps too Ziggy can't help but believe that fags don't deserve love, or happiness, and that the mechanisms of god or fate or epidemiology will destroy them wherever these things seem to be found.

'Malcolm?' The doctor reads his name off a clipboard. Ziggy takes Malcolm's hands and gives them a reassuring squeeze. Malcolm gets up and crosses the room. His heart starts to beat arhythmically. An odd riff runs through his head, very fast and not pleasing to the ear, a formidably complex series of staccato permutations with an edge like a scream.

The doctor gestures for him to sit. Malcolm sits. The doctor closes the door, goes over to his desk.

'The test I performed on your blood sample contains no antibodies for HIV,' he says, showing Malcolm a flat rectangle of glass into which his blood has been injected. It is a clear, fake-looking red. 'If it had contained antibodies for HIV, crystals would have formed,' the doctor continues. 'Since there's no ambiguity in this result I shall now dispose of the spare sample I took - ' He drops another rectangle into a sterile bin. 'Have you had unsafe sex in the past three months?'

'No.'

'Good. If you had, any infection you might have picked up then wouldn't show up in this test, okay?'

'I understand.'

And now the screaming, fluid music in his head has a title: *Death Crystals*.

Back in the waiting-room he hugs Ziggy.

'Clear,' he says, although he knows Ziggy already knows, could feel it in the pattern of energy in his musculature as he held him. The receptionist looks at them out of the corner of her eye, but benevolently.

They leave hand-in-hand and free.

When George gets home he finds Luke sitting cross-legged on the living-room floor. Four or five newspapers are spread out in front of him on the polished beech boards, and he's studying them intently. His mobile sits beside him, unanswered.

'Hey, sweetness.' George dumps the bike-lock and his pack down by the door. He is shiny with sweat from cycling back from the West End in the summer heat.

'Hi, man,' Luke says, not looking round.

'You didn't answer your phone.' George hooks the damp lycra one-piece off his shoulders and rolls it down to his waist, enjoying the feel of the slightly cooler air inside the flat on his bare skin.

'Sorry.'

Luke keeps on staring down at the papers in front of him. His back is tense and hunched.

'What's wrong, sweetness?' George asks.

'This.' Luke gestures at an article in one of the papers.

George sits on the floor behind him, fanning his legs and sliding himself into position so his crotch is pushed up against Luke's butt. He wraps his arms around Luke's waist, hooks his chin over Luke's shoulder and scans the newspaper-pages for whatever it is that could have troubled his young lover so much. Half of him wonders if it'll turn out to be something trivial or sentimental, but the other half is uneasy as his eyes move from headline to headline.

It takes him a while to find what he is looking for, the one story common to both the broadsheets and the tabloids. It isn't front-page news.

'Not our area anymore,' locals complain following violent attack on refugee.

Council Housing Policy on migrants 'to be challenged in High Court' in interests of community cohesion.

Asylum-seeker dies in hospital.

George is aware of the prelude to these loosely-connected headlines. A week earlier Yusuf Mohammed, a twenty-two-year old Somali asylum-seeker (or refugee, or economic migrant, depending on which paper you read), had been beaten into a coma by a gang of white youths outside a chip-shop on an estate in East London. The attack had happened next to a block where many Somali refugees had been housed by the local Labour council, creating among poor whites the belief that scanty resources would now have to be competed for with the newcomers. White resentment had built up, fuelled by the activities of far-right groups like the BNP and Combat 18, and violent incidents such as the attack on Yusuf had become too commonplace to be front page or even page two news, except in the local papers.

Towards the end of the week four members of the gang who allegedly carried out the attack had been arrested and charged. On a news report George had only been half-watching they had concealed their faces from the cameras by pulling their sweatshirts up over their heads, the comic, Muppet-like effect that seeming headless produced undercut by the swagger of their walk. Luke had been out of the house at the time and George had been doing something, fixing supper maybe, and hadn't registered their names. Why would he?

Today he does. They're printed below grainy, skew-angled CCTV-derived stills. One name stands out to him, one surname: Bourne. Derek 'Del' Bourne. And a blurry photograph that you'd never mistake for Luke in a million years, even if he shaved off his blond dreads and his goatee and worked up a double chin, because it turns out he was right: how we live is marked in our flesh, so even twins can cease to be identical. But still -

The story is news today because late last night Yusuf Mohammed died without regaining consciousness and the four are to be charged with the comparatively new offence of racially-motivated murder. If found guilty, it will add to the severity of their sentences.

'Oh, baby,' George says. Suddenly the weight of the world is on him. He fights a sudden impulse to withdraw from Luke. From white Luke, the nigger-loving brother of the nigger-killer. For a moment it would be easy to do that, to protect himself from that involvement, that impurity. But Luke is his lover, and the love between them is a fact as much as any other, a counterweight. George sighs.

'Yeah,' Luke says, his voice catching. He clears his throat but doesn't say any more. Right now he has nothing else to say. He slides the tip of his tongue over the bridge that conceals the loss of his right front tooth. *You can say it's not yours,* he thinks. *You think you can escape from it. But it claims you anyway. Blood.*

Powerlessness overwhelms him. Only George's thighs and arms around him stop him flying apart. He feels a sudden impulse to beg George to fuck him brutally, to punish him physically and symbolically with his cock, and that impulse disgusts him: as always, Del contaminates him. He feels rotten from the inside out, and has to struggle not to pull out of George's embrace, so unworthy of it does he feel. He wants to beg George to love him even though he knows George loves him already; as if the idea of begging for love would be symbolically liberating, because liberation must be both actual and symbolic to be complete.

'What are you going to do?' George asks, rocking Luke gently back and forth.

'I don't know, man.' Luke says. 'What is there to do?' The rocking calms him a little.

'That depends on what you feel, baby.'

'You mean do I feel like he's family? Or *I'm* family? Do I feel like I've got to, I don't know, show up at the court, sit there through it and...'

'Be a witness?'

'Well, yeah. Not like a giving evidence witness, a witness to a bit of justice. Well, what's supposed to be justice. Or a bit of family history. Of my different families, you know? Chosen and not chosen. *Un*chosen.' He almost smiles. 'Fucked up, ain't I?'

'Not especially, baby.'

'No?' Luke says. 'Well, maybe not, man. Maybe I'm just ordinary. But I don't know if I could go there and just - watch, you know? Because he is my brother, ain't he? My twin. My dead twin, in a way. You know something?' Luke twists round to look at George and his green eyes are vivid. 'When Ziggy found out I was a twin he said it was like a big deal in traditional African beliefs. In Vodou. Like there's a power in it, in being one of two, exactly the same, or mirrored, like I am with Del.'

'Power for good or bad?' George asks, only half-seriously.

'Just power,' Luke says. 'It can go either way, I guess. Like electricity can be a toaster or the electric chair. But knowing we - well, we come out the same egg, the same exact sperm, the same fanny, that's weird shit and it makes me feel - dirty, you know?' He shakes his head. 'Funny, ain't it? Being with another man, making love with another man, fucking arse, being fucked, that makes me feel clean. But this - ' He kicks out at the spread papers, sending their pages scattering. A topless glamour-model flies into the air then slides back down, landing face-up in front of them, smiling brightly. She's just turned sixteen.

'Don't tear yourself up over what you can't do anything about, sweetness,' George says, echoing what he said to Joe earlier today. He nuzzles Luke's neck. There are traces of citrus and cinnamon on his skin, George's own scents, freely shared. He feels a strong, bittersweet compassion for Luke. *Where are our connections strongest? Can we avoid betrayal?*

'I wonder if the boy they killed was gay,' Luke says disconnectedly, arching his head back and closing his eyes, inhaling George, his relief at the intimacy between them so overwhelming as to be almost unbearable.

'Is there any reason to think so?' George asks, nipping Luke's earlobe gently between his teeth, his voice warm and resonant in Luke's ear.

'The first way I saw him was in that headline,' Luke says. "Asylum Seeker Killed'. When I read that I thought, what a shitty planet, you cross half the fucking world and end up getting murdered by racists. And maybe your country was fucked up by white people and that's why you had to leave in the first place. But then I saw he had this like Islamic name and I thought, well shit, Muslims ain't doing nothing good for gay people in the world, so - I felt cold about it, you know? Even a bit - nasty. Like, plus this, minus that. And then I saw he was African and - fuck, ain't this the shallowest, man? - he was kind of nice-looking too, and I felt for him again. Like I was on his side when maybe a lot of people weren't going to be for that exact reason. I mean, him being black, not the good-looking bit. And *then* I thought, well, he could of been gay. I mean, why not? A gay Muslim. There must be a ton of 'em. And that's a cross, ain't it? Or, well, not a *cross*, but you know - he could be all those things, Somali, a Muslim, a asylum-seeker or a refugee or a economic migrant *and* gay. And we won't never know the truth of that, cos even if he was gay no-one'll want to say. They wouldn't reckon it'd make no-one shed more tears for him, would they? I guess I feel like if he *could* be gay then he's family. Like Del ain't. You know?'

And as he says that Luke remembers Malcolm's words to him: 'You're at least a part-time nigger, my

Nubian. And that's not a job you can quit.'

George kisses his temple. 'You're family to me,' he says.

Chapter Ten

*T*he graves weep. Oh my country that I have never seen in adult life. Oh my Orishas. It is in dreams you come and in dreams I wait for you. I wear iron on my chest and metal round my cock and balls for Ogun the warrior, I wear a quartz crystal around my neck for Shango against the lightnings in my head. Sometimes I think you speak to me. Sometimes I think you cannot speak because you have been confined within a weeping grave, the stone pressed down and weighted heavy-heavy with Bible and Koran bullshit the stone blinding white under a blind white sun. I close one eye and squint and see coffins carved and painted like carnival floats, this one an airplane, that one a Cadillac for a big man, here an orange crab for the dead man was a fisherman. What would my coffin be? A great curving cock of ebony?

I want to reach out to Malcolm. He is offering me his hand and I need his strength so much. But I cannot take it. There are a thousand rules that prevent me. I do not know who made them. They penetrate me like radiation, like isotopes. I try to slow my mind's decay by staring at the wall If I stare hard enough it may work if I turn my eyes to stone Petrification is resistance -

Do not try to decode. It is not susceptible to logical analysis -

It's earlier. I am comforting Joe over the loss of his son. My family lost their son too, to faggotry. I am someone else even though I look like myself. Sometimes I am dead but when I am alive the Orishas keep me strong. They know what has to be done. They do

not care that I love men: they understand. I do not tell
Joe that there are certain things you must do to stop
the spirit of the dead one troubling your house because
he won't want to hear that, he might even want to
cling onto it to keep some contact with his dead son
although it can cause sickness and even death for him
and for others. And truly I think that a spirit is troubling his house because he never wants to be in there
with his wife and he cannot sleep. I stay up three
nights carving a death doll for him. I make it elegant
so he will have it in the house, so his wife will allow it
in her house. She is a Christian. It will protect him, it
will protect her despite her beliefs, because of this
power of mine. I am an artist, I can do this.

My intensity disquiets Malcolm.

My mother is sealed in her Christian grave on her
long wait for world destruction and bodies getting up
and going back to where they were. It is so unreal. My
parents' faith gives me nothing for this. God moves in
a mysterious way is all they can say. There is nothing
you can do for your dead child. God wanted your child
dead. God is good. Praise His name.

In Vodou there is always something you can do. I
do what I can for Joe, something that is worthwhile
when others are wringing their hands and crying. His
wife senses I am doing something she does not understand and she does not like it because she can feel that
I am giving Joe something that she cannot. Maybe for
the first time she wonders if he has sex with other men,
seeing that we are sharing something, seeing my hand
gripping his hand and his fingers closing reflexively
around mine. Maybe he does have sex with other men,
I don't know, but I think that she had never really
wondered about it until that moment. I give him a
metal pendant to wear. Symbol of Ogoun, the warrior.
For protection in the fight. He puts it on at once,

ignoring his wife's eyes on him.

I sense the dead child Leo. He is a twin to me. Luke has a dead twin. Dead to him. Such living dead are dangerous, both physically and spiritually.

There are things that must be done.

When I was a child my grandmother told me stories of spirits and charms and things found in your house that meant you knew a curse was put upon you. Witches who come into your house as black cats. Snakes that vomit money and demand the sacrifice of a loved one as payment, and people know that in advance but still pay to keep them. My mother scolds my grandmother. 'Don't fill his head with that witchcraft nonsense.' I am left with puritan Christianity and bourgeois materialism, longing for the spirits to come to me.

And they do.

I never speak of this.

I am not stupid-oh.

They will take you away if you speak of this.

They took me away anyway.

No no no, it is not you who is taken away. It is everything else: freedom, clothes, music, books, sex, everything. TV where you choose what channel to watch. Even your name is taken. I am Ezekiel here. I do not tell them I prefer to be called Ziggy. I would not prefer them to call me Ziggy. I would prefer to be elsewhere.

I do not tell them that.

I say I understand I am here for my own good.

When they ask why I did what I did to end me up in here I say it is confusing and I cannot remember. I say the pills help when all they do is cut off my connections. I need my connections to heal myself.

But I have to admit something is broken, it is true. Something inside my head. I was wearing metal, more and more metal all over my body. Metal and mirrors, tied on with string or taped rippingly to my skin with duct-tape. I wasn't coping. One of their words. But that is a different thing from the spirits. The voices are different from the spirits. The spirits protect me from the voices. The pills divide me from the spirits and the voices get worse even though they are silent.

Cutting helps when the spirits are not allowed.

When I was taken away, though, I did not cut. All my thoughts were 'do not cut' because I knew that if I could achieve that one thing, not cutting, then I would be allowed back into life. I was a zombie but I didn't cut myself. I drew cuts on paper but I made them decorative. I kept them secret. I didn't use red. I told my doctor they were motifs from African skin scarifi-cation rituals. This only half-pleased her, but she was worried about being seen not to understand my culture, to be a racist, so she didn't make any marks against me in my file. No scars there. No cuts. With her I talked in a put-on Nigerian accent I took from my grandmother. I thought if I didn't sound so English then she wouldn't judge me so much by English standards of what is mentally healthy.

That should have been a joke, but wasn't.

In there, though, it was all jokes, all games. Acting. Performing. It was all about being super-normal in a way no normal person would be if he or she was locked up. You had to learn to perform in a manner considered normal by the people who hold the keys in order to get out. You had to learn to perform as if you weren't performing, as if you were sincere. Sincerely normal. You retreated behind one glass wall then another then another but you kept the glass so clean it was transparent so they wouldn't know it was there. No fingerprint-smears, no chips or cracks. No give-aways that you were faking it, that you were only as *sane as everybody else who is walking free in the streets.*

It is before.

They are hammering at my door.

It is four a.m.

I shout to drown the hammering out. It is outside and inside my head at the same time. I don't know if I am only shouting inside my head or with my mouth as well. I don't know how long things have been going on. I keep thinking there is one thing that if I could do it would make my mind clear. If I could just think what that one thing is but I can't. My thoughts go on and on. I smash the mirror and tie the pieces to my body. Here and there I am cut but it's not about self-harming, the blood is just a by-product of protecting myself, making myself invisible to Them, the ones who are hammering on the door now, who have been hammering for a long long time, since, ever since -

I am at school. They are hammering at the door. A chair-back rammed up under the handle blocks it but it can still be forced open by strength. I pull the sheets up over my head. The boy in the bunk below mine pulls the sheets up over his head too. He is Bengali. He is afraid. I am afraid. They are hammering at the door and yelling things. Our faces are covered like shrouds like we are already dead I am fourteen years old Damballah I will cut myself for you I will give you blood protect me Legba protect me. They are hammering at the door. I know what they want to do. I am the only African boy in the house. He is the only Bengali boy in the house. Perhaps he has gods too.

I walk the streets in metal and mirrors. I wear sunglasses with one lens pushed out. I see the spirit world and the physical world, one eye for each.

Sometimes I am button-down and normal. But this is when I am most controlled by the things outside me.

It is like being a deep-sea diver in a metal suit, waiting for the glass face-plate to crack and the pressure to rush in and crush me and make my eyes explode. The spirits are the oxygen tube to the surface the sun and sky.

Things get in. Electro-chemical misfires, synaptic ruptures, neurological dysfunctions occur. Protect me from them, Damballah.

I could never explain it is the spirits that keep me sane.

What would *my coffin be? A split skull?*

Malcolm, Malcolm. I must let you in.

Ziggy starts to cry. Tentatively Malcolm touches his arm *Fingers like penetrant entities bone-knives inside No stop this Let him heal this flesh rebuild this temple Yes Damballah* – Ziggy shifts round and lets Malcolm hold him, pushing his face into Malcolm's chest and sobbing uncontrollably.

Malcolm can feel Ziggy's tears hot and wet on his bare skin. He rocks Ziggy as George rocks Luke on the other side of the city. *When did this begin*, he wonders. Luke had told him Ziggy was crazy but Malcolm hadn't believed the word meant what it meant. He had thought Luke just meant drink-and-drugs crazy, or existential-void crazy, not spiralling-into-mania crazy. And Malcolm had been so happy. So simply happy.

Two weeks ago, on a crowded bus, sitting upstairs at the back, heading home, Ziggy's arm draped round his shoulders in an easy half-embrace. Malcolm leaning into him in a way no two straight male friends would ever do. A black man with cane-rows came up the stairs, sat a few rows in front of them, rode for a couple of stops, then got off. As he passed Malcolm and Ziggy his eyes met Malcolm's and he shot Malcolm a look of venomous contempt.

He was gone before Malcolm realised it was

Marvin.

Before, Malcolm would have shrunk under Marvin's gaze, or the gaze of any seemingly straight black man. Now he realised with a sudden, almost shocking excitement he didn't care. It was at that moment that Malcolm knew he was in love with Ziggy, and he turned and kissed him on the lips with simple naturalness.

Perhaps because it was such an unusual sight, two black men kissing on the mouth in public, no-one on the over-full upper deck of the bus said or did anything. A freckle-faced mixed-race teenage boy with a light-brown afro shot them a blushing glance as he went down the stairs, his eyes bright with something. Every-one else carried on as if nothing out of the ordinary had happened. And of course, they were right: it was just an everyday miracle.

Charmed days followed. Malcolm made music, Ziggy painted and sculpted fetish figures that were full of colour and vitality and, it seemed to Malcolm, and for once Ziggy didn't deny it, African essence. They idled in galleries and bookshops and second-hand clothes-shops, around market-stalls and in parks and cafés, lolled in bed until the late afternoon, and made love often and passionately. They got caught up in the Notting Hill Carnival at the end of August, and Malcolm was able to embrace the event in a way he never had before, liberated by Ziggy's visceral enthusiasm for it despite the millions of white tourists and the oppressive corralling tactics of the police.

As both he and Ziggy lived on the Carnival route they were grudgingly permitted - after displaying bills with their names and addresses and bank-cards to prove they were themselves - to clamber over the crash-barriers and duck beneath the cordons and leave the dancing crowds where they wanted when they wanted to go home. It was like being VIPs, a small thing that added to the magic of those days.

On the Sunday of the bank holiday weekend they ended up at the Champion, a gay pub on the edge of the carnival, in Notting Hill. Normally sedate, for this one weekend it was vibrant and loudly overflowing with brothers, and Malcolm and Ziggy caught up with old friends not seen since time. It was both the peak of summer and the beginning of its end.

Three days later Luke called them to say Joe's baby had died.

Son
Brown as
   Autumn
      Leaves/
Leaves
Us/
Leo

- words Malcolm had written on a paper napkin while waiting for his order in a Jamaican takeaway on Uxbridge Road. He and Ziggy liked Joe a great deal, and the death of his baby felt like a crime against nature to Malcolm.

'It's a crime *by* nature,' Ziggy said as they walked along eating greasy, deep-fried dough-balls. His voice was harsh, and his words laid Malcolm's sentimentality bare.

'Is it true,' Malcolm asked, 'that when you were born your mum's umbilical cord was strangling you?'

Ziggy nodded. 'That's why my given name is Ajyi, although only my family would use it. I had to be slapped into life. So I understood certain realities before I even drew my first breath.'

In the face of death and loss they turned to art. Malcolm worked on a sad, sweet piece of music, Ziggy on a small, stylised sculpture of a young African-featured boy. They didn't know Joe well enough then to

go to the funeral, though Luke went as George's partner. Even joining the mourners at the graveside afterwards would have been inappropriate, they both felt, as
neither of them had, as far as Malcolm knew, met
Leonie before. But they did go to visit Joe in what they
knew would be the blank and endless days that followed; gone to his home, to which he had invited them
in a happier time.

It had been awkward at first, being welcomed in too
enthusiastically, stumbling through offers of coffee,
which Malcolm drinks and Ziggy doesn't, then finding
words and even breath swallowed up by the heavy
silence that emanated from deep within Joe once the
pleasantries were used up, a silence that spread
through all the spaces of the house. There had too been
a terrible pulling from somewhere upstairs, and a bar
of merciless sunlight that extended from the half-open
nursery door across the landing and slowly inched its
way down the staircase towards where they sat.

Ziggy broke the mood by saying that Malcolm had
written a commemorative piece for Joe, could he play
it? And Joe nodded and Malcolm played, and in
between the floating, melancholy phrases he was
sending out Ziggy read the shards of words that Malcolm had written: 'Son/Brown as autumn leaves/
Leaves us/Leo,' his voice throaty and resonant and
somehow intensely African, if Africa can have a single
voice, even for a moment.

And Joe got up and started to move in response to
the music and the words, bare-footed, in baggy sweats
and a dirty white vest, stubble on his slick face. Ziggy
pushed the furniture up against the walls, Malcolm
played the piece over and over, and Joe's movements
became wilder, harder, more punching and kick-boxing
than dancing as Malcolm's licks got shorter, sharper
and more breathless and Ziggy shouted the words of

the poem: 'Son brown! As autumn! Leaves! Leaves us! Leo!'

Joe's body wept sweat as he flung himself around the axis of his pain, purging grief. (Joe: *And I felt, and I felt, this is the ritual, this is the warriors together, this is the elders in the hut this is something to be done.*)

Afterwards Ziggy gave Joe the sculpture he had made. Touched by the unexpected gift, Joe took it and set it at once on the shelf above the fireplace. He didn't ask what it was for, understanding it in the Western sense as simply commemorative. The sculpture had a sort of Afro made of long nails hammered into the wood that looked both decorative and harsh. Earlier Malcolm had watched Ziggy banging the nails in with odd, random violence: to complete the sculpture in some symbolic way, he guessed.

'You've seen what they call fetishes in books and museums, right?' Ziggy said, when Malcolm asked what the nails signified. 'All covered with iron spikes and broken-up looking?'

'Yeah, sure.'

'And maybe you thought they looked creepy, like something out of a horror movie. Devil-dolls, all spiny and spiky and nasty, coming to get you.'

Malcolm nodded.

'Well, it isn't like that,' Ziggy said. 'You make a sculpture of a god or spirit and this is how you use it. You carve it and you perform certain rituals to bring the god or spirit into it. And then you have to anger the spirit into action, you have to kick-start it. So you strike the carving, or you shoot it, or you hammer nails or spikes into it. You anger the power. And then it will work for you, if the sculpture has been done right. If it is a good house for the spirit. Even a protective sculpture is powered up in this way. So that is what I am doing. For Joe, and for his wife.'

'Do you believe in it?' Malcolm had asked. And Ziggy had shrugged and hammered in another nail, *bang-bang-bang.*

They are banging at the door they are inside the room they are looking at me with eyes wide-wide I drop the hammer and look down at my arm the long black nails protruding from the flesh I cannot twist my wrist it makes the nail-points scrape against the bones radius ulna the hammer hits the floor with a dull thud blood is streaming I hit the floor with a dull thud I have got to a certain place All I was trying to do was kick-start the power I needed to move forward, malleus incus stapes hammering in my head They are my ancestors they have come at last to answer my call I drag to my feet and stumble down the stairs shedding mirrors as I go mirrors I now know I was tricked into wearing by evil spirits that meant me harm -

Later I am told I was found in the street amongst bin-bags and dead flowers. I cannot separate the split fence-posts of time the bang-bang-bang on different doors.

Carnival, carnival helps. It takes the pressure off. I can dance for days. Dance, drink, smoke. And this year Malcolm was with me and it felt so good, it felt so right. He disliked there were so many whites there, I liked it. Everyone drinking from the same cup. He asked about the marks on my arm from the nails and I said they were marks from pins to repair my bones after a motorcycle-crash and it was true I did crash just there were no pins. He didn't need to ask about the faint white lines going up and down my wrists even if I hadn't said already he knew what they were suicide scars and he could see what mattered, that they were old.

He thinks it is Joe's baby dying that has brought me to this point. He is wrong: with that I knew what to do. Now I must explain I must try to explain I must let him all the way in. But I am afraid, I fear the pain of such a demanding penetration psychic rupture prolapse extrusion agony Breathe deep relax into the pain Open a flesh flower You are allowed to cry out it even helps -

A breeze springs up. The sun has sunk behind the broken outline of the city and the hazy sky is now pricked with stars. Ziggy palms tears away, sniffs and snorts mucus, turns and hawks it onto the tarpaper. He makes himself meet Malcolm's gaze and finds he is calmed by it, even though he knows there is a wall of words building behind Malcolm's eyes like the uprush preceding a tidal wave. Ziggy gets to his feet. He takes Malcolm's hands in his and pulls him up. Malcolm is bare-footed. They are on top of his and Luke's block, up on the roof. The door to the roof is supposed to be kept locked as there is no safety rail, just a concrete lip, but junkies broke the door down months ago and no-one has bothered to repair it. Syringes glint here and there on the worn, warm asphalt, and Malcolm has to watch where he puts his naked feet.

Malcolm brought Ziggy up here because he thought if he brought Ziggy to a high place, somewhere with a view extending as far as the eye could see in every direction, that somehow that might help. Gazing into Ziggy's unrevealing eyes he wonders if it has.

Ziggy's been this way for three days and four nights now: distracted, depressed, disconnected. Sometimes - as now - he is uncommunicative, tearful; sometimes he rambles on interminably. His talk when he does talk alternates between hyper-articulacy and incoherence as his mind makes strange connections that are some-times clear and brilliant, and sometimes opaque to anyone but himself.

Things have gone into more alarming territory too:

two evenings ago, while he was in the kitchen doing the washing-up, Malcolm felt his hackles rising as though unfriendly eyes were on him. He turned to find Ziggy leaning in the doorway, staring at him with his brow deeply furrowed. From the hard, unfriendly look on Ziggy's face it was clear that he not only didn't know who Malcolm was, but saw him as an intruder in his space, possibly even a threat who would have to be dealt with.

Malcolm had been frightened then, and hadn't known what to do. The thought that he, and everything he meant to Ziggy, could somehow just be switched off in Ziggy's head and replaced by blank hostility disturbed him on the deepest level.

That night, for the first time, he had felt physically afraid of Ziggy.

He had hated that more than anything: the idea that the intense, beautiful, visceral physicality of his lover could be twisted round against him, against them both, through some neurochemical dysfunction of the brain.

Then something in the room had changed and Ziggy had seemed to recognise Malcolm again. His expression and his body language shifted and the sense of physical threat evaporated. But before Malcolm had time to draw a breath the hostile look was replaced by one of terror. Ziggy sank slowly to the floor, hunching in on himself, all the while staring up at Malcolm with bulging eyes.

With only the slightest hesitation Malcolm crossed the room and knelt facing Ziggy.

I must –

Ziggy had the expression of a frightened child, a shell-shocked soldier, his face suddenly shiny with sweat as he radiated raw, choking vulnerability.

I must –

His anguish at realising that he hadn't recognised his lover, and that therefore something was seriously wrong with his brain, drew Malcolm to him. *Your pain is my pain. Your fear is my fear. Lover. Comrade.* Violent shudders began to run the length of Ziggy's huddled body. 'Sorry sorry sorry sorry sorry,' he said, his eyes locked on Malcolm's. 'Sorry sorry sorry sorry sorry.'

Tears spiked Malcolm's eyes. 'Don't apologise, man,' he said, kneeling and hugging Ziggy to him. 'There's nothing to be sorry for, you hear me?' He let the tremors pass from Ziggy's body into his own, not thinking of anything as he held Ziggy tight, remaining as far as he could in the absolute present, intending nothing except that their breaths, their heartbeats should fall into synch, hoping that might somehow bring a wider harmony and stability.

'What can I do to help, man?' he whispered into the groove of Ziggy's small, hot ear as Ziggy's trembling subsided, his voice catching as he repeated, 'What can I do?'

'Don't leave me alone,' Ziggy said, his voice muffled in the bunched shoulder of Malcolm's jacket. 'Promise me.'

'I promise, man,' Malcolm said. 'But that's part of a deal, okay?'

Ziggy pulled back until he could look Malcolm full in the face. His eyes searched Malcolm's. There was doubt in them, but neither fear nor confusion. 'What deal?'

'Don't you ever leave me alone either,' Malcolm said, trying to keep his voice light and even. 'Alright?'

Ziggy smiled then, a sudden, shy, sane smile, but he didn't reply.

'Deal?' Malcolm pressed him with an earnestness that was childlike in its insistence.

Ziggy's smile faded. 'Deal,' he said. And he kissed Malcolm on the lips.

The nights and days that followed were restless and broken for both of them. Malcolm thought many times of calling Luke for advice, or just to share the burden, but in the end he couldn't: he had to work this out on his own. Or rather, he and Ziggy had to work it out together, and no-one else, not even Luke, could be part of that process.

Malcolm focussed on talking to Ziggy, making sure he never let what Ziggy was saying become a monologue, keeping the flow interactive, grounding the conversation in reality, in real exchanges between two people. In doing this, and it was difficult but he did do it, Malcolm found he was more resilient and sane than he had ever imagined himself to be. It almost disappointed him, as if a surcease of sanity was a threat to the artist he knew himself to be. But too he learnt the lesson that there is a difference between the fire of art and the fire of madness. One consumes itself, burns itself out while producing only darkness, and leaves nothing behind it but ashes and rubble, while the other gives out light, and heat, and warmth. Sometimes the two fires burn together, one as it were within the other. But not always; not even often; and the one does not intensify the other.

Standing side by side Malcolm and Ziggy look out over the glittering city. Seen this way it's almost magical. On the shifting air the sound of a police-siren comes to their ears. It grows in volume then fades away. Trouble, going in another direction. Ziggy takes a deep breath. 'Let's go in,' he says.

Holding hands they make their way over to the grid-iron steps that lead down from the roof to the top floor of the block. From there they take the lift.

Luke isn't in, he's rarely there anymore, but his

presence is still everywhere, in the canvases, brushes and paints, the books and CDs, the ornaments and junk; in old bars of soap and splayed toothbrushes and almost-finished bottles of scent. His presence is not unwelcome to Ziggy or Malcolm; it even comforts them: he is home, family, memories that are mostly fond, the reassurance they are loved.

Malcolm risks a bottle of wine, lights some candles, and he and Ziggy sit and talk, more normally now. The TV, which got put on at some point, murmurs in the corner at a low volume.

'These fuckers,' Ziggy says, interrupting whatever he was talking about to gesture at a news item about an Islamic march that has flashed up on the screen, the marchers angry, male, mostly in full beards and skull-caps, dressed in robes that are intended to prevent the fabric hugging the genitals. 'These fuckers are lucky to be here however angry they act, and they know it. So they should shut up.'

'You reckon?' Malcolm says, wishing he'd kept the TV turned off. A sagging banner reads, *Sharia Law for the UK.* Some marchers hide the lower halves of their faces with Palestinian shawls and wear dark glasses.

'We're lucky to live in this corner of the world with all its stuff and possibilities,' Ziggy says.

'But still - '

'And I can know I'm lucky even when I'm cutting my wrists.'

'Ah, Ziggy, man, don't even say that - '

'It's having perspective even in the dark, when you can see nothing with your eyes.'

'So we've lucked out materially,' Malcolm says. 'But there's still lethal racism here, lethal homophobia, genuine poverty and spiritual emptiness to fight.'

Ziggy nods. 'But there's also a type of bullshit here that doesn't even want to fight for what is worth holding onto,' he says. 'I don't mean white racists and their childish futile clinging on to a dead fantasy past, I mean foolish liberals who are eager to stick their tongue up Islam's arse to show they aren't judgemental. Because they don't see that they can choose to do that, choose to be tolerant, only because they have the real power. For now. And we are the objects of their judgement too, because they have that power over us, to tolerate or not to tolerate. But if they give away their power to others then we will be judged by those others.'

'You're sounding like an anti-Muslim Nazi,' Malcolm says, muting the TV with a flick of the remote.

'It's easy to be liberal about something you think will never have power over you,' Ziggy says. 'All those religions are just power-machines, control systems. Churches and mosques are barrack-blocks and prisons for the spirit. And if you are gay - ' He shrugs. 'I turned to Vodou to undercut all that shit, that murderous shit of crusades and jihads. The shit of evangelical arseholes and Sharia law. I went underground and joined the spirits.'

Ziggy drags on the joint he's been smoking, offers it to Malcolm.

'Why're you taking it so personally, man?' Malcolm asks, taking it from him and toking.

'Don't you ever feel the weight of it?' Ziggy asks. 'Don't you ever feel it crushing you down?'

Malcolm exhales. 'Sure,' he says. 'But you have to put that aside to keep sane, don't you?'

Ziggy smiles lopsidedly at him. 'I feel my ancestors,' he says. 'I'm cut off from them but they call out to me. The spirits of my biological family of course, although my parents' Christianity fucked up that connection, but also the spirits of all Nigerian gay men, all black African faggots across the continent, across the world. They are with me always, only speaking quieter or louder. If I was without them I would feel alone. Don't you ever feel alone?'

'I don't know, man,' Malcolm says. His heart is pounding oddly in his chest, perhaps due to the dope, which is unusually strong, and he feels dizzy.

'It's all personal, it's all present,' Ziggy says. 'It is not some abstract college debate. I am British but I am also Nigerian and there is Sharia Law gaining ground in Nigeria. Christianity is bullshit too, but they're mostly not killing people who won't believe in it. ' He takes the joint back from Malcolm. 'I claim the ancestors I'm going to claim,' he says, and tokes.

Malcolm sips his wine. 'But you don't choose your ancestors,' he says.

'You do.'

'How?'

'They come to you. In sleeping or waking dreams. They call you and you welcome them in, or you close your ears to them and go on with your life alone. You chose John Coltrane, Thelonious Monk, Charlie Parker, Miles Davis to be your elders. Your artistic ancestors, who mattered more than family to you. And why? Because we no longer live in small villages. We live in the whole world. We don't have the continuity of land, the stools of the ancestral spirits in the family shrine, the altar with the blood of generations of sacrificial offerings on it. We have something shattered. We have to reach out and find the pieces, wherever they are, whoever they are, and draw them together in ourselves. The time of blood ancestors is passing, it's past.'

'The break of slavery.'

'For you. And for all of us the rushing in of the modern world. The global village.'

They sit in silence then. Malcolm's mind drifts back to an earlier round in this long bout, one won on points, maybe, that they had over at Ziggy's studio, beginning with Ziggy scolding him for 'this big-time romance you've got going with the Black Muslim African-American thing.'

'The bebop Black Nationalist cats of the Fifties and Sixties? I'll cop to that, my Negro: that style – and before you say it, yeah, the style was the content, how you blew became a revolutionary act. You won't see me down any mosque, but there's a vibe - '

'How you blow is always a revolutionary act,' Ziggy interrupts, leaning over from where he's working squatting on the floor to briefly kiss the bulge in Malcolm's trunks.

Malcolm sprawls back on a bentwood chair, thighs spread. 'We've all got a romance,' he says, his dick stirring in response to the intimate contact. 'We're all looking for revolutionary love.   I know what you're gonna say,' he adds, as Ziggy buffs with a rag the surface of a lino rectangle that will become his first *African Pride* series print. He has smeared it with globs of different-coloured paint and is working them into the gouges in the fleshy surface, gouges which through visceral association will lead him to ultimately rename the series *Tribal Scars*. Seeing his current rag is becoming paint-clogged Malcolm reaches round and hands him another. Flecks of red, blue and green are transferred from Ziggy's fingers to his own.

(Ziggy: Luke asked me do I remember Africa and I told him no, we left Nigeria when I was only four and I have no conscious memories though I have dreams of ancestral places but sometimes those are English too.

My parents were looking forward, and going into the past, into the end of empire was their way. Nigeria was a fallen house then and though things change, wheels turn and rise, it's a matter of when: no good if Nigeria rules the world in ninety years because we'll all be dead then.

Lagos Pride 2020: the title of a series of monoprints I did, the work I made after Tribal Scars, *the work that's closest to Luke's though Tracey Emin-casual, gay African men dancing under a banner a rainbow flag Lagos Pride. Yoruba float Hausa float Igbo float, a future dream.*

Not sponsored by Shell.)

'What am I going to say?' Ziggy grunts as he moves round the rectangle of lino on the floor, keeping crouched down. He is wearing just his leather kilt and bike-boots, a fantasy warrior out of legend or its bastard child, comic-book kitsch. Malcolm loves this. He used to get hard as a boy looking at Spiderman, the Human Torch, the Black Panther.

Me and Luke, he thinks, *We were T'challa and Johnny Storm.*

> *Flame on in Wakanda*
> > *(Afro-romance by way of*
> > *((yeah white)) Jack Kirby –*
> *physically flawless Muscled Superhero,*
> > *First*
> > *love in*
> > *Fetish lycra like so many*
> > *Young men who like*
> *men*

'You're gonna tell me that romance is a projection and we need to resist all projections.'

'*That* is the revolution,' Ziggy says. 'Or at least, it is the resistance. This is ready.'

Malcolm gets up and goes over to the trestle-table, takes a sheet of paper from the waiting pile and brings it over to Ziggy, It is hand-made, uneven in texture and rough-edged. Ziggy places it carefully on top of the lino rectangle. 'But romance is a valorisation not a projection,' Malcolm says.

'How do you mean?' Ziggy picks up a bent tin spoon and starts to rub its curved underside on the back of the paper, forcing it down into the paint-filled incisions.

'It's a way of saying 'this is important, this is what I am most.' A musician. An artist. A gay man. A black man. A jazz-man. A bohemian. A radical. My romance is with all those things, those aspects of myself. It's a heightened focus, and where my meaning is. The projections you mean are other people's shit forced on us, what we have to fight off to find who we really are: the nigger imposed on the black, the faggot on the same-gender-loving, the loser on the artist.'

Ziggy doesn't disagree, and they fall silent. Time passes, meditatively. Notes wander through Malcolm's head, the piece they start to shape themselves into untitled then, though later Ziggy will suggest *Lagos Pride*, and Malcolm will take his suggestion. Ziggy grunts and flicks cramp from his aching wrist. 'You want me to take a turn?' Malcolm offers.

Ziggy nods and relinquishes the spoon. Malcolm kneels and imitates his technique as closely as he can. 'You have to test your shit out, though,' Ziggy says. 'To make sure it's not just your own mental confusion. That's the bullshit paradox of faith. What is a true belief?'

'I fell for a musical spirituality out of a decade I wasn't even born in, a jazz-man's version of Islam that didn't exclude fucking, drink or drugs,' Malcolm says. 'Okay, part of the kick was rejecting Church bullshit, I admit that. A different black way.'

(Crucified Lord keep
        The nails handy
    For
Other
    Thieves and martyrs)

'And I heard the music, I read the sleeve-notes, and I was home. But that isn't romance the way you mean it, because I didn't choose it. It chose me.' *Like Luke and Negritude*, Malcolm thinks.

'Some dreams you should wake up from,' Ziggy says. For him Islam is a straight-up enemy. As a man and as an artist rooted in both Western and traditional African modes of representation it is exterminatingly hostile because no images are permitted.

(Serene faces of giant Buddhas hacked off and smashed, somehow a sort of murder, the excision of a spirit tongue.)

One drizzly afternoon, Ziggy and Malcolm lying in bed smoking and flicking through books of African art, Ziggy pointing out how African art, uniquely in all the world, so loved, so prioritised the human form, that its makers used it everywhere, from the statues of gods to the handles of spoons. 'And militant Muslims would destroy all that in blind rage,' Ziggy says.

'But formal constraint can make great art,' Malcolm says. 'Like Islamic calligraphy: the writing's brilliant art because all that focus had to go there. There's a purity to that. Like the architecture.'

'Yes, but the difference is I don't want to smash that,' Ziggy says. 'And I can see that beauty. But they can't see this beauty. And the constraint comes out of a hatred of human love, of the human body. All that is a very bad mistake that leads to wickedness and harm.'

'What about Christianity? Religion of the slave-masters?'

'Only a little less bad. But don't forget Muslims began the slave-trade, selling Africans to Christians. Don't fall for that Nation of Islam romance.'

A Fela Kuti tape is playing on a dusty cassette-player by the bed. Ziggy fantasises a new Kalakuta Republic, a Yoruba evolution. This romance he will admit, though he knows so little about it really. His parents told him, Yes, we are Yoruba, but, staunch Christians, they went no further than stating that familial allegiance. What lay beyond and below he had to find out for and from himself, creating from necessity a synthetic new form for a new world.

And in this I understand Luke because he too required a self-invention, a shrine to worship at, though he would call it essence and I would not –

Malcolm would -

Something to sacrifice for, and to. Yes.

And Luke he knew had had no models, no Negrophile avatars (though these he would trip over later, in all their problematic paradoxicality: Robert Mapplethorpe, Carl Van Vechten, Nancy Cunard, flawed nigger-lovers, Fanon right in that: the hypervalorisers).

'I've got time for Nancy, though, my Nubian,' Malcolm said to Luke, some other long blue evening. They had been dissecting Mapplethorpe while read-sharing Patricia Morrison's biography of the photographer, its dispiriting revelations – despite the protestations of black models like Ken Moody and Joe Simmons - of his cold-blooded search for 'the super-nigger with the biggest dick,' coming one bleak chapter at a time.

'Yeah?' Luke said. 'Them Black Arts brers hated her guts.'

'She was the heir to a fortune,' Malcolm said. 'The Cunard shipping line. They said leave your nigger lover or we'll disinherit you. And she didn't, and they did. Not many people have given up millions for love. So I give her that. It wasn't a pose. Or if it started that way she ended up living it for real. Like most of us do.'

This kind of conversation required from Malcolm a particular sort of double-consciousness: to talk to Luke as though Luke both was and wasn't white – and the corollary: to talk of black men as though he both was and wasn't black. And so he and Luke lived: inhabiting that provocative, endlessly-oscillating space between essence and social construction. That neither of them would want to live elsewhere was perhaps their truest commonality.

It's all about love, Malcolm thinks. *Love, and anger at injustice.* Rubbing with the spoon is making his fingers ache, not good for his playing. 'Back to you,' he says to Ziggy.

One of the candles Malcolm lit earlier gutters and goes out. Smoke drifts across the room in twists, and there is the scent of beeswax. The wine is finished.

'I had a cousin,' Ziggy says. 'Eze he was called.'

'"Easy"?'

'Ee, zed, ee. My mother's brother's son. He was my age once.'

'Once?'

'Yes.'

The graves are weeping.

'He lived in a village in the north of Nigeria. Outside the village was a very old wall, all that remained of a palace that had stood there, long ago. Eze's family were Christians but they also honoured the ancestors and the spirits of place and the plains and forests. These old beliefs were the bricks of their buildings and Christianity was the decor, the soft furnishings, present, but exchangeable. In the village were also many Muslims. There were contestations and struggles, both political and religious, throughout the region, and after a time the Muslims gained the upper hand in Eze's district. They imposed Sharia law. Women were forced to go veiled and forbidden from public life, which created much hardship as they could not work to support their families. Baskets of hands cut from thieves rotted in the town square by the gallows the Imams had erected there, and fear hung over the quiet, well-ordered streets of the village. The ancestors grew pale and the blood on the shrines blackened and the gods were not fed. Eze had a friend who was dear to him and rumours went about saying this and that, and they came to certain ears and he was killed for it, and his friend was killed for it. There is no wall outside the village now. Just rubble over bones.'

Ziggy falls silent. The joint has gone out. He puts it to his lips and flicks the lighter.

'Because that's how they execute homosexuals in Islam, right, man?' Malcolm says. 'They pull a wall down on them?'

'On *us*,' Ziggy says. 'It is always us.'

Malcolm gives Ziggy a look. 'Did you say *baskets* of hands?'

Ziggy watches him, doesn't say anything. Smoke trickles from his wide nostrils dragonishly.

'Easy,' Malcolm says. 'Eze. Ezekiel. Ziggy. That's your name, isn't it, man?'

Ziggy doesn't answer. A second candle's wick slips into clear molten wax and goes out. His profile is now silhouetted by the flickering television-screen. Malcolm remembers Luke saying Ziggy taught him lessons. At the time Malcolm hadn't understood what that meant, or at most he had thought they would be lessons in race or racism that Luke would benefit from, even if he was never a fool like so many white boys: he had never imagined that Ziggy could teach him anything in that way. 'Do I have a name in your story?' he asks.

'Do you want one?' Ziggy drags on the spliff, making its tip glow orange. Seeds crack and pop and fall from its end. He seems pleased that Malcolm has seen through his story, or rather seen it for what it is, a fable. A legend.

'We could have left the village,' Malcolm says. 'We

could have run away.'

'It's not easy to leave what you know and what is yours,' Ziggy says. 'Look at the Jews in Germany. Many of them had education and knew the world. But they stayed despite everything that was happening around them. Because you never believe it will happen to you.'

'You think it could happen here?'

'I think I would pick up a knife to prevent it.'

Malcolm has no answer to that.

You understand now, Ziggy thinks. *A little, at least. Madness and sanity, they are a matter of where you are speaking from. Who in the rest of the world defines freedom as we define and desire it? We want freedom from systems of belief, systems of authority, systems of morality, obligations to family, to custom, to God: we long to be free of all the things that to a billion other human beings make all the sense of life there is to be made of it. To them we are mad. Intriguing, exciting, but mad. And therefore dangerous.*

'I hammered nails into my arms,' he says out loud. 'That's why they sectioned me. That's where I was. Before.'

'Okay,' Malcolm says carefully. 'What - why did you do it?'

'To anger the spirits within me, so they would protect me from the voices.'

'Did it work?'

'For a while. But it was too much of a physical fuck-up.'

'So you don't wanna do it again?'

'No. It was a wrong turn.'

'Why was it a wrong turn?'

'Because I do not need to anger the spirits for them to help me.'

'What do they need to do their job?'

'Passion.'

'Yeah?'

'Yes.'

'How?'

'Lips on lips, love, cock, arse. Your spirit in mine. Because now I know for sure what maybe I always knew: that homosexuality is powerful magic.'

Malcolm smiled at that. 'Do you hear voices now?'

'Only spirits and ancestors. Not bullshit white noise mind-rapers.'

'Good.'

And with that finally they can talk about the things that up until now have been off-limits between them: drugs and medication and rejecting medication. Self-mutilation, self-medication, self-annihilation and the lure of suicide. They talk the remaining candles down and the sun up. At around ten in the morning, with hard, dope-reddened eyes and throats aching from smoke and conversation, they make their way down to Portobello Market to buy fruit for breakfast. They walk slowly and wordlessly. After being up all night the hot brightness of the day has an almost hallucinatory quality to it, and, despite the bustle around them there is the curious sense of time slowed to near-stillness. *Amber era.* They go on to Ziggy's flat to eat because it's nearer. Ziggy buys Greek yoghurt and combines it with oranges, peaches, raspberries and strawberries in the blender to make a healthy drink for them to share. After such a long, strange night watching Ziggy do something as everyday as click the lid down and turn the blender on seems somehow unreal to Malcolm: heightened and oddly moving.

After sharing the contents of the blender they undress and collapse onto Ziggy's bed, squirming round to face each other, then lie there in each others' arms. For all the dazzle of the day, soon they are asleep.

And they dream.

Ziggy

The drums beat. I am in the forest. It is night. Before me is the shrine. Yellow light spills out. Over and over I approach it. It is hard to find the right path. What makes you a man what makes me a man what do we need to do to become men? We lack the rites the rituals the ceremonies the ordeal survived I am not circumcised that is not my tribe.

My ritual.

This I do not tell Malcolm, it is too unbearable:

Every time I cut myself, every time I hammer nails into my flesh I am replaying the ordeal that made me a man or failed to make me a man, and with each self-inflicted wound I am connected to the world of agony. My blood flows for all Africans, for all faggots, for all faggot Africans. I know it is no use, I know it achieves nothing for them. But it is also an offering to the spirits and to the ancestors: my blood, my tears feed them and give them power. To protect others as they have protected me. I only lied a little, Malcolm my lover. I think you would forgive me if you knew.

I am fourteen again. The chapel bell is sounding. It is Easter. Christ will rise but He is dead now. It is after this that I read Fanon, Lumumba, Saro-Wiwa and the works of every black revolutionary I can get my hands on. There is a hammering at the door. My parents saved and sacrificed to send me here. Sacrificed. My body is the altar and I am the offering to the God of their vision. My grandmother cannot reach me here cannot stretch out her hand to me, cannot throw me a lifeline. They are hammering at the door This is it this is it Do you want to belong? Me and Karim look at each other scared scared Do you want to belong? Reflecting back at each other black mirrors of submission. He has always wanted to belong he will let them do anything to him if it means afterwards he belongs. He won't fight what they do to him strip him boot-polish his bare genitals stick him in a cold shower hold him there laughing and drag him into another room a room with no light-bulb in the socket and I only hear later what happens in that room and I don't know if it's true but I do know he will not tell me afterwards and in that room later I smell dark sour smells I do not think I am imagining.

It didn't happen to me. I fought them off I kicked them off I smashed a mirror and cut my arm and they got scared and they left me Damballah Damballah I give you my blood Protect me. And He did, and I knew at that moment I would never belong to that world it would never own me and I would never be part of it I would be free. And my thoughts raced faster and faster as I watched what they did to Karim who wanted to belong and always afterwards I wondered Did I refuse this thing that would have made me a man, afterwards when no-one would talk to me, all of them afraid I would say something to someone, to my parents, to the teachers. I think they all fucked Karim. I had gone down on him in small private moments but afterwards he would not let me, he would not permit that simple release: he had been changed. Become a sort of man. My thoughts all started to move at different speeds, like lanes of traffic getting faster and slower until the pile-up occurred, the voices in my head yelling sobbing and contradictory. And I begged Damballah to silence them and when He didn't I offered him more blood and then more and that was how it all began.

I am an outsider seeking an outsider and I have found him. He solves nothing but answers everything. I have seen the markings of our tribe on him where I saw them on Luke, where they are always found, on

the wrists. I have kissed the place where the knife cut.
Malcolm, I am yours.

Malcolm

Africa
  Afrika
    Afreaka/
You are
  O -
  My
  Ni-
    gerian
Freak. Sweet
  as sugared
  hot
  Black
  coffee/
    and as
  Strong.
Give me my horn
  cos you
Give me
  the
    horn/
    And you draw
the sweetest,
  hottest
  sounds
from me/
    Night
        after indigo
          Night.

Chapter Eleven

The dressing-room backstage at the Jazz Café is small, unheated, and packed past capacity with musicians and dancers. Condensation runs down the gloss-painted brick walls and steams the mirrors, and the air is blue with cigarette-smoke. Outside, icy, driving rain sets the prematurely-hung strings of Christmas lights in Camden High Street swinging wildly above a sea of shiny black umbrellas. Inside Luke is hunched awkwardly on his knees, carefully outlining in white paint the shape of a femur on George's smooth, bare, sinewy thigh. When it's filled in it will complete the skeleton design that covers the rest of George's near-naked body. Luke has already painted the same design on Ziggy, who is leaning back against the dressing-room's grubby partition wall, arching his body and keeping his arms akimbo in order to avoid smearing the still-wet paint on himself or anyone else in the crowded space.

Both George and Ziggy are wearing low-cut black trunks, army-boots and nothing else, and seem comfortable like that. Ziggy because he's an exhibitionist, George because he's a professional performer - though his professionalism is, of course, not untinged by pleasure in showing off in public his still remarkably lean and well-shaped physique.

Luke's dreads brush the bulge in George's trunks as he starts to quickly fill in the outline of the femur. The teasing contact makes George's dick twitch, as does the soft stroking of the wet squirrel-hair brush on his freshly-shaved skin.

George has shaved his body ever since he was seventeen. It began with shaving his chest because the coils of hair spoiled the look of the scoop-neck leotard he wanted to wear to dance-class. The hair in his armpits went next, sacrificed 'for a clean line.' Then he noticed that most of the older male dancers shaved their legs, and he liked the way it emphasised the shapes of the muscles, so he shaved his legs too. And if he was shaving his legs it seemed somehow ridiculous, and unhygienic, to have a hairy butt. That left only his pubic hair. He began by shaving across the top of it so he could wear low-cut thongs and briefs without overspill. Then he started to trim the sides too, and what remained became a narrower and narrower strip until one day he shaved it off altogether, and felt clean and free, more fully himself, and only a little perverse.

One time George let Luke shave his body. Luke has sensitive hands, and he slid the razor deftly over George's crotch and balls until the skin there was glassy-smooth, and didn't nick George once. George then rolled onto his front, pushed his large, muscular butt back and up, spread his thighs as wide as he could, and offered Luke full access to his most private, receptive places. The lather felt cool on his trembling sphincter, the soft bulk of the brush warm, and George's cock was rammed into a sudden, almost painful adolescent erectness as Luke used the razor on him there. The extreme sensuality of the experience left him breathless, and he urged Luke to fuck him right away. Luke, flush-faced and heavily-aroused himself, had been eager to oblige, briefly lubing his substantial erection while tonguing the gasping, writhing George's glossily-smooth hole. The sex had been extremely hot, and Luke had come inside George, and George had come for the first time in his life without touching his own dick.

Luke shifts position to ease the cramp in his calves and squeezes more white paint out onto the saucer he is using as a makeshift palette. He glances over at Ziggy to make sure he is following the same stylisations of the skeletal form on George.

Being unheated the pokey dressing-room is fundamentally chilly but has grown dense with body-heat. Malcolm isn't there yet, but the other Urban Afro-Nubians are, sharing joints and beers and chat, leaning where they can find a space that won't get in Luke's way or get paint on their clothes. Trevor, the drummer, runs a sovereign-ringed hand over his slickly-shaved head, laughs at something one of the others has said and passes an almost-spent joint to Don, a lean, mixed-race brother and the group's bass-player. A gold front tooth flares as with a smile Don takes the joint and tokes. A Black Power pick rides high in the back of his large Afro. Beside him a dark-skinned, round-faced young man with a porkpie hat pushed back on his shaved head sips from a can of Bud: Percy, the quartet's pianist and clown.

Hot jazz filters through from the auditorium - the Urban Afro-Nubians are only one of twelve acts on this evening - and the room is filled with pre-gig static and upbeat anticipation. Don moves his head to the bassline; Percy's fingers drum and snap.

Ziggy puts his hands up sharply to avoid being hit on the chest as the dressing-room door bursts open and Malcolm comes hurrying in with Joe, who has been having trouble getting backstage. They have to turn sideways to fit into the room, and only with difficulty manage to close the door behind them, then have to lean against it in what is now the only space left in the room. Malcolm kisses Ziggy on the lips, then touches fists with Trevor, Don and Percy. He squats down by Luke, running his hand through Luke's dreads and down to his butt.

'You got enough time to paint Joe too?'

'Just about,' Luke says, not breaking off from what he's doing.

'Cool.' Malcolm straightens up and, seeing Ziggy's back is unpainted, slots in behind him. He slips an arm carefully round Ziggy's waist, his hand coming to rest on Ziggy's hip just above the curve of pelvic bone Luke has painted on the front of Ziggy's trunks.

Coming out to the Afro-Nubians was a strange experience for Malcolm. Freighted as it was with his fear of their disapproval, even rejection, it was also exhilarating: if they couldn't deal with who he was, then fuck them. There had been no grand announcement on his part, just mentions that he was seeing a genderless 'someone', combined with talk about the show he, Ziggy, George, Luke and Joe wanted to put on, and what they wanted to express with it. When he introduced Ziggy to Trevor, Percy and Don he simply said, 'This is Ziggy' in a way that sounded like the answer to a question, and the only question anyone was asking at that time was who was Malcolm dating.

To his relief and gratification none of them had cared, though inevitably it caused a shift in their pre- and post-gig banter. Trevor's tales of romantic conquest acquired a slippery, bisexually-eroticised quality, although whether that was an oblique confession of greater sexual openness on his part or a playful desire to include the now out-as-gay Malcolm in his exploits, Malcolm didn't know. Perhaps, like Joe, Trevor was simply a straight man who liked gay men.

It was Trevor who had got them the gig at the Jazz Café, of course: he was the only member of the quartet who focussed on the practical, work-chasing side as much as the music. He had charm and boldness, and was prepared to use both to get the band engagements. The owner of the venue, a wealthy middle-aged white guy, had a penchant for black skin, male as well as female in Trevor's estimation. Trevor had been able to exploit that penchant at a party he had tagged along to with a black girl singer acquaintance.

'I flexed my arms,' Trevor told Malcolm later, 'and she - well, she *flexed*, man.' He laughed. 'And we both got the gigs we wanted.'

They are performing as part of an evening showcasing more experimental material than is usually presented at the Jazz Café, and are billed as *'The Urban Afro-Nubians featuring The Baron Samedis with Surprise Guest Vocalist'*.

The Baron Samedis are George, Ziggy, Joe and Luke. Luke has been responsible for the body-painting and sourcing some of the costumes - top hats with red feathers for the dancers, cowry necklaces and bracelets for the musicians - and along with Ziggy, and helped by the others, he has designed and painted a large, African-inspired canvas backdrop that will be hung at the back of the stage for their performance.

This isn't Luke and Ziggy's first collaboration: they've been working on paintings together off and on for the last three months, sometimes at Luke and Malcolm's flat, sometimes at Ziggy's studio, whichever has the more free floor-space at any given moment. Collaborating has been liberating for them both, and has allowed them to find their way to a new level of friendship, one that isn't threatened by Ziggy's relationship with Malcolm or Luke's with George. Luke has reconnected Ziggy with the sensuality of the brush, and Ziggy has pushed Luke away from the folksy and small-scale. The work they have been creating is vivid, garish, crowded with symbols, jaggedly intense. It is Vodou-inspired junk art, daubed and scraped on scrap board and crudely nailed-together planks. The art of reclamation, Ziggy calls it.

And the surprise guest vocalist?

One drizzly Thursday afternoon a fortnight before the show Luke, Ziggy, Malcolm and George had been hard at work colouring in the outlines of the still-unfinished backdrop on the floor of Luke and Malcolm's front room. All the furniture had been pushed back against the walls or taken out of the room altogether to make enough space to fully spread the backdrop out and work on it from all sides.

They'd been working for maybe three hours when the entryphone sounded. Luke got up with a grunt and went and answered it. It was Joe. Luke buzzed him into the block, and a few minutes later, in response to a rattle at the letterbox, opened the front-door to find him standing there, looking self-conscious, with Leonie at his side.

Luke felt slightly awkward as he pecked Joe on the cheek and invited the two of them in. He had met Leonie only once before, and that had been at the funeral, where they had barely spoken. He shook her hand lightly. Seeing her made him aware that Joe had been spending a lot of time with George, Ziggy, Malcolm and himself over the last month or so, and that while this male companionship clearly gave Joe something he needed, it shut his wife out. Luke suspected that Leonie was trying to challenge this exclusion by imposing on it, and that Joe was at best ambivalent about her doing so.

Luke also felt awkward because he knew how negative Ziggy could be towards black women. He didn't want Joe to have to stand there while Ziggy froze Leonie out. But there was nothing he could do about it. He ushered them in.

Joe wore a grey tracksuit and vintage hi-tops, and had a neat, barbershop-fresh fade. Leonie had on no make-up and wore pre-worn jeans, a white basketball sweatshirt, and slightly platformed powder-blue trainers. Her hair was cane-rowed so fiercely it pulled at the corners of her eyes. She hung back slightly in the doorway of the living-room, unsure of herself, and also, perhaps, both afraid and resentful of the four gay men who had become so close to her husband.

Ziggy looked up at her with hazy, red-rimmed, almost blank eyes. After taking a long moment to size her up, and without any change of expression, he gestured for her to come into the room. With only the slightest hesitation she did so. Reaching round behind him he picked up a paint-brush and offered it to her, handle-first. Her face was expressionless as she took it. Without a word, Luke and Malcolm shifted round to give her room to kneel next to Ziggy. Without a word, she knelt. Joe picked up another brush and knelt on the other side of her from Ziggy. *(This is my tribe these are the men of my tribe I want you to join with them)*

Ziggy gestured to sketches he and Luke had made showing what colour should go where. Leonie nodded and dipped her brush into one of several dishes of paint, as did Joe. The CD that had been playing in the background - Thelonious Monk piano solos - finished, and they worked on in silence. The tension that Leonie's arrival had created slowly dissolved into the common purpose, the shared activity. No-one spoke, except to make the odd request for more paint or a rag or clean water.

I can see why Joe comes here, Leonie thought as she worked. *To be among these men. I was angry with him at first, even though I could see why his old friends weren't enough for him. Because my old friends weren't enough for me: they made me feel trapped. In my grief. In my situation. Like a CD stuck on repeat. Here something is open, there's a sense of something that can expand. Expand away from family. Away from failure. There are suns in this pattern I'm painting, and I know they're for Leo, suns and lions.*

My mum and my aunt and even some of my girl-friends are already saying, Well, you can try again. It's not consolation or advice, more like just an obser-vation: you can try again. And it's true, and I know we will try again, probably even quite soon. But none of that helps. But then what else are they supposed to say? My auntie's had several miscarriages, one almost came to term. Even in this I'm not special. I wish I was a poet or something so I could at least make the ordinariness into something that stood out, but I'm not and I can't.

God helps, Church doesn't. You get sick of being pitied real quick. My aunt cops a competitive attitude, so now I just shut up about it.

My full breasts nightmarish, perverted. Needing draining like some awful backed-up sewer.

They knew he was dead - I knew he was dead - but I still had to go through all of it. The labour. The delivery. All the colour was bled out of everything, all the life was gone out of everyone's faces. Joe was there the whole time. Holding my hand sometimes. Not quite looking at me. Everything was right and every-thing was wrong. It took six hours and seven minutes. They cut me so I wouldn't tear. Later the cut throbbed like a brain full of thoughts that won't go. The injec-tion made me numb below the waist. It was frighten-ing but a relief to not feel for a bit. With my body. I was already numb above the neck.

But still - but still when he came out with a sudden rush I immediately propped myself up to see him. I was so afraid they'd take him away get rid of him before I even saw him. Still I was waiting for them to hold him upside-down by the ankles and slap his pale little behind, and for him to cry his way into life, still I was hoping even though I knew there wasn't any hope. And seeing him actually seeing him made it worse in a way because he was so complete, so fully formed, so new and ready. He should have been alive. They wrapped him and let me hold him and I did and Joe did and his little fingers were perfect and he was even warm from being inside my body and then the warmth slowly went from him and the dead weight of the world and everything in it was pressing down on my heart, and everything became unbearable.

And you think you can't, but you go on. And on. And friends and family members offer the usual words in the usual ways over and over, and you do what needs doing and then it's done and you're into the blank time and soon you can feel people getting bored with your grief, your loss. You can feel them needing new news, a new twist to the story of your dull, dead days. You think about suicide sometimes, just to end the feeling and the lack of feeling, but adding more death to death doesn't make sense. Or not to me, anyway. And you avoid your husband and he avoids you because your faces have become reflections of each other's loss.

So Joe walked out one evening and came here, and now I've come here. Before I came I didn't believe that men, or any men apart from Joe, could offer me anything, could help me in any way. I don't even understand how, but somehow they have. Here in this room. Here, despite what you'd think, the difference between men and women is somehow special. Here I am special and my loss is celebrated.

For the first time in a long time the colours around her seemed bright. She reached out for more yellow, accidentally brushing Luke's arm as she did so.

'Oh, I'm sorry.'

'S'alright,' he said, shooting her a crooked smile.

Leonie gasped at that, in sudden recognition of something, and dropped her brush, flecking cadmium over a patch of orange. Ziggy kissed his teeth in irritation.

'What?' Luke asked.

'Nothing,' she said, giving Ziggy a glance as she picked her brush back up. 'I just realised where we met before. I mean apart from at the service.'

Luke tilted his head in curiosity, his green eyes feline. 'I didn't think we had met before,' he said.

'Joe,' Leonie said. 'Look at Luke and Malcolm.'

And Joe looked at Luke and then at Malcolm, and although he already knew, he knew that Malcolm and Luke did not, and so he said as if it was a new realisation, 'That night on the bridge.'

And suddenly it was the meeting of old friends, comrades and veterans, and there was a flurry of excited talk of changed looks, of the impossibility of none of them having recognised each other before.

'Context,' Ziggy grunted, affecting disinterest, carrying on painting but watching from the corner of his eye as their recognition bound them together and filled the room with the roar and uprush of predestination.

Even as she experienced it Leonie knew a lot of that feeling was ephemeral, but as it swept through her she felt some of the tautness leave her face and not return. And what would not leave her, what she would be permitted to take from this room, was the knowledge that she was no longer outside the world of meaning. And if it was odd that she gained this comfort through these four gay men, she could once more accept what she, like Joe, had railed against: that her God moved in a mysterious way, and He was good.

'What happened on the bridge?' George asked.

'It's where me and Malcolm met,' Luke said. Then as simply as he could he told George the rest, the others chipping, telling their own legends. And for Luke their telling answered a question that had always troubled him: would Joe and his friends have helped them if they'd known that Luke and Malcolm were gay? Now he knew the answer was yes, and it made him feel more real in the world: it wasn't some assumed straight boys who had been saved that night, it was him and it was Malcolm. He felt both loved and set free. *This was my offering: ties blooded with my blood when my birth-brother's boot hit my face, when he kicked out my front right tooth while I was trying to defend my black brother Malcolm, who I didn't even know then, just that he was a brother. Blood for blood. Blood against blood. And I guess my offering was accepted cos Joe and his friends come to our rescue.*

Until the day of Joe and Leonie's recognition Luke had felt Del there, an albatross, an ankle tag.

'So are you going to go?' George asked.

'I don't know.'

To attend the trial or not, to find himself liberate or have his parole revoked: either choice was a psychological hazard. Whatever he decided, Luke felt he should do something for the family of the murdered boy. George offered no suggestions at the time, but two days later he borrowed a disconcertingly flash silver Mercedes Sport from his friend Lester, Luke bought a large bouquet of white lilies, and they drove to the spot where Yusuf was attacked, where his death began.

It was on the edge of the estate where Luke grew up, just east of Poplar and the Isle of Dogs. Drab high-rises scabbed with satellite dishes jutted up into a compressed and sunless sky, and there was no view of the river. The odd Goldfinger block, ironically fashionable among the tombstone rows of vertical slums, beckoned brutalistically to investors. Luke recognised the architect's work now in a way he never would have before he left this place, before he met Ziggy, his first friend who knew about stuff.

'What's it like coming back here?' George asked, glancing over at Luke as they drove through residential streets that were disconcertingly devoid of inhabitants, taking in the flexing of his jaw, the hard brightness of his eyes.

'Like visiting a prison you was in what's been closed down,' Luke said. 'Well, kind of closed down.' He pointed out a surveillance camera on a pole. It was one of many: they were at every corner, every crossroads, and those were the ones that were visible. 'A prison you was in for a crime you didn't even commit.'

They didn't have to go into Luke's estate to get to the spot where Yusuf was attacked, only drive along the western edge of it. And there it was: a featureless length of pavement overlooked by disused council offices, distinguishable only by the several bunches of dying flowers that were tied to a lamp-post partway along, some with cards attached. Rain had already made the messages on the cards bleed and blur. A brand-new CCTV camera had been fixed to the side of the council building and was trained on the meagre memorial, a red light blinking on top of it. George pulled over and they got out, feeling self-conscious. Luke tied the bunch of lilies to the lamp-post. It was large and top-heavy, and he had to crumple the cellophane and tussle with it to get it to stay the right way up. He swore. Rain began to spit.

The case wasn't high-profile. Yusuf didn't die at the scene of the attack but a week later, in hospital. The police didn't crack the case after months and thousands of man-hours: the perpetrators got caught because one of them bragged about it while pissed in a local pub that weekend, and was then grassed up by a mate for the £5000 reward. The CCTV footage of the attack wasn't good quality, but it was good enough to confirm identities once there were actual suspects to compare it against. When the police searched Del's flat they found a bomber-jacket with a ripped sleeve that matched footage of the jacket of one of the assailants being torn during the attack. Yusuf went down fighting, and as a consequence left behind that one crucial piece of corroborating evidence that did for his attackers. The police also found racist and neo-Nazi literature in Del's flat, on his hard-drive, and in the flats of the others. Circumstantial evidence, but damning nonetheless.

All five were found guilty of something: two of manslaughter, one of grievous bodily harm, one of actual bodily harm, and one, Del, of racially-aggravated murder and incitement to racial hatred. He was re-manded to Brixton Prison to await sentencing, and no doubt to appeal against his conviction.

'I wondered, you know, man,' Luke said to Malcolm later. 'What if he got off? Would I of had to, I dunno, do something? And if I did, what?'

But he didn't get off.

In the end Luke decided not to attend the trial, even after George offered to go with him. The near-ecstatic, almost apocalyptic vision of himself sitting there with his black lover at his side, claiming him in front of them all, tempted him retinally. But he didn't want to see Del. He didn't want to see his mother and father or be seen by them. He didn't want to have to account for his life to them. *Del is their son, not me. I've got other ancestors now.*

Almost he felt the need to test that. Somehow.

Flags against flags. Sequinned drapeau versus Union Jackboots. Carnival of life versus carnival of death. Skulls against skulls –

He didn't attend the trial but one afternoon he did

cycle past the courthouse. Twenty or so anti-racism protestors were gathered on the steps, placards at the ready, waiting for something to happen. They were mostly young, a mix of races, in jeans and combat gear. Above them a group of Somali men in suits were talking quietly amongst themselves. Further down a woman reporter and TV cameraman smoked cigarettes. A white youth in a camouflage jacket was hawking *The Socialist Worker* while a woman in a headscarf half-heartedly offered *The Big Issue*. A special constable stood nearby, looking bored.

The doors swung open and two uniformed security guards came out. The cameraman hefted his camera, the reporter trod out her cigarette and moved into position, and the protestors raised their placards and began chanting, 'Say no to race hate!' as a middle-aged couple emerged from the building.

Standing straddling his bike on the far side of the street Luke watched his parents refuse to talk to the reporter as they hurried down the steps to a waiting minicab, which he noticed had a driver who looked North African. They walked with their heads up, unashamed, perhaps even proud to claim their moment in the spotlight. It was seven years since he'd last seen them, and they both looked old, fat and ill. *Only seven years,* he thought. *Since my life began.*

The policeman kept the protestors out of the road as the minicab pulled away. The security guards went back inside. The protestors fell silent and returned to the steps to await the emergence of the accused. A security van, boxy and white with small black-glass windows, drew up where the minicab had been, stoking their anticipation.

Nothing happened. Then a white girl with a nose-ring and a Tibetan pixie-hat appeared at the corner of the building. 'They're taking them out the back!' she yelled, before vanishing back the way she had come. The protestors broke ranks and followed her, throwing down their placards as they ran. The reporter and cameraman followed them. The policeman muttered something into his radio.

Luke pedalled away.

He didn't tell George he had been to the court-house.

Luke's birthday, which was also, of course, Del's birthday, came a week after the trial ended. Seeing how low Luke was feeling, George surprised him with tickets on the Eurostar and a weekend away in Paris.

Luke was childishly excited. Except for a cigarette-and-booze run to Calais with a mate of Del's when he was fifteen he had never been out of the country. That had been a drab drive along featureless roads to a featureless Hypermarché which had all the signs in English as well as French. They had loaded up with spirits, lager and fags then driven straight back to the ferry. The only thing that had made it feel like being abroad was driving on the wrong side of the road. 'Fucking stupid Frogs,' Del's mate had said.

This trip was totally different, embracing as it did the particularity and magic of place, the wilfully tour-ist-romantic. Through some beneficence the train was efficient, customs were unharassing, and when they arrived in Paris the weather was cold, but crystallinely so, and sunny. They dropped off their bags at the pensione George had booked in Pigalle, then wandered along the banks of the Seine and through the Tuileries; visited Notre Dame and Sacre Coeur; climbed halfway up the Eiffel Tower and looked out over the city. They saw a Klee exhibition at the Pompidou Centre. In the square outside, a black man on a soap-box harangued a crowd in English: 'All Englishmen are homosexuals!'

They visited the Orangerie and the Louvre and looked at the great art of the West. Outside the galleries skinny African men with striped bags tried to sell wind-up birds to queues of stony-faced, resistant tourists. George bought Luke one, having a small conversation with the African seller in French, which he could speak well, and Luke could not speak at all. The man smiled, and he and George shook hands. Luke would have been ashamed to buy a bird himself - *I'd of only been doing it cos the guy was cute as well as a sufferer* - but he was proud of George for making the connection.

They had supper that first evening in a small restaurant on a cobbled square in the centre of which was a large fountain made up of three green-stained tritons. Conches were hefted on their marble shoulders, from which water trickled into half-shells below.

After they'd finished eating and the plates had been cleared away George produced a small box from his pocket and slid it towards Luke. Violin music was playing softly over speakers and candles lit the low-ceilinged room kindly, enriching skin-tones and glinting on glasses and bottles. Luke opened the box. Sitting side by side on a black velvet pad were two silver rings. Flowers with intertwining stems were incised into their outer surfaces, the petals some pale blue semi-precious stone.

'They're Victorian friendship rings,' George said. 'The flowers are forget-me-nots.' He gestured for Luke to give him his hand. Luke did so. George slipped one of the silver bands onto his wedding-finger. It felt right there. Luke took the other ring from the box and worked it onto George's wedding-finger. Then he took George's hand and kissed it.

On the Metro back to the pensione, in an almost-empty subway carriage, they were serenaded by two African buskers with a guitar, who sang Bob Marley's

'Redemption Song' for them in English with sweet, clear voices. The pensione itself was in an area where there were many Africans, Arabs and Algerians, which surprised and pleased Luke, who had imagined Paris to be pretty much all-white. He and George fitted in where they were staying in a way that was both unexpected and gratifying, and Luke was pleased to discover that the two of them didn't seem particularly English to the French-speaking people around them.

Unexpectedly too, Luke found that he loved the age of Paris, the sense of history embodied in its buildings and streets. On the estate where he grew up history was a forgotten slum followed by a bomb crater, followed by a concrete slum that was already rotten without having acquired any of the integrity of age. Not a brick or breezeblock reached back further than the jerry-built Sixties: no connections beyond that were possible.

From that void to Del's eugenic pure-race fronting. From there to my voyage to the Afrosphere.

Luke enjoyed going round the galleries of Paris, getting more out of the older art than he had expected he would. He thought of Ziggy as he passed through room after room of Monet *Waterlilies* in the Orangerie. It was through Ziggy that he had become connected to Monet, to the whole of the rest of art, and he took pleasure in sharing what he knew with George, that retransmission part-payment for his birthday treat.

They said 'Bonsoir' to the concierge - a plump French queen who was friendly without being intrusive - as they passed his window a little before midnight on their second night, then climbed the three flights to their room. The steps were stone, and worn. The gleaming brass handrail rose up alongside them, a sinuous Art Nouveau curve.

Their room had no curtains, only shutters, which they unhooked and closed, on the outer side against the glare of streetlights, on the inner so they wouldn't be overlooked by the many windows that looked down into the narrow, washing-line-criss-crossed interior courtyard, the one directly opposite theirs no more than twenty feet away. The double-bed was soft, the sheets bright white and clean. A fresh spray of carnations stood in a pewter vase on the bedside table, releasing traces of scent. Arabic music came drifting up from the street outside, and from somewhere there was the sound of people having a party. Kissing passionately and pulling at each others' clothes, they fell onto the bed.

The next morning they woke early. Snuggling up together under the covers they listened to the dawn chorus and talked quietly about art and love and life. About each other, and the odd, fated as it seemed, way they had met, and finally, about the trial, and Del.

'Don't you want to know exactly what happened the night that boy was attacked?' George asked.

Lying in bed with his lover in a Paris pensione it didn't seem threatening or lowering to Luke to talk about all that, just natural. 'I know what Del's capable of,' he said, resting his cheek on George's smooth, bare chest. 'I don't need to hear every last thing. It won't exonerate no-one. He won't have been saying, let's not do this, or, let's call a ambulance.'

'Isn't it too easy, though, to dismiss him, your twin brother, raised the same as you, as a total villain?'

'You don't know him,' Luke said softly. 'You know me, but you don't know him. I know him like reverse telepathy. Right now he'll be seeing himself as a martyr. He'll never regret none of what he did except getting caught. He'll never feel remorse. Like them whites what lynched black people in the States and took photos, you know? Of themselves with the bodies, like they was proud hunters, and they even had the photos made into postcards they sent to friends and family cos they had no shame. Cos they was even proud.'

'But maybe later - '

'Do you believe that, man? That they felt torn up about it later?'

'Some of them, perhaps. In the raw light of day.'

'I don't, man. I reckon the ones still alive now are probably still smug about it. And Del'll be like that, man, he'll be one of them. Probably he's got a tape of the CCTV footage stashed away someplace, like a proud record of his one big moment. Like kiddie porn, like paedos filming themselves molesting kids and keeping it. Showing it off, like to be a bragging point with their mates. And more than that, man, he thinks what he did was right. A blow for something. Cos if he accepted it wasn't right, he'd fall to pieces. Like, what would happen to us if we really believed being gay was a mortal sin? Or we're mentally ill for being gay? What'd that do to you? Totally destroy you, right? That's how come I know he'll never change. He can't afford to, you know? Psychologically. I get it.'

'But you're different.'

'I'm a chequer-board bumboy and proud of it.'

'You make it sound like that came before everything else,' George said, his cock stirring, stiffening. He found Luke's anger oddly sexually exciting.

'Maybe it did,' Luke said. He felt safe and loved as he lay there with George in that history-steeped Parisienne hotel-room. The contrast with the bleak grey streets in which he had grown up, and which he feared still ran through him in some hidden, toxic way, was strong in him. (*Make it into something you can be proud of Yes, I survived that I'm strong.*) He gripped George's now-rigid dick. George groaned and Luke was reassured: here was life. Life was here. 'Maybe it's in the genes,' he said, moving his fist slowly on George's erection. 'Or maybe it's like a gift from God. What's there in you before your parents booze it up and fuck you up. Maybe for every hate there's got to be some love.'

'Maybe so, baby,' George said breathlessly. Luke moved his fist faster on George's dick, enjoying his lover's helpless tensile responsiveness. 'Maybe – oh fuck, yeah - ' Luke twisted round and kissed George on the mouth, giving himself over to his lover's pleasure as if love was an unlimited resource to be freely given away. And it was.

One time Malcolm asked Luke if he felt that only being attracted to black men in a majority-white environment limited him. 'I guess if I felt like it did then it'd be a sickness in me, you know?' Luke said. 'But most people aren't attracted to as wide a range of people as from Nigeria to Jamaica to the States, are they? Not culturally, for sure, but not even lookswise. And more generally, who really don't care if a guy's tall or short, fat or a bodybuilder, femme or a bear? Practically no-one ignores all that and just goes for the pure skinless person, cos all them things do signify. And with me I've got that one up-front thing, but - how many people would go out with someone where they had to learn a new culture, or maybe had to fight immigration? Or if you're white, having to feel and face off racism, cross onto that side, take that stand. Most people who'd say I was limited won't go that far out. So fuck 'em.'

And Malcolm had laughed and said, 'You're getting better at sticking up for yourself, my albino brother.'

After coming back from Paris Luke decided he would write a letter to Yusuf Mohammed's family, but he only posted it to them after the trial was over. It was the last time he signed his name Bourne anywhere.

'I reckoned it was time for a change the day Joe and Leonie recognised me and Malcolm,' he told Ziggy later. 'It made me feel kind of reborn, you know? Like I could put certain shit in my life behind me for good, finally. And I looked at my name and I thought, well, so change it. But then, you know, it's my history and I don't wanna deny it cos denial stops you letting go. I just wanna move on with it where it belongs, in the past.' And Ziggy had nodded: he understood the power of names.

In the end Luke only changed the spelling of his name, from Bourne to Born. But it was enough. Several months of tedious bureaucracy followed, involving getting hold of a copy of his birth certificate, changing his name by deed poll, changing the old spelling to the new one on his bank account, credit card and billing accounts, his tenancy agreement, driving license and passport, but then it was done.

'Dear Mr and Mrs Mohammed,' he wrote, when he finally put pen to paper, *'I wanted to write to you to say how sorry I am about your son Yusuf. One of his attackers was my brother. Me and him, we haven't spoken for seven years, we fell out. Because he was a racist and I'm not. I know I can't say anything that helps. But I wanted you to know for sure that not everyone here is like my brother and there are people who care about what happened to you're son. You probably don't want to hear from me, but I did cry for your son. He deserved a lot better than he got.*
Yours Sincerely,
Luke Born (Bourne)'

It was only barely good enough, but it was the best he could do after more than twenty efforts. At least as Del had been convicted it couldn't be misinterpreted as some sort of obscure, creepy effort to be manipulative on his behalf.

Luke had felt uneasy putting his address at the top of the letter; as if it might somehow rebound on him and lead to his being hunted down for some sort of retribution, black or white, he wasn't sure which. He sent the letter to the Mohammeds' lawyers, whose names had been in the papers. He didn't expect a reply, and he didn't get one. Sending a handwritten letter had felt strangely old-fashioned.

Joe quickly strips to black trunks identical to the ones George and Ziggy are wearing. With deft strokes of his brush Luke starts to sketch out the white rib-cage motif on his bare brown chest. Joe is lighter-skinned and shorter than George but has larger pectorals. At the same time he's less generally beefy than Ziggy. So Luke has to alter the shape of the design to make it work on him. Joe's skin goosebumps and his nipples prickle as the cold, wet brush glides over his chest, and he laughs in surprise. Malcolm lifts his trumpet to his lips and plays a lick. Trevor says something Luke doesn't catch but Malcolm does, because he breaks off to laugh too.

It took time for Luke to tell Malcolm and Ziggy about Del and the killing of Yusuf: to stop being silenced by shame. He had also to tell Malcolm that it was Del who attacked him on the bridge. Afterwards he told Ziggy too, because Malcolm called the coincidence 'Freaky Voodoo shit' that he said, 'Relates to twins. You should ask Ziggy if it means something, because that's deep African shit happening there, my albino Nubian. It could mean something you ought to know about.'

Luke had never thought about it as anything other than a grotesque coincidence. If he also had a vaguely Christian sense of a guilt through association that had to be expiated through suffering it didn't rely on Del being his twin, or even his brother, only on the shared colour of their skin. But when he told Ziggy Ziggy nodded, seemingly unsurprised by the revelation, and said that Del was a 'dead' twin, and that he believed that, as the 'living' twin, Luke had been drawn to that particular place at that particular time to offset Del's bad deeds.

'But what about Yusuf?' Luke asked. 'Why couldn't I be there then?'

'Because it's not straightforward in that way,' Ziggy said. 'Maybe you and Malcolm, even though you're white and he's British, are open to African beliefs in a way Yusuf wasn't. You don't have that door closed between you and the spirits. Maybe being gay even brings you closer because it forces you to resist all those big-time one-god religions with their books of rules and regulations. Maybe Islam got in his way.'

'Do you think, man?'

Ziggy nodded. 'Because I've discovered that I'm a witchdoctor,' he said. 'I learned that just recently, in a dream. And I was told homosex is powerful magic. I believe fucking men was your protection, and Malcolm's protection. That was your magic that night, that was what you believed in.'

Malcolm and George had asked Luke more expected things: did he feel any psychic rapport with his twin? Had he had any premonition that had guided him to that particular place on that particular night? Did he believe in fate or did he think it was just a coincidence?

'Fate, maybe,' Luke said uncertainly. But he knew he meant no more by that than the universal sense that what happens in one's life ought to mean something. As for being a twin, he had never, as far as he could recall, shared any psychic affinity with Del, or shared with him any of the commonplace things that twins are supposed to share. *Well, we wore the same clothes, but only cos our mum doled 'em out at random. And later cos that's what we all wore at school, a uniform. But we never tried to pass me off as him or him off as me.*

Didn't we? Really?

We must of done and I don't remember. Won't remember. But he did remember:

She got our hair buzz-cut the same. Zero crop. I got sent home from school for that so Del must of too.

And then he flashed on his mother dragging them both into the staff-room, they would have been nine then, and saying loudly in front of everyone, in a voice edged with grievance, 'You let the niggers do it, why not your own?' and his form teacher's face going scarlet. *Our first exclusion, a fortnight till our hair grew back, a taboo, a split: for him transgressively white, for me latently racially transvestic.*

But that is not the romance of twinnedness.

Dad made us box one time. We was twelve. Get in there you poof Was that snarled at me or Del? It didn't feel like father-son stuff more like we was pit-bulls getting bet on, and even more than money the punters want to see our blood. I punched Del in the face and his nose bled or did he punch me I forget. Okay I'll give you that much. I'll cry that much for the both of us. Neither of us was much cop at fighting. Then.

That evening he had been out on a date with a guy he had exchanged numbers with in a bar the week before. What was his name? Trevor? Tyrone? Tall, black British, short hair, mid-twenties. A goatee. He had lived in a flat on a Peabody estate off Southwark Street. Luke had gone back with him, they had smoked several joints together, and Trevor-Tyrone had talked on and on about himself and how he hated his job and hated the scene until Luke had completely gone off the idea of sex and was desperate to escape. Eventually he had got to his feet and said he had to be going home.

Wanting to clear his head of dope and dull talk he

had decided to walk up to Trafalgar Square and catch a night-bus from there. Which was how come he had been crossing the bridge one way at the same time Del and his mates were crossing it the other. And Malcolm had been at the apogee, staring down.

He said he would of jumped, that that saved him.

After their talk of twins Ziggy made Luke a small painting of racially-ambivalent twin male figures, their shaved heads anointed red as if with a blood-offering. One held a spear, the other a shield. Luke placed it on the mantelpiece in George's flat as though he was setting it on an altar.

Off to one side of the dressing-room George is demon-strating hand-movements to Ziggy, and Ziggy is imitat-ing him, reminding himself of bits of the routine he's still unsure of. Most of the time, because of the easy way he interacts with them, Ziggy, Malcolm and Luke think of George as being around their own age, but the flair he's demonstrated over the past two weeks for coming up with simple, practical solutions to problems in the work they've been creating is self-evidently the product of long experience as well as talent and imagi-nation.

Luke is proud that George can fit in with his friends so well. He's also proud of his lover's pure physical stamina: at fifty George has repeatedly put both Ziggy and himself to shame. The first day they joined in with his dance-session with Joe George was barely breaking a sweat by the time Luke and Ziggy were sodden and gasping for breath.

For his part George has been enjoying himself greatly. Working on a personal project with younger people full of passion and commitment has made his energies surge. He has even enjoyed coming to the situation with no rep, as an equal, mucking in with everyone else to get things done: it has reconnected him with something that had got buried under years of decently-paid but superficial commercial gigs, and teaching.

George likes teaching, and it pays the rent, but it has its dangers: becoming too fond of the sound of your own voice, striking a pose of omniscience that you fall for yourself, artistic dead ends. And its inevitable perpetuation of orthodoxies constrains the questing spirit that must push past limits and transgress un-afraid of potentially humiliating self-disclosure. His work with Luke and Joe and the others has been a liberating corrective to that, and if there are elements of mentor and student, father and son to his relation-ship with Luke that is natural enough, and it fills a need in both of them they can, and do, freely acknowledge.

'But it's father *and* mother to son to me,' Luke said one rainy weekday afternoon. He was lying on his back on George's kitchen floor, his head in the cupboard under the sink, dismantling the u-bend with vigorous twists of an adjustable spanner. 'Not just father.'

'Weren't you ever close to your mother either?' George asked, squatting down next to him.

'Well, you know, I don't remember really, man,' Luke said, grunting as he forced the spanner round. The sinews stood out in his smooth, butter-peach forearms. 'The thread on this is fucked. She was brutal to us kids. I didn't see her as a victim, I know that, not till ages after, cos she'd yell back at my old man and smash shit up till he battered her, so it felt more like Tyson v. Holyfield, a fair fight till the ear-biting, you know? And after, she'd take it out on us. She'd hit the bottle, then us. He did too, but she was more thought-out cruel. And your mum's meant to protect you, ain't she? And she never, so I probably hated her more than him. Thinking about it now, I suppose she hated herself for loving him, but I could be just making that up. Maybe she blamed us for trapping her so she couldn't bail on him when the love died. Or maybe she just kept on loving him despite everything. Maybe I got my whole wanting to run thing from her because she never could. Run away to where everything'll be different cos different had to be better.'

He handed George the spanner, wrangled the u-bend free and pushed himself out from the undersink cupboard. There was a smudge of dirt on his small nose. George thumbed it away and Luke smiled.

'But I gotta reckon there was something there once,' he went on, going through to the bathroom and upending the u-bend into the bathroom sink. Black sludge dripped out and there was a rank smell. He ran the tap through the pipe to clean it out. 'There has to of been. Because it's like, it's ironic, man: I mean, I'm totally gay, you know? I don't fancy women. And I do fancy men, I love men's bodies, and men are who I fall for. There are women I like a lot, who are beautiful, who I even love. But not in that central way. But the truth is, who do you learn to love from? What makes you able to love another human being? It's your mum, man. The way she loved you when you was just born. The way she looked at you and held you and breast-fed you and all of that. So when I look at you and I know I love you so fucking much - ' Luke said that not looking at George, too shy to say it to his face. ' - I know that comes from my mum doing something right when it mattered.'

'What's her name?' George asked, wrapping his arms around Luke from behind as Luke sluiced water into the sink to wash the muck away, sloshing it around with one hand.

'Penny.'

Like a camera flashing, the saying of Luke's mother's name took George back to his own childhood and a sudden vivid image of himself dancing with his mother and aunt to Ska 45s in their front room. The front of the Dancette glowed amber. Colourful, heavily-patterned curtains were drawn tight against the damp grey world outside. His mother had made those curtains up herself, out of yards of fabric she'd bought from a stall in Shepherd's Bush Market, using a sewing-machine she'd borrowed from her sister to hem and line them. Good as professional they had looked, the motif turquoise chrysanthemums and orange peonies on a satin saffron background.

There was an off-cut left over that his mother gave to George after he badgered her repeatedly about what she was going to do with it. He kept it rolled up in a drawer in the bedroom he shared with his brother, and sometimes, when everyone else was out of the house, he would take it from its hiding-place and wrap it round his head like an African priestess's headscarf. Then he would go down to the front room and mime to records by black girl singers with a hairbrush for a mic, all the time staring into his own eyes in the geometric mirror that hung on chains above the fireplace.

His mother is sixty-nine now, his father seventy-one. George has seen them only intermittently since leaving home at the age of seventeen. At first this was because he was often out of the country for months at a time touring. In those pre-Internet, pre-mobile phone days, when international calls were both difficult and expensive, he was effectively unreachable. Later, when he could have seen his parents more often because he was regularly working in London, he found that 'once in a while' had become the accepted degree of contact between them, with neither side it seemed needing or wanting more.

He used to invite them to see his more crowd-pleasing work, like his stints in *Starlight Express* and

Cats, and to the shows he choreographed that didn't foreground his sexuality too explicitly. Not that his mother and father didn't know he was gay, of course. But he could never bring himself to be direct about it with them, and for their part they avoided asking him any question that would demand too direct an answer. *Mum, Dad, I'm seeing a white boy half my age I take his cock up my arse and I love it and I love him -*

George's father had retired early, at fifty-five, from his job as a bus-driver, and he and his mother had moved back to Jamaica straight afterwards. *Our plan. Our dream.* Using the savings of a lifetime they had built a house in his father's parish, three-storey and marble-floored, fulfilling the thirty-five year dream of a prosperous return to the place of their birth. But Jamaica had changed since they were young: it had become poorer and more violent. And they had changed too, in ways they hadn't noticed until they returned there: they had become more English, more urban, used to a faster pace of life however azure the sky and warm the breeze. So they had rented out the house and moved on, to Miami, where the sky was equally blue and the sun just as bright, but there was a general air of First World efficiency and prosperity. They lived there still, regularly flying north to Canada to visit George's brother and his family.

George had visited his mother and father several times at their home in Miami. He had never visited them in Jamaica.

The last time he saw his parents was two years ago. He had flown south to stay with them after the short run of a show with an AIDS theme he had been invited to choreograph a segment of in New York. Called *Obeah Spell*, it had been commissioned by an all-female African-American dance troupe, and had been a critical success. The dancers had been fun to work with and he had been decently paid, so he had arrived at his parents' home in a buoyant mood.

His mother and father had seemed well, but there was a fragility to them both that hadn't been there on his visit the year before, a sudden delicacy even in his father, who had once been so broad and solid, as if mass and muscle had somehow become bird-bones and feathers in anticipation of the final migration of the spirit. But the sun had been warm, the sky clear, the house clean and comfortable, and the plans they'd made for their life together in their old age had turned out about as well as they could have done, so there was no real sadness. And if it was a small life, would a larger or more public life have brought them anything more? His father's anger at the white world and his mother's anger at his father were long gone. And George blamed them for nothing, and as they waved him off at the airport he surged with love for them both.

On his return he told Luke things about his child-hood that even Lester didn't know: gave him small jewels that could have meaning only to himself and the one he was closest to, the one who had been inside his body, and not as a baby but as a man, a primal reversal.

The piece they will be performing tonight has evolved out of lengthy, open-ended get-togethers at one or other of their homes, dancers and musicians throwing in ideas as they jammed, drank and smoked. George or Joe would kick off with a movement or sequence of movements, and Malcolm and Percy or Trevor or Don would respond to it. Their response would pose a challenge that required a solution, and so the piece wound this way and that, moving in directions, some of which were dead-end, but none unworthy of explora-tion. Themes mutated, fragmented, exploded like fireworks, recombined. Motifs evolved, imploded, emerged remixed and revealing new truths. Ziggy and Malcolm and Leonie added words and phrases to the piece, and these too challenged and altered what was there, what was becoming.

Everyone has something he or she wants to express through this evening, but one theme is dominant: that the dead must be honoured, and that that can best be done by asserting life in all its muscularity. And so they are all Baron Samedis for the night, dancing fear away.

George has read about other Barons too, how some of them are said to be male lovers of males, gay *lwa*, so if he and Joe are dancing as Samedis, then he, Ziggy and Luke are also dancing as those other *Ghedes*, Limba and Lundy. And Trevor picked up on the Vodou vibe that George and Ziggy were bringing and pushed the drums forward in a way he wouldn't normally do, making them voice the spirits, the dead, and lovers past.

The sessions were chaotic even as the piece was coming together but all of them wanted to honour that chaos: to shout out that dissonance is the fundamental truth of life; that life is not orderly and the world is not orderly, and that being alive is both painful and joyous. And then to allow art, for the length of their performance, to assert order, and allow that assertion to bind and heal.

George has been the conductor, the collager, but his role has been responsive and organic, not controlling.

For so many reasons he is the happiest he has been for a long time tonight. His years are in him but not on him, weightless as light.

The door shoves open a foot, forcing Malcolm and Ziggy to hutch up. A burly, shaven-headed white man in a tuxedo sticks his head in. 'Up in five,' he says, then withdraws.

'Shit.' Luke struggles up with a grunt, knee-joints clicking, and quickly strips to the same black trunks that George, Ziggy and Joe are wearing: he too will be dancing tonight. Like Ziggy he is untrained but a good enough club dancer to follow George and Joe's moves. Even if he hadn't been he would still have danced, both for Joe and Leonie, and because he knows George and Ziggy want a white dancer onstage too, to show that Vodoun and Orisha energies can inspire people of every race and background.

Ziggy came round to Luke's earlier that afternoon and painted a version of the skeleton-pattern on his body, outlining the bones in black so they'd stand out against his pale skin. Luke wandered around the flat with nothing on until the paint dried, feeling like some young male being prepared for initiation into manhood and the tribe. Afterwards he dressed carefully in loose clothing, trying not to tear the fragile skin of paint. The design has survived fairly intact, but parts of it – in particular the knees, elbows and shoulders - have been worn away. 'Ziggy, man,' he says.

As Ziggy takes the brush from him and squats down Leonie arrives, looking nervous but beautiful in a simple white dress that reaches her ankles and leaves her arms bare. Her hair is pulled back in a tight lattice of braids. She kisses Joe on the lips, Malcolm and Luke on the cheek, and touches hands with the other musicians. She air-kisses George, not wanting to get paint on her face, then bends down and kisses the top of Ziggy's head. He grunts an acknowledgment, not looking up as he squeezes out black paint next to white on the dish Luke has been using as a palette, then rapidly fills in the damaged patches of the design on Luke's knees, hips, elbows and shoulders. That done, he gets up and outlines a skull on Luke's face, scooping under and accentuating his cheekbones, blacking in his eye-sockets, blacking out his nose.

Behind him George is thumbing white crosses on the foreheads of the musicians, and Leonie. She and Ziggy will be singing tonight. Her voice is small but pure, his is large and coarse, and both are human.

Leonie and Ziggy have become, during the course of the devising and rehearsals, if not friends, then certainly comrades. She has come to find him oddly comforting, a bright splinter in the grey flesh of her grief. He has given her something that nobody else, not even her husband, has been able to give her: freedom from shame. Perhaps because, unlike almost everyone else, including Joe, Ziggy is not ashamed of death. And if that sometimes makes him brutal Leonie prefers that to the evasions of family and friends, who alternately indulge, belittle and deny her loss. Even his African witch side has come to seem like freedom.

And so it was Ziggy, Malcolm, Luke and George that Leonie and Joe asked to accompany them for the placing of Leo's headstone: comrades, not family.

Funny what you learn, she thinks. For instance, that the stone cannot be placed for at least a month after the burial because the dug-up ground needs time to settle. A small rite of passage for the bereaved, the acquisition of that kind of particular knowledge. The marble had been as shiny as if it was lacquered, and that had felt both right and wrong. It had been an unseasonably hot October afternoon, the sun dazzling.

Ziggy fills in quickly around Luke's eyes. 'It won't be dry by the time we go on,' he says.

'It don't matter on the face,' Luke says, patting the repainted design on his shoulder. It's already tacky.

'Close your eyes.'

Luke does so and Ziggy strokes black over his trembling eyelids. Their breath mingles as he leans in close. Both of them are nervous about dancing tonight, especially with two trained dancers, and being busy until the last second is helping them keep down the jitters.

The act that's onstage now is performing an encore, even though all performers were expressly told before-hand that no overrunning of sets would be allowed, on pain of having the plug pulled.

Of the twelve bands performing tonight the Afro-Nubians are up fifth, which is perhaps ideal: the earlier acts have warmed up the crowd nicely without blowing it away, and there haven't yet been so many of them that the audience has got worn out and succumbed to the lure of the bar. They were originally slated to go on second, which would have relegated them to being virtually a warm-up act, but got shuffled back to fifth after Trevor managed to lure the club's owner along to one of their rehearsals. He had liked what he saw and heard enough to rejig the running order and promote them into one of the best spots.

The delay caused by the encore frustrates the musi-cians, but Luke and Ziggy are glad to have a few extra seconds to tidy up the skeleton designs. Paint-laden brushes in hands they move about quickly, checking for errors and missed spots. The wetness of the paint in the cramped room means that everyone's movements become exponentially restricted. The dancers hold themselves at increasingly awkward angles to avoid smudging the skeleton designs while the musicians tuck their elbows tight to their sides to keep paint off their tuxedoes. If Leonie seems to mind less it is only because her dress, like the paint, is white.

At first Luke had worried about the designs getting rubbed off during the performance, concerned it would look amateurish. But Ziggy said the damage would echo the way Vodou dancers kicked over the *vévé* patterns the priests marked out on the ground with flour or coffee grounds before a ceremony. For the make-up to still be flawless at the end of the performance, Ziggy said, would suggest a lack of commitment on the part of the dancers.

For Ziggy tonight is full of meanings hidden from the others, and has a spiritual significance that he knows resonates only vaguely for them. He doesn't push this religious, ritual side to what they are doing, but it is there nonetheless. He feels the dying of the year, and the need to do something to let go of the pain, anger and madness he has gone through during it. *Exorcise it Sacrifice it Leave it on the stage.* And too he wants to celebrate, to offer thanks for his enduring friendships, for his new-found love.

Love can't heal everything, he knows that. The spirits, the ancestors can't heal everything. Drugs - imposed or self-medicated - can't heal everything; nor can work, or sensual self-indulgence, or friendship. But all these things help you bear what you have to bear. He hasn't cut himself, or hammered nails into his arms, or overdosed in the last five months. With Malcolm's help he has got through his dark days, and the backwash of chaos that he had come to believe was a permanent feature of his damaged psyche has receded, leaving him strong and well.

Did it make a difference that Malcolm, too, was black? Was there some essence Malcolm could bathe him in that Luke could not? And if that was so, as on some level it seemed to be, was that essence really to do with race, or was it more simply and more complicatedly the essence of Malcolm himself? Ziggy has spent his life resisting being claimed by any group, any individual, any cause except self-expression, which is no cause after all, only a psychic function. At times he has even resisted the claims of the spirits and the ancestors. But now, finally, Malcolm has claimed him, and he is glad.

*And his dick penetrates me and his music pene-
trates me and his seed libates my gut and each thrust
of his hips against my ass, each slam of his dickhead in
the shrine of my ass each punch of pain and pleasure
fires up my fetish.*

Ziggy knows that claim is not without a price for
Malcolm, though he doesn't resist paying it –

'It can be tough,' Malcolm says. He and Luke are
browsing Portobello Market. It's a Friday, the day when
the second-hand fashion- and book-stalls are there and
bargains are to be had.

'The talking him down a zillion times?' Luke says.

'That for sure, but it's more the assumption every
time that I'm gonna be the sane, sensible one with all
my demons in check.'

This conversation is rare for them – discussing
Malcolm's relationship with Ziggy – but today Malcolm
needs to offload.

'But they *are* in check, though,' Luke says. 'And you
are the sane one. That's the fucked-up fact of it. I
mean, I love Zig, but he is kinda deranged.'

'Yeah, but so am I, sometimes. So are you. We've
got scars too, my Nubian, and they're not even that
old.' *(I bound your wrists that night, do you remember? You never could tell me a reason why/Just life in
all its horrors and weight/I ripped strips from an
unstretched canvas and we skipped*

A&E, psychiatrists and neat sutures)

'It's like his pain swamps yours.'

'Yeah. Not intentionally, but basically, yeah. Like I
don't have the right to - '

'George is twice my age,' Luke says, picking up a
book and flicking through it. 'It means my insights are
always gonna be duds compared to his. He doesn't
mean it to be that way, he doesn't act like it is, but...' He

shrugs, puts the book back down.

'How did it end between you and Ziggy?' Malcolm asks. 'You've never really said.'

'You're just forgetting,' Luke says, 'because you hadn't met Ziggy then. It blew out on a bipolar loop. He thought I wasn't there for him. Then he thought he was projecting onto me that I was supposed to save him from his own brain, and he knew that was crazy, because I mean how, you know? It's not a possible thing someone can do for someone else. So it was okay for five seconds. Then he didn't know that anymore and I was piking on him, I was betraying him. He was up and down and up and down and suddenly there just wasn't a relationship any more. There was him and his brain and the voices and I was way back in fourth place and I couldn't shout loud enough to be heard. But it was him broke up with me, though. Because I could of never, you know?'

Malcolm nods. 'I think he's found a way forward,' he says. 'Like he's using the spirits to beat down the schizo shit, if that makes sense.'

'You're a big part of that,' Luke says. Malcolm smiles.

They leave the market. As they head home a police-car kerb-crawls them, the officer on the passenger side staring at them with bold bovine hostility, because what could a nigger and a wigger be but criminal? What could their association be but burglary, mugging, drugs? Ironically Malcolm gets more of this kind of harassment when he's with Luke than when he's with Ziggy. It's because with Luke his defiance of the assumedly natural affinity of like for like is criminally visible; and with Luke it's even harder to catch a cab.

One time they were stopped on Oxford Street in front of Selfridges and accused on not the slightest evidence of being purse-snatchers. To compound the stupidity the lead officer of the pair had been a young black woman. 'What are you doing in this area?' she asked.

'Shopping.'

Searched in the street under the eyes of non-nigger shoppers, reminded of how power works, how randomly and easily your freedom can be taken away, he almost thanked her for laying it all so bare.

In the dressing-room they hear lively applause as the band that's onstage finally winds up its set. The security-man sticks his head round the door again. His shaven scalp is now lobster-pink and shiny with sweat.

'You're on,' he says.

Chapter Twelve

From the moment Joe, George, Ziggy and Luke lined up at the front of the stage in their Baron Samedi body-paint and, heedless of frayed cables, poured libations of wine, water, beer and whiskey onto the dirty black boards at their feet, and Trevor began to pound the drums, there was a visible turning away from the bar and a curious crowding through from the seated area beyond it. Leonie was so shy she couldn't bring herself to face the audience, so she kept her back to it in what she was unaware was a time-honoured tradition as she sang snatches of the poetry Malcolm had written with and for her, her fragile shoulders hunched over the microphone, her inadvertantly oracular reticence adding to the ritual feel of the performance. Sometimes the words were very male, and for many reasons that too seemed appropriate. *'Veins in autumn leaves,'* she sang, *'And the trees scream/Blood should never be/This still and low...'*

The music rose up, then burst like a breaker shattering white over black rocks. The musicians played wildly from jump, pushing themselves repeatedly into that place where structure strained until it seemed it must yield to chaos. The drums pulsated under Trevor's palms, the piano was sharp and glinting as a stabbing knife beneath Percy's jabbing fingers, and the sound of Malcolm's horn was piercing as he arched back and blew, thighs tensing, electric soul energies coursing through his crotch and criss-crossing his chest and biceps and fingers, his lungs channelling powers sacred and profane, his throat throbbing as he pushed the power higher, the music feeding the dancers as they threw their arms up and thrust their thighs down warrior-hard, earth against sky, cosmos as calabash. And Ziggy took the mic at the front of the stage and sang chants in English and half-assed, half-remembered Yoruba as though he too was channelling something long time gone but now returned.

'*My tongue is not your tongue,*' he sang, his voice hoarse. '*I cannot twist my palate into your words. I will not twist my palate up to make your words.*

There is a brand upon my tongue
A tongue that must be heard
A song that must be sung
Orishas hear your son
Your son is coming back to you - '

The sinews in his neck serrated as he sang, the veins dilating and inflating spectacularly, and the necklace of cowries he was wearing burst, scattering shells across the stage. He fell to his hands and knees and moved fast among the other dancers' legs, snatching up and looking at the fallen shells like a witchdoctor divining the future, his eyes rolling up in his head. And Trevor pounded the drums until his palms were bruised and his shoulders ached.

They over-ran their set by fifteen minutes, at first unwilling then unable to stop, unable to cut off the flow of energies, and the audience was with them.

Afterwards, in the cramped dressing-room, wet with sweat, radiant with applause, and flushed with pumping blood and discharging adrenaline, everyone hugged and kissed everyone, and none of them cared what they revealed in kisses or embraces that normally they would have concealed or denied.

They are driving to the airport in Joe's hatch-back. There are six of them in the car. Joe and Leonie sit up front; George, Luke, Ziggy and Malcolm are crammed in the back. It is 7.30 a.m. Traffic is unexpectedly heavy but they've allowed plenty of time. They're on the M4 heading for Heathrow Terminal 4, intercontinental departures. It is ten days before Christmas.

Joe is driving. Ziggy and Malcolm's numerous bags are piled up in the back, blocking the view in the rearview mirror. Most of the bags are Ziggy's. Malcolm is travelling light. He is confident that Africa Will Provide, Ziggy is not. They had a row about it last night, but it wasn't a serious one, just pre-flight nerves. Now they sit squeezed in alongside Luke and George, not looking at each other. But their thighs are pressed together in a way that comforts them both, and Ziggy's arm is slung with casual fondness round Malcolm's shoulders. They both wear shades against the grey, hungover morning, and in anticipation of the dazzle to come.

The car smells of sleep. No-one is talkative. After listening to the traffic news Joe puts on a CD Malcolm gave him, Max Roach's *Freedom Now* suite, at a low volume. *So I am going for real*, Ziggy thinks. None of the others can really know what this journey means to him. He has telephoned aunts, uncles and cousins all over Yorubaland to tell them he'll be visiting with a friend and ask them if they'll be available. It was unexpectedly easy to do. But that was because he was performing, not being himself: *I will be bringing my homosexual boyfriend-o!* was not a piece of information that came out of his mouth during any of those numerous short, enthusiastic conversations. Also, speaking to relatives he had never met in a country he had never visited in adult life was easy because they weren't yet real to him, just voices in the wires and he was used to that, *oh yes*.

Not just a country he has never visited: a land.

My land?

He both hopes so and not. Today he feels wholly British. As, he suspects, does Malcolm, though he wouldn't admit it.

Unable to decide what to do about his hair, he has shaved it all off.

Paradoxes haunt him. Going to his perhaps-homeland in the hope of being in some way liberated he has never felt the pressure to conform imposed on him so savagely, aware as he is that there will be a danger in looking above all sexually deviant that could literally be lethal.

How much of me am I taking with me? If I leave too much behind I should not go at all. But if I take too much of things people will not be able to cope with, then their reactions to those things will take up all my time and energy, and I won't see many things that I will want to see, may even need to see. And hear.

His fissuring indecision led to him filling bag after bag with every sort of clothing, relevant and irrelevant, practical and impractical, until every case was straining at the seams and the locks couldn't be forced shut. It was the increasingly manic way he was doing so that had eventually led to the row with Malcolm, who had forborne to say anything until Ziggy, having over-filled every travel-bag and case he possessed, then started cramming things – including small carvings and sketch-books - into old carrier-bags while muttering repeatedly, 'I must bring gifts for everyone.'

Malcolm does not know how this works but still he is my witness, the griot of the tribe of me. He makes this journey I am about to take worth something. Before it just felt like some family thing I did not want to do and so did not do. Now it is an adventure.

When did my decision begin? Perhaps when I be-gan to believe I was dreaming his dreams, when I began to feel the black monoliths he was planting in my mind.

We talked, we debated. To go or not go. He was afraid of disappointment for both me and himself, I was afraid of becoming burdened with a new set of mechanisms of control to add to all those that are operating on my personality at this exact moment.

To focus on Africa, on Nigeria, was something I had never done. Before, always, I saw or considered it through the camera obscura of family and madness, myself in the dark, the panorama poorly-focussed and shadowed by obligations. Even now I have said I am going I don't know whether I will actually visit any family: can I bear smiles that are only for a projection of what I am not and not for the real me?

We both fear rejection, Malcolm and I. Exploring the landscape of that fear was an expedition we could make together before physically setting out, and sharing its dangers brought us closer. I conquered my fear for him, he conquered his for me. It is easier to do it for one you love. And we will take our black heathen faggot energies with us.

My father, who I had not spoken to for eighteen months, was so happy when I told him of the trip. It would have pleased your mother, he said, God rest her soul. Yes, I said. You won't go with funny hair, he said. I didn't answer that. Instead I asked for the numbers of various relatives and as he gave them and talked on about family trivia, children and grandchildren and great-grandchildren, my head began to pound and I felt a desire to vomit. Malcolm asked me why was I not closer to my father and I could not explain to him, a son of the do-as-you-please West, the pressure of being the first-born son, under the thumb of a thousand bullshit expectations, a thousand obligations that destroyed my mind, a thousand programmes run to

destroy my faggotry, erase my freakishness. To speak
to my father is to be a butterfly mashed back into
caterpillar pulp. And I know my bullshit madness has
tortured him and it tortured my mother before the
tumour killed her and I don't feel any shame because
shame requires the possibility of choice, but still -

I want to see Nigeria. I want to open my channels
to the Orishas all the way, and silence the false voices
that are, I think, the product of here and its racisms
and bigotries, forever. I want to see my own land. But
the truth is I do not want to see my father's land. I'm
sorry Daddy because I do honour you. And Mummy.
In the ways I can. But I will always be unmaking your
crosses. You were sent back to be buried, Mummy. I
understood you then. I was twenty-two. I came to the
service we had here late and all in black latex and a
black eye-mask of make-up, scary as Ghede and
Daddy looked at me with silver crosses in his eyes that
spun like Ninja throwing-stars and cut tears from his
eyelids and we didn't speak after that for two years,
three weeks and two days.

I hope you have a good trip, son, he says.
Thank you, Daddy.
Did you pack gifts?
I'm bringing art, Daddy.
He grunts, doesn't say anything.

Ziggy is wearing tight orange jeans, a flaming orange silk shirt with outsize lapels, orange DMs, and his
sunglasses have orange rubber frames. He wears cowry
shells round his neck. Here, in the grey UK, he looks
garish. There, in Africa, he hopes the hot colours will be
adaptive. But he can't resist one defiant touch: orange
nail-varnish on one hand. *Because I must.* Probably, as
he's not effeminate, they will take him for an American
rapper.

Malcolm is wearing a white skinny-rib vest under

an unlined indigo cotton jacket, and tight hipster trousers. A faun porkpie hat is pushed back on his freshly-shaved head. He wears gold on his wrists, in his ears, and around his neck.

Gold to the Ashanti Kingdoms
 Coals to/
  New/
  castle?
Am I
 (going)
Home?

Two weeks ago Malcolm bought a Yoruba phrase-book, and since then in every quiet moment he has been stumbling through the handful of words and phrases he has committed to memory. Not that he expects to be expected to speak any Yoruba when he gets to Lagos, just it seems the respectful thing to do, as well as, of course, practical. Also, to know at least something of one of the languages spoken there makes Malcolm feel that his first experience of Africa will be as immediate as possible.

As real as possible.

'You don't have any dope on you, do you, man?' Luke asks him as they leave the motorway, following the signs to Terminal Four.

'What do you mean, man?' Malcolm says. 'No, of course not, why d'you ask? Anyway, it's too early in the day.'

'I don't want any, man,' Luke says. 'I just mean don't accidentally take any in the airport with you. And definitely don't take any on the plane with you. And even more definitely don't bring any back. Zig?'

'Don't worry about it,' Ziggy says. 'Anything obtained there will be consumed there.'

'I just don't want you taking any chances,' Luke says. He is staring ahead, his eyes dull sea-green.

'So are you jealous, man?' Malcolm asked him, one afternoon about a fortnight before he and Ziggy were due to fly.

'What, that you're going to Africa?' Luke asked, flicking through the phrasebook Malcolm had just bought from Foyle's.

'And that I'm going with Ziggy and he's pretty much your best friend and he's African and we're going as a couple.'

Luke looked at him. They were in the kitchen. Malcolm spooned tea from a dented brass caddy into two mugs.

'And I guess I'm feeling bad because you and me have spent the last two Christmases together and now we're not going to.' He looked down into the caddy, which was almost empty. 'Those were tough times,' he said. 'And you helped me get through them big time. I mean, I don't know if I'd have survived the shit that was happening to me then if you hadn't been there. I know I gave you something too, but... And now this year I'm gonna be flying off to spend Christmas in Lagos with Ziggy as my lover. And Ziggy was your friend first. Your lover.'

'Generous, ain't I?' Luke said.

'No, but seriously, man.'

'I guess the reality is if I hadn't met George then yeah, I'd of been weird about the whole situation,' Luke said. 'I'd of been pissed off with you and Zig. Because it'd've felt like being dumped by your partner and stiffed by your best friend at the same time. Your two best friends. But I did meet George, so...' He shrugged. 'But I am jealous though,' he added. 'Just a little bit.'

'Because of the trip?'

'Yeah, but not exactly. How can I say it so it makes sense? I'm jealous you're going with Ziggy, and I'm jealous he's going with you.'

'Well, we are two phyne brothas - '

'You know I don't mean nothing like that, man. I mean it would only really mean something for me to go to Africa if I went with someone black, you know?'

'You mean African, Nigerian, whatever,' Malcolm said. 'Not just black.'

'No,' Luke said. 'I said what I meant: black. Like going with Ziggy would obviously be amazing cos he is actually Nigerian, but so would going with George. Or you. Sharing your reactions, you know?'

Malcolm nodded.

'Maybe I'm afraid too,' Luke said.

'Of what, my Nubian?'

'That I'd never really be allowed to share in that. That in the end a black person would only ever want to share that with another black person, so even if I was there I'd end up as just some white tourist tagging along. And what would I be doing there?'

Malcolm reached out and took Luke's hand. 'You're not a tourist, man,' he said. 'And it would be different but yeah, I would share it with you. With my albino brother.'

'For real?'

'For real.'

They stood in silence then, just as they were, holding hands as the kettle boiled, each feeling the gentle, insistent pulsing of the other's blood.

'Does George want to visit Africa?' Malcolm asked.

'I don't know, man.' Luke swung Malcolm's hand back and forth like a little boy would, his arm loose at the shoulder. 'He never has done but I think he does, yeah. I mean, he's mentioned it a couple of times since you guys said you were going.'

'Well, okay, then,' Malcolm said. 'If it goes well, and if it's cool with George, then maybe next time the four of us can go together.'

'I'd like that,' Luke said.

Malcolm wonders what the gay scene in Lagos is like, and if he and Ziggy will be able to connect with it. He had hoped to find some relevant information in the Spartacus gay and lesbian traveller's guide, but it didn't have much to offer when it came to Africa, just a couple of dispiriting paragraphs saying that 'in every country south of the Sahara apart from South Africa homosexuality is at best taboo and at worst heavily criminalised.' The guide was written with predominantly white travellers in mind, of course, which leaves Malcolm hopeful that he and Ziggy will be able to make connections few white travellers could to reach black gay Africa.

Not that partying on the no-doubt-clandestine Lagos gay scene was initially Malcolm's number one priority; nor even meeting gay Africans: what mattered to him most, he thought at first, was experiencing the land and the way its history – his history - was embedded in the rock and soil of it. Gaining a generalised sense of the people in relation to their culture, geography and history; experiencing and exploring Ziggy's responses to all that and, even more, his own. Listening for the erased and forgotten names of his ancestors crying out in the bush, answering from the sacred grove of his own heart.

Malcolm longs for healing on some deep level. Is that a romance? Would Ziggy call him on it? He hopes that floating in a sea of black faces in a vibrant, self-confident black nation will repair some wound in him, and in Ziggy.

Despite all that, as the departure time drew nearer Malcolm's sense of what he wanted from the trip changed. He found himself losing interest in the grand Afrocentric narrative that had initially possessed him: that passionate fascination with an epic history of mighty warriors and kings and queens and leopard-hunts; the belief, ridiculously sentimental in the face of his disdain for British royalty, that he, had his fore-bears not been stolen, would no doubt have been the son of a chief or a prince, someone of legendary stand-ing. And as that romance, as ultimately adolescent as his love for T'Challa and the fictional kingdom of Wakanda, faded, so his desire to connect with real gay African men grew stronger, in fact came to seem to him the most important thing of all. Because they are his family in a very particular way: the family he hopes is waiting to embrace him, that above all others he wants – needs - to claim him. If there is healing, he has come to believe, it is there.

He has never felt this way towards gay men as a group before, perhaps through being all his life in a white country where race-loyalty habitually trumps common ground based on sexuality. It is in an oblique way a sensibility he has picked up from Ziggy, and now it fills him with something luminous and slightly intoxicating, and makes him stand taller. And if it too is a romance - gay African brotherhood - it is at least focussed on the human, the particular and the actual, not on sentimental dreams of golden empires lost and won by long-dead obsidian warrior-kings.

Though they are only going for three weeks Mal-colm is taking his trumpet. Partly it's that he can't imagine not wanting to make music while he's there; partly because his skill with his instrument is a gift he can share with those he meets when words, as they will, fall short.

He and Ziggy tell the others they don't have to hang around till the flight boards, but having got up this early and come this far together they decide to anyway. Joe finds a space in the short-stay car-park, Luke goes and gets a trolley for the bags. Sleet lashes them with brief wintery violence as they hurry across to the terminal building, but once the doors sigh shut behind them it could be any season: the air is warm and neutral, the lighting artificial, and the feel windowless.

In the lengthy queue at the check-in desk are Nigerian men and women in traditional dress or expensive-looking Western business suits. Almost commuters they look to Malcolm and Ziggy, who immediately feel out of place.

'Are you sure you really want to do this, man?' Malcolm asked Ziggy one last time, just before ringing up to finalise the booking.

'I won't wig out on you if that's what you're asking me,' Ziggy said. 'You don't need to worry about my mind blowing out under the pressure of 'going back to my roots'.'

'I didn't mean that,' Malcolm said.

'I know you didn't,' Ziggy said. 'Keep your head still, enh.' Ziggy was plaiting Malcolm's hair, which Malcolm had briefly let grow out Don King-style on top.

Malcolm sat cross-legged on the floor between Ziggy's thighs with the phone on his lap, the flex trailing across the room. 'Just I know you hadn't spoken to your dad for like – eighteen months, right?'

Ziggy's fingers moved deftly over his scalp. 'I had to speak to him so I could get all the family phone numbers,' he said.

'I didn't mean that either, man.'

'I know. Anyway, the answer is, yes, I do want to do this.' He tipped Malcolm's head back and gazed down into his eyes. 'I want to do this with you.' And he bent forward and kissed Malcolm gently on the lips.

One bright autumn afternoon Malcolm took Ziggy to visit his Uncle Milton's grave, in Kensal Green cemetery.

An ancestor I do honour.

The pink marble headstone, though still sharp-edged, was weathered and discoloured, the gilt inlay dulled. The pewter flower-holder was tarnished and long empty, and all around the grave grass and weeds had grown long. Once green and full of sap and vitality, now they were brittle, brown and dusted with frost. Where the sunlight struck them they sparkled. Malcolm poured a slug of whiskey on the stone's head and left a bunch of pink and white carnations, Milton's favourite flower, in the holder.

He and Ziggy walked through the cemetery arm in arm, their breath white in the crisp air. His father seemed remote to him then, his mother and step-mother remoter. But he could remember Milton holding him that night his young heart was broken for the very first time as sharply as if it was yesterday.

Perhaps all parents who can't deal with their son being a faggot remove themselves from the life of that son, he thinks. *Perhaps the silence that yawns is their silence, not his, however it appears to be.*

Because they always know really.

Malcolm's father is an engineer, his stepmother is a social worker, his mother a piano teacher. He has an older brother and sister he rarely sees. His truth does not reside in this. Ziggy's father manages transport policy and financing, his mother was a businesswoman, import-export. He is an only child. His truth does not reside in that either. He is a painter, Malcolm is a musician, and they love each other. If they have a truth, that is it. *Other connections.*

After checking their bags they have nothing to do but wait about until a Starbucks opens. The shutter rattles up and they go in. Their conversation, over cappuccinos and hot chocolates and mint tea, is incon-sequential: just easy-listening words to fill time. There are smiles dusted with soft, companionable laughter.

By the time they sit down with their drinks it's gone nine a.m., but because they had to get up so early it still feels like some nebulous pre-dawn hour, and so they are low-key.

'Bring us back something if you can, man,' Luke says to Malcolm. He is holding George's hand across the table.

'What would you like, my Nubian?' Malcolm asks, stubbing out his last-but-one cigarette before the flight.

Luke shrugs. 'I don't know, man. Whatever you think would be right, you know?'

Eventually their flight is called. Without haste they make their way to the departure gate. There, carry-on bags tugging at their shoulders, Ziggy and Malcolm hug Luke, George, Joe and Leonie goodbye.

As he follows Ziggy through to the departure lounge, Malcolm looks back at his friends.

George has his arm around Luke's shoulders. He is wearing a black vinyl puffa jacket with a white, furette-lined hood, and black lycra leggings that show off his long, lean legs and disappear into chunky, buckled bike-boots. His shaved head gleams and glints. Luke has his arm around George's waist, his hand resting easily on George's hip. It looks like it belongs there. He's wearing a silver-grey jeans-jacket, matching hipster jeans and faun Timberlands, and leans in towards George affectionately. His blond funki-dreds glitter under the fluorescent lights. Joe wears a loose grey tracksuit, and has a black stocking-cap on his head. His arm is around Leonie's shoulders. She wears a close-fitting black leather trench-coat and Cuban-heeled boots, and her hair is a flawlessly Afroed haze.

Malcolm is struck by this momentary image of simple parity. *If the world was always this way,* he thinks. He lifts his hand in a gesture of farewell as the doors swing shut on his waving friends. Something unbearable rushes up through his chest. He turns, and runs to catch up with Ziggy.

THE END

Also available from Team Angelica Publishing

'Reasons to Live' by Rikki Beadle-Blair
'What I Learned Today' by Rikki Beadle-Blair
'Faggamuffin' by John R Gordon

Coming soon from Team Angelica Publishing

'Fairytales for Lost Children' by Diriye Osman